Misalliances

Misalliances

Misalliances

Book Two of
'The Allington Accounts'

Nicholas Jones

Misalliances

Misalliances

Part One

Misalliances

Misalliances

Chapter One: Kate

'Hello, Sir Thomas.'

Even though the young woman's face is in shadow, shrouded by the hood of her coat, he knows who she is. He has been watching her and her companion ever since they turned the corner of the privet hedge and approached. 'Good morning, Kate,' he replies, raising his eyes but retaining his seat on the bench.

'Kate? You *are* forward, Sir.'

'Everyone calls you Kate,' he says, 'so why shouldn't I?'

She pulls back her hood to expose the features he has caught occasional glimpses of these past few days. They are up close now, and all the more pleasing for that: the dark auburn hair, brown eyes, finely shaped nose and mouth. With raised eyebrows she is turning to her companion, as if to say 'what do you think of this man?' He knows the other young woman, too. It's the Basset girl, as blue of eye as when, at the age of eight or nine, ten or more years ago, she was introduced to him at the Lisle House in Calais. She gives him a smile and half-curtsey.

The enclosure behind the Palace kitchens is somewhere he has been once or twice before when in need of fresh air but wanting nobody's company but his own. On this warm autumn morning the gardens are busy with people who, these days, he barely knows, so he's followed the path and settled himself here, amid the scraps and slops, where assorted aromas from ovens and spits are presently wafting not unpleasantly to his nose. Even though he is not much in a mood to be courteous to two young, and probably silly, women, Wyatt's innate sense of mannerly behaviour gets the better of him. Removing his hat, he rises.

'This is an odd sort of place to find you,' Catherine Howard says. She gestures to the pile of kitchen detritus to her left.

'And you,' he returns. Catherine's pretty face reflects her search for a plausible explanation. He helps. 'If I were of a mind to flatter myself, I might think you had followed me.'

Catherine laughs. 'Well, we did, didn't we, Anne?' She warms to her tale. 'I said to Anne here, look, there's Sir Thomas Wyatt, not long back from Spain. He must have a story or two.'

'Oh, I have stories enough.'

'Then you must come and spend an afternoon with us,' Catherine says. 'Mustn't he, Anne?'

'I think not, Mistress,' he says.

'Oh.'

Wyatt is not sure how to read her face. Is she disappointed?
Affronted? A Howard woman typically thinking too well of herself? It must be the latter because her demeanour has become cold. 'Then we'll leave you, Sir Thomas,' she says, tugging on her friend's sleeve and turning on her heel.

Misalliances

He watches them go, considers resuming his seat, but decides he should move on. To go back the way he has come would mean having to follow the girls. No one would much mind if he made his way back in through the kitchens.

Later that afternoon, having been told the King is still busy with the party from Kleve and that he should report again tomorrow, he makes his way back to his lodgings. The letter he received from Thomas Cromwell said he should come in the second week of October, by which time the Germans would have gone, but they haven't apparently and he's not been able to get a room in the palace.

'I'm very sorry, Sir Thomas,' the household clerk said on his arrival. 'There's nowhere I can put you.'

'I'm here on the King's business. He's summoned me.'

'Well...'. A ledger consulted, a head scratched. 'There's a place on Thames Street vacant.'

Thames Street! It was a double assault on his dignity. Courtiers lowlier than he are lodged there and fifteen years ago he had come across his wife copulating with Charles Brandon in one of its houses.

Though not the one he's entering now. The location of Elizabeth's adultery is four doors down. It's doesn't much bother him. What does is that he's here at all. Henry will want to send him away

Misalliances

again, he's sure of it. And what he wants is to be at home, especially now he has another child coming. He'd like to be there for good if only they'd let him. He pulls off his boots and slumps down on the settle.

He's four months back from two years in Spain where he served as the King's ambassador to Charles, the Holy Roman Emperor, and in idle moments he falls in to reflecting on those times. His brief had many strands to it, though they could all be framed thus: improve relations between the King and the Emperor. If Henry's divorcing Catherine of Aragon, the Emperor's aunt, had created a fissure in those relations, then the means by which he had secured the annulment – decreeing the English Church's independence from Rome – had blown open a chasm, and prompted murmurings of war from the Vatican. So, it wasn't a simple brief, and making headway with it was stymied by the peripatetic nature of attendance at Charles V's court. He had spent twenty months of the twenty-four trailing after Charles as he toured the provinces of Spain: from Valladolid to Zaragoza, from there to Monzón, then down to Barcelona and finally on to Toledo. He still has dreams which resurrect that tortuous Imperial progress, from town to town, lofty castle to lofty castle, on stony, rutted, at times barely discernible roads, with the horses losing their shoes and the pack mules forever strung out behind. But something must have been achieved, because though beacons are still in place on hilltops across the south coast, ready to be lighted if Spanish or French ships are sighted coming up the Channel, the King has received repeated assurances from the Emperor that, whatever their differences, he has no plans to join Pope Paul's campaign for a Holy War against heretic, renegade England.

    His thoughts shift to a question that has been nagging at him all day. What to make of his encounter with Kate Howard that morning? There's one thing he's sure of: she's interested in him, not his stories. She's at most eighteen. Half his age. And the word is she's far from averse to some pastime in bed. Hmm. Kate Howard in bed. With this pleasant thought, he begins to relax. He gives in to the wave of sleepiness washing over him.

*The mule train has fallen behind again, the Spanish are cursing, John Mason is tapping him on the shoulder...*He wakes to a knocking. Someone's at the door. He gets up wearily. It's dark. He fumbles to light the candle. 'A moment!' he calls.

    The candle flame is guttering, but there in the pitch black of the alley is the unmistakeable figure of Catherine Howard. She gets her words in first. 'Sir! You are rude!' Her tone is petulant and her lips are set in a childish pout.

'What in God's name...!'

'I try to be friendly and you...' Wyatt can't believe what's in front of him. The girl seems on the verge of tears. She goes on between gulps of breath. 'And you rebuff me...as if I were...as if I were nothing.'

He holds the candle up to her face. 'Come now. I don't think that. And you *are* following me!'

'I saw you crossing the green...' She lets down her hood and peers at him, like she's expecting a reaction and is curious what it might be. There is rouge on her cheeks, kohl on her lashes.

'You've come alone? At this time of night?
'Yes.'
'No one following?'
'I don't think so. I slipped out.'

He sets off down the alley in his stockinged feet, looks this way and that and comes back again. 'You're in the clear.'

'I only came to...'

He takes her by the arm. 'Come inside.'

Passive, she stands motionless as he undoes her coat and pushes it back over her bare shoulders. 'Well, Kate,' he says, 'I can see why all the gallants at court are after you. What is it you want from me?' She raises her eyes. 'Oh,' he says, 'that.' He brushes a droplet of rain from her brow. It would be a shame for the kohl to run. She steps forward and kisses him on the lips.

Chapter Two: Lizzie

Lizzie Darrell puts down her book. 'Oh, he's so loud!

    Jane Wyatt raises her head from her knitting. 'Poynings? He is, isn't he?' She shows Lizzie her work. 'That's a fine enough stitch, don't you think?'

    'You're doing well.'

    'For someone who's still a novice I am.'

    The two women are in what the family calls the parlour. It's at the rear of Allington Castle on the ground floor. The big window faces south-west and this afternoon the room is getting some sun. Their chairs are on either side of the fireplace, though in this spell of warm October weather there's no need yet to light the kindling and set up a blaze. Both have fair hair, but Jane's is of a duller shade than Lizzie's and in its natural curliness has a tendency to escape from her coif. She envies Lizzie her well-behaved locks, and her good looks. She has known from childhood that her round face and large nose were not likely prerequisites for adult beauty. She is the younger of the two. Not long back from burying her father, she's all in black. Lizzie, in her late twenties, ten years the elder, has put on a plain grey gown this morning, not out of any kindred feeling for Jane, but because in the last few days she's concluded

Misalliances

she is pregnant and she likes its looseness, the feel of the soft wool against her skin.

There's another guffaw from the chamber next door. 'God, Tom! You really are the very worst of card players.' Tom's voice, still that of a boy, can be heard giving a grumbling response.

Jane is concentrating on her needles. 'I don't know why he's still here. That bit of business he's doing with Sir Thomas was sorted out weeks ago. It's about time he went back to his wife.'

'He was a help while Thomas was away, wasn't he?'

Jane lets the garment lie in her lap. 'He did take over the management of his money when my father fell ill. He did do that.'

'It sounds like he's been a good friend these last few years.'

'About the only one Thomas had.'

Lizzie knows this. He was close to Henry Norris and William Brereton, and while he kept his head when all the business over Anne Boleyn blew up, they lost theirs. As one of Queen Catherine's ladies, and out in the fens at the time of Anne's fall, she didn't hear he'd also been one of the men implicated in her alleged adultery until after the executions. When the news came of his release from The Tower and appointment as the King's ambassador in Spain, she had burst into tears.

Jane is holding up her knitting, scrutinising it. 'I take it he's pleased?'

'He is.'

'I hope it's a boy. Then Henry'll have a playmate.' Jane pauses, like something's struck her. 'But it's going to be strange for Tom, isn't it? Having a brother – a half-brother - younger than his own child.' If she had not been preoccupied with her knitting, she might have seen a blush rise to Lizzie's cheeks, for whether the child will be Tom's sibling is a question that's been troubling her ever since her monthlies stopped. She puts her face in her book. 'Does he know?'

'I told him last night.'

'What did he say?'

'He just nodded and went off to the stables.' Jane looks up. 'I know you don't find him easy.'

'We get along well enough.'

'You did serve Catherine all that time.'

'I don't think that matters.'

'It might.' Jane picks up the ball of wool to prevent it falling to the floor and moves it closer to her. 'It goes back a long way. He had a bad experience as a boy when he was visiting his father in France. Saw a young woman being burned at the stake by the priests. He hates everything to do with the Pope. He wants this new Church they're talking about. Everything done in English.'

'That's not a bad thing. What I don't like is all the monasteries being shut.'

Misalliances

'I'm surprised they still are. I thought it'd all come to a stop once Anne was gone. It makes sense, I think. If we're not going to have anything more to do with Rome, then why not close down its religious houses? Some of them have terrible reputations.'

'There are good ones.'

'I hear the man driving it doesn't have the purest of motives, though.'

'Thomas Cromwell, you mean?'

'They say he's got rich on it. I think Queen Jane would have been good for the King, don't you? Such a shame we lost her after she'd given him a son. Oh, I've dropped a stitch.' The clicking halts and then resumes. 'What was it like, being with Catherine when she died?'

'Oh...' Lizzie gathers her thoughts. 'Well, it was hard, as you'd expect.' She puts down her book. 'But it had been for months. Nobody came to see us at Kimbolton. Neither when she became ill, nor after she died. I learned later that the King had forbidden it. I think Thomas would have come if he had been allowed to. He liked her. He'd done what he could to help her.'

'That's Thomas for you. And then he helped you.'

'He did.'

'I remember when you came. You *were* in a state.'

'I'd had to walk from Maidstone.'

Misalliances

'And you'd had all that trouble over the Exeters. Did you have no idea what they were up to?'

Lizzie feels Jane's eyes on her. 'I wouldn't have stayed with them, if I had.'

'No wonder the King sent them to the block.'

'Not all of them. Lady Exeter's still in The Tower. I thought for a while I might be heading there myself.'

'There's no danger of that now is there? You're safe, surely.' Jane puts down her knitting and pulls on her slippers. 'It's time I went and checked on my little boy. And the kitchen. That new girl is hopeless.'

Lizzie hopes she's safe. Whenever she looks back at her time living with Gertrude and Henry Courtenay, the Exeters, who had been kind enough to take her in after the old Queen died, her stomach turns over. Thomas had done his best to impress upon her how much peril she was in.

'You do know what sort of house you're in?'

'Yes, a good one. Friends of Queen Catherine.'

'And in league with Henry and Geoffrey Pole to raise a rebellion against the King.'

'How do you know this?'

'Because Reginald Pole has been heard talking about it.'

'He's in Rome, isn't he?'

Misalliances

'In Spain not long ago, trying to drum up support for the Pope's war to return the English Church to Rome. And that's what your friends the Exeters are about.'

'Plotting to topple the King?'

'That's what Pole's saying. Look, I have to be back on the road first thing tomorrow. The Emperor's expecting me and I'm already late. You need to get out of here. I'll call at Allington and tell them you're coming.'

'Thomas, I can't just up and leave. It's not as if I know anyone there.'

'They're good people and they'll look after you. When have I ever been wrong about such things?'

He had not been wrong. And as for seeking refuge at Allington, what other choice did she have? It's gone well, she thinks. There'd been the mistake with Tom, but they'd reached an understanding, and she's confident that won't be a problem. What she's not entirely sure of is whether, in the end, Thomas Wyatt will be good for her. For one thing, he's at the beck and call of the King, which is why he's at Greenwich now.

There's a clash of swords out in the yard. It's been quiet next door for a while.

Jane comes back in. 'Can you hear?' she says. 'They must be fighting with grandfather's swords!'

'Shall we take a walk?' Lizzie says. 'I'm sure we can skirt round them.'

In their exertions the men have wheeled themselves round by the kitchen door They step to one side when the women come out but continue to fight. Tom is getting the worse of things. As Lizzie and Jane watch, he receives a blow on the arm and then on the shoulder.

'It's alright,' he says, backing off to take a breath and rub his shoulder. 'We've blunted them in the forge.'

'Good job, you did,' Lizzie calls, 'otherwise I think you'd be in pieces by now.'

Jane is not to be appeased. 'You should have left those swords where they were, Tom. Your grandfather fought King Richard with them.'

'I don't think grandfather's in much of a position to mind.'

'And you were supposed to be going to Malling Abbey to do the inventory your father wants,'

'I'll do it tomorrow.'

'He might be back tomorrow.'

Tom ignores her and raises his sword to the en-garde position. Thomas Poynings, who has remained silent during these exchanges, does the same.

Tom sends a smile in Lizzie's direction. She's embarrassed by it and turns away. She hopes Jane hasn't noticed.

Misalliances

Chapter Three: Cromwell

In the dimness of dawn, Catherine Howard is quizzing Thomas Wyatt about her cousin, Anne Boleyn. Wyatt would prefer her to lie quiet, her nakedness soft and warm against his own while he strokes her arm, a precursor, if she would let him, to their coupling again, but she's insisting. She wants to know the full story.

'No. I've told you,' he says. 'There was nothing between us after the King showed his interest. Do you take me for a fool?'

'You might be. You're in bed with me.'

He finds her laughter, the low throaty chuckle she does, arousing. A ray of sunlight has succeeded in piercing what he takes to be a morning of low cloud and in flickering across the room it illuminates her face. Though sleep has made it puffy, it has divested it of the rouge and kohl she came wearing the previous evening, and in the momentary burst of light he sees how young she is. Also, he has begun to feel uncomfortable with the levity that underpins her questions.

'And he did put you in The Tower,' she adds, digging him in the ribs.

He knows he has to be careful; she is Thomas Howard's niece. 'I would lay down my life for the King. But if he has a fault, it's that he's too quick to mistrust those around him.'

'And take their heads. He does do that a lot.' She laughs again. Wyatt thinks it best not to comment. 'I suppose,' she goes on, 'being mistrustful comes with being King. My uncle's like that.' She props herself up on one elbow and peers into his face. 'You don't think he had anything to do with it, do you?'

'To do with what?'

'You being suspected of tupping Anne Boleyn…'

'Tupping? We weren't sheep.'

'Fucking, then.'

It's not the word he has anything against, but she has gone too far, strayed into memories he cherishes. And it's not just that. He can tell from the way she hesitated before saying the word, the way her eyes danced, that she thinks it's daring of her. How silly, he thinks. She has no compunction about doing the deed, but she's shy of the word.

'Let's not talk any more about Anne,' he says.

She exhales a gust of bad breath. 'Oh, sorry,' she says, wafting it away and rolling back. It stings him that she is quick to offer an apology for the sourness of her mouth but doesn't see another might be in order.

'It was a serious question,' she continues. 'Are you sure he didn't have anything to do with it? He's one of the few people who has the ear of the King. At least that's what he's always telling me.'

'It was the other Duke who did for me.'

Misalliances

Catherine lets the remark sink in. There are only two dukes in the kingdom. 'Oh, you mean Suffolk. Brandon. He's always trying to pinch my bum.'

There's a hammering on the door downstairs. He swings his legs out of bed. 'Who can that be? No one knows I'm here.'

'I did.'

And someone else will, he realises, as he reaches for hose, undershirt and doublet.

'I've been looking for you in the palace,' Thomas Cromwell complains. 'What in God's name are you doing here?'

'They said there was no room, because of the Germans.'

'The Germans have gone. How long have you been here?'

'Two days. I told the clerk to let you know where I was.'

'He didn't tell me till this morning.' Cromwell surveys his surroundings. He shakes his head, balances himself on the edge of the settle and gathers his fur coat around him. 'You smell of the whorehouse. Have you got a woman here?'

'There's no one but ourselves.'

'In one last night, were you? A whorehouse, I mean.'

'I haven't been in one for ages.'

23

'Not since Barcelona, I suppose. What was that place you went to? Where you consorted with nuns, according to Bonner? Jonkers, was it?'

Edmund Bonner. Wyatt could see the fat little cleric now, strutting up and down indignantly because they wouldn't let him near the Emperor. The lies he had told about their closeness to Charles, to the point of making an accusation he was in league with the traitor Reginald Pole, required a reckoning some time.

'Jonqueres,' Wyatt says, giving the word its Spanish pronunciation. 'And there was none of that. Have you come here just to have a row?'

'Now, now, just joshing. Sit down. We have business to discuss.'

Wyatt is wondering about Kate Howard upstairs, but all is quiet. Cromwell is looking tired, as if he's under strain. He is known for his unperturbed, imperturbable physiognomy, but there are bags under his eyes and some hollowness has infiltrated the usually smooth plane of his cheek.

'Henry will see you this afternoon,' he says. 'He thinks you've been out to pasture long enough. Something is going on with the Emperor and King François.'

'There always is.'

'It looks like the peace between them amounts to more than signatures on paper. And since we know the Pope is still pressuring them to send a fleet and make us all Catholics again, he needs your eyes and ears over there.'

'He had them for two years in Spain. There's nothing in it. I've told him that and so has Charles more than once.'

'Since then the Spanish and French have signed their treaty.'

'They may have, but it doesn't make them allies. They were killing each other outside Milan up to the end of last year.'

'We'll see. Our spies tell us the Emperor is planning to go up to Flanders. The City of Ghent is refusing to pay its taxes and because it's the most important town he has in the Low Countries, it's a rebellion he has to put down. Do you know it?'

'I know of it. It's run by its merchant guilds. They're rich and powerful.'

'Hence its importance. Well, it seems the guildsmen have got above themselves, and Charles wants to put in an appearance himself. Show off his authority by putting down the insurrection personally, presumably with his sister's armies.'

'Why isn't she doing it herself?'

'She hasn't got the appetite for it, apparently. She may be his regent up there but she hasn't been finding it easy. So he's going. Now, here's the thing. He's going by land, presumably because he's afraid we might blow him out of the water if he came by the more obvious means.'

'Soon?'

Misalliances

'Next month.' Cromwell makes one of his familiar hand gestures, a sideways motion with the palm upwards, as if to say 'make of that what you will'.

'He does travel up and down Spain throughout the year.'

'It still strikes me as odd, making that journey in winter. Anyway, however you look at it, Charles and François will be spending time together. And Henry wants you there when that happens. So you'd better get yourself back in Charles' favour.'

'I was never out of it.'

'The Inquisition declared you a heretic!'

'That was nothing to do with him.'

'You kept begging me to get you home.'

'After Henry, or you, ordered the destruction of Thomas à Becket's shrine. In a Catholic country that would have made any Englishman *persona non grata*.'

'Whatever. We want you to meet him in France and follow him into Flanders.'

'Stay with him till then?'

'Yes. In case Ghent isn't the only thing on his mind. Let's not get into that now. I'll give you what we know about dates and itinerary once we've seen Henry. I shall be there too. I make sure of that these days.' Cromwell steadies himself on the settle and picks up his hat.

It's still quiet upstairs. 'What else have you got to tell me?'

'What else? As I said, I'll tell you later.'

'You don't look well.'

Cromwell sighs, like there's a knot of exasperation within which he might just be considering releasing. 'It's nothing physical.' He repositions himself on the settle. 'I'm struggling to get the new Church off the ground. We always knew Henry was only really interested in getting his divorce. At heart, he's no different from Norfolk and Suffolk.' The voice trails off. 'The last straw was when some Lutherans came over from Schmalkalden last month. One of them said he met you in Spain.'

'In Barbastro?'

'If you say so.'

Wyatt doubts he'll ever banish the memory of the weeks he spent in the town waiting on the Emperor, who was presiding over the regional parliament in Monzón. It had nothing to offer in the way of taverns, but then they met the Saxons, the envoys from Schmalkalden, with their own brewer. The many evenings spent supping German beer had made Barbastro just about bearable.

'I think they're serious people,' Cromwell continues. 'I told the King that since he's marrying a German princess, he ought to consider an alliance. The states in the north have a big army and they're willing to take on the Emperor and the Pope. But he's not interested. Once they'd gone, and they stayed barely more than a day, he issued a statement saying the English Church is not going to be like Martin Luther's.'

'He was addressing those who fear it already is.'

'That's most of the people, isn't it? You'd think they'd like the idea of having The Bible in their own tongue. That's the only bit of Luther in *my* new Church. Apart from getting rid of the paraphernalia that places the Pope second to God. High time we were done with all that nonsense.'

'Does Henry no longer agree?'

'Oh, he's happy enough to fill his coffers from all the monasteries I've closed down. But, as I said, when it comes down to it, he still thinks like a Catholic.' Cromwell rocks back and forth on the settle. 'What about this? Norfolk and Suffolk have absented themselves from court in protest against the German marriage. But we've just signed the contract so that's one in their eye.'

'On the subject of eyes, do we know what she looks like?'

'Pretty enough, I'd say. Holbein went over and did a portrait. We need this. Otherwise, we'll be under the heel of the Pope and the Emperor forever.' Cromwell gets up. 'Now, as I said, I shall be there this afternoon, but tread carefully all the same. Air your own views if he asks for them but not otherwise. You've seen what he's like these days.'

'He's fat.'

'Claps it on with each passing day. Do you think it can affect the brain?'

'I've no idea.'

'Well, something's wrong up there.' Hat back on, coat gathered round him, Cromwell makes for the door. On the other side of the doorstep he stops and turns. 'I meant to ask you. The Darrell woman. Did she come to you?'

'She did.'

'Good. I told her to.'

'*You* told her to?'

There's no reply; Cromwell is already halfway down the alley.

Catherine Howard is dressed. 'I'd better go', she says. 'They'll be missing me.' She doesn't meet his eyes before scuttling off down the stairs.

Chapter Four: The Sister

That same morning, at exactly the time Catherine Howard and Thomas Wyatt are talking about Anne Boleyn in his Thames Street bed, a nun silently descends the stairs from the dormitory of St. Peter's Convent. She goes into the dark kitchen and lifts from the griddle the loaf she baked the previous evening. In the larder is a basket, which is full of apples fresh from the tree. She chooses one that is ripe and two that are still green and puts them with the loaf into the canvas bag looped over her arm. She goes to the outside door, quietly slides its heavy bolts, takes its key from the hook on the adjacent wall and unlocks it. She returns the key, pulls open the door and looks out. It's almost light. Some of the monks next door will already have risen and made their way across the yard into the Abbey. A handful of them have abandoned it, as she is about to do, but those who remain are fierce in their condemnation of such deserters; a few weeks ago Sister Margaret had hands laid upon her when word got out she was about to leave. It took the intercession of the Prior himself to allow her to go on her way. 'I fear we shall all have to leave in time,' he said. 'Let our sister go on her way.'

Sister Damaris steps outside, closes the convent door behind her and walks briskly in the direction of the river. On the early morning breeze

Misalliances

the sour, fishy odour of the Thames enters her nostrils.

The street narrows as she approaches the water. The road alongside it will soon be bustling with carts and men on horses making their way to the bridge or to the warehouses, docks and workshops down river. She turns to the left, for she is sure her destination lies that way. All the sisters have been permitted to walk out twice a week with a companion. In her case that used to be Sister Margaret. She has walked many times alongside this particular stretch of the water, where the town houses of the ennobled and wealthy cluster. The tide is low, exposing some yards of the littoral. She stops and looks across the river. It is a disconcerting feeling being on her own today, free to make her own choices. The word 'free' is at once an exciting and frightening word. She's not sure yet what it signifies or how she will manage her knowledge of it once it comes.

The river is beginning to be busy: just a few yards along a wherry is putting out with a single passenger aboard. Directly opposite from where she is standing, there are signs of activity over at Lambeth, figures scrambling about on the deck of a similar craft. She knows about boats, though the knowledge belongs to another time, before she took her final vows. The margins of the river are always littered with this and that, odd items that the current rejects: shards of pottery, vegetable peelings, clumps of half-burnt wood and other stuff she refuses to consider long enough to name. Almost under her feet is a severed arm from a child's doll.

As she follows the curve of the river, beyond the limit of her excursions with Margaret, she comes to a place where an embankment of sorts has been built up. Patches of grass and several bushes have taken hold on this rise. She has to stop again, this time to wipe from her eye a speck of grit thrown up by a passing wagon. As she opens and closes the eye to ensure it is cleared, something catches her attention, a flash of white. Minding where she places her feet, she goes down to take a closer look and realises she's looking at a soiled petticoat. She crosses herself. No one takes a dip in the Thames. The item is more likely the cast-off from some carnal encounter, because she's now among men and women in all their baseness. She prays: *Sancta Maria, Mater Dei, ora pro nobis...*

Whether to conceal her origins or openly wear her head-dress is something she hasn't yet made up her mind about. Under her long surcoat she has on her newest and thickest tunic because she has no other kind of clothing to wear, but at present she is covering her head with a shawl; her wimple is in the bag. She dislikes subterfuge, but she doesn't know how a nun, alone, will be received on the city's streets, or at the house she's intent on finding. She knows it stands on a side-street above the horse-ferry. 'Be who you are,' she says to herself. She squats down behind the nearest bush, removes the shawl, opens her bag and takes out the one thing which will unequivocally identify her as a nun. Once the wimple is tight to her face and secured at the neck, she climbs back on to the road.

The horse-ferry, with its railed enclosures and staging, is not far ahead. A barge is waiting for its first freight of the day. The city is waking. Traffic was desultory a while ago but riders and carts are passing her continually now. When she comes to the junction, she turns left and then, relying on instinct as much as memory, left again. She finds herself in a quiet street and enclosed once again by tall, well-appointed houses.

It's twelve years since she spent time in this house, but she's sure it is the one. Double-fronted with tall, narrow window embrasures and a steep tiled roof, it's as she first saw it, though not as big as she has pictured it in her mind's eye all this time. Her understanding then was that Thomas Wyatt stayed there only occasionally. If he's not there. she's hoping someone will be. As she crosses the forecourt she sees a lamp is burning in one of the front rooms. Hoping her status as a nun will give her some sort of welcome, she undoes her coat to display her black habit, straightens her wimple, and knocks on the door. A woman in servant's cap and apron answers.

'Sister?' The woman's tone is friendly.

'Good morning,' she says. 'I am Sister Damaris from St. Peter's Convent. I believe this house belongs to Thomas Wyatt.'

'No, I'm sorry. It belongs to Sir Richard Southwell. He bought it from Sir Thomas two years ago.'

'Oh. Do you know if he moved to somewhere else in the city?'

'I don't.'

'Then I'm sorry to have bothered you.'

'He used to spend a lot of time at court,' the woman adds. 'At Greenwich.'

The Sister nods. She knows that. 'Thank you for your time,' she says, before returning to the street and back to the river.

There is a milestone opposite. The letters on it say: 'Westminster 1 mile.' After waiting for a gap in the procession of carts and riders, she crosses over and perches herself on it. She takes the loaf out. Laying it in her lap, she reaches into her bag for the ripe apple. She has come so short a distance, but she left without breakfast, and taking a few minutes to remedy that will also give her time to think.

Perhaps her plan was always a foolish one. Not for the first time, she wonders if she should be putting her faith in Thomas Wyatt. But all those years ago he had been her saviour. Her hand is sticky with apple juice and she wipes it on her coat before feeling for her purse. She knows that were it not for Sister Ann, her gift of a handful of florins, she would not now be sitting where she is, chewing on bread and apple beside the river, a mile from home. She would still be at the Abbey, waiting on the pension that's been promised to all the nuns and monks turned out of their houses but which she doubts will ever come.

She has rehearsed this moment, what she would do if she were out on a city road with nowhere to go. On the day she left her father's house, she resolved never to return to it. He will be in his fifties and more lecherous than ever. What little experience she has of life outside convent walls has told her that is often the way with men as they age. But Thomas Wyatt is not like that. He's a good man. And she's not ready yet to abandon her quest for his assistance.

She's always dismissed the idea of taking a boat up to Placentia. Who's to say he would be there? And even if he were, what kind of reception would a nun get at the King's palace, when it's he who's ordered the closure of the religious houses. There's only one thing to do. It'll be a long journey, but if the pilgrims of old could walk all the way to Canterbury, she certainly can to Maidstone. She knows the road to Kent starts on the other side of the river. To find it she must go across the bridge.

It's a forbidding structure, but even more terrifying are the masses of people coming off it and scrabbling to get on. With a deep breath, she plunges in. The narrow passage through the gate throws everyone into a tussle for space to lay their feet. No one is averse to making their way, coming or going, with a push or a shove. She feels fingers working at the pocket of her coat and she slaps them away. Once through the bottleneck and free of its competing feet and elbows, its creeping, criminal fingers, she relaxes a little, only for a young workman - a handle of a saw protrudes from his sail-cloth sack - to take her arm and pull her to one side. 'Careful, Sister,' he says. She's grateful, as much for the respect she's been shown as for being prevented from stumbling over an overturned handcart.

She's on the bridge proper now. The road is narrow, straitened by the buildings upon either side, many of which are connected overhead by what appear to be extensions of this house, that shop. Here is a draper, its business proclaimed by a sign high on the wall, over there a costermonger loudly advertising his wares. A boy stationed directly in her path is selling comfits from a box strung round his neck. When the wall she's trying to stay close to admits a gap, she takes advantage of the fresher air and takes refuge against the few yards of railing. She dares to look down at the river below. The water beneath her is turbulent, its currents crowding in on themselves to find their way through the arches, much like the people above navigating their way along their own constricted pathway. For a moment her progress, for all its unsteadiness, is obstructed by a woman with bent back and bow-legs. A man of middle-age edges past them both. He smells of soap and rose-water. She imagines him on his way to his lover, now that her man has left the house to go to work. A butcher in a bloodied apron hurries by.

She spies the building she's been told of. St. Thomas's Chapel is indeed seemingly built out in mid-air. The miniature church beckons her and she's drawn to it, longs to spend some time there away from the noise and commotion, but her journey has barely begun and she walks on, over the drawbridge which marks the half-way point. To her alarm she can feel it swaying.

Ahead, a handful of people are staring at something raised above the barrier. Realising what it must be, and wanting to avoid it, she crosses over. It's something else she's been told about, the heads on spikes. She tells herself she's not going to look, then does, quickly, and sees a face, distorted by rigour and weathering. Most of those around her are taking little notice of the spectacle so she pretends to be one of this indifferent party and walks on. Bad enough, she thinks, for men and women to lose their heads for disagreeing with the King, but to display them in such a public fashion, that's an act as barbaric as any heathen's. While she can find it in herself to excuse the people who find entertainment in such a show, she can't her King.

Misalliances

Once through the second gate, she sees respite, the *terra firma* of Southwark. She knows it only by its reputation. On this October morning the sun is bright and she has felt too warm in her coat for a while. She decides to reveal fully who, or rather what, she is, to stuff her coat into her bag and walk proud, if not fearless, through these streets.

The cozeners and cut-purses Sister Ann warned her of must still be in bed, for Southwark, like the bridge, appears to be populated only by folk off to their daily toil. The street she's on is lined with grocers, fishmongers, poulterers; she passes a glover, a draper, a shoemaker. Compared to those in Westminster, the frontages of the shops are worn, shabby. Occasionally she catches someone glance at her. She comes upon a barrow piled with carrots, cabbages and turnips. 'Which is the way to the Kent Road?' she asks the boy behind it.

He points to her right. 'Over that way, missus.'

'Is it far?'

'Not far.'

The chooses the street opposite. It looks as if it's going in the right direction. But she's not gone far when she starts to worry it might be a dead-end because what at first appeared a well-trodden footpath has deteriorated into little more than an alley. To her relief, it eventually opens out into small square. A rough voice calls out 'Hello!' and she jumps. It comes again. 'Lost your maidenhead yet, Sister?' Raucous laughter follows. Two men appear and begin to caper around her. Ugly bignosed faces, thread-bare shirts and hose. They gurn and grimace, poke their fingers at her. She spins round and tries to push past them. There's shouting of another kind. It sounds like it's coming from a woman and it's angry: 'Get off her! Get off, I say!'

A balloon of a figure in yellow and red taffeta breaks into the frenetic circling. It strikes one of the men with its fist. The other man backs off, still leaping about in a crazed simulacrum of a dance. 'Meant nothing by it, Mary!' he cries. The woman hoists up the waistband of her skirt so it sits more securely on her expansive belly and waves the fist after him: 'Get back to your kennel!' She swings round to face the Sister, who is finding the garish make-up of her rescuer as frightening as the bulk of her. 'What're you doin' 'ere? This is no place for you.'

'I'm looking for the Kent Road.'

'Kent Street?' The whore straightens her cap. 'It's not that far off. Go straight on as you're doing.' She considers the other type of female before her. 'Listen, you may be a nun, but the blackguards round here won't be put off by that. You're pretty and comely and you're on your own. A cunt's a cunt to them. 'Ave you got something to protect yourself?'

'What sort of thing?'

'Stay there.'

The woman goes off into a house with sagging eaves and comes back with a thick stick in her hand. It's been planed and polished. 'It's briar wood. Hard wood. Anyone else tries to waylay you, you hit 'em with it. You'll soon be out of the city once you're on Kent Street. It's all open country after Saint Thomas a Watering. Where you goin'?'

'Maidstone.'

'That's a fair stretch. *I* wouldn't fancy doin' that on me own. Listen. Make sure you're not still on the road at dusk. Don't wait too long finding somewhere to bed down. The light evenings have gone and the road at night is no place for a woman.'

No one has ever told Damaris she's pretty. Apart from her father, that is. Reduced to drunken, mumbling sentimentality once she had yet again rebuffed him, he would sit back down in his chair and say things like that. Didn't Thomas Wyatt also find something in her looks that he liked? He might never have said as much but she thinks he did. As she pushes on, trying to keep a straight course through the maze of narrow by-ways, she smiles to herself. She knows she's on Kent Street when she comes out on to a wide thoroughfare which soon takes her beyond the tight-packed streets.

Misalliances

On either side are hedge-rows crowded with berries. The bright red ones tempt her but she's not sure what they are. The black ones are safe, she knows, and using the stick she pulls the brambles towards her and carefully picks a handful. A cart comes up behind her and she hopes its occupant might see what she is and stop, but it doesn't. She meets two women carrying baskets of apples and exchanges nods with them. A young man is striding towards her, a sack over his shoulder. 'There's been a hanging at Watering, Sister,' he tells her. 'Don't drink the water.' She doesn't know what he means. 'Is it far?' she calls after him.

He spins round, walking backwards. 'The next bend.'

She feels she has been walking a long time, but it can't be so long because she can tell by where the sun is that the day is not far advanced. Her feet are sore and her legs are beginning to ache. Pilgrims used to stop at Watering - it's how it got its name - and she'll rest there a while too.

At first she has no reason to suspect it's anything other than what she was hoping for, a patch of ground with a stream running across it where she can sit. She can hear the babbling of the water before she gets there. It's only then she sees the scaffold and the three hooded, dangling corpses. Her feet want the weight taken off them but her head is telling her not to stop. A breeze stirs the

Misalliances

trees and assaults her with the smell of rotting flesh. Up comes the bread and apple. Some of it goes down her front. She staggers back, wipes her mouth and, staggering a little at first, walks on.

A while later, less than hour, she comes to a hamlet, a scattering of cottages, a big house on a hill, and it's there she sits at last, on a grass bank. Slipping off her shoes, she massages her throbbing feet. Though her coat is still in the bag, she's become uncomfortably sweaty. She's about to remove her wimple to get some air to her scalp, when she hears a wagon coming down the road. She puts her shoes back on and, doing her best not to appear as desperate as she feels, looks up. She sees a man and a woman, some years older than herself, ordinary folk by the looks of them. The man is calling out to the big drayhorse: 'Whooah.' They're actually stopping.

'Come, Sister,' the woman says, getting off the seat. She climbs down. 'You look worn out,' she says, as she helps Damaris up. 'Have you come far?'

'Westminster,' Damaris murmurs.

'And where are you going to?'

'Maidstone.'

'This is James and I'm Marion.' James gives her a shy smile and a nod of acknowledgement. He lifts the reins and slaps the horse's rump with them.

Misalliances

'That's a Benedictine habit, if I'm not mistaken,' Marion says.

'Yes,' Damaris says, still catching her breath. 'We're Dominican. Or we used to be.'

Bit by bit, stories are exchanged. Marion's and James's house, Dartford Priory, was closed earlier in the year.

'Don't feel guilty about leaving St. Peter's,' she says. 'Looking back. I wish we'd had the presence of mind to do something like that. Then we wouldn't have had to face the indignity of being turned out. And having to deal with the men who came to do it. Oh, they were respectful enough, even polite one or two of them, but we quickly learned what would happen if we resisted. You must have come past Watering?'

'I did. It was horrible.'

'Three men?'

'Yes.'

'One of them was ours. Brother Michael. He refused to swear allegiance to the King and barricaded himself in the sacristy. So they took him to Watering and hanged him.'

'It's because it's a revered place,' James says. 'It's their idea of making a point. Cromwell and the zealots around him.'

'So you renounced your vows?'

'And took the oath acknowledging the King as head of the new Church,' Marion says. 'It was either that or face the consequences. And it was the only way to get their pension.'

'I don't want to renounce my vows,' Damaris says.

'Well, I think you have to ask yourself what they mean now, since you've left your house. The fact of it is, I'm no longer a nun and James is no longer a monk, but we still have our breviaries. We still make time for prayer every day. I'm a good Christian woman, and he's a good Christian man. Listen. We're going to the other side of Dartford. It'll be getting dark by then. Spend the night with us and in the morning we'll see about getting you where you want to go.'

Chapter Five: The King

Wyatt is received in the outer room, which he prefers to the more private ones because he finds them stifling with their chintzy daybeds, damask wall-hangings and overperfumed air. It contains just one item of furniture, the large estate chair the King likes to occupy when visitors come on business.

Henry looks ill-at-ease today. The way he's wriggling his bottom back and forth suggests there's a problem there. Perhaps Thomas Heanage, who has the honour of being Groom of the Stool, needs to find a softer cloth to wipe the royal bum.

'I expect better than this,' Henry is saying. 'The Emperor and the King of France are now in bed with one other. How is that, Wyatt?'

'If you remember, your Majesty, I did tell you that was in the wind.'

'When?'

'When I came back to put the Emperor's offer. About the marriage.'

Wyatt had journeyed from Nice to Greenwich at pell-mell pace. Five post-horses, stopping only to eat, drink, empty his bowels and snatch a few winks of sleep. He'd been so saddle-sore when he arrived, he could hardly walk. He'd done it in eight days. The Emperor, who never in his life had ridden post-horses, had said he had to be back in fifteen. He was never going to make it. By the

Misalliances

time he did get back to Nice, Charles was on his way to meet François.

Henry has bent down to scratch his calf. His ulcer must be playing up. 'The marriage? It was no more than a sop, to keep me quiet.'

'Hardly a sop, your Majesty, to propose you take his niece as your Queen.'

'Don't tell me what is and what isn't a sop! You were a fool, Wyatt. Charles hoodwinked you. Wanted you out of the way while he cosied up to France. We'll give you another chance. Get yourself over there and worm your way back into Charles' good opinion. Find out what they're up to and if the Pope's involved. And remember whose side you're on.'

'I know that, your Majesty.'

'Do you? I began to wonder whose ambassador you were last time, Charles' or mine.'

Wyatt knows where this has come from. Bonner's report. He's seen it. What were the words? *Wyatt aims to please the Emperor and be in his favour.* The King is pointing at him. 'And tell Charles that if he wants our help with the Turks, he'll first have to break with the Pope.'

'Break with the Pope.' Wyatt looks to Cromwell for aid but he's studying the floor. 'Understood.'

'What do you know of Robert Branceter?'

'He took himself off to Rome last year. He's on our list of traitors.'

'He's now working for Charles. I've told Bonner to look out for him in Paris. The trouble is Bonner likes to do things by the book, so I'd rather you saw to it.'

'Saw to it...'

The King tips sideways in the chair, like he's trying to fart. 'Are you having trouble understanding me this afternoon?'

Wyatt takes a step back. 'Not at all. No.'

'I'm not expecting you to do it yourself. But I want it done.' Henry pulls his furs round his shoulders and directs his attention to Cromwell. 'Mister Secretary, you've said nothing till now. Why are you here?'

'Sir Thomas needs an itinerary, to be advised who is likely to be in the Emperor's train, which of those he already knows and might successfully cultivate. He needs to know who to avoid and who to obstruct...'

'I don't need the details.' The King struggles to his feet, waves away the page hurrying to help him and limps off.

'Break with the Pope!' Cromwell scoffs, when they are back in his office. 'I'll leave you to decide whether to tell the Holy Roman Emperor to do that.'

'I'm not going to.'

'Look, the way I see it working is that you meet up with the Spanish before they get to Paris. Then take advantage of whatever credibility you

Misalliances

do have with Charles to find out if an alliance is on the cards. Personally, I'm hoping there is.'

'Are you?'

'Well, leaving aside the fact that it probably wouldn't last much longer than it takes Henry to fart – did you see that? - it'd make an alliance between ourselves and the Germans more appealing. And that brings me on to what I suspect is Charles' second reason for coming up into the Low Countries. There's something else going on in Kleve that he's going to be unhappy about. The question of Gelderland, who it really belongs to.'

'It's his, surely.'

'Yes and no. It borders the duchy of Kleve and was once theirs. By one means or another it came into Charles' possession. Years ago. The old Duke made noises now and then but he never had the courage, or the muscle, to take Charles on. The old man's dead and his son William – the princess's brother, a youngster, barely in his twenties - has inherited the dukedom. He wants Gelderland back. You can see where I'm going with this. If Charles, with a big army behind him, decides to take on William once he's finished with Ghent...'

'Henry might feel obliged to side with his new wife's brother...'

'And to form an alliance with the Germans. It's the obvious counterweight to one between France and Spain. So while you've got your ear to the ground about that...'

'Find out if Charles is planning to march on Kleve.'

'You've got it. Who will you want to take with you? It only needs to be a small party.'

'John Mason, if he's safe to go.'

'Why shouldn't he be?'

'Because when I sent him back from Spain you had him arrested for spending time with Reginald Pole.'

'That was Suffolk, not me. You know all this. I told you.'

'That I was the real target. But where does that leave Mason?'

'He's in the clear. As are you.'

'Is Lizzie Darrell?'

'What?'

'After the Exeter business.'

'What's made you bring that up?'

'You mentioned her this morning…'

'She's been in the clear for ages. She put herself there. I thought you'd know.'

'I didn't.' Wyatt is momentarily lost for words. He moves quickly on to safer ground. 'So, when should I start?'

'The beginning of next month. No later, because you'll have a lot of riding to do and you'll need to present yourself to François first. You'll not be doing anything without that. And you need these.' Cromwell hands over a packet of documents. 'Rouge Croix safe conduct papers and where we think Charles is going to be and when.

You shouldn't have any trouble. Unless you kill Branceter, that is. Whether it's wise to do that, given the consequences it would have for our relations with the Emperor, I'll leave you to decide.'

'We might decide he's impossible to find.'

'Bonner might decide the same, I suppose, with some help from you.'

'Understood. We'll do what we can. Is that all?'

'For now.'

'I'll go straight from Allington.'

Cromwell stands and offers his hand. 'God speed, Thomas.'

He's on his way out when he sees his wife coming towards him.

'Elizabeth.'

'Thomas. Don't look so surprised. I do come up to court sometimes.'

'I see you do.'

'Has my brother been in touch?'

'I've had a letter.'

'And...?'

'I'm amazed you think I still owe you anything.'

The bright eyes harden. 'I have a right, Thomas. I have a son and grandson at Allington. And a daughter-in-law.'

'You can visit for an afternoon as long as you give us notice. It's no distance from Cooling.'

'I'm entitled to some rooms of my own.'
'I think not.'
'Is it because of that woman you've got there?'
'That's none of your business.'
'I have met her.'
'I know. You came down when the child was born.'
'Well, you weren't there...'
'I am now.'
'And how long will it be before the King sends you off again? Tom needs his mother.'

Wyatt slips the pouch of documents into the inside pocket of his jacket. 'Strange he's never said. Goodbye, Elizabeth.'

As he crosses the green, he notes how the shadows are lengthening. It's too late to set off for Allington. It'll have to be first thing in the morning.

Chapter Six: Kate Again

Catherine has taken to spending her afternoons in a room above the Queen's floor with Anne Basset. As a newcomer to Greenwich, she's made friends with Anne because she's pleasant enough and she thought she'd need someone to show her what's expected of a lady-in waiting. But there's no queen so the situation is altogether odd. Some of the women who served Queen Jane still meet daily in her Presence Chamber; others are who knows where. It means Catherine and Anne have the place upstairs to themselves.

It's high on the west side of Placentia, overlooking the green which separates the palace from the village, a crow's nest for someone who wants to see who's coming and going. Catherine, in just her shift, has been doing this for much of the afternoon. When Anne wakes from a doze and sees her friend still in the same position, she says: 'Kate, don't you think you should leave off? You're going to catch cold.'

'This was the time he walked back last night.'

'It'll be dark soon. You're not going to see him then.'

'I'll go anyway.'

'You'll be caught.'

Catherine turns from the window. 'I wasn't coming back this morning.'

Misalliances

Anne crosses to the table, pours herself some beer and returns to the bed. 'You won't be able to behave like this when we get a new queen.'

'There's still no sign of one.'

'It'll be the German.'

Catherine jumps up and lets out a shriek. 'He's there! It's him, I'm sure of it.' She picks up her coat and hastily shoves her arms into it. 'Cover for me at supper. Say I'm unwell.'

'You can't go like that.' Anne jumps off the bed and chases after. 'Kate! You need to get dressed.'

But Catherine is already tumbling down the stairs to the next floor. It's supper-time, so there'll be nobody much about. When she reaches the ground floor she slows, because there are always guards there and though they wouldn't stop her it's best she's not seen. She's tempted to run, but she restrains herself, just in case. The side-door is unmanned. She's outside and free.

'No,' Wyatt is saying, 'you should go. I need a good night's sleep, and you, lady, mustn't risk another night away from your bed.'

Catherine snuggles up to him. 'What do you need a good night's sleep for? Am I getting too much for you?'

'I have to be back in Kent tomorrow.'

She abandons her exploration of his beard and sits up. 'Dear heart, no!'

It hits him hard. He's not seen it before, the likeness, but it's there, not simply in the use of her cousin Anne's favourite endearment, but in the emotion so unguardedly exposed. And in the voicing of vulnerability, of loss. It's Anne when she came to him at Beaulieu, and afterwards here at Greenwich, by which time she was Queen but still in need of him. He hasn't seen it before in Kate because he hasn't been about to leave.

He strokes his hand down her bare back. 'Don't be upset.'

'I thought you liked me.'

He's at a loss. This pretty young woman has become attached to him, whereas he thought she was simply having an adventure, like girls do. 'I do like you. Of course, I do.'

She's crying. 'When will I see you again?'

'I don't know. I've got to go to France.'

'Now?'

'In a few weeks.'

She rolls out of bed. He watches her pull on her shift, slide her feet into her shoes and grab her coat. She's scrabbling in its pockets for something. He reaches for his jacket and extracts his handkerchief. 'Here,' he says.

She snatches it, wipes her eyes and throws it on the bed. Then she's gone.

Misalliances

Chapter Seven: James

Having found the straw pallet no less hard than her bed at St. Peter's, Damaris has slept well. It is almost light. The air in the room is chill.

Marion's told her the two-room cottage used to belong to her mother. Luckier than some, she and James came there when they were evicted from Dartford Priory. There's an outhouse-cum-stable attached and a sizeable vegetable garden. Damaris, uncertain of her own future, envies them. There's no sign of life from Marion in the other room and James must still be asleep in the outhouse. She wonder if this is how things normally are. Something in the air last night suggested otherwise, though it was nothing more than an exchange of glances when, with the dark pressing against the window and the candles wilting, James declared it was time for his bed and went out. Setting to one side the impulse to rise as she would normally be doing at the crack of dawn, she recalls the evening's conversation.

'Take my advice,' Marion said. 'Put off your habit. Wear ordinary clothes. You'll draw attention to yourself as you are. I've got something you can have. You'll find it easier, believe me. There'll be fewer questions, fewer problems. That's how James and I have managed to live together.'

'Because you look like an ordinary couple…'

Misalliances

'We're not a couple. That's a threshold we've not crossed. I'm fond of him. And I shall miss having his company tomorrow while he's taking you to Maidstone.'

She likes riding in the wagon, seated high above the road. As they have moved away from Dartford, the highway has broadened out from its banks of hedgerows and overhanging trees.

James has become unexpectedly talkative. 'So, what's in Maidstone for you, Sister?'

'It's actually Allington I'm going to. Do you know it?'

'It's just before you get to Maidstone. There's not much there apart from Sir Thomas Wyatt's place. Is he the friend you mentioned?'

'I don't know I'd call him a friend. He did me a good turn once and I'm hoping he'll help me. You've heard of him, then...'

'Heard of him? Everyone in Kent has heard of him.'

'Why's that?'

James gives the reins a flick and clucks at the horse. 'Don't you know? He was one of those sent to The Tower when it all came out about Queen Anne. Anne Boleyn.'

Damaris can feel the blood rushing into her cheeks. 'But I was told yesterday he's still at Greenwich.'

'He probably is. He was the only one the King let go. The rest went to the block. You must have heard about it.'

'About Anne, yes. I'd no idea Sir Thomas was involved.' It's only a flutter of a laugh, but it's all she can manage.

'He's done well since. The King sent him to Spain as his ambassador. So he's still a favourite.'

They are coming to a steep hill. James gives the horse a light slap on the rump with the reins. 'Go on, boy!' He says to Damaris: 'Samuel came with the wagon. He's getting on a bit but he'll make it.'

At the very top, she wonders if they're going to. Once it's been crested Samuel's pace picks up a little and then as the downside of the hill evens out he settles to his characteristic plodding speed. At the very bottom, there's a tight bend. As if out of nowhere a powerful horse appears, cutting the corner. It's coming straight at them. Its rider steers it away at the very last moment but Samuel, whinnying in alarm, has pulled them too far to the side of the road. They're pitching into the ditch.

James lets go of Damaris's arm. 'You alright?'

'I think so.' She steadies herself and straightens her bonnet,

'I need to get him out of his traces.' He helps her down. 'We've lost a wheel. I'm sorry. We'll have to start walking to find a wheelwright.' Unlike the wagon, Samuel is upright. He's tossing his head and puffing.

Fellow travellers are numerous, galloping by on their daily business. Damaris expects the one coming up behind them to go on past like everyone else, but he's slowing, coming alongside. He takes off his hat, gives it a shake and wipes his brow.

'Good morning,' he says. 'Is that your horse and wagon back there?'

James looks up. 'It is. We've lost a wheel.'

Her heart skips a beat. It's him. Older, of course, and his hair is thinning, but it's him. He hasn't recognised her, but why would Thomas Wyatt see in this ordinarily clad woman the nun he had known years before? As his eyes settle on her, she takes fright and draws the shawl round her face.

'Mistress,' he says, before returning his attention to James. 'Where are you going?'

'Anywhere there's a wheelwright.'

'You'll not find one much before Rochester. I'll be there within the hour. I'll get a man out to you.'

'I'd be most grateful if you could. It'll need a team.'

Wyatt replaces his hat. 'A team, yes.'

'Thank you, Sir.'

'Not at all. I'm happy to help. You might as well go back and wait.'

Damaris, still rooted to the spot by indecision, feels Wyatt's eyes flicker over her again. She's about to say something, like 'Sir, do you remember me?', but she can't formulate the right words and his horse is moving.

'That was good of him,' James says. 'I wonder who he is?' She says nothing. 'I can't see anyone coming out this afternoon, can you? We could be out here for the night, Sister.'

It's another cold one. She wraps her coat around her, glances at James who has settled down a decent space away, and the next thing she knows, she's waking to him climbing back in.

'I'm sorry,' he says. 'Go back to sleep.'

She can guess where he's been. 'Is he alright?'

'He is. He's still cropping the grass over there.'

She's wide awake now. 'Couldn't we sit together? I'm frozen.'

Chapter Eight: Histories

In the stable-yard Thomas Wyatt takes Lizzie into his arms. 'How are you, my love?' He places his fingers on her belly. 'All well?'

'All well.' She pecks him on the cheek and picks up beneath the staleness of his hair just the feintest trace of something feminine, a hint of fragrance. His smile persuades her to dismiss it.

'And everyone else?'

'Well enough.'

'Even Tom?'

'Even Tom.' She walks him in. 'A good journey?'

'Yes. A clear run, apart from stopping to help a couple with a broken down wagon.'

'And other news?'

'I'll tell you later,' he says.

At the supper table, Tom is being defensive: 'You don't even want them!'

'That's not the point.' His father wags his spoon at him. 'I told you to go to Malling Abbey and start an inventory. Instead, you've been idling here, playing cards and fighting with grandfather's swords. Apart from whatever you've been up to in town.'

'I haven't been up to anything in town.' Tom swirls the custard round. 'Can't Edward do it?'

Misalliances

Wyatt lays down his spoon. 'Edward's getting things ready at Boxley.'

'We're almost done,' Poynings says. 'I'll bring Katherine up in a week or two. She's looking forward to being closer to the city.' He wipes his mouth. 'That was good. I'll be in the other room.'

'We'll talk later,' Wyatt calls after him. He lays down his napkin. 'Lizzie, Jane, will you excuse us?' He beckons his son. 'Tom, let's go next door.'

Lizzie and Jane, still at the table, hear everything that follows.

- You're right, I don't want them.
- Then tell that to the King.
- I can't.
- Why not?
- Sit down.
- No.
- Sit down! Listen, because this is about you, and this place, your wife and son and God knows what else. Some of it you will know, some you won't, because you were small when it happened. Tom...?
- I'm listening.
- When the King put me in The Tower three years ago...
- Not that again…
- Just listen. When I wound up in The Tower your grandfather told you it was because of

something I'd said about the King. But that wasn't the reason. And it's time you heard the truth. After your mother and I stopped living together...you know about all of that...I became involved with Anne Boleyn. Nobody knew. And then the King became smitten with her...

Jane says: 'Do you really want to hear all this, Lizzie?'
   'Yes, I do. I was there for some of it.'

- Did he know about you and her?
- Not at first. Then he got wind of things and I told him the truth.
- So *that's* why you were arrested when things came out about her...
- That's why. I hadn't done, or said, anything wrong. I certainly wasn't one of the men she'd been entertaining in her bedchamber. I can't explain why he sent me off to Spain after he had me released. I thought Thomas Cromwell must have had something to do with it, but he says not. I didn't want to go, but I was back in favour so I'd have been a fool not to. You need to understand this. If you want to prosper at court, you have to stay in favour. So, to go back to what you said, I can't return the gift of the Abbeys. The King would be offended and then where might I be?
- Out of favour.

- They are ours and we must make the best of it. I explained why we had to make a start on the inventory as soon as possible. Why I wanted you to do it while I was in London.
- Because the Treasury will be waiting for it. So they can say what they want from it. Its valuables.
- Mostly.
- We have to send them.
- We do. It's a condition of the gift. There'd be trouble if we didn't. I could wind up in The Tower again. You can't play the King false. That's how I've stayed in favour. I play by the rules. So, you will go to Malling tomorrow and make the start you should have made a week ago. I want this to be *your* job.

They hear movement. Tom and his father are on their feet. 'Let's go into the parlour before they come back,' Lizzie whispers.
    'Anything new?'
    'Yes.'

Lizzie and Wyatt are back at the supper table. He's telling her he shouldn't be away for long; he'll certainly be back in time for the baby.
    'How can you be sure of that?'
    'I'll make sure. It's not like it was in Spain. I'm not going to be a resident ambassador. If it's the end of April, or early May...'
    'I think so.'

'If we're still there at the end of March, I'll leave things with Mason. It's only France. I can be back in a week.'

'Is it going to be to be dangerous, what you're doing?'

'No, no. We'll be there as Rouge Croix, which means we're entitled to safe passage.'

'Because I don't want this baby losing its father before it's come into the world.'

The servants have left a pepper pot on the table and he's moving it around. 'I didn't know you'd been to see Cromwell after the business with the Exeters.'

'He's told you.' She pushes a glass across the table. 'Give me some of that, please. I wrote to him.'

'Why?'

'Well, for one thing, I was expecting to be dragged off to The Tower any day.'

'This was after you'd been questioned...'

'Yes.'

'And you'd told them you didn't know anything.'

'Except that wasn't entirely true.' She takes the pepper-pot from him and begins to play with it herself. 'Look. I know I haven't been straight with you, but it was for the best of reasons. I didn't know anything until you turned up out of the blue, frightening the life out of me.' Lizzie's eyes flash. 'What was I to make of that? I haven't heard from

Misalliances

you for over a year and then you come and tell me I'm living in a nest of traitors!'

'I had no idea where you were. I told you.'

'And then you were off again, back to Spain!'

'France. And that's unfair. I explained the bind I was in.'

'Anyway, after you'd been to see me, I started to think. Henry and Geoffrey Pole were always coming to the house and then all of a sudden they weren't. Instead, Lady Exeter and I began going to them, to the Poles. It was easier to spend time with Jane and Constance that way, they said. We always took a letter. Sometimes I went on my own.'

'You became their messenger.'

'When I was first taken in for questioning, I saw Richard Rich. Then Cromwell came in and took over. I didn't think I was important enough for him. I was frightened, Thomas, so I told him. How many visits I'd made. How many letters.'

'And then he let you go.'

'He did, but he said he'd have to speak to the council and they might want to speak to me again.'

'You should have come straight here like I told you.'

'How would it have gone for you if they'd then turned up to arrest me? I didn't want to put you in danger. When I wrote to him, it wasn't to find out where I stood. I'm not that naïve. I needed help. I was on my own and what money I had was nearly gone. I threw myself on his mercy, said that

Misalliances

since I couldn't very well stay at the Exeters any longer, could he help me? To my surprise, he told me I should come to you.'

'Would you have come if he hadn't told you that?'

'What?'

'I came to see you in June of last year. I know exactly when it was because I was on that madcap mission – riding all the way from Nice and back again - to persuade the King to take Christina of Denmark as his wife. I walked into a house that I knew was a nest of traitors with the single purpose of convincing you to get out and come here. You finally came eight months later. What took you so long?'

'I've just told you.'

'Did Cromwell know I'd been to see you?'

'He didn't say. I wasn't going to tell him.' Lizzie empties her glass. 'I should have come when you said.'

'You should.'

'If I'd known I was in the clear, I would have. Nick Carew was executed in March for his part in things. Lady Gertrude and Margaret Pole are still in The Tower. And for all I know, *I'm* still on their list. That's why I've never told you any of this.'

'I saw Cromwell yesterday. He said you've known for ages you're in the clear.'

'I didn't know.'

'You should have.'

'Because I'd betrayed my friends?'

Misalliances

'No, because you hadn't committed treason. They had.' Wyatt fills his glass. 'I wish you'd had more faith in me.'

'I'm sorry.'

'This betrayal thing. It eats away at you if you're not careful. After Anne went to the block, I thought I was to blame. It nagged at me for months. Whether what I had once told the King about her loose behaviour in France had convinced him that the stories about Brereton and Norris and her brother were true. And that's what did for her. It took me a while to get over that, to make myself accept that it had to be whatever she had done since, not ten years ago. None of us is responsible for the actions of others. Whether that's the Poles plotting against the King, or Anne's wanting the company of other men. Or the King executing her, come to that.' His voice has slowed. 'When it comes down to it, we have to look after ourselves.'

'Was Anne really like that when she was in France?'

'She was. I got that from someone who knew her. She was very young then, of course, and…well…I'm sure you've heard about the French court. Its licentiousness.'

'Will you be going there?'

'I shall have to.'

'Then you'd better be careful. I don't want anything else coming between us.'

Misalliances

Later, with Lizzie asleep beside him, he's wide awake. What he hasn't told her about Anne, and never will, is filling his head again, not something he'd said, as Tom had thought, but something he didn't say. He knew Thomas Cromwell was having her watched and he didn't tell her. At the time, he couldn't see it would do any good. She would have demanded Cromwell's head and the King, once told why she was being spied on - what reportedly went on in her rooms late at night – would most likely have taken hers there and then. How could he have foreseen that Henry was going to do that anyway, two months later, after the reports from Cromwell's spies had been supplemented by the confessions of those accused of having carnal relations with her? Smeaton, Norris, Weston, Brereton, and her brother George. Never Brereton and George, he thought. But the other three? He thought they might have been admitted to that inner sanctum where on pain of death it was forbidden to go. What was certain was the King wanted a new wife, desired Jane Seymour so hotly that he married her fourteen days after having Anne put to death. There it was. There was no point in reproaching himself. Nothing anyone could have done would have made a bit of difference.

Chapter Nine: Changing

Their second day on the road is without sunshine and for the past hour they have been trundling through a steady drizzle. 'That's it,' James says. He draws Samuel to a halt. They are now beside the river, which they've had only glimpses of till now. The small castle a quarter of a mile away on the opposite bank has to be Thomas Wyatt's home. In the rain its grey walls don't look welcoming.

'Are you sure?' she asks.

'They said at Sandling it's across the bridge. And this is the bridge. We are right, Sister.' He yawns. A cart comes up behind them and he urges Samuel on. 'I'll come in with you,' he says.

'No. You must get back. It's already the middle of the afternoon and Marion'll be worried you've been away so long.' Her eyes fix on the turret tops she can see above the mottled leaves of the trees. 'I can do it.'

'I'll wait until I'm sure.'

'You mustn't.'

'If they don't want you, you'll come back with me.'

She tuts. 'That'd never do. You know it. You need to find your way with Marion.'

'I don't trust all that man woman stuff.'

'Neither do I,' she says. Though, truth be told, she's been aware of James in a different way today after their night huddled together.

Misalliances

They are coming out of the trees. She looks into the back of the wagon where her tunic is hanging. 'If you can stop for a moment,' she says.

****

'Good work, Edward,' Wyatt says, though he would have expected no less. His confidence in his bailiff's abilities goes back to the time when he was his manservant, a wide-eyed boy following him through Italy.

They're at the long table in the great hall, going through Boxley Abbey's inventory. 'It's a lot of stuff,' Edward says. 'Most of it from the abbott's place, which isn't the kind of house I'd expect a friar to have.'

'He wasn't a monk. I heard he spent most of his time out and about making deals.'

'That explains it, then.'

'What about the place itself? It looks in good repair.'

'It is. But it's been a religious house. Mister Poynings will have some work to do if he wants to make it a home. Has Tom started at Malling?'

'He's gone today. I want it done before I leave for France.'

'When's that?'

'The week after next.'

'And you don't know for how long?'

'Two or three months, I'd say.' Wyatt rolls up the sheaf of papers. 'We're done.'

'Right. I'll go back to this month's accounts.'

'I'll walk out with you. I need to go to the stables.'

On the edge of the close they come to a stop. Standing there, as if uncertain of the way in, is a nun.

'What is it?' Lizzie asks.

'Thomas wants us in the hall,' Jane says from the doorway. 'Something about a visitor.'

Lizzie goes to her mirror, pushes her hair into place and puts on her coif. 'What sort of visitor?'

'I don't know.'

Edward is waiting below.

'Who is it?' Jane demands as they reach the bottom stair.

'Someone from years ago,' he says. 'I'll let Sir Thomas tell you.' He leads the way into the small sitting-room.

Wyatt stands up from the table. 'Jane, Lizzie, let me introduce Sister Damaris.'

The Sister puts down the slice of custard pie she's eating and gets to her feet.

'Edward and I first met her when she was fleeing from a convent that was in trouble,' Wyatt continues. 'It must be ten years ago.' He looks to Edward for corroboration.

Sister Damaris speaks for the first time. 'It was twelve.'

'Was it? We brought her to London and I got her into St. Peter's at Westminster, where she tells me she's been happy. But St. Peter's is about to be closed, and Sister Damaris once again has nowhere to go. So she has come here. We will offer her sanctuary for as long as she wants it.' He beckons Lizzie and takes her to one side. 'God knows how long she's been on the road. Will you see what she needs? Madeleine's getting a room ready for her. Would you take her up?'

The bedchamber is on the south-eastern side of the castle, with a window which offers a view down the Medway. It is plainly furnished: an iron-bound wooden chest beneath the window, a stool in the opposite corner, and a bed. Damaris lays her hand on the counterpane. 'You're all being very kind.'

'Are you sure you've had enough to eat?'

'Yes, thank you.'

'We'll be having supper early,' Lizzie says. 'We do when the nights start to draw in. After the journey you've had, you'll want to bathe, so I've sent for some water.' Her eyes stray to the stain on the sister's tunic. 'I see you've spilled something…'

'A mishap on the road,' Damaris says. 'I've tried to get it out...'

'We should wash it. But...I don't know...would that be alright?'

Damaris goes to her bag. 'I've got something else to wear.' She pulls out the skirt and blouse she'd been wearing till they reached Allington and

Misalliances

lays them on the bed. 'They're not very smart, though.'

'And they're all creased. Are you comfortable in this sort of thing? In garments that aren't...you know...religious?'

'I shall have to be.'

'Well, in that case.' Lizzie is having to think fast: what she wears when sitting down for supper is never any old thing. 'The other lady, Mistress Jane, is more your build. I'll ask if she'd mind letting you have something while this is being washed. Would that suit?'

There's a knock. 'Is that you, Peter?' Lizzie calls.

'Robert, Mistress. Tub's filled.'

'You go and bathe,' Lizzie says. 'It's the room opposite. There are wash cloths, soap, and some linen to dry yourself with. Leave what you're wearing outside the door. You can tell me later what you'd like me to do with it.'

Damaris's eyes stray to the swell of Lizzie's belly. The question comes without her willing it. 'Are you with child?'

'I am.'

'Is it Thomas's?'

'Yes.'

Damaris begins to undo her wimple. It has been chafing her for the past hour and she wants it off. 'I'm sorry,' she says. 'That was rude.'

'It was,' says Lizzie. 'But it's a fact, so you're excused. I'll go find you something to wear.' The

Misalliances

nun is shaking out her hair, which is the colour of chestnuts, and as glossy. In an instant, she's become another person.

Chapter Ten: Ripples

Damaris tests the warmth of the water. At Saint Peter's she always washed in cold. And as for the porcelain tub…they used to have a wooden one at home, which her father had to caulk with pitch when it began to leak. She undresses. At the convent, there was no opportunity for being naked and at one with your body.

As she goes to step into the tub, she catches sight of herself on the opposite wall. The mirror is fogged with steam, so it's only reflecting her faintly, like the rippled images she has glimpsed when she has sat by a window, bent over a bowl of water, or crouched over a stream. She goes across and wipes it. She has never appraised herself in this way, stared into a real mirror and assessed what she sees. She has always thought such self-regarding as vain and sinful.

She's familiar with most of what she sees: a woman with a shock of dark hair and a small but straight nose. But the shape of the mouth takes her by surprise. There's been a change there. She's always thought of her mouth as little different from the Madonna's, but she's never seen the *Sancta Maria* of her prayers with a mouth like this. Now in this strange room, it strikes her as pretty. It's a nice mouth.

The woman in the back streets of Southwark, the one who gave her the briarwood stick (which

Misalliances

she has been reproaching herself for having left in James's wagon), called her 'pretty' and 'comely'. She would never have used the second word about herself, but looking down at the fullness of her breasts she knows what the woman meant. She goes back to the tub. Before she gets in she touches her breasts with the tips of her fingers, not unconsciously as she would once have done while washing, but deliberately, to enjoy the sensation. There are two voices in her head. One is saying 'You shouldn't do that', whilst the other, more persuasive, is saying 'Why shouldn't you?'

There are footsteps outside. A man, the same one as before, says through the door: 'I've been told to bring up some more hot water, Mistress.'

She waits till the footsteps recede before opening the door a crack and peering out. There's no one there. She picks up the jug.

Wash cloth, soap. The warm water rippling over her skin feels good. The censorious voice is speaking again, telling her it's sinful, indulging the self, the sensations of the self, in this way. But she's listening to the other voice and it's saying: 'It's alright. Why shouldn't you?'

She likes what little she's seen of Allington. It has big fireplaces and settles and couches. Carpets even. The people have welcomed her. She doesn't know what she thinks of Lizzie having Thomas's child. It's the way of things, she supposes: you have a special memory of someone, but years go by without seeing them and changes occur in their life that you've no knowledge of the reason for. No matter. As for the other woman, there's something in her she dislikes. Thomas seems much the same. Older, that's all.

She ripples the water over her thighs. She can't really tell what time of day it is since the room has no window but it must be getting on for late afternoon. James will still be on the road. It'll be dark by the time he gets home. There had been nothing improper about the way they had snuggled up to each other in the night. It was simply to shield themselves from the cold, to give each other warmth.

She touches her breasts again, cups them and lifts them. James won't leave her head. No, she tells herself, but her finger-tips have a life of their own. Down they go, making their way through the thick tufts of hair to that part of her she will not name. The woman on the street used the coarsest one there is for it. She mouths it to herself. She ignores these lips except when daily and monthly bodily functions compel her to tend to them. Neither of those is the reason she's parting them now; it's the one she's always refused to acknowledge, where she really shouldn't go. The voice is loud in her head. 'Why shouldn't you? Do it, do it!'

Chapter Eleven: Identities

The family is gathering for supper in the small sitting-room where she met everyone earlier. A fire has been lit. Thomas's son is here. He looks like his father – the same dark brows and strong nose – but there's some slight or resentment simmering in him and how far that's an aspect of character or something temporary she has no way of knowing. So far he has not met her eyes, and when they first spoke his manner was off-hand. Throughout the meal Thomas's friend Poynings has been staring at her. She doesn't know what to make of him. He's handsome and has a self-assurance about him – a swaggering, typically masculine kind - that unsettles her. The woman named Jane has dressed herself in an elaborate silk thing, pale green with interwoven silver filigrees, whereas Lizzie – she feels they're already close to being on first name terms - is still wearing the grey woollen gown she had on earlier. It's a similar shade to the blouse Marion gave her. She's had to wear it and the skirt after all. Jane wasn't keen to part with any of her gowns. 'So let me have these pressed,' Lizzie said, when she returned with the news. They still look poor things. When she came down in them, Lizzie had the presence of mind to quickly explain the tunic needed washing. It's the clothes she was wearing when Thomas stopped on the road, but he's shown no sign of recognising

Misalliances

them or her, the woman with the man and the wagon. He's insisted she sit next to him, which has pleased her but now he's begun to tell the story of when they first met it's making her uncomfortable. She can feel herself reddening. Not because she's being taken back to when she was a young, undeveloped girl - in itself that doesn't bother her – but because all these eyes are on her. After what she did in the tub she's not feeling at all herself; her senses are on edge and what she'd most like to do is crawl away into herself, hugging her guilty secret.

'So we go down to this monastery,' he's saying, 'and there's this young nun there…'

'At a monastery?' Tom pipes up.

'I said earlier. She'd run away from a nearby nunnery.'

Tom persists. 'And you'd been sent by Cardinal Wolsey?'

Wyatt chews on his chicken for a second. 'Yes. I was working for him at the time.'

'Doing what?'

She forces herself to speak. Participating might help her feel less self-conscious. 'Sir Thomas had been charged with closing the monastery. St. Wilfred's.'

Wyatt nods. 'Yes, that was it. The Sister here had gone to St. Wilfred's, for reasons we don't need to go into, unaware that it was about to be closed.'

'And where was this?' Lizzie asks.

Misalliances

'Near Southampton.'

Jane's eyebrows shoot up. 'You went all the way to Southampton, just to close a monastery?'

Everyone has finished their chicken, it's time for pudding, and Jane turns to the two young women waiting in the shadows. They begin to clear away dishes. Jane chivvies them, reminders of this, reminders of that.

Wyatt is picking at his teeth. 'It was Cromwell who sent me. He was Wolsey's secretary at that time. I thought it would help advance me, working for him and the Cardinal, and it did.'

'I didn't know they were closing monasteries in those days,' Lizzie says.

'Oh, they were,' Poynings puts in. 'It was Wolsey who started it.'

'He closed a few,' Wyatt says. 'They'd fallen into disrepute for one reaon or another or had so few monks it was no longer worth keeping them open. Like St. Wilfred's.'

The table has been silent for a few minutes. Then Tom picks up the thread again. 'There were treasures there, I suppose,' he says. He sticks his spoon into the confection of blackberries and cream that has been put in front of him.

'There were,' Damaris interjects. Her eyes are on Wyatt. 'We talked about it.'

'So it's the same old story, is it?' Tom's eyes are on his father. 'Close the monasteries, and plunder them. Not that I mind them closing. It's high time. But I've spent the day unearthing pieces

Misalliances

of gold and silver, which should all be going to the people, to the parishes, to pay for English prayer books. Not to the King's coffers.'

Wyatt's face darkens. 'It's not our place to question where it goes, Tom.'

'I think it is.'

Damaris hasn't touched her dessert. 'So that's what you're still doing?' she says to Wyatt. 'Emptying houses for the King?'

'It's not like before,' he says. '*I* don't empty them.'

'The ones we own you do,' Tom says.

Damaris is looking round the table. 'How many do you own?'

'Two,' Tom says. 'Malling and Boxley.'

'They're gifts from the King,' Lizzie intercedes. 'Thomas doesn't really want them.'

'I'm taking Boxley,' Poynings says.

'The thing is, Sister,' Lizzie says, 'Sir Thomas can't very well turn them down.'

'It's about favour,' Tom says. 'Staying in favour.'

'Yes, it is,' Wyatt says. 'And keeping my head.'

Jane picks up her empty glass. 'More wine, anyone?'.

Damaris goes straight to her room. For a minute or two she paces up and down. 'Mistake, mistake,' she says to herself. 'He turns people like me out of their homes. I should have known.'

Misalliances

Wyatt is in the doorway. 'Can I explain?' he says.

'I'm in your house,' she returns.

'You're disappointed in me. Come and sit. Please, Sister.'

Turning her face away, she lets herself down on the window side of the bed. Wyatt doesn't move from the doorway. 'I no longer empty monasteries. I support the new Church, but that doesn't mean I like the way all the Catholic houses are being shut down. That's something I've only told Lizzie. She was a lady-in-waiting to Queen Catherine, so her views on the Roman Church are probably close to your own. Recently I've been the King's envoy to the Holy Roman Emperor. I spent two years in Spain. While I was there, I went to Mass. Before I went to Spain, the King came close to ordering my execution. Did you know?''

Damaris looks at him over her shoulder. 'Not until yesterday.'

'It means my position will always be fragile. What Lizzie said at the table is true. I don't want the abbeys. But if I turned them down, it would displease the King and I can't risk that.'

'Why do you work for him?'

'Because I daren't do otherwise.' Silence hangs between them. 'Sister,' he says, 'you are most welcome here. Lizzie has taken a liking to you. As for Tom, he needs to grow up a bit. Will you come down and sit with us?'

'I'm very tired. I'm going to bed.'

Misalliances

'Then we'll talk again tomorrow.'

Early the next morning, before breakfast, Lizzie finds him in the stables grooming his mare. 'She's gone,' she says. 'Her tunic's gone, her bag's gone, she's gone.'

Wyatt puts down the comb. 'Saddle her for me,' he says to Arthur.

Damaris, wearing her nun's tunic, has only got as far as the outskirts of Sandling. She backs into the hedgerow when she sees him coming up the road.

He dismounts. 'Sister! What are you doing?'

'I'm going back to Dartford. I have friends there.'

'You're going to walk the thirty miles to Dartford?'

'I can't stay. I was wrong to come.'

'Do you remember when I saw you outside Saint Peter's that day? It gladdened my heart. I've never forgotten you.'

'Yet you didn't recognise me on the road yesterday.'

'On the road?'

'With the wagon.'

A farmer on a big shire horse is coming by. 'Mornin',' he says.

'Good morning,' Wyatt replies tersely. He waits till the heavy horse is past. 'How was I to know that was you? You were wrapped up in a shawl. And you were with a man.'

Misalliances

Damaris puts her bag down. Her eyes are everywhere except on Wyatt. 'It doesn't matter. I didn't want you to see me like that.'

'Why?'

'Because I wanted to come to you as you once knew me.'

'Is that how you want to stay?'

'I don't think that's possible.'

'Neither do I.'

She wipes her tears away with her sleeve. 'Then don't call me Sister. I'm Damaris Althorpe, from Southampton, in the county of Hampshire.'

'And I'm Thomas Wyatt from Allington in Kent.   Let's   start   again.'

Chapter Twelve: Fledgling

Catherine has taken to calling it their aerie. 'We're not eagles, Kate,' Anne says.

'I am,' Catherine says, 'and when I see what I want I'm going to swoop.' She has taken up a new position so that she can see the side-door of the palace. It's the way visitors familiar with it normally enter. It's the door through which she made her escape two weeks ago to chase after Thomas Wyatt. Her foolishness still pains her.

'We're fledglings,' Anne says. 'Or you are.'

'Alright. Don't rub it in.'

'Who are you watching out for?'

'No one in particular.'

'Are you still lovesick?'

'No point, is there?' Catherine pulls her skirt down over her woollen stockings. The afternoon's becoming chilly. Fingering a pimple that has erupted on her chin, she returns her attention to the vacancy below. 'He's off to France. And he's bound to have a woman at home.'

Anne eases herself off the bed and goes to the table. 'He does. Someone by the name of Dabble, Durrell. Something like that.'

'Where'd you hear this?'

'Well, if you mixed a bit more, you'd pick up all sorts of things.'

'I know. The pox most likely.' Catherine comes down off her perch. 'Anyway, what do you mean? We went dancing the other evening.' She stretches out on the bed. 'Any beer left?'

'That's all of it,' Anne says.

'We'll have to get some more when we go down for supper.'

Anne is shaking the jug. 'You can get some for yourself. I'm busy tonight.'

'You're not coming back up?'

Anne still has her back turned. 'No. I can't.'

Catherine sits up. 'What's this? Are you seeing someone?'

'I don't know yet.'

'Who?'

Anne returns to the bed. 'You have it,' she says, offering the cup. 'There's not enough for us both.'

Catherine takes the cup and drinks. 'Are you going to tell me?'

'Not yet. Budge up, I want to lie down'

'Someone important, is it?'

Anne, looking straight ahead, holds out her hand. 'Let me have a mouthful.' She takes back the cup. 'I'll tell you if, or when, it becomes something.'

'Tell me more about this Durrell woman.'

'Well, she lives with him, so she's not exactly a mistress. He does have a wife. One of the Cobhams.'

'I don't know them.'

'Been apart ages. The Durrell woman used to be with Queen Catherine.'

Misalliances

'That's going back a bit.'

'That's all I know.'

Catherine is smiling to herself. 'Queen Catherine has quite a ring to it, don't you think?

'You're not serious!'

'Why not? Though he is a bit old and, for all we know, thorough-goingly pox-ridden.'

'He's not that old.' Anne likes her joke, and in nudging Catherine's arm she spills what's left of the beer.

'Damn it, Anne!' Catherine pulls out a handkerchief to mop her skirt and then wipes her mouth with it. 'He couldn't take his eyes off me at the dance.'

'Who?'

'The King, silly!'

Part Two

Misalliances

Misalliances

Chapter Thirteen: Paris

'I am zoory to zay dat lettrers of creddance muzt be prezented do ze King.' Wyatt takes off his hat and throws it across the room. 'Why does he insist on presenting us with his pitiful version of English when he knows we speak French?'

Mason slumps down on one of the settles which partition the room. 'He's the Dauphin, He can do what he likes.'

'So we've got to go to Blois.'

'We've got time. We can afford a couple of days here, can't we?'

Their apartment, a large room with a bed at each end, is on the second floor of a house in the Petit Nesle quarter of Paris, a short walk from the Seine, with a view across the river to the fortress of the Louvre. In the shadow of the city wall, it's a *pension* reserved for visiting foreign envoys.

'We ought to get off as soon as we can,' Wyatt says.

Mason takes off his jacket. 'Pitcher and Rudston will need to find us some horses first. Let's go and see what Courrières can tell us. Good thing we ran across him.' He's stripping off his white linen shirt. 'This,' he says, 'is the only one I've got so I'm saving it.'

Wyatt turns his face away from the sight of Mason's milk-white body and its rust-coloured chest hair and begins to change. He's also worn his best clothes for going to see the Dauphin, but something plainer is better for walking the streets of the city.

'Where did you say we're meeting?' Mason asks.

'On the Mouffetard, *à l'Enseigne d'Ange.*'

'At the Angel? Just like home. I used to go to the one in Southwark.'

Jean de Montmorency, Seigneur de Courrières, made it clear at their very first meeting in Valladolid that he is not related to Anne de Montmorency, Constable of France, and that he prefers to be known, and referred to, simply as Courrières, after the Flanders village he comes from. As ever, there is a faint air of perfume coming from him. He's a traveller like themselves, so how is it, Wyatt wonders, he's so well groomed – neatly trimmed beard, hair coiffed just so – and that his pink silk jacket shows no signs of the creases Wyatt's velvet has suffered during a week in his saddle-bag. He assumes it's one of the benefits of having the Emperor as a friend. Courrières probably has a team of servants attending him in Paris and a carriage to ride in.

Wine has arrived at the table. 'So,' Wyatt says, 'Charles is planning to sort out Ghent with the army he has up there, is he?'

Courrières pours for himself and passes the carafe to Wyatt. 'He was hardly going to march one through France, was he? His sister Mary has men enough. That's not a problem. Let me ask you a question. Why are you and John here?'

'The plan was to present our credentials to the King, but he's at Blois.'

'I meant here in France.'

'I'm sure you know why.'

Courrières leans back, sips his wine and gives one of his arch smiles. 'I doubt it's to propose an alliance with the French.'

'Why are *you* in Paris?'

'There are things I have to do. Charles is coming.'

'That's why we're here.'

'You want to find out what he'll be saying to François...'

'You could tell us, I suppose.'

'Even if I knew, you know I couldn't. You won't get near him. The French won't allow it.'

'They won't have a say in the matter if we get to him first.'

'You'd have to reach him before he arrives at Tours, then. That's where the Dauphin will be mounting an official welcome before taking him on to Blois to meet François. By then he'll be folded into so tight a Gallic embrace, you'll not get within a mile of him.'

'Where is he likely to be now?'

'At Bayonne, I imagine, having just crossed the border.'

'Let's add it up,' Mason says to Wyatt. 'It's must be four-hundred miles or so from Bayonne to

Misalliances

Tours. Given the speed the Emperor travels at, it's going to be...' Mason counts the days '...the second week of December before he's anywhere near there. So, let's say it takes us a week to reach Blois ourselves, and several days waiting attendance on the King, that'd still give us time to get to the other side of Tours.'

'I wish you luck,' says Courrières. 'As you know, I'm all for keeping King Henry's hand in the game.'

The tavern has two new customers. One of them is a corpulent cleric with a square face. Mason jumps like he's been stuck with a pin. 'God! I thought that was Bonner for a moment.'

Courrières glances over his shoulder at the newcomers. 'He's on his way to Blois, on a mission much like yours.'

'What do the French think of him? Do you know?'

'Your ambassador is not much liked.'

'He's not much liked anywhere,' says Mason.

Courrières leans forward, his face serious. 'Thomas, you say you have a good relationship with Charles. I think you once did. This is a public visit. The Pope's people will be there. And the Holy Office has decided you're a heretic.'

'I'll not be entering Spain.'

'The Emperor had a visitor after you left Toledo. De Tavera, the Chief Inquisitor. He told Charles the Holy Office disapproved of him entertaining you as often as he did.'

'It wasn't that often.'
'You met with him privately.'
'To talk about books.'
'Now, Charles was annoyed, of course, but since the Inquisition believes you're an enemy of the Roman Church…'
'He's had to take heed.'
'He *is* the Holy Roman Emperor. What I'm saying is, he might not be as welcoming as you would like.' Courrières gets up. 'I have things to do. I might see you at Tours, gentlemen. Or Blois. If I don't, I'm sure our paths will cross at some other time.'

After seeing Courrières, Mason says he wants to go to a place he knows. Wyatt knows what sort of place it'll be and isn't in the mood for it. Glad of some time to himself, he returns to the *pension*, takes out pen and paper and tries to write. He has subjects in mind: the arrival of the Sister, his two nights with Kate Howard. It's gone through his mind more than once, on the chill, choppy crossing to Calais, the ride from there to Paris, that he treated her with a nonchalance she didn't deserve. But if in seeking him out she'd been giving more of herself than he'd had reason to realise, that was hardly something to be laid at his door. Where there was blame, it was that he'd let her in at all. What he most feels guilty about is his betrayal of Lizzie, who is having his child. There really ought not be another Kate.

Misalliances

But even as he tells himself this, he has no confidence he'll be able to resist the temptation of another pretty face, another firm young body. There was a time in his life when he did. While he was with Anne, and in love with her, the thought of going to see Alice, a fresh-faced whore in Rochester, never crossed his mind. Anne's love was enough to keep him from Alice, so why hadn't Lizzie's been enough to keep him from Kate when she came knocking? Anne. It always came back to Anne.

Mason's back. He's got a candle from somewhere and he's eyeing the other end of the room in the arcs of light it's casting about from his unsteady hand. 'Oh, you're awake,' he says. 'Sorry, I'll put this out in a minute.'

'Did you have a good time?'

'Yes. Had this beautiful girl from Normandy. Younger than the ones who usually come on to me. Couldn't have been much older than your Kate.'

'*My* Kate?' Wyatt sits up. Mason is still in his hose.

'You know what I mean. She was lovely. I'd like to see her again but I know I won't.'

'You might.'

'I doubt it. Girls like her move on.' Mason lifts the candle. The movement plunges his lower body into shadow and illuminates his face, which looks untypically sad. 'It doesn't matter, Thomas.' He blows out the candle. 'Goodnight.'

Chapter Fourteen: Malling

It's not quite light and Damaris has needed a candle lantern to make her way to the chapel. One part of her says she should aim to break away from the routine she's followed for most of her adult life, going to say her matins at dawn. She's felt like an imposter anyway, ever since she stopped wearing her habit. Though the gown she's wearing – one of three she's got with Lizzie's help from the seamstress in Maidstone - is sober enough for a place of worship. Once she's finished the set prayers, she says her own. They've been the same ones for weeks. Thomas comes first: a plea to God to keep him safe and bring him back soon. Then she thanks God for her new home and for Lizzie. And this morning, something new, she asks Him to make Tom a friend. He's taking her to see Malling Abbey this morning.

****

They are coming into the village and having to wait for a herd of sheep to go past. 'It's market day,' Tom says.

While they're stationery, she asks how much he still has to do.

'A few days,' he says, his eyes on the last of the animals meandering by. 'Could finish today with a bit of luck.'

Misalliances

'Your father'll be pleased.'
'Whenever we see him again.'
'And you will be.'
'I think it's a bad business, so I will.'
'Do we have no idea when Sir Thomas will return?'
'It's not going to be before Spring, I reckon.'

The road is clear. In the middle of the village, her attention is caught by a group of women gathered round a stall. She is certain one of them – a youngish woman, not much older than herself - is wearing a coat like her own.

After Westminster, with its grand church, extensive cloisters, chapels and dormitories, Damaris finds Malling Abbey diminutively pleasing. It stands within its own grassy circle, enclosed by a low wall. Its frontage, for all its smaller scale, has borrowed something from that of her own house.

Tom anticipates her. 'You'll want to pray,' he says, drawing out a key.

'Won't you?'

'No.' He unlocks the door for her. 'I'll be round the back.'

She stands at the head of the nave and looks towards the apse. From here it looks little different from any other village church. It's still being looked after for the pews show no sign of dust and in the air is the familiar smell of beeswax. The altar table is bare apart from what must be a Bible.

Misalliances

She drops to her knees and prays. She remembers something Marion said to her, about being a good Christian woman finding her way through a time of darkness. It's certainly that. But she doesn't feel she's in the dark herself. Allington has brought light.

The nuns' dormitory is on the second floor above the sacristy. It's arranged in conventional fashion, the beds set out in two rows facing each other, blankets and quilts neatly folded at the foot of the bed. It's familiar but at the same time foreign.

She finds Tom in the chapter house. It's become a treasure trove: chalices, monstrances, patens, jugs and chasubles - all the silver and gold things an abbey would have - are spread out in ill-assorted piles across the floor. He stands up quickly, like he's been caught doing something wrong.

'So this is what you're doing for your father,' she says.

He nods unhappily. 'I had to go round and collect it all. There'll be other stuff they want as well. Anything of value. But this...' he gestures to the shiny things around his feet. 'This is what really matters.'

'What'll happen to it?'

'They'll melt it down. The lead's been stripped off the roof in other places but we weren't having any of that here.'

Misalliances

'One evening at supper you said something about prayer books.'

'It's what Anne wanted when she was Queen. For the new Church. You probably wouldn't have heard.'

'No. I was part of the old Church.'

'Let's go outside,' he says. 'I need some air.'

It's one of those uncertain November days, pitched between the last warmth of autumn and the first truly cold days of winter, the imminence of which a sharp breeze occasionally announces. The garden is overgrown, except for some distant vegetable beds, which have been newly turned over.

'It was her idea,' he says, once they've sat down, he on an upturned wine keg, she on the rickety stool, which she takes to be where he normally sits. 'Anne has a bad name now, but she wanted them in English in every parish. Every worshipper entitled to one. The wealth from places like this was going to pay for them.'

'And you don't think that's going to happen now.'

'I don't.'

'Why do you think the Church needs to change?'

'Because it doesn't give the people what they need. As things are it's blind worship, Sister. I bet if you asked any ordinary person what they had just been listening to, or been reciting, they wouldn't be able to tell you. Not with any understanding. For instance how much of The Bible do you know?'

'A lot of it.'

'You've read it in the Latin...'

'No, I couldn't. But that doesn't mean I don't know it.'

'You know only what's been passed to you second-hand, then. What Latin you have is what you've learned by rote, right?'

'That's true.'

He hooks a thumb over his shoulder. 'Your Church has all this wealth. But it keeps those who follow it, even someone like yourself, in a state of ignorance.'

'I don't think it's deliberate.'

'I think it is.'

'The gold and the silver are about glorification and celebration.'

'But Christ was a humble man. It's all in The Bible. He didn't go around wearing gold round his neck. He didn't drink from silver cups. And he gave his message to the people in words they could understand. Your Church celebrates *itself*, not God. So we need a new kind of Church. Though what I'm doing at the moment isn't helping it much.'

'It's your father you're helping. Otherwise he'll be in trouble with the King.'

'I know. I'd better get back to it, Sister.'

'What is it you're doing exactly?'

Misalliances

'I've got to put all the same things together. Count them up and list them. It's taking ages.'

'It'd be easier with two of us. Let me help.'

'Why would you do that?'

'Because it has to be done. Come on.'

Side by side, they take a piece at a time and put it with other like items in a place on the floor. Tom keeps a record on the paper he has. They're finished by early afternoon. As they're leaving, they meet the woman Damaris saw in the village, the one wearing a nun's coat. She's carrying a basket with a trowel.

'What are you doing here?' Tom asks her.

'Getting our vegetables,' the woman says. 'We sowed them and we'll sell them, since your father's turned us out.'

'It's the King who's done that,' Damaris says. 'Not Thomas Wyatt.'

The woman tightens her lips and draws herself up, like she's getting ready for an argument. 'Same difference. Who are you, anyway?'

Tom intercedes. 'You shouldn't be here. I've told you. You have to move away once you've taken your pension. There'll be trouble if they find out.'

'Threatening us now, are you?'

'He's trying to help you,' Damaris says. 'To *stop* you getting into trouble.'

'And what do you know about it?'

'A great deal.'

Misalliances

The woman puts down her basket, comes up to Damaris and peers at her. 'What do you know about someone like me?'

'I was in Holy Orders myself.'

'You don't look like a nun.'

'You don't sound like one.'

The woman lands a globule of spittle at Damaris's feet. 'Judas,' she snarls, before walking back to her basket.

When they're half-way home, Tom says: 'I have a copy of The Bible in English, you know.'

'Lizzie said you had.'

'Is it anathema to you?'

'No, not at all.'

'Would you like to read it?'

'I'd very much like to.'

'You should have said, Sister.'

'Please call me Damaris.'

Chapter Fifteen: The Gallic Embrace

Blois. An invalid King, grey of complexion, says he's pleased to see them, always pleased to see them. He peruses their letters of credence for a moment or two and returns them.

As they walk back down the long gallery to the grand hall, Mason says: 'All that *bonhomie*. He knows full well we're here to spy.'

'Bonner wasn't there,' Wyatt says. 'I thought he would be.'

'Courrières did say François doesn't like him. Unless he doesn't know we're here.'

'You think he's not been told we're coming?'

'It's possible, after all the mischief he made last time.'

Two women have come out of one of the side-doors and are walking towards them. Wyatt touches Mason's arm. 'Here's a kind of beauty we don't see very often.'

It has nothing to do with artifice, the tints applied to their cheeks and lips, the jewels on their French hoods, their glittering necklaces or the fineness of their gowns. It dwells in the symmetry of their features, the elegance of their carriage. Both have chosen to wear velvet this morning: one purple, the other, and younger of the two, black. On the bodice of the latter's gown an 'A' is embroidered in gold. It recalls another woman, who was fond of putting her initial, the same one,

Misalliances

on her gowns and jewellery. It's too painful a revisiting for Wyatt to draw Mason's attention to it and, anyway, his companion has stopped to watch the women as they proceed down the gallery. 'Do you know who they were?' he asks him when they resume walking.

'I think the older one's Diane de Poitiers, Henri's mistress. I saw her once in Paris. I don't know the other.'

They hurry on, tapestries from floor to ceiling lining their way, rugs from the Orient soft under their feet,

It seems the grand hall is where others like themselves – ambassadors, emissaries, petitioners – gather to await the moment they are called into the King's presence. To the left, behind a row of arches, is a place for relaxation and while Mason is sipping his wine he's eyeing the couches on offer and the half-dozen gaudily dressed women who are passing along them, soliciting opportunities for their specialised trade. Wyatt says: 'Drink up, John. We need to be off. Let's see what Frank and Robert have found in the way of fresh horses.'

They chose Frank Pitcher and Robert Rudston for different reasons, Pitcher because his ten years' experience as a King's messenger qualifies him to be their courier when needed, Rudston because he learned in Spain how to look after the requirements of a party on the road. Both have a more than adequate grasp of French, enough to

Misalliances

barter in a market or order food and drink in an auberge, but they have returned from the nearby post-house with a problem beyond them. It's forbidden to hire horses for Tours because the Dauphin has ordered the road to be closed in view of the imminent arrival of the Emperor.

'I've never heard such nonsense,' Mason says. 'We don't close roads for the King.'

'I'm sure there's a way round it,' Wyatt says, taking out his purse and checking its contents. He finishes buttoning up his riding coat. 'Come. Let's go and see.'

At the post-house, a disgruntled ostler repeats the edict: until the Dauphin brings the Emperor to the King, travel without a permit between Blois and Tours has been banned. Wyatt takes out his purse and counts out a dozen gold *écus*. The ostler, from whose singlet and breeches all the varied smells which accumulate in a stable are rising, looks at the coins laid out before him. 'Quatre chevaux?' he queries.

'Quatre,' Wyatt affirms. 'Vos meilleurs.' He draws the coins towards him. Only when the man nods his head does he release them. 'Go with him, Frank, and check them out.'

The horses aren't young and they bear the signs of the many miles they've travelled. 'They're alright,' Pitcher says. 'They'll get us there and back.'

Misalliances

'We don't know how far *there* is,' Mason says.

Wyatt's checking the shoes on his mount. 'It's about fifty miles to Tours,' he says. 'Let's aim to get south of there by the end of the second day. If we haven't met up with Charles' cavalcade by then, someone'll know how far off they are.' They mount up. 'And watch out for soldiers,' he adds.

The road follows the river between screens of skeletal trees. A frost lies over the land, giving it a certain severe prettiness. There's no one else on the road. They're at Amboises by the end of the first day.

The *pension* is several cuts above the average. At supper, they receive the attention of the proprietess herself, who's similarly of a different order from the conventional tavern hostess. She's wearing a necklace with an emerald pendant and her greying hair is pinned neatly under a French hood that would not be out of place on the head of Diane de Poitiers. On this royal road, she must be used to catering for wealthy, well-placed, clients and Wyatt and Mason apparently give off enough of that kind of *cachet* to bring her to their table. Or it could be because the place is otherwise empty which, with contemptuous gestures towards the unoccupied tables, she blames on the restrictions imposed by the Dauphin. How these English travellers have eluded them, Madame Escoffier doesn't ask. She's handsome in a way

Misalliances

that Wyatt knows is typically French, a complexion kissed by the south, a face that owes much of its animatedness to her mouth with its pouts and smiles, and a figure that is broad in the hip, full in the bosom. He estimates her age as close to his own. It's him she mostly addresses, asking how the veal is, if they would care for more wine, presenting him with this or that tidbit of information about the hostelry, telling him that she, a widow, runs it herself.

When the two serving girls have cleared the dishes and Pitcher and Rudston have gone to the stables to feed the horses, Mason says: 'She likes you, Thomas. I think you could have her tonight.' And when Wyatt says nothing, he adds: 'If you wanted to, that is.'

Wyatt drains the last of the wine. 'My bed will have only one occupant tonight. I am under orders.'

'Whose?'

'My own.'

Why, then, after Mason says he must go to bed, does he continue sitting in the cold, empty tavern? The truth of it is that the attentions of the proprietress have piqued his interest. He's not convinced Mason was right. Surely, it was simply a show of attention on an evening when *any* personable customer was welcome.

When Madame Escoffier does appear - with a 'Monsieur, are you still here?' – she's in her nightdress, a shawl over her shoulders. She laughs and gestures to what she's wearing. 'I thought I might get to bed early for once, since things are so quiet.'

'I'm sorry,' he says. 'Sleep and I are not the best of friends at the moment.'

'Too much on your mind? Your mission, perhaps?'

'My mission?'

'You are an Englishman on a road *interdite.* I assume that's to do with the important man coming this way.'

'It's not that which keeps me awake.'

She is fussing with things at the counter. 'Then it must be something personal.'

The dregs in Wyatt's glass are barely worth emptying, but he makes a show of doing so. 'Perhaps.'

'It's a woman,' she says, 'and she is making you sad, la-la-la. It's an old story.'

'But still maddening.'

'Come and tell me. It's warm in the back.'

The fire has burnt low and she pokes it into flame. It's a room small enough to keep its heat, and after his days on the road and the chill next door, he's glad of it. It's a homely space. On the wall is a sampler, the needlework roughly done, possibly the work of a child.

'Sit,' Madame Escoffier says, directing him to a cushioned settle. She sits down opposite and pours a dark liquid from the bottle she has brought with her.

He sniffs the glass she gives him. 'Eau de vie?'

'From Armagnac,' she says. 'A cousin brings it.'

Now she's cast off her finery and her public role, Wyatt suspects he's seeing the person she most likely is in her private moments. The samplers suggest she has children, probably grown-up now and no longer at home; and there is something matronly about her nightdress with its embroidered neckline. She wants his company, he assumes, because she's lonely, a widow, running the hostelry by herself. He doesn't find it difficult to talk to her. When she poses the first of her questions, he tells her who he is and who he is working for, though nothing more. Her given name is Louise, she tells him.

'So this mission you are on,' she says. 'It must be a secret one.'

'Nothing untoward. Making contact with an old friend, that's all.'

'To say what?' She forestalls his answer by showing him the flat of her palm, with the fingers spread. 'No, let me guess. You are obviously more than a messenger. And you're a learned man, I saw that as soon as you came in the door…'

'As soon as that?' He raises his glass. 'You have unusual powers, Madame.'

Misalliances

'I think you are a person who argues, who disputes, who negotiates. And you do that with powerful men. Like the Emperor.'

'Something of the sort.'

She shifts in her chair. 'My husband was educated. He instructed the royal children at the palace in Tours. And he wrote poems.'

'As do I,' he says. He raises his glass to her again, though it's almost empty. She brings the bottle over and tops it up.

'I guessed as much.'

'Come now, Madame...'

The pout is an unhappy one. 'Now you are making fun of me.'

'I assure you I'm not.'

She waves her glass at him. 'It's easy to recognise. Educated men who have a way with words are often writers. Others will have seen it in you. Women especially, I imagine. The clever ones, those you do not frighten off.'

'Perhaps...'

'And you write about the women who make you sad...'

'And those who please me.'

'Just for yourself?'

'No. For the like-minded at King Henry's court as well.'

'Are you famous in England?'

'Not famous. But known.'

'Let me hear one.'

'Recite one? I can't do it in French.'

Misalliances

'I understand some English.'
He thinks for a moment. 'I write my verses and they're gone. There are one or two, though...'
'Choose the one you remember best.'
Wyatt clears his throat and begins.

> 'I see that chance has chosen me
> Thus secretly to live in pain...'

Her eyes are on him; she is all attention.

> 'Unto myself sometime alone
> I do lament my woeful case
> But what avails it me to moan
> Since truth and pity have no place
> In them I sue and serve
> And others have what I deserve...'

He pauses before the final stanza.

> 'Such is the fortune that I have
> To love them most that love me least
> And in my pain to seek and crave
> The thing that others have possessed.
> So thus in vain always I serve,
> And others have what I deserve.'

'That's all of it,' he says.
She applauds him, clapping her hands in dumb show. 'It's about someone you loved.'
'Yes.'

Misalliances

'And the woman gave her affection to another.'

'Yes.'

'Where is she now?'

'She's dead.'

'That must make you sad.'

'Sometimes.'

'Did you never find another?'

'Oh yes. Several others.'

'But you are still in love with the woman you lost.'

'I did love her.'

'Are you with someone now?'

'I am.'

'Married to her?'

'No. I already have a wife. We have lived apart for many years.'

'Then you need to follow your King Henry's example and get an annulment.'

'You need to be a King to do that.'

'But then, if you don't love the woman you're with, you wouldn't want to marry her anyway...'

'I didn't say I didn't love her.'

She purses her lips. 'Does she love you?'

'Yes. And she's carrying my child.'

'Then learn to love what you have. You mustn't allow yourself to be haunted by a ghost, by what you can never have.'

Wyatt takes a sip of his *eau de vie*. 'Tell me about your husband.'

Misalliances

'He was learned but not wise. At the palace he was surrounded by pretty women. He became involved with one who was much too young for him. She had important, powerful relatives. One of them, an uncle, challenged him to a duel. Jacques was not a fighter. The uncle was, so that was that.'

'I'm sorry.'

'He was a fool. Beware young women with powerful uncles. Especially those who are skilled in weaponry.'

The absurd image of the Duke of Norfolk brandishing a broadsword flits into his mind. He flicks it away. 'I'm quite skilled myself on that count,' he says.

'That's not what I meant. Some men are never satisfied. They are always yearning for the young and pretty.' She holds his eyes with hers. 'You might be one.'

'It's a constant temptation. It comes with being a man.'

'It's not very manly to pursue the young and inexperienced.'

'That depends on what you mean by inexperienced.'

'Being experienced in what we do between the sheets is not the same as being experienced in life necessarily. The young woman who became entangled with my husband was destroyed by what happened. She's now in a nunnery.'

'And you?'

'I was devastated but not destroyed. I too was at the palace. I used to serve the Duchess D'Étampes, Anne de Pisseleu, who is now the King's mistress. She spends her time in the palace at Blois these days.'

'I was there a few days ago.'

'She always wears her initial on her gowns, the letter A.' Wyatt says nothing. 'No,' she goes on, 'I wasn't destroyed by Jacques' death. In fact, the Duchess was more scandalised than I. When she told me I had to retire – disappear, not make a fuss - and gave me money to do it quietly, I agreed. And came here.'

'That's quite a story.'

'Oh, I'm sure you have some of your own. A man who works for King Henry, who reads poetry at his court, who rides the Tours road when it's closed…'

'Another time, perhaps.'

Louise Escoffier rises. 'It's time we took to our beds.' She reaches out to him. 'Come! Let's embrace as friends.'

She smells of garlic and armagnac. 'Goodnight,' he says.

'I liked your poem,' she whispers. 'Sleep well.'

'Wake up, Thomas!' Mason is shaking him. There's daylight outside.

'What?'

'Soldiers. Downstairs.'

Misalliances

'So?' Wyatt sits up and rubs his eyes.

'We're on the road to Tours. No one should be on the road to Tours!'

'For God's sake, John. Someone has to be.'

'But not us. Get dressed. Robert and Frank are waiting at the stables. There's a back door.' Mason throws him his clothes.

At the foot of the stairs, Wyatt looks into the main room and sees three of them, their tabards embroidered with the *fleur de lys* of the King's household. Their helmets are on the floor beside them. Two of them are in the act of removing their gauntlets while another is filling goblets from a flagon of wine. He hears a snatch of conversation. Down the passage stands Madame, gesturing to them to hurry. At the door, she says, 'Stay safe, my friends,' and points across the yard.

It's well after noon when they first catch sight of Tours, its tall towers and turrets hazily visible against the grey sky. Pitcher knows the city. 'There will be lots of soldiers here,' he's said. 'So we stay on the this side, away from the palace.'

It's an hour since Rudston rode ahead to look for somewhere to spend the night and as it's now almost dark they're becoming anxious. At the junction of three equally unpromising roads, they stop to confer. As they discuss whether to wait where they are or arbitrarily choose one of them, mounted soldiers carrying torches emerge from the gloom. They are wearing Spanish helmets.

Misalliances

'Buenas Noches, Señores!' Wyatt calls out to them, relieved to see that a smiling Rudston is among their number.

There's a moment's hiatus while the lead rider, a Captain of the Emperor's guard, brings his horse closer. He holds up his torch. 'Señores Hoyet y Mason,' he says, breaking into a smile

Chapter Sixteen: Stories

'She's crying again,' Catherine says. 'And she doesn't want breakfast, so someone'd better tell the kitchen.'

'Any signs?' Anne Basset asks.

'They didn't.'

'Did he sleep with her?'

'Stayed in his own rooms all night according to Margaret Douglas. Unless he's taken her into the bushes while out hunting, they still haven't done it.'

'And there's not been blood or anything?'

'No. But who's to say she's a virgin.' Catherine takes her friend's hand. 'Honestly, you are naïve. Whether she's a virgin or not, there'd still be signs on the sheets. Stains and things. And even when he has slept with her, there's been nothing. I'm going for breakfast. Coming?'

Anne hesitates. 'I'm on duty. Shouldn't I go in…?'

'Margaret Douglas is with her, and the countess. Come on.'

Now that the Christmas and New Year banquets are over, the hall has been returned to its everyday function of the main refectory. It's crowded. As they look round for somewhere to sit, Anne says: 'I like your gown. Is it new?'

Catherine runs her palms down over the hips of the green skirt, raises her hands to the yellow

Misalliances

brocade of the bodice and lifts her bosom. 'French,' she says. 'My uncle brought it back. He's been over in Calais for a week. He brought back six of them.'

'Six new gowns!'

'Now I'm one of the Queen's ladies, he wants me to shine.'

Space comes available at the end of a table by the far wall. 'That'll do us,' Catherine says.

Anne hangs back. 'It's Sir Thomas Cheney and John Russell. Baron Russell. Are you sure?'

'I'm the niece of a duke,' Catherine replies. All she knows of Cheney and Russell is that they belong to the select circle of serious, secretive men who the King calls on for advice. She's sees them now and then, waiting to be taken up to his floor.

The elderly men look up as the girls go to seat themselves. Catherine does a half-curtsey and Anne does the same. Neither Cheney nor Russell respond.

There is bread and fruit and enough beer for the two of them. 'Go get us some cups and plates, Anne,' Catherine says. She listens in. It's Russell who's speaking.

- So Cromwell thinks the Emperor's campaign against Ghent could be a feint...
- Not that exactly. But if it does have a dual purpose, his coming into Flanders, and he eventually moves his army against the new Queen's brother, that could be a problem.

Misalliances

- And Wyatt's been charged with learning more...
- If he can get near.
- Why shouldn't he? He was quite the favourite in Spain.
- But one of the reasons he left was because the Inquisition were sharpening their knives for him. Charles might be wary of renewing their former intimacy, particularly while he's in France.
- You're still happy working with Cromwell, are you?
- I am.
- Good luck, then. Because if Henry doesn't develop a liking for his new wife, I wouldn't want to be in Cromwell's shoes. Though what liking's got to do with it is beyond me.

  Cheney is in the middle of laughing at Russell's remark when he becomes aware of Catherine's attention. 'Mistress...?'
  Catherine is all pertness. 'Did I hear you mention Thomas Wyatt?'
  'You did.'
  'Is he well?'
  'He's in France.'
  'Oh. That explains why I didn't receive a reply to my invitation.'
  'Your invitation?'
  'To come and visit our new Queen. To read his poems to her.'

Misalliances

Russell pitches his words into the air, between his cup and her, as if he's not much inclined to look at her. 'She wouldn't understand them, would she?'

Catherine pretends naivety. 'Oh! I didn't think of that.'

Russell fixes his gaze on Cheney and shakes his head, as if to say 'who is this silly girl?'

Cheney reads his mind. 'Catherine Howard, the Duke's niece,' he murmurs. He does look at her. 'You're serving the Queen, I hear.'

'Yes, Sir.'

Anne Basset is back with cups and plates. She looks from Catherine to the gentlemen and gives them both a wan smile. Cheney's eyes settle on her briefly before returning their focus to Catherine.

'And how is she?'

She tells her second lie of the day. 'She's very happy.'

'Do you know Sir Thomas Wyatt?'

'Yes, of course. That's to say, we have met.'

'And that's when you asked him to read for the Queen...'

'It was.'

Anne is pouring herself some beer. She casts a shifty glance at Cheney and Russell. 'Didn't he offer to?'

'That's right. He offered to and then I wrote to him.'

'Where?' Cheney asks.

Misalliances

'Where?'

'Where did you send your letter?'

'I dropped it off at the Household Office.'

Cheney's smile is that of a parent, or grandparent, indulging a wayward child. 'I should tell you, Mistress, that while Sir Thomas is in France, I'm picking up his personal letters.'

'Oh.'

'And I don't recall seeing one with the Howard seal on it.'

'I don't think I used the seal.' Catherine shrugs. 'Either that or it must have got misdirected.' She turns to Anne. 'You did take my letter down to Household, didn't you?'

'What letter?'

Catherine giggles, all silly girl now. 'Oh, don't tell me it's still in our rooms! Gentlemen, forgive me!'

Russell, caught up in a piece of silliness he patently has no patience for, pulls a face. 'Never mind.' He pushes his breakfast crockery into the middle of the table. 'Come on, Cheney. Since I'm here, let's find a card game.' He takes a moment to straighten his cloak. 'When did you start picking up Wyatt's letters?'

'I never have,' Cheney says, lowering his voice. 'She was obviously lying and I wanted to catch her out.'

Anne is furious. 'Kate, what were you thinking? They saw right through you!'

'Sorry.'

Misalliances

'Don't ever do that again. You and your stories. Honestly!'

'Don't make a scene.'

'Why in God's name did you ask about Wyatt in the first place?'

Catherine chooses some bread and pulls the dish of apricots towards her. 'I was interested, that's all. Are we going to eat?'

Catherine takes the stairs and walks the length of the corridor towards the King's side of the palace. The men who serve him in roles similar to hers with the Queen can sometimes be found in the outer chamber. She is wary of entering alone, partly because it would necessitate having to pass through the guards' station, a place where gets looks she doesn't care for, but primarily because it's only permitted in the case of carrying a message or summoning this or that courtier, which in present circumstances - with the Queen desperately unhappy and keeping to her private rooms - are both unlikely events.

Catherine is on the look-out for Thomas Culpeper, her cousin, who has recently been made one of the King's grooms. In the past few weeks they have become acquainted again, exchanged words on the stairs and in the great hall. Culpeper is taken with her, she's sure of it, and it pleases her. She has become used to the attentions of men, it's been happening since before she entered her teen years, and invariably she finds it

Misalliances

wearisome. To make matters worse, the persistent ones are always old enough to be her father, or are ugly, or have nothing in the way of personable manners. But occasionally one comes along who does take her interest, a man who has a certain *je ne sais quoi*. She doesn't know quite how it works, but she thinks it's to do with an independence of spirit, an indifference to the opinions of others, a refusal to go with the herd. Those qualities are rare at court, where everyone's looking over their shoulder to check they are making the right impression. Men of this sort have an air of danger about them, and that thrills her. Thomas Wyatt has it (he was indifferent to her till she made him take notice!). And Thomas Culpeper does too. What's more, he's definitely noticed her.

She has reached the entrance to the guards' chamber. Does she have the front to walk in there, through there, without a reason for doing so? Without even a made-up one?

Culpeper takes hold of her elbow. 'Kate!'

'Hello,' she gasps, embarrassed she's been caught off-guard, didn't see him coming. The picture Culpeper is presenting doesn't quite square with the one she has in her head. Yes, he's handsome in his dark grey doublet, his fair hair neatly combed, but there's an excitement about him, an urgency, that hasn't been there when they've spoken before.

Misalliances

'Come!' he's saying, steering her towards the passage that leads to the stairwell, 'I have to ask you something.' He drags her into the shadows.

'Cousin...!' She pulls her elbow free from his grasp. 'Honestly!' She straightens her sleeve.

He looks around to check they are not being observed, places a hand on the rise of the staircase above her head and leans into her. 'Is it true? They haven't done it?'

She wriggles away and reverses their positions. 'What kind of question is that?'

'He hasn't lain with her...'

'Yes, he has.'

'He's slept with her but they haven't done the deed.'

'That's not for me to say...'

'I bet they haven't.' He takes her by the waist, pulls her back into the shadows and lowers his voice. 'The word is he can't get it up any longer!'

Despite herself, she lets him hold her. It's not unpleasant, feeling him against her here in the dark of the stairwell. His breath is on her cheek.

'I can, Kate,' he whispers. 'Any time you like.' He plants a kiss on her cheek. 'When? Just tell tell me when and where. Send me a message.'

****

The pavane transitions into the galliard and Culpeper is showing off, leaping into the air and laughing as he takes her hand to lead her down the floor again. The ladies do not have to leap, thankfully. She's finding it hard to manage even the occasional hop.

'Is that what you do in the lists?' she asks. 'Jump?'

'Definitely, if someone's coming at me with a big sword. But then I close…' He draws her to him. 'And I thrust…'

The dance is almost done and with a little laugh she walks away. He follows. 'You can't have the next dance,' she says, 'or people will talk.'

'What if they do? We're cousins.'

'People will think we're together.'

'What's wrong with that?'

'Lots of things.'

Nearby is a cresset and she leads him away from it into a well of shadow. 'Someone has his eye on me.'

'Someone else? Who?'

'The King. Don't look.'

'What?'

'He was watching us.'

'He was watching everybody. It's all he does, now he doesn't dance any more.'

'His eyes were fixed on us. On *me*.'

'You're imagining it.'

'Very well. You go and leave.'

'Leave?'

'Someone else will then to ask me to dance and you can watch.'

Misalliances

'What if nobody does?'

'They will. They always do. So when when the music starts, you come back in and watch.'

'Watch the King watching you while you're dancing with another...'

'I'm not imagining it.'

'It better not be anyone too handsome or I'll run him through.'

'Go!' She pushes him away. 'Off to the jakes or somewhere.'

The thing about the presence chamber is that it's large enough to host an evening's dancing for the King's favourites and their wives but small enough for him to be close to them and, needless to say, them to him. It's true: he himself hasn't danced since the days of his marriage to Anne Boleyn. Apparently, he's quite happy to be an observer, seated in his throne-chair on the dais. Tonight he's here with his new Queen, and though protocol decrees one shouldn't stare, there's a lot of discreet glancing at the pair, particularly from those in the know. To Catherine, she appears to be more settled than she was the other morning. But Anna of Kleve will know how to present herself on such occasions. Never much of a one for protocol, Catherine isn't just giving the occasional glance at the royal couple. She's staring at them, because she wants to catch the King's eye.

The musicians are readying their sheets of music for a new dance. She's afraid she'll be left in the rare and - after what she's said to Culpeper -

Misalliances

embarrassing position of having to stand on the side-lines. Then two things happen at once: for one heart-stopping moment the King's gaze meets hers, and Surrey sidles up, slips his hand in hers and says: 'May I, cousin?'

She and Henry Earl of Surrey, one of her first cousins, have never been close. When she was still a very young girl, barely on the cusp of puberty, he - then in his late teens - had twice attempted to take liberties with her and she's certain he wouldn't hesitate to do it again if the opportunity presented itself. Not that it's going to, thank you, because she finds him as unattractive five years on as she did then.

They make small talk. 'Where's Frances?' she asks, though she knows what he's going to say, for his wife is not far off giving birth to their latest child. How many is it now? Four, five? Surrey's no fool, so she's curbing the impulse to look towards the dais. Culpeper can report on that later. He's back and has stationed himself by a pillar half way down the room.

At the end of the dance she makes her excuses to Surrey and leaves the chamber. A number of couples are lingering in the vicinity of the refreshment table. 'Not here,' she says to Culpeper as they come together outside the door. She walks to the head of the stairs and waits for him.

'Did you see?'

'Yes. You made a lovely couple, you and Surrey.'

Misalliances

'Don't be ridiculous.' She lowers her voice. 'It is constant, isn't it?'

'I wouldn't say that.'

'He caught me looking, you know, before the dance started.'

'He was bound to. You were staring at him.'

'He stares at me.'

'Yes, he does.'

'You do think so?'

'You're a pretty young woman.'

'We had better be careful.'

'We? I think *you* might. He's just got married again.'

'It doesn't seem to be much of a marriage.' Catherine ignores his laughter and takes hold of his sleeve. 'Come. You can have one more dance.'

He takes her in his arms. 'I don't want to dance. Or not that way. You know what I want.'

She accepts his kiss and kisses him back.

'Poor Henry,' he says. 'Doesn't have much luck with women, does he?' He tightens his arms round her. 'But I tell you this, he's not having you.'

Chapter Seventeen: Loches

While Wyatt is with the Emperor, John Mason is seeing how far he can go before someone stops him. His thinking is, if the man himself is lodged on the ground floor of the chateau's keep, who's above on its other many floors? Up he goes, stone step by stone step, until he comes to a landing. A voice shouts in Spanish: 'Stop!' And then: 'Señor Mason, what are you doing here?' It's gratifying to be known to the Emperor's personal guard. It made the journey to locate him the previous evening a straightforward matter, and now it's easing the way up this huge tower. He recognises the man, though he was just one of many on the endless journeys he and Wyatt made across Spain. Fortunately, he's known by name to these men even if it's a courtesy he can't return.

'I'm looking for Robert Branceter. Is he up here?'

The guard is smiling. 'Señor, you remember me? I came to your house in Barcelona.'

'With messages from the palace?'

'Yes, many times. You always offered me a glass of wine.'

'Did I?' Mason accepts the guard's hand and shakes it. 'It's good to see you,' he says. 'Branceter. Is he here?'

'Señor Roberto?' The guard nods. 'He is.'

'Tell him I'm here to talk.'

Mason has met Branceter only the once, in the County's palace in Nice, before Wyatt set off on his doomed journey back to England with the marriage offer, but the vague image he has in his mind's eye – a large man with sandy hair and a florid complexion - is sufficient to recognise him when he appears at a door across the landing. 'It's John Mason,' he says, taking a step forward.

Branceter, his shirt half open, doesn't move. 'I know who you are. What do you want?'

'Just to talk. I don't have a weapon.' Mason opens his jacket. 'Please, Robert. If I was going to harm you, would I really do it here?' He indicates the Spanish guard. 'And we've got Juan or Felipe, or whatever his name is, keeping an eye on things. Can we sit down somewhere?'

'He comes with us.'

'As you wish.'

In the square, stone-flagged room is a young woman buttoning up her bodice. At a word from Branceter, she leaves with a sideways glance at Mason. 'Female company, a daybed in front of a roaring fire, a flagon of wine and a bowl of sweetmeats,' he says. 'You're well provided for.'

Branceter reaches for his jacket, puts it on and pours wine. 'He has no English,' he says, indicating the guard, who is by the door and still smiling.

'It's as well he hasn't, because I've come to tell you the King has ordered us to kill you.'

Misalliances

'He's mad.'

'Nonetheless, I thought I ought to tell you.'

'Are you planning to do it here?'

'We don't have much interest in doing it anywhere.'

'That's good news.'

'But Edmund Bonner will have other ideas and he's the official ambassador.'

'Whereas you and Wyatt are unofficial...'

'This visit is strictly unofficial. You're safe for now. But when you get to Paris it'll be a different matter. I'd stay close to the Emperor if I were you.'

'I shall.'

'Good. But we both know the pleasures on offer in Paris. Unless you're taking that young woman with you...'

'Don't be ridiculous.'

'Comes with the château, does she?'

'French hospitality.'

'All I'm saying is be careful if you're planning to go out and about.'

'Why are you telling me this?'

Mason laughs. 'I'd like to say it's because you're an amiable fellow, but to kill you - or Reginald Pole - would have consequences that we think it's best to avoid.'

'Meaning you, Wyatt and who else?'

'Just me and Wyatt. We're ploughing our own furrow in the absence of good diplomatic sense elsewhere.'

'Pole's convinced you're out to kill him.'

'Not us, though others might be. You *are* traitors.'

'Because we've chosen to side with the Roman Church?'

'Because you campaign against Henry and *his* Church.'

'It'll never last. Give it a few more years and he'll be begging to be back with Rome.'

'Perhaps. But I doubt that'd save you.'

'I'm safe for now.'

'You are from me and Wyatt. But as I said...' Mason downs his wine. 'What is it you do for Charles exactly?'

'Do for him?'

'You're here. You're travelling with him.'

'I liaise between him and Pole.'

'Doesn't Reginald have any French?'

'No. Nor Spanish.'

'So you translate his messages?'

'Not exactly.'

'But he writes to you and you tell Charles what he's thinking.'

'If you like…'

'You'd lose your head for that back home.'

'I know.'

Mason rises. 'You've heard what I've said. Keep this conversation to yourself, 'cause if the French or Spanish were to hear what we've been *ordered* to do, that wouldn't serve your turn at all, if you take my meaning.'

Misalliances

'I haven't seen you.'
'Nor I you.'

Mason waits downstairs in what passes for a great hall, a cold space without furniture, its bleakness only marginally relieved by the murals which decorate its walls. The place is empty, apart from the guards stationed on either side of the door. Their eyes alight on him every now and then, and he knows that if it had been a French patrol they'd run across the previous evening they wouldn't be here. When Wyatt finally appears, his face says it all.

'The Dauphin's arrived,' he says. 'We've been told to leave.'
'How did it go otherwise?'
'We can't talk here.'
'Neither of these clowns is going to have any English,' Mason says, flashing a smile at the guards.
'Let's say I've had friendlier receptions.'
'Courrières was right, then.'
'I'll give you the details later. Did you track down Branceter?'
'I did and succeeded in frightening him, I think. We'll see.'
'Let's go meet Robert and Frank.'

The tavern is down a narrow side-street, a dim room with two or three tables, a row of tapped barrels at the rear and a patron who responds to

Misalliances

their greeting with a grunt. It does have things to recommend it: there's a yard at the back for horses, it's not the sort of place that will give a fig about their being English and, as Mason remarks, it's unlikely to be visited by anyone attached to the chateau.

'So?' Mason begins.

'Charles says we'll be enemies if we enter an alliance with the Germans.'

'In light of Henry's marriage...'

'It's the first thing he brought up. We didn't have time to get on to anything else, because that's when the Dauphin arrived.'

'You don't think Cromwell might be right, about its balancing the power?'

'I think he's wrong. You and I know Charles has never thought of himself as our enemy. So why make him one? On top of that, an alliance with the Germans would mean us having to make a pact with the Lutherans. If Cromwell goes out on a limb about this, like he's done with the marriage, he'd be making a mistake. Henry doesn't like the Lutherans.'

'His new wife might change his mind. Does he know Charles might be marching on her brother?'

'Cromwell said he hadn't told him yet.'

'Well, he wouldn't have. He's been pushing for the marriage, so he'd be the last to raise an argument against it.'

'We need to tell the King what Charles has just said. Get Frank to take a letter.'

Misalliances

'Direct to the King, then. One for his eyes only. In the meantime, we do what we've been sent to do. Pick up what we can about the new accord with the French.'

Pitcher, sitting to one side with Rudston, has been listening. 'You want me back at Greenwich?'

'I'll tell you later,' Wyatt says, his attention having been drawn to the two young women who have slipped into the room. With their low-necked gowns and rouged lips it's obvious what they are. They take up position near the stairs in the further corner. The one in orange is intently eyeing them. The other, in yellow, has her back to them as she adjusts her hose. 'I see they start young over here,' he says to Mason.

The second girl turns round. 'They evidently do,' Mason replies, 'but what's more interesting is the one there, the yellow one, was with Branceter up at the chateau.'

'I'm not surprised,' Wyatt says. 'It's a common practice, bringing in the local whores as a sign of welcome. It happened to me in the Vatican once of all places. But they were seasoned courtesans, not youngsters like these two.'

'No, what I meant was, she might be able to tell us something.'

'Such as what?'

'I'm going to have a word with her.'

'Wait...'

But Mason is already crossing the room. Wyatt turns to Pitcher and Rudston. 'Go and get the horses ready. In case we have to leave in a hurry.'

The other girl is making her way towards the table. She has made no attempt to tidy her blonde hair under her coif. Indeed, the impression is that this raggedyness might be deliberate, because she thinks it's provocative.

She addresses Wyatt with a brazenness at odds with her youth. 'You want me, Monsieur?' She juts out a hip and places a hand on it.

Her prettiness still has traces of the child about it, in the plumpness of her face, the clearness of her eye, the willowiness of her figure. Wyatt feels no temptation to reply in the affirmative. She's an ingénue, caught up in a business that will quickly age her and might even prematurely kill her. 'No,' he says, 'but come and sit.'

'Sit?'

'I'll see you right.'

The patron is impatiently eyeing Mason and the girl in yellow. He addresses them with a few curt words and the girl immediately takes Mason's hand and leads him up the stairs. Wyatt is familiar with the type the patron is: he will not be slow in coming forward to set the terms of business, and it's no surprise when he approaches the table.

'You pay for her,' the Frenchman says.

'I'll pay for her time,' Wyatt says.

'You pay for her whether you fuck her or not.'

'That's what I said.'

Misalliances

The fighting abilities of this back-street pimp are questionable. He's younger, but he's running to fat. He's not wearing a sword, but he does have a dagger in his belt. More than likely, he fights dirty. If there's someone else on the property, they haven't shown their face. If it came to a fight, Wyatt fancies his chances.

The girl shuffles up next to him on the bench with a practised smile. Close up, she's even younger than he thought. She's adjusting her grubby neckline, either at some artfully coy attempt at modesty or to reveal even more of what she has. With one hand raised to play with her hair, she tips herself forward. It's the latter, then.

'Monsieur?'

'How old are you, M'am'selle?'

'Old enough.'

Wyatt shakes his head. 'That won't do. How old? Fourteen?'

'Does it matter?'

Wyatt studies her. 'You're thirteen,' he says. 'Not much more.'

'It's better than working in the fields,' she says unexpectedly. The pellucid white and cornflower blue of her eyes really are those of a child. 'I work all day and my mama and I still don't have enough to eat.'

'Listen to me,' he says. 'You're too young for this life. Go back to the fields and in time find a man to marry.'

'Pouf! The only men with any money are up at the chateau, and they only want me for the one thing.' She's trying to push the errant strands of hair back under her coif, but they're greasy and unco-operative. He imagines her clean, in a fine gown.

Wyatt takes out his purse. 'How much do you earn here in a day?'

She shrugs. 'What's that to you?'

He takes out a sovereign and holds it up. 'However many times you lie down on your back, it'll be nowhere near this much.' He puts the coin in her hand and lets her turn it back and forth. 'It's solid gold. If you can't spend it here, get a blacksmith to melt it down.' He takes the coin back. 'If you want it and another for your friend, leave when we do.'

'That's impossible.' She looks across to the counter where her boss is busy tapping a barrel. 'He won't allow it.'

'I'll take care of him.'

Mason and the other girl are coming down the stairs. Wyatt's rushes over, grabs her friend by the arm and takes her off to the side.

'He'll do what?'

'Give us gold, chérie. Gold.'

'What for?'

'What's going on?' Mason asks Wyatt.

'We're getting them out of here.'

'We are? How's that come about?'

Misalliances

Wyatt's girl is at the counter. 'We're leaving,' she announces to the patron, 'and you will not stop us because that man has a sword!'

Since the girl's ferocious pointing at him has precipitated the inevitable, Wyatt clears himself of the table and draws his weapon.

Mason, still in his seat, says wearily: 'Thomas? What are you doing?'

'I've got this, John.'

It's mayhem on the other side of the room. With agitated repeatings of 'Non, non, non!' the patron is pushing Mason's girl up the stairs, while Wyatt's, wedged between the two of them, is pulling her back down. It's a tangle of flailing arms, elbows and knees. A raised boot is repelled by the stamp of a slippered foot, the grab for a narrow wrist countered by a rake of finger-nails down a greasy neck. Raining expletives down on her, the patron drags Wyatt's girl off the stairs and throws her to the floor.

Mason comes and stands next to Wyatt. He draws his sword. 'I've got this,' Wyatt says. 'I've told you.'

'Just in case,' says Mason.

The Frenchman's dagger is out. He turns on them in a fighting stance, feet apart, and tossing the dagger from one hand to the other. There's a threatening flurry of French. Wyatt says 'Enough,' more to himself than anyone else, dances forward as he's done many times in the tilt-yard, feints to the side and puts his thin-bladed sword, his *espada ropera,* straight through the man's upper arm. The patron falls back against the table with a 'Merde!' that's more than an exclamation of surprise than a cry of pain. Cups and jugs tumble to the floor. The air is ringing with the shrieks of the girls.

Wyatt calls to them. 'Now!'

Feet flying this way and that, their thin gowns up round their knees and their caps skew-whiff, the girls rush to him. Wyatt's throws herself into his arms. 'Be careful,' he warns, detaching himself from her. He takes out his handkerchief, wipes the blade of his sword and puts it back in its scabbard. 'Come,' he says to them.

Outside, he gives them their sovereigns. 'Straight home,' he says. 'Don't come back here.' They exchange glances. The one in the yellow dress comes up and kisses him on the cheek. 'Thank you, Monsieur,'

'Go!' he says, shooing them off.

Mason is looking anxious. He still has his sword drawn. The street is long and narrow, opposing eaves almost touching, and if something more does go off it'll be easy to get hemmed in. He waits while Wyatt sees the girls out of sight. Then, his patience exhausted, he takes hold of his friend's arm. 'We have to go.' Pitcher and Rudston are coming down the alley with the horses. 'Now, Thomas!'

It's a good mile before they draw to a halt. The road, such as it is, has a vineyard on one side, a fallow field on the other. 'Ride up to the bend,

Frank,' Mason says. 'See if anyone's following.' He turns to Wyatt. 'Well, that was diverting on a dull afternoon. What got into you?'

'They were too young.'

'When did you become so righteous?'

'It was wrong.'

Mason gives a derisive snort. 'You do know they'll be back at work when your money runs out.'

'I don't know that.'

Pitcher is back. 'All clear,' he says. They jog their horses into a walk.

Mason says: 'In case you're wondering, the girl and I only talked.'

'Now who's become righteous?'

'About Branceter. She had information.'

'I bet she did.'

'Not that sort. He's going to Paris tomorrow.'

'Not on to Tours?'

'Straight to Paris. We know what he does for Charles. I think he could be meeting Pole.'

'But that wouldn't make any sense. If Pole is in France, he'd be with the rest of the Pope's people, at Tours or Blois, with Charles, the King and the Dauphin.'

'True. But Branceter must have had permission to go on ahead. Perhaps he's meeting someone else on Charles's behalf.'

'If he's in the city on his own, he's at risk of being picked up by Bonner's men.'

Mason draws his horse to a halt. 'Do we need to be back in Paris, then? How much do we want to put into saving his skin?'

'If Bonner takes him, we can kiss goodbye to whatever chance we have of talking to Charles again.'

'We're not going to do that down here, anyway, after the way you were dismissed this morning. And it mightn't be a bad idea to find out what Branceter's up to.'

Wyatt wheels his horse round. 'Frank. The Paris road. Which way?'

'I thought I was the only one heading back.'

'We all are.'

'Then we need the road we came in on. Where we met the Spanish. I can find it from the town'

'Let's hope there's no one waiting for us,' Mason says.

'We'll be in and out. He'll be getting his arm dressed.'

'Thomas, I've got to say this. You need to cast out the mote in your own eye.'

'What mote?'

'Kate Howard.'

'I don't follow you…'

'She's not much older than the girls back there. Didn't you know?' Mason spurs his horse into motion.

Chapter Eighteen: Lust

'Which are the penitential psalms?' Damaris asks Tom one morning.

'Don't you know?'

'A lot of them are asking for God's forgiveness, I know that. But penitential psalms? Is that a particular group?'

'It's not a question I've ever asked myself. Why do you want them?'

'Thomas said he was working on them.'

'Look for the ones which mention repentance, I suppose. David wrote most of them, didn't he? So I imagine there'll be a few like that.'

'Why's that?'

'He had need to repent. Don't you know the story? About how he came to marry Bathsheba?'

'No.'

'Where's the book?'

'Upstairs.'

'Fetch it. I'll show you.'

Once up in her room, she begins to read.

And about the eventide it happened that David arose from his resting place and went up to the top of the King's palace, and from there he saw a woman washing herself and the woman was very beautiful. And David sent to ask who the woman was.

Misalliances

She can't take it in. How could a godly man like David behave like this? Be so consumed by lust? She goes to find Tom but Lizzie tells her he's gone to Malling with Arthur to pack up the stuff that has to go to the King.

'I'll catch him later, then,' Damaris says. By way of explanation, she holds up the book; she has her thumb in it to mark the place. 'I wanted to ask him something, that's all.'

'How far have you got?'

'The books of Samuel.'

'I don't know those. I did take a look at some of the Gospels when we first got it.'

'I don't know it as well as I thought I did.' Damaris removes her thumb and closes the book. 'I was wondering,' she says, 'couldn't we take turns reading it to each other to get to know it better?'

'You, me and Tom could. I don't know whether Jane'd want to.' Lizzie shifts awkwardly in the big chair, a manoeuvre that requires an effort disproportionate to the result. 'That blue gown suits you,' she says. 'I think that's the nicest of them.'

'It's the most comfortable.'

'Comfort.' Lizzie laughs. 'I'm not getting much of that at present. I need to send Edward to see if the new ones are ready. I could undo the laces on this but then I'm showing my back.'

Misalliances

'There's no danger of that while you're sitting down. Do you want me to do it?'

'Could you?'

'You will need to stand up.' Damaris opens the placket and loosely ties it again. 'Is that better?'

'Oh, it is. Thank you. I suppose you'd be used to that sort of thing, living among women?'

'Not really. Very few of them ever got pregnant.'

Lizzie's laughter spills out of her, like a long-submerged well of merriment has been tapped.

'As for me,' Damaris says, 'I went into the convent a maid and have remained so.'

'Was that about faith? You felt called to Christ?'

'It was about escape.'

'From what?'

'A man.'

'Oh.'

'Are you expecting Jane?'

'She's upstairs with Nurse. Henry has a cough.'

'May I keep you company?'

'Please. Come and sit.'

'When is it due?'

'Not before the end of April, I think.'

'Thomas will be back by then, will he?'

'He said he would.'

'Have you heard from him?'

Misalliances

Lizzie shakes her head. 'He said it'd be hard. It's because of what he's doing.'

Damaris wants some air, even though it's going to be bitterly cold outside. It's been freezing since Christmas. January was never as cold as this in the city. The tall buildings must have acted like a shield. She resolves to take a turn around the close and goes upstairs for her coat. In front of the mirror, she removes her coif and unpins her hair. It's longer than it's been since she was very young, and she likes it, so much that she's tempted to leave it as it is; it's not as if she's likely to meet anyone. At the last minute she pins it up once more and replaces her coif. On the way down she meets Tom's wife. 'Are you going out?' Jane asks. 'I'll come with you.'

'How's the little boy?' Damaris asks as they set off towards the park.

'Much improved, thank you.'

To Damaris's relief, it looks like they won't be doing much small talk – it's never come easy to either of them – but it makes her wonder what this companionable excursion is about. That becomes clear when they reach the edge of the close and are looking out over the deer park, and Jane says: 'You and Tom seem to have become friends.'

'Yes. I think so.'

'You must have read the whole of The Bible by now, all those hours you spend in grandfather's study.'

Misalliances

'We talk about it as well. I like to hear Tom's views. I was a nun for twelve years.'

'I know that.'

'What's in The Bible is of great interest to me.'

'I'm sure.'

'And no one else here seems to have read it.'

'We don't get the chance.'

The continuing sourness in Jane's face releases the anger Damaris has so far suppressed. 'This isn't about the Bible, though, is it?'

'No, it's not. I tell you what, Sister. I would feel more comfortable if you and my husband had your discussions downstairs.'

'I beg your pardon?'

'I need him sometimes of an evening. And I really shouldn't have to traipse upstairs to find him.'

'He doesn't spend every evening with me.'

'Doesn't he?'

'He plays cards with Edward and Arthur two or three times a week.'

'You seem to know a lot about his routine.'

'More than you, it seems.' To take the sting out of the jibe, Damaris forces a smile. 'Look, I enjoy talking to Tom about matters of religion. That's all it is. You really have nothing to worry about.'

'I should hope not, you a nun and all.' Jane steps away. 'Do your discussing downstairs, please.'

Misalliances

At supper, Tom's question crosses the table: how her reading is going. 'The second book of Samuel,' he says. 'The story of David and Bathsheba.'

'I've read it.'

'Do you want to talk about it?'

'I do, yes.'

'Then sit next door,' Jane says, as she takes a second piece of pork from the platter. 'It's too cold to be up in grandfather's room.'

Lizzie, looking from Jane to Tom to Damaris, says: 'Damaris has suggested we take turns reading one afternoon or evening. That would be good, wouldn't it?'

'It would,' Tom says.

Jane says nothing.

Tom has the book open on his lap. Damaris, next to him, taps the page. 'It's all there. David might have been favoured by the Lord and yet he behaved like a son of Satan.'

'That's a little strong.'

'No, it's not.' She takes from her pocket a sheet of paper. 'I've made a list of his sins. First, he covets another man's wife…'

'He didn't know that when he set eyes on her.'

'Yes, he did. And he still orders her to come to him. He uses his power as King to summon and seduce her.'

'That is what kings do.'

Misalliances

'They shouldn't. After that, when Bathsheba finds she's with child, he tries to make it appear it's been conceived in wedlock, to protect his reputation.'

'That is sinful...'

'And how he does it is more so. He orders an honourable man, Bathesheba's husband Uriah, to return from where he's been fighting the Ammonites. To come home.'

'So that he'll sleep with his wife...'

'But that would mean neglecting his duty, so Uriah refuses.'

'That is honourable.'

'You do know what a mortal sin is?'

'Yes, it's intentionally doing harm.'

'If you commit a mortal sin you put your immortal soul in peril.'

'Does David do that?' Tom turns over a page. 'Ah, I see. Uriah refuses and David sends him into the front line of the battle, where he knows he's likely to be killed.'

'Uriah *is* killed.'

'Doesn't David redeem himself. I seem to remember reading something about Nathan...'

'Nathan confronts him with his sins. And then he repents.'

'And makes amends. He takes Bathsheba as his wife.'

'That wasn't making amends! He doesn't do it out of pity for her or from any sense of guilt. He's driven solely by self-interest. He gets his woman and makes her child by him legitimate. The fact he repents – or expresses repentance - doesn't absolve him in my eyes. He sins again and again and profits from it.'

'The child dies. God punishes him.'

'If you like…'

Damaris takes the book. 'I think lust is wicked.'

'What?'

'I've been the victim of it. At the hands of bad men. And now I'm thinking…if it can lead a good man like David astray, then it must be the devil at work, mustn't it?'

'Not always. It's the way we're made.'

'So all men have the devil in them…'

'All men have lust in them. Otherwise, there'd be no babies.'

'And where is love in this?'

'Love?'

'I think lust without love is sinful.'

'I don't know, Sister.'

'Why do you insist on still calling me Sister?'

Tom picks up his wine. 'Do I?'

'You know you do. I keep telling you to call me Damaris, but you won't.'

'It's out of respect, I suppose. Because you were a nun.'

'Exactly. I *was* a nun. And I don't think it's that.'

'What is it, then?'

Misalliances

'I think it's because you're frightened of getting close to me.'

'That's nonsense.'

'Or have been told you mustn't.'

The colour has drained from Tom's face. 'I don't know where all this has come from, Sister…'

'There it is again!' From where they're sitting, she can see into the dining room. There's no one left at the supper table. They've all gone into the parlour. 'We'd better join the others.'

Chapter Nineteen: Bonner

Edmund Bonner's room in the two-story building on the St. Honoré ill befits a man who is, both literally and figuratively, of little stature. It's big, with a high ceiling decorated with gold-leaf and a window almost as tall. It's in front of this that Bonner has placed his massive desk, a piece of furniture that does little for him, since it serves only to reinforce the impression that this is a small man in a big office.

'Do we have to go?' was Mason's response, when they received the summons. 'We don't have to report to him.'

'He is the King's ambassador.'

'Damn it, Thomas! What are we, then?'

It's a question that Wyatt is asking himself, sitting here before the big desk, reduced to a disdainful silence by the ridiculousness of this middling cleric lording it over them. Such is the absurdity of being subjected to Bonner's crowing monologue about the festivities at Blois, his prominent place in them, how grand it all was, that his mind has wandered.

'I'm sorry, Edmund,' he says. 'What did you just say?'

Bonner tuts. 'Do keep up. I said I had to speak to François about the traitor he was harbouring.'

'A traitor to him or us?'

'To us, of course.'

'You mean Robert Branceter...'

'Who else would I mean?'

'That was clever of you, vicar,' says Mason.

The glow of self-satisfaction fades from Bonner's face. 'I must warn you not to speak to me in that fashion.'

Wyatt cuts across them. 'Mason's right. What you've done is alert the French to our interest in him.'

'And the Spanish...' Mason adds.

'I don't understand. They already know we're interested in him. All I said was that in a just land, a traitor to a fellow king would be handed over.' He pauses and something like appeal enters his voice. 'It's understood, isn't it? That's what must happen.'

'Edmund, let me explain how this sort of thing works,' Wyatt says patiently. 'When you have orders from the King to seize someone the last thing you do is tell the very people he's with. That's what the King told you to do, wasn't it? To seize Branceter?'

'To seize him and take him back to England.'

'Well, that's impossible now, because the French and the Spanish will have gathered him to their respective bosoms. But what you've also done is wrecked whatever chances Mason and I might have had to carry out *our* instructions, which are newer than yours.'

'What are your instructions?'

'To kill Branceter.'

Misalliances

Bonner starts, his fingers fluttering. 'Well, I know nothing about that.'

'What you've also done by the sound of it,' Mason says, 'is insult the King of France.'

'How have I done that?'

Wyatt huffs impatiently. 'My God, Edmund! Do you understand nothing? There's nothing wrong in asking a king to hand a traitor over to one of his fellows, but there's a manner in which it must be done. And that's with small steps, not by casting aspersions on the way he runs his country!'

'François'll have someone on his way to Greenwich now, I reckon,' says Mason.

'For what purpose?'

'To complain about you, you blundering fool. What else?'

Bonner pushes his chair away and rises to his full, if modest, height. 'I'm not telling you again, Mason,' he says, with a jab of a finger. 'If you insult me once more…'

Mason wafts the show of temper away. 'Oh, sit down. You've made all the mischief for me you're ever going to. All those lies you told me about me and Reginald Pole...'

'They weren't lies.'

'They weren't the truth…'

'That's enough,' Wyatt says. 'We need to decide what we're going to do when Branceter finally gets here.'

'He's already here,' Bonner says, his face a picture of self-satisfaction.

'What do you mean?' Mason sits forward in a show of surprise.

'That's my understanding. He's here in Paris.'

It's Wyatt's turn. 'Where did you learn that?'

'At Blois.' Bonner sits back, preening. 'I have my sources.'

Wyatt's skill at pantomime is the equal of Mason's. 'He must have come on ahead,' he says to him.

'We don't know exactly where he is...' Bonner says.

Wyatt, incredulous: 'You don't know where he is?'

'But I have posted men at Fontainebleau and the Louvre.'

'He'll be at the Louvre if he's anywhere,' Wyatt says. 'And if your men do find him, I assume they've been instructed to seize him?'

'As per my instructions.'

Mason shakes his head. 'No, no. That'd be cutting across *our* instructions.'

'I have mine in writing.'

Wyatt gives a theatrical sigh. 'Edmund, listen. From what you've told us, you're already *persona non grata* with François.'

'And more than likely with Henry as well,' Mason puts in.

'So if you do locate Branceter and seize him Heaven knows what kind of row that's going to spark with the French, not to mention the Spanish.'

'It's what I've been instructed to do. I'm not afraid of a row.'

'The King must have thought again because he's given us new instructions. He must have realised the diplomatic furore it would cause, his ambassador to the French court grabbing someone close to the Emperor while he's a guest there. Because that's what there'll be, and I tell you this, it'll destroy what remains of your credit here, and damage however much you have of that at Greenwich.' Wyatt gives Mason an eye-rolling glance that wouldn't be out of place on a playhouse stage. 'You must leave it to us now. Our traitorous friend will still be dealt with but in a manner that's commonplace in the seedier parts of this city. He will meet with a dagger-thrust – an anonymous one, needless to say - in some back alley or other. Tell your men to report to us as soon as they know his whereabouts, and we'll take it from there.'

'Why couldn't my men do it?'

'Because if they did there's a risk of it coming back to you, after what you said to François, and you're in enough trouble.'

'Whereas if you leave it to me and Wyatt,' Mason says, 'it'll have been done on your watch, which'll please Henry, but it'll have absolutely nothing to do with you. At least, not as far as the French and the Spanish are concerned.'

'The King will be enormously pleased to see him gone,' Wyatt adds.

Misalliances

'You're sure you can see to it?'

'Are we sure?' Mason recoils from the affront. 'Don't you know us yet, vicar?'

'Oh, I do, I do. That's the trouble. Very well. I'll have my men report to you. And please don't call me vicar.'

'Good,' says Wyatt. 'So, why else are we here? I assume Branceter wasn't the only reason.'

'No. You'll be meeting your good friend Charles when he arrives.'

'Now, now, Edmund. Enough of the sarcasm. I've been instructed by the King to do that.'

'I shall want to be present.'

'That will not be possible.'

'I advise you to make it possible.'

Wyatt claps Mason on the back when they're back on the street and doing up their coats against the snow that's started to fall. 'We brought that off rather well, I thought.'

'We did, didn't we?'

They begin walking. 'So let's see where we are,' Wyatt says. 'Branceter's at large in the city, as we thought he would be, and Bonner's on his trail, as we thought *he* would be. So as soon as we find out where he is, we tell him that. Just in case Edmund can't resist having him seized after all. He's daft enough. Branceter needs to see you weren't frightening him with phantoms and he must lie low till the Emperor gets here.'

'And then there's what he's been up to.'

'I've been thinking about that. It could be something personal. Nothing to do with Charles at all. In any event, if *our* mission is to succeed, we have to do what we can to keep him safe. And since we don't trust Bonner, let's hope your friend and his gang of scally-wags find him first. When are you seeing Fitou?'

'When he's got something to tell me.'

Precisely what services Patrice Fitou did for Mason when he was stationed in Paris, Wyatt hasn't asked, because he can guess what they were. About the time he himself returned from Calais and was negotiating a new relationship with Anne Boleyn, one that would still eventually imperil him, Mason was apparently navigating his way through his own set of dangerous liasons in the brothels of Paris. He knows this much of his friend's history from the tales they told one another late at night in Spain, while sampling the produce from the local vineyards or, in Barbastro, the beer their German friends had given them. It was testament to Mason's continuing standing with the denizens of Paris's underbelly that he located Fitou within a few hours of their arriving back in the Petit Nesle. The Frenchman still runs a small army of thieves and pickpockets. 'If an Englishman is out and about,' Mason said, 'they'll spot him.'

But as yet they haven't, Fitou tells them, when – his coat dusted with snow – he finally rises from

Misalliances

the pitch-black streets and ushers himself into their room. With his crooked nose and darting dark eyes, he looks every inch the villain, and there's a bluff, blustering manner about him which – even allowing for the French tendency to be over-demonstrative – does little to persuade Wyatt to set aside his first impressions and incline towards trusting him. Whatever Mason is paying for the man's cohorts of sharp eyes and ears, the fact they have picked up nothing suggests it might not be money well-spent. 'We will keep looking,' Fitou assures them. 'Tomorrow. You'll see. Tomorrow we'll be lucky.'

Three days after Fitou's visit, they get word the Emperor's about to enter the city. 'Are we going?' Mason asks. Wyatt's view is that it's politic for them to stay away after the manner in which the French treated him at Loches, even though it's an event of some moment, a celebration of Spanish and French reconciliation which, publicly at least, promises continuing amity. The man who rules Spain, the Low Countries, large chunks of Germania and Italy and the newly discovered, ever expanding territories of the New World has been at war with France for over a decade and he's now about to enter its capital city in the company of its king, his ostensible new brother.

So Wyatt and Mason do not see the procession, but since its route passes close by them – it begins at the Hôtel de Clermont, the mansion along the river, and follows the Seine until it reaches the bridges of the Île de la Cité, where it crosses to the other bank – they do hear it, the murmurings and hurrahs of the crowds, the sound made by the footfall of hundreds of soldiers, the metallic clop of a similar number of horses. Later they hear from the concierge that it was 'a grand show, though – *hélas* - you couldn't make out the Emperor because he was hidden by a great big canopy'. 'What did he need a canopy for?' Mason spluttered. 'Anyone'd think it's high summer.'

    In these January days Paris has battened itself down beneath the icy privations of a winter habitually found further north. Wyatt and Mason sleep late, take their food and drink in a small establishment beyond Notre Dame, and spend their evenings according to their own individual bents, Mason repairing to his favourite back-street haunts, Wyatt going back to Petit Nesle to write. He has had no choice but resort to the channels provided by Bonner's office to request an audience with the Emperor. But there's no reply. The first days of the new year unwind in this torpid, static fashion until two of Bonner's men come to the door one morning.

'Lots of churches named Saint Denys in Paris,' Mason says, as they're buckling on their swords.
    'It's the one next to the Porte Saint Denys.'
    'And a house with a green door? Could be a number of those, too.'

Misalliances

There's been no more snow and the day is clear and bright with a high blue sky. They cross the river, follow it for a short distance and then head north through the Marais, where the street widens and there's a succession of big houses, standing within airy courtyards behind iron gates. The quality of the neighbourhood deteriorates as they approach the wall: they come upon a livestock market and have to pick their way through pens of chickens, geese, pigs and sheep. They keep their hands on the hilts of their swords. The wall no longer represents a true boundary of the city – dwellings of one kind or another have long sprung up all the way round it - but King François has until recently been at war with the Holy Roman Empire. Paris remains the symbolic heart of his kingdom and he protects it with this ramparted circle of stone. There are only two gates in the wall and Wyatt and Mason are on a narrow street near the northern one.

'So where's this church?' Mason queries, more to himself than Wyatt.

Wyatt points. Further down, standing proud above several tiers of low roofs, the segment of a stone pediment is visible, grey against the blue sky. 'That has to be it.'

Mason stops to survey the porticoed frontage when they reach it but Wyatt walks on to look at the houses beyond the adjacent patch of scrub.

'This one's got a green door,' he calls, drawing his sword.

Misalliances

Mason, catching up, takes his arm. 'Put that away. He'll think we *have* come to kill him.' He knocks on the door. An old woman wrapped in a shawl crawls by, and gives them a quizzical look. Someone has begun to move about inside.

Several things happen at once. A young woman throws open the door and assaults them with a barrage of obscenities, and soldiers spill out of a gap on the other side of the road. A group of them, all with their swords out, surround Wyatt and Mason; the rest push past the woman and enter the house. A captain rides up. 'Thank you for taking us to him, Messieurs,' he says. 'The King and the Emperor will be pleased.'

'They've followed us,' Mason murmurs.

'Take it easy,' Wyatt whispers. 'How do you think they knew?'

'Fitou,' Mason says. 'Who else?'

'You need to learn who to trust in Paris,' the captain says, with an amused smile.

Wyatt speaks up. 'We came to talk, that's all.'

'It's all the same to me.' The Frenchman looks off to the still open front door. 'My orders were to retrieve Monsieur Branceter and that's what I've done. In view of who you are, I recommend you go on your way.'

Once they're well down the road, they stop to look back. Branceter is being shepherded to a waiting horse. 'So all he was doing was seeing a woman,' Mason chuckles. 'The same old story...'

Misalliances

'How do you think this'll play when it gets back to Henry?'

'We were at his door. Our motives for being there, which as it happens were the same as the French, can remain between ourselves.'

'We led them to him, John. That'll get back, too.'

'We'll say that was Bonner's fault. If he hadn't tipped them off we were going after Roberto once he entered France, they wouldn't have been looking for him.'

'Roberto?'

'That's what the Spanish call him.'

They're still laughing, out of relief as much as anything, when they reach the Marais, with its stately houses. Wyatt stops by a pair of iron gates and peers inside. The yard is as long as it's wide. At the bottom of it there's a broad-fronted stone house with a balcony. 'Have you ever been in one of these?' he asks.

Mason shakes his head. 'Never invited. They all belong to French nobles. François' favourites. I went to Fontainebleau once or twice. But only on business.' They walk on.

'We'll need to tread carefully once we're home,' Wyatt says when they're back in the Petit Nesle. 'We might think we've come out of it well, but Bonner will do his utmost to make sure he does.'

'Then we need to give Henry our side of it before he hears it from anyone else.'

Misalliances

'We don't have Frank...'

'Even if we did, we need to speak to him in person.'

'Rudston's no good for that.'

'No, it has to be me.'

'Take Robert with you. For safety.'

Chapter Twenty: Resonances

Damaris has returned to the very first books of The Bible. In reading Leviticus she has come across this:

> I am the LORD. You shall not uncover the nakedness of your father, which is the nakedness of your mother; she is your mother, you shall not uncover her nakedness. You shall not uncover the nakedness of your father's wife; it is your father's nakedness. You shall not uncover the nakedness of your sister, your father's daughter or your mother's daughter, whether brought up in the family or in another home. You shall not uncover the nakedness of your son's daughter or of your daughter's daughter, for their nakedness is your own nakedness.

It puzzles her. If this is Holy Writ, why is there nothing about a father uncovering the nakedness of his daughter? She reads on, statute after statute condemning various kinds of wickedness: you must not lie, you must not steal, mistreat the poor, wrong your neighbour. Then, two chapters later, the unknown author of Leviticus returns to the topic of vice within the family and lays down a further set of prohibitions: you must not lie with your stepmother, with your mother-in-law, your daughter-in-law, your uncle's

Misalliances

wife, your brother's wife. Still there is nothing about a man wronging his daughter. She begins to wonder if Leviticus truly is God's word, or rather an ancient writer's personalised, corrupted rendering of it, for there is one thing she is certain of: her own father wronged her, and that must surely be condemned.

Now that she is, for good or ill, out in the world, or rather in it again, she's finding her thoughts returning to the time before she entered the Convent of St. Agatha, to the world she was born into in Southampton. There, in the big house on Oxford Street, she soon enough came to realise, however undeveloped her young mind was, that some behaviour was indisputably wrong.

The difficulties between the two of them which led to her requesting admission into the nunnery were the culmination of a series of things going wrong. Or rather, she now thinks, those calamities paved the way for their subsequent problems. First came the death of her mother when she was six. Three years later, her father's business collapsed, after the Vintners Company decided it could no longer rely on John Althorpe to supply their wines (she learned later he had been selling the barrels imported on the Company's behalf for ready cash). And last of all, the forced move from the fine house to the little cottage out at Millbrook, a poor district above the docks.

In that constricted space, she did her best to keep her distance from him but he was always

Misalliances

there, pulling her to him in too tight an embrace, attempting to kiss her or caress those parts of her which, for any girl her age, were forbidden to any man. To echo the language of Leviticus, he never succeeded in uncovering her nakedness but his behaviour left her in no doubt that was what he desired. After several years of this, she knew she had to get away, and St. Agatha's was only a mile up the road. Eventually she was to discover this revered convent was also tainted with lust, so she fled from there too. And that was when she met Thomas Wyatt.

Love and lust. She wishes she were clearer in her own mind as to the relationship between them. Her conversations with Tom have ceased, and she misses them. Actually, if she's honest with herself, and she always tries to be, she misses him.

It's time for her morning walk. January came to an end with a spell of mild weather. That and the longer hours of daylight have given the impression that spring might be arriving early. But February has entered icily and she's swaddling herself again in a woollen shawl and a long scarf before she puts on her coat.

This particular morning there's something new to see. Propped up in the angle between the wall and the kitchen door is the walking-stick she left in James's wagon. She picks it up and strokes her fingers along it. She's glad to have it again. Surely he hasn't come all this way to return it? He must have been on his way to Maidstone. Yes, that'd be it.

With the thought of him, the feelings she had on their last day together are disturbingly reawakened. What a hypocrite she is, to be so strong in her condemnation of lust, when she's as much prey to it as anyone else! Or had she fallen in love with him, in the course of the three days she was in his company? Does love work like that? Going out of his way to return the stick is a kind of act of love. She raises the collar of her coat and, stick in hand, walks out.

Skirting the spot where Jane upbraided her about Tom, she thinks back to the unpleasantness of that conversation. It still rankles, and she thinks relations between her and Jane will be forever affected by it, though in truth they have never been particularly good. Thomas's having to leave for France so soon after she arrived did make her wonder how far his patronage was going to upheld by the others. She needn't have worried about Lizzie and Tom; not for one moment has either of them failed to make her feel accepted. She has even come to think of Tom as a friend, despite their silly crossed words the other evening. The only check in proceedings – the only thing that has prevented her from feeling fully settled at Allington – has been Jane Wyatt's determination to be anything but friendly towards her. For months she's been putting that down to something in the woman's character; perhaps she's like that with everyone. Now she knows better, of course. In fact, she'd lay a pound to a penny Jane's only like that with women, or more precisely any woman she identifies as liable to take her husband's interest away from her.

Sitting down on the felled tree-trunk below the row of alders, she laughs at the idea. If there was anything between her and Tom to warrant his wife's jealousy, it'd be quite flattering. But what does it say about their marriage, that Jane is so prone to jealousy? There doesn't appear to be much affection there. Anyway, enough of Jane. She's going to be away for a while at Bishopsbourne, settling her father's estate. Please let it be weeks rather than days, because her absence has brought a decided lightening of the atmosphere in the house. Lizzie's been in better spirits and even baby Henry seems to be crying less. As for Tom, he didn't offer to go with his wife, as far as she can make out, so perhaps he's welcomed the respite as well.

She starts, because he's crossing the park towards her. His nose is red and his breath is escaping in foggy wisps.

'Good morning,' he says. 'This is where you come.'

She's glad he's stopped. 'Only this far,' she says, 'I wouldn't want to frighten the deer.'

'Oh, there's not much chance of that. They're used to Edward and Arthur. One or two are with

Misalliances

kid. But they seem to be alright. This is a nice place to sit, isn't it?'

'I don't think I'll be here long. It's too cold.'

'May I?'

'Of course.'

He sits. 'Are you still reading the Bible?'

'I am. I'm on Leviticus. They puzzle me, those first books.'

'Most of the Old Testament puzzles me.' He takes off his hat, ruffles his hair and gives his head a scratch. 'Lizzie would like us to read some of it to her.'

'She can read, can't she?'

'Oh, yes. But we said we would. And since you and I know it, she'd like us to choose some passages.' He's passing his hat from one hand to the other, twisting it.

'Have you really read all of it?'

'I have. In the Latin. I used to hate it, you know. But my father insisted. This was when I was small. So later, at the University, I was well ahead of the others. In the course of my two years there I read most of it. And as time went on I learned enough Greek to tackle the original Apostles' books. I had to lean on Tyndale for that, though.'

'You had Tyndale's books?'

'Only his New Testament. My father gave it to me. Goodness knows where he got it from. It was banned back then.'

'And now we have the whole thing in English.'

'We've made progress. Let's hope it stays that way.'

'Don't you think it will?'

'I don't know. For what we're doing, reading the Scriptures in English, I saw a woman in France put to death. That was only ten or so years ago.' He puts his hat back on. 'I don't trust the times.'

'Neither do I.'

'You wouldn't.'

'Do you want us to read this evening?'

'Yes. If that's alright with you?'

'It's fine. I have some thoughts.'

'Are you walking back?'

She gets up. 'I think I will.'

Lizzie's new gowns still haven't come and when they sit down for their usual midday bread and cheese she looks so uncomfortable it prompts Damaris to go up to her room and take out her tunic. It'll be a bit long but it'll be roomier than what Lizzie is wearing. If the idea was simply put to her she might reject it, but...a better idea...what if it was shown to her? It is that time of the afternoon when she goes to lie down.

She has never been to the side of the castle where the family's private quarters are. She considers summoning Madeleine or Miriam to show her the right room, but decides it's a matter best kept between Lizzie and herself. How many rooms can there be?

Misalliances

    She ventures out into the long gallery. Two of the house-maids are on their knees polishing the floor and they raise their heads at her approach. One of them smiles at her. It's the girl who gave her the beeswax for the chapel pews. Is it Abigail? She has yet to attach names to any other servants who work behind the scenes at Allington, those who clean and polish in the house, who mow the grass and cut back the trees in the park, and she's had no reason to explore as far as the farm, where she assumes another small army of workers contributes to keeping the castle going.

    Resisting the temptation to ask the girl for directions, she returns her smile and walks on. At the end of the gallery, she finds herself looking down a narrow corridor similar to the one outside her own room, with a half-dozen anonymous doors, all of which are closed. She stops and considers what to do. She can hardly go along tapping on each of them. Tom could be up here, taking his own afternoon nap. At that moment, as if she's willed it, she hears his voice. And Lizzie's. They're in the chamber at the far end. The reason she doesn't know this part of the castle is because she's never been invited to it. She's always assumed that's by design: the family want to keep it to themselves. And since Lizzie's not alone, her arrival will be an intrusion, won't it? Just go and see, she tells herself. Where's the harm? If she's not wanted, she'll apologise, retreat and explain later.

Misalliances

The door is ajar, and she's about to knock when her courage fails her again. The gap between the door and its frame is wide enough for her to see in. Tom and Lizzie are seated on the bed. She crouches down to get a better view and immediately wishes she hadn't. He's fiddling with Lizzie's gown, with the laces at the back. 'Let me,' he's saying. 'It'll give you ease.'

'No, Tom, you mustn't.'

'I want to comfort you.'

'Tom, no!'

Damaris claps a hand to her mouth to silence the gasp that's risen there and tip-toes away.

Back in her room, her heart still pounding, she struggles with what she saw. But surely, all Tom was doing was trying to give Lizzie some relief, like he said. He's a good man. At the same time, she doesn't need to look far into herself to understand why the incident has disturbed her so. It was what she heard in Tom's voice. She's at her window. The sun has come out and its wintry beams are shimmering on the river. Birds are chattering in the eaves as they settle down to roost for the night. But she registers none of it. All she can hear is Tom saying 'Let me' and Lizzie saying 'No!'. She's back in the cottage at Millbrook with her father. It's what he used to say, what she did. She shakes herself free. It's not the same. The tones of voice are similar, but the situations aren't. And she had no right to be there, invading their privacy. The word brings her up short. Because in whatever way she tries to explain it, what she witnessed *was* a private moment, and – dear God! - she knows better than most what privacy can hide, what can occur behind its shutters.

It takes her a while longer to impose proportion and perspective on these wild thoughts. These are people she has been living with for five months. Tom has helped her arrive at a better understanding of The Bible. And her Church. Lizzie – in offering her company and friendship - has helped her to think of herself not as a sister, one of a community of sisters, but as a woman, one newly out in the world. She has come to know them, to like them, to understand how they relate to one another. That's the thing. If Tom has strayed beyond the acceptable bounds of familiarity, and if it's really upset Lizzie, she'll discern it in their faces. She'll see it at supper.

When she goes down, they're seated side by side, their heads bent over a letter. Far from being distant with one another, they appear to be closer than ever.

'It's from Thomas,' Lizzie explains, picking the paper up to show her. 'In Paris. The Emperor is still in France. Thomas is under instructions to follow him into Flanders. At this rate, he says, he's not going to be back till May.'

'At least,' Tom says.

'We'll manage,' Damaris says.

Misalliances

'We will,' Lizzie says, her tone suggesting determination rather than confidence. 'Jane'll be back soon, and the midwife in the village will come at a moment's notice.' She signals to Madeleine and Miriam. ' Let's have supper.'

'Now,' Lizzie says, once the table has been cleared, 'let's see what all the fuss is about.'
'It's a fuss,' Tom says, disgruntled, 'because people have died for reading it.'
Lizzie straightens her back and rubs it. 'The Church must have had its reasons.'
'Just one,' Tom says. 'To maintain their authority over the people. They don't want them reading it for themselves.'
'There are things in it,' Damaris says, 'which explain, I think, why they wouldn't.'
'Which things?'
'Take the gospels,' Tom says. 'After Jesus's crucifixion, when Mary Magdalen sees the risen Christ in the sepulchre. He says to her *Touch me not.*'
'Does he?'
'He does,' Damaris says, 'because he's no longer the mortal Jesus. He's the risen Christ.'
'*Noli me tangere* in the Latin,' says Tom. 'And that's the way even Coverdale translates it. But in the original Greek, it's written differently. In the Greek, he says to Mary *do not cling to me*, which to me has a different ring.'

Damaris lets Lizzie ask the question. 'Something more intimate, you mean?'

'I think so. That sort of thing, which suggests Jesus was very much a man with human feelings, has always been outlawed by the priests.'

'Read it to us.'

'I only have this version,' Tom says, opening the book. 'But think about what I've said. I'll put in the Greek when I get to it. This is from John's gospel. Mary's in the sepulchre, and Jesus is speaking to her. *Jesus said unto her: Woman, why wepest thou? Whom sekest thou? She thought it had been the gardener and said unto him: Sir, if thou hast borne him hence, then tell me where thou hast laid him, and I will fetch him. Jesus said unto her: Mary. Then turned she about, and said unto him: Rabboni, which is to say, Master. Jesus said unto her: Don't cling to me*...that's the bit...*for I am not yet ascended unto my father. But go your way unto my brethren and say unto them: I ascend up unto my father and your father, to my God and your God.*'

Damaris says: 'And you think that implies an intimate relationship between Mary Magdalene and Jesus?'

'I do. She was special to him.'

'But not necessarily in the way you're suggesting,' says Lizzie.

Tom shakes his head. 'I think she was. The Roman Church has always been censorious. That's why it's always had difficulty with the Old

Misalliances

Testament, the Hebrew books, because they're full of things which the Roman Church considers unchristian.'

'Are those books so bad?'

'Not bad,' Damaris chimes in. 'But they do deal with human passions, especially illicit passions.' She takes the book from Tom and opens it near the beginning. 'Listen to this, from Leviticus.' She reads them the passage which had perplexed her that morning. 'That's a troubled view of the family, isn't it? It suggests there was a lot of uncovering going on.' Lizzie and Tom are still; if they have a view, it's not forthcoming. 'And then there's this,' Damaris says, rapidly turning pages. 'This. *If any man lie with his fathers wife, they shall die both of them, for they have wrought abomination: their blood be upon them.*' She raises her eyes to look at Lizzie. She wasn't sure what to expect from her mischievous foray, but she's shocked.

'You must excuse me,' Lizzie says, her face red and her mouth opening and closing like she's struggling for air. 'I don't feel well.' As she gets up, the flush ebbs from her face, leaving it chalk white.

Tom is up too. 'Fetch Madeleine,' he says to Damaris.

She slips her arm round Lizzie's waist to support her. 'Is it the child?'

'It's moving,' Lizzie says.

Misalliances

Damaris takes her by the elbow and leads her round the table. 'It's alright,' she says to Tom. 'I've got her. She just needs to lie down.'

'I think I should call Madeleine,' she says, when they reach the room she fled from earlier.
    'You're here. Just untie my laces.'
    That done, she helps Lizzie lower herself on to the bed. 'There,' she says. 'Is that better?'
    'Thank you, Sister.'
    'It's Damaris.'
    'Thomas should be here.'
    'I know. Lie back.'

Chapter Twenty-one: Richard Pate

It's a wet evening in Paris. Wyatt, at his window, is watching the rain as it flickers into the circlet of light thrown by his candle. It's turning to sleet. The black street contains different shades of darkness and one of them, one of the darkest, is moving. What's more, it's crossing over towards his side. He thinks nothing of it and returns to the table where he's refining some lines.

> *I cannot speak and look like a saint,*
> *Use wiles for wit and make deceit a pleasure,*
> *And call craft counsel, for profit still...*

Some minutes later, he hears feet on the stairs. The concierge is rapping on his door. '*Monsieur Weeat, un visiteur.*' Wyatt puts down his pen, gets up, straightens his hose and, taking the candle with him, crosses the room.

Richard Pate is in the doorway. 'Hello, Thomas,' he says. They know each other, have had similar careers; Pate was ambassador to the Emperor before he took up the post. Wyatt likes this man, has always admired his integrity and competence, if not his fondness for Rome. 'Richard,' he says, ' welcome! What are you doing here?'

'It looks like I'm going to be here for a few months,' Pate says, taking off his hat and shaking

Misalliances

the rain from it. He removes his damp riding coat, lays it over the nearest chair, unbuckles his sword and places it on top. He offers his hand. 'And then I'll be going on to Spain, to be ambassador to the Emperor again.'

'He's here.' Wyatt goes to the window, retrieves the flagon of wine and looks around for a clean cup. 'Sit, Richard.'

'I know. But first things first. I talked to Mason before I left.'

'How is he?'

'He's well. He can't be far behind me.'

'Has he seen the King?'

'He has. And so have I. I've to tell Bonner he's being recalled.'

In other circumstances, Wyatt might have clapped his hands and danced around the room. 'Thank God,' he says. 'At last.'

Pate stretches out his legs. 'You've had problems.'

'As have others.'

'Not least François...'

'He wrote to Henry...'

'Most pointedly.' Pate is surveying the state of the room, the sheets of scribbled paper littering the floor, the half-eaten chicken leg by his feet, the stack of dirty dishes on the side. His eyes settle on Wyatt's wine-stained shirt-front. 'Is everything as it should be, Thomas? With you, I mean?'

'I'm well, thank you.'

Misalliances

'Are you on your own here? You've not got a manservant?'

'He went with Mason. There's a concierge.'

Pate looks round the room again. 'You'd have been better off on the St. Honoré with the rest of our people. You'd have a team of servants there.'

'Too close to Bonner.'

'I see.'

Wyatt pours the wine. 'Here,' he says to his guest. 'It's a good one. Have you come in today?'

'From Chambly. Yes.'

'That's a good ride.'

'Not too far. We've done well. Three days from Calais. You covered some miles yourself, I hear.'

'Not so many. But enough.'

'And you've seen the Emperor...'

'Just the once, at Loches. He's across the river, or I believe he is. All my requests for audience have been ignored.'

Pate pulls up his chair and straightens his back. 'That'll be about our old friend Branceter, won't it?'

'You've heard...'

'That's the second complaint the King received. Good job you had the presence of mind to send Mason back with your account of things.'

'I didn't want Henry thinking we'd colluded with the French.'

'He doesn't think that.'

Misalliances

'We were betrayed and, consequently, exposed.'

'You came close to getting hold of him. Which is more than I ever managed to do...'

'When you were in Spain...'

'It's been going on that long. But we have to leave it for now. In the meantime, when you do see the Emperor, you'll have to have your explanation ready.'

'He'll know what we were about. Branceter's a subject of the King, after all.'

'Your orders were to kill him, I take it?'

'What do you think?'

'Probably be as well not to admit that to Charles, though he will have surmised it, of course.'

'I'll say we just wanted to talk to him.'

'Which is all we should be doing, in my view. Though don't quote me. Give me a day or two and then I suggest we try Charles again.'

'The two of us?'

'If you've no objection. I have to present my credentials.'

'None at all. So will you be coming on to Ghent?'

'No. My orders are to stand in for Bonner until they've found a replacement. I didn't want it. Much rather be in Spain. So I'll go on to Vallodolid once Charles has returned there. As far as Flanders is concerned, he's all yours.' Pate reaches into his bag. 'Which reminds me. New instructions. On how you take things forward. Now, before I go off to my bed, tell me exactly what's been going on. Apart from François, is there anyone else I need to make peace with?'

Wyatt turns to the second page. He can't believe what he's reading. What Bonner said to François is mild by comparison. Raising the hackles of the French King can be weathered, but addressing the Holy Roman Emperor in such a manner could sink the ship of diplomacy altogether. Cromwell couldn't have had a hand in it, of that he's sure. Wriothesley could have. Unless the King has put these directives together all by himself. As for how he presents them, he'll not have much lee-way. A response will be expected, from Charles as well as himself. To not deliver them as they stand simply won't wash. Everything gets back. Which is why, when he does get an audience, he can't do anything other than adopt the role Charles will be assuming he had in the Branceter debacle. To let on that he and Mason, contrary to their instructions, were actually trying to *prevent* harm coming to the man is out of the question. If that got back he'd be standing at the block one morning with his neck bared. And despite his best efforts at preventing one diplomatic crisis, here's another coming down the track. 'Buck up, Thomas!' he says to himself. 'You're a word-smith. You have a silver-tongue.'

Misalliances

    In the absence of John Mason, he thinks about confiding in Pate. Then, just as he's considering this, he receives a message from him. Alas! The Emperor left for Brussels two days ago. His first thought is thank God Mason is on his way back; his second, he was right to tell him to get a message to Lizzie. Because by the time they catch up with the Emperor, whether that's at Brussels or Ghent, he's not going to be home before May.

Chapter Twenty-two: Higher Things

Catherine is in one of the King's barges on her way across the river to Lambeth. Her uncle wants to see her, and when he demands her presence there's no saying no. So she's making a visit to Norfolk House, a place she hates because it's her grandmother's, and she doesn't like the Dowager Duchess, let alone love her.

As she eyes the broad-shouldered frame of her guard, Coxon, standing tall at the prow of the boat, bracing himself with his pike against the moment it comes to the customary juddering halt, a wave of indignation rolls through her. Why couldn't her uncle see her at Greenwich? She'll make up an excuse, so she can get away before dark. Coxon. She and Anne call him Cocksman. She giggles to herself.

She's glad to get away from the river, what with the stink wafting over from the horse-ferry and the miasma that rises from the marshes even on a winter's day like this. They're on solid ground at least, and what if she is, tiresomely, having to lift the hem of her dress away from the filth on the street? It's only a few minutes to the house.

Cocksman is striding on ahead. She's ignoring his occasional stoppings and head-turnings. She'll proceed at her own pace, thank you. He does have a knack of making her feel like a recalcitrant child, but it's a role she doesn't mind embracing because it allows her to be naughty. It's fitting, really, since she'll soon be in the glowering, judgmental presence of her grandmother. They're passing the grounds of a big house with a wall that's not especially tall. Letting her skirts fall, she leaps up, hooks her hands over the the top, pushes herself up with her toes and takes a look. The garden is neatly laid-out and well-cared for. She hoists herself up higher, rests her belly on the crest of the wall and secures her position with her elbows. There's a lawn below the house, though it's the cleanly weeded flower beds that most invite her attention. If she leaned over a little more, she might be able to reach the snow-drops immediately below. Cocksman is calling from where's he's stopped, further down the road: 'Mistress! Take care!' Out of the corner of her eye, she can see him retracing his steps. Well, he can go whistle. If he'd been doing his job, he wouldn't have let her climb up in the first place. She's going to hover here, swinging her feet and scuffing her toes against the rough-cast stones a while longer.

He's by her side. 'Mistress.'

She lets herself down. 'It's all Church property round here, isn't it? This must be a bishop's house.'

'I expect so.'

She senses that beneath the decorum, his unsmiling demeanour, Coxon is quite shy. And he's not bad looking for someone like him. 'So

Misalliances

there's no need to be worried. It's not as if someone's going to attack me for peering over their wall.'

'I didn't want you to fall.'

'If we were further down river it'd be a different story, wouldn't it? In Southwark.'

'The likes of you don't go there, Mistress.'

'More's the pity.' She teases him with a giggle. 'I bet you do.'

Coxon stares at her and says nothing.

'I wouldn't have fallen.' She leads off. 'Come on, then.'

From the outside Norfolk House is a handsome place. She likes its red-brick facade, the symmetry of its proportions, the tall chimneys and mullion windows. Inside it has the makings of something fine, too, but she knows it'll be bare and austere, with none of the decoration she's become used to at the palace. As ever, it'll be as unhomely as a religious retreat.

The porter must have seen them coming, because the Duchess is waiting in the vaulted chill of the vestibule. The old woman levers herself up on her stick. The expression on her face – what Catherine can see of it, because it's shrouded by the side-panels of her old-fashioned hood – is apprehensive, like she's anticipating the arrival of bad news. 'How are you, granddaughter?' she says. 'Have you been behaving yourself?'

Misalliances

She steps forward, gives the requisite curtsey, and plants a dry kiss on the old girl's bony knuckles. 'I always do, Grandmama.'

'The Duke's in there,' the Duchess says, gesturing to the front sitting-room. 'I've had a fire lit.' She takes hold of the swathes of thick material that constitute her skirts and shuffles off with what little speed they, and her elderly legs, permit.

Catherine has never found much in Thomas Howard that's kindled warmth or made her smile. As long as she's known him, he's been old, and she realised when still a child that his customary dourness is not a function of advanced years, but of character. She can not imagine him ever making a woman laugh or, come to that, attracting one's interest. She used to find him intimidating, and seeing him now – after many months of their paths not crossing while she's been her making her way at court - she still feels a little of that. The sombreness of his dress – ink-black, with furs – does little to lighten her sense of the weight of him in the room.

'Welcome, Catherine. I hope I find you well?'

'You do, my Lord.' She curtsies. 'And yourself?'

'It's time we talked. Please sit.'

She unbuttons her coat. The servant at the door didn't offer to take it and no one has come forward since, which makes her think she might get away before too long. She's chosen to wear a high-necked, yellow woollen dress – as expected, it was bone-chillingly cold on the river – and though it's more sedate than what she normally likes to wear, it does show off her figure and contrasts strikingly with her red hair. She settles herself and waits for her uncle to continue.

'You are how old now?'

He knows her age but she'll play along. 'I'm fifteen,' she says, not curious at all about his reasons for asking. She's been anticipating something like this ever since her monthlies began.

'And you're a maid still?'

'My Lord?'

The set of Norfolk's face remains rigid. 'I assume you are.'

Catherine lifts her chin and meets her uncle's pale grey eyes. 'Your assumption is correct.'

'Is anyone paying you suit?'

'Trying to court me, you mean?' Catherine is adept at adapting her laughter to a given situation and a trill, pitched high enough to convey a degree of scorn, is appropriate to this one. 'Come, now. If there were, I'm sure you'd know.'

'I don't. I haven't been at court these past few months.'

She knows this. 'There are no suitors,' she says. It's not an untruth. She may have been frequenting Culpeper's bed, or whichever bed was available and safe, but she doesn't want to marry him.

Misalliances

Norfolk smiles at her. It's an unusual kind of smile for him, because there's an attempt at warmth in it. His thesaurus of bodily language is a spare thing, and this – this attempt to charm her - is new. She senses he's about to put something to her he fears she might reject. 'Then listen, Kate.' She notes the transition to familiarity. 'The King has noticed you, my love.' My love? 'And you would do well to return his attentions.'

'His attentions? What attentions? He hasn't paid me any.'

'But he may. Being favoured by the King is a prize you mustn't disregard.'

'I wouldn't. But he's newly married. If I were to respond to his attentions, as you call them, isn't there a risk of *my* attentiveness being misconstrued? I serve the Queen.'

'Don't worry about that. Listen closely. The King will be going to Hampton Court for Easter. With the Queen, which means you will be going too.'

'That's weeks away.'

'It is. Nonetheless, I have reason to believe it could well be the last time they're seen together.'

'What do you mean?'

'The marriage isn't working. You must know that.'

'I know there are difficulties.'

'Henry will be seeking an annulment.'

'Who have you heard this from?'

'I can't tell you that. But it's a reliable source.'

Misalliances

'Your sources aren't that reliable. They didn't know if I had suitors.'

'Who might be flirting with you is a minor matter.'

'Not if it's the King who's supposed to be doing it!'

'Take it from me, there will be changes come the spring. It's better I let them play out. Since I didn't approve of the marriage, it would not be politic of me to have any involvement in its unravelling. There will come a time when I have his ear again, of that I'm sure. Which is where you come in.'

'I don't see how.' Though she does see, has for some time been in no doubt of where her uncle's words are leading. She's pressing her fingers into her waist just below her rib-cage, such is the thrill it's bringing her.

'Would you not want to be Queen?'

'What?' She lets out another trill.

'I'm serious.'

'And how do you suggest I go about that?'

'You simply have to be there. At Easter, I mean. Wear your colourful gowns. Though not as high-necked as the one you've got on today.'

'You want me to show myself off...'

'Don't be coy, Kate. You may be still be a maid but you're not telling me you don't know how to play on men's fancies.' Norfolk's gaze shifts from his niece's face to where her fingers are still working. It lingers there too long.

Misalliances

Catherine stops stroking herself and puts her hands together in her lap. 'Now,' her uncle says, 'I shall have to stay in the shadows, as I said. And I shall be busy for a while with another matter. Just make sure he sees a lot of you when you go to Hampton Court.'

'He sees a lot of me now.'

'You know what I mean.'

'And what if he's not interested as much as you think.'

'Looking at you, I'm sure he will be.'

Back in the vestibule with Coxon standing by, she's being helped into her coat when she sees Mary Lassells - pinch-faced, long-nose Mary, never one of her favourite people - gesturing to her from the other side of the vestibule.

'Good morning, Mary,' she says.

'What are you doing here?'

'I've been seeing my uncle.'

'I've something to tell you,' Mary says, opening the door she's standing by. It leads into a room, little more than a cubby-hole, where coats and hats are put on the rare occasion the house has guests.

'What?'

'Dereham's gone.'

'And why should I want to know that?'

'I thought you would.'

'Where's he gone?'

Misalliances

'He told Joan he was going to Ireland to become a pirate.'

'A pirate?' Catherine can see Joan Bulmer's face as she relayed the story. Gullible, little Joan. Dereham was probably spinning this tale while he was in her bed. It's like the ones she had to listen to when he was in hers. 'I'll believe that when I see it.'

'Joan's out walking. She can tell you herself if you want to wait.'

'I don't want to. I'm expected back.'

'Couldn't your uncle have seen you at Greenwich?'

'He could, but it was family business. Better here.' She touches Mary's arm. 'I really must go.'

'What's she like?'

'Who?'

'The Queen.'

Catherine raises her coat collar and opens the door. 'She's lovely. And very happy.' Outside, Coxon hasn't moved. 'Goodbye, Mary.'

As she is rowed back up river, her thoughts swing back and forth between the prospect of becoming Queen herself – oh yes, she'll have that if it's on offer - and what to make of her uncle. It surprised her, how easy it was to hold her own with him. Not that it should have, for she knows the power she has. The mighty Duke of Norfolk is looking to that, and some of the power he has he's promised her. She'll have power over him if she handles it

Misalliances

right. The trouble is, there are so many things she knows nothing about. For instance, what's the other piece of business he's working on? It might be useful to find out. Culpeper will know, though he mustn't know the rest.

****

'I don't understand,' she says, pulling the blanket up over her because it's freezing in the room and she still hasn't thawed out from her trip across river. 'I thought we had our own Church now.'

Culpeper is caressing her with the back of his hand, up from the curve of her hip to the soft flesh of her midriff and back again. 'We do, up to a point.'

'What do you mean? We do or we don't.'

'It's not that simple. In the last few months the King has moved closer to those who want us to go back to where we were. And that has put him at odds with Thomas Cromwell, who's already in trouble because it was he who got Henry to marry Anne.'

'The Anne we have now…'

'The first Anne, too. And that was also a disaster.'

'And my uncle wants to bring Cromwell down…'

'They've always hated each other. How much do you know about the first queen?'

Misalliances

'I know the King divorced her to marry my cousin.'

'He had to cut us off from the Pope to do that. Cromwell was the one who drove it all, in part because he wants an English Church that is protestant.'

'What does that mean?'

'One that rejects the Roman Church and all its frippery. More like the one the German Martin Luther has devised. Your family and the Suffolks have never forgiven him for that. They were on Catherine's side and they still want us to return to Rome. How do you not know any of this?'

'I was only little when it happened.'

'Your uncle has scores to settle. And power to recover. We might not see him at court much, but he's working behind the scenes at Parliament. As for the King, he sways one way and then the other. All for the new Church one week, and then against it the next. Last week, for instance, two priests were taken to The Tower because they were said to be preaching what Luther had written. Both of them were close to Cromwell. I tell you, if I was intent on bringing him down, now'd be the time to do it, given the state the marriage is in.'

'I think there's some wine left.' She gets out of bed and reaches for her shift. As she pours, a draught of bitterly cold air wafts through the broken windowpane behind her. 'This is a shabby little room. Doesn't anyone look after it?'

Misalliances

'Nobody comes here now the jewel house has been moved. That's why I chose it.'

'This was the jewel house?'

'Not this, silly. This would have been for a clerk, but *I* think someone else used to use it.' …' He reaches down beside the bed and retrieves a crumpled sheet of paper. 'I found this the other day. Down the side of the mattress.'

'You've slept here?'

'I just came in to see if it was good enough for us.'

The 'us' unnerves her, but she shrugs it away and returns to bed.

'So there I was bouncing up and down on the bed, testing it, and this popped out. It's a poem. Thomas Wyatt was once the keeper of the jewels. You have heard of him?'

'I know the name,' she says.

'He's the King's favourite poet.' He laughs. 'After himself, that is.'

She starts to decipher the scrawly script.

That time that mirth did steer my ship
Which now is fraught with heaviness
And Fortune then bit not the lip,
But was defence of my distress,
Then in my book wrote my mistress
'I am yours you may be sure
And shall be while life does endure.

Misalliances

She gives Culpeper the paper back. 'I don't know much about poetry,' she says. 'And even less about him.'

Chapter Twenty-three: Sweetlips

Mason finishes his tale and drains his cup. 'So that's that. We're in the clear.'

Wyatt reaches for the bottle. 'He's not expecting us to try again, then?'

Mason stretches and stifles a yawn. 'Oh, you know Henry. He's moved on. He's more concerned with what the Spanish and the French have been up to. How've you been getting on with that?'

'Charles left for Brussels a week ago.'

'Without granting you an audience, I take it…'

'We'll have to chase him. I've been waiting on you.'

'Right.' Mason gets wearily to his feet. 'I need a wash and then let's go and find somewhere to eat. We'll take the other two with us.' He takes out of his coat a leather pouch and throws it on the table. 'Don't bother with this now. I'll explain over supper.'

À l'Enseigne d'Ange, the house on the Mouffetard where they met Courrières four months earlier, has become Wyatt's favourite bolt-hole. He lets the three travellers make inroads into their potage and patiently sips his wine. Eventually, Mason wipes his mouth and says: 'We came across two Englishmen not long after we'd left the Pale. Where were we exactly, Frank?'

Misalliances

Pitcher retrieves a sliver of carrot that's fallen into his beard. 'Tilques. Just before you get to St. Omer. The Eastern end of Calais is at Balinghem, right? After that you're in France proper. Tilques is beyond Balinghem, before you get to St. Omer.'

'I know where it is,' Wyatt says.

'So we're just coming up to the village,' Mason continues, 'and these two riders come galloping up the road. And I mean galloping. We had to pull our horses over to let them by.'

'I recognised one of them,' Rudston puts in.

'Two Englishmen outside the Pale, in a devilish hurry, one of whom Robert thought he knew. What would you have made of it?'

'I'd have been curious to say the least,' says Wyatt.

'So was I. And what really made me smell a rat was the name he came up with.'

'Which was?'

'I'll come to that. So I tell Frank to go after them, find out what they're up to.' Mason gestures at Pitcher with a chicken leg. 'You carry on.'

Rudston does. 'I went as well. By the time I'm in the village, Frank's got the other one, the one I didn't know, up against a wall.'

'They'd slowed down by then,' Pitcher says. 'Worn out their horses. Neither of them was up for a fight.'

'So who were they?'

'Gregory Botolf and a certain John Browne,' Mason says. 'Either of those names ring a bell?'

'Botolf, otherwise known as Sweetlips.'

'Sweetlips himself. Known Catholic sympathiser. Belongs to the Lisle household in Calais. Or did.'

'I was with the Lisles for a while,' Rudston says. 'Botolf was their chaplain. And a right sort of chaplain. He had something going on with one of the girls.'

'Hence Sweetlips, presumably.' Mason's remark elicits a round of chuckles. 'In fact, they said they were on their way to see some woman or other. An assignation with a mademoiselle in Tilques. I didn't believe that for a minute, but in the absence of evidence they were up to no good - of the kind that would concern us, I mean - we couldn't hold them. Luckily, I'd had the presence of mind to tell Robert to take a look in Sweetlips' saddle-bag while we were talking...'

'They didn't see me,' says Rudston.

'And he'd come up with this.' Mason takes out the pouch and places it on the table.

Wyatt picks it up. 'What's in it?'

'Letters. A plot against Calais that will make your hair stand on end. Don't open it here. Wait till we get back.'

Mason pulls off his other boot and returns to what he's laid out on the table. 'Look at this one,' he says, selecting another letter and unfolding it. 'This is from Reginald Pole to Arthur Lisle.'

Misalliances

Rome vi January

Thank you for your kind words in recommendation of your servant Gregory. We have met him and agree he is indeed a good Christian. We will consider his words.

Cardinal R. Pole

Wyatt takes the letter. 'This doesn't show Lisle was in on it. He's the Constable of Calais, for God's sake. I know Lisle. He inclines to Rome, there's no doubt about that, but as for plotting on its behalf, I can't see it. I doubt he knew what Sweetlips was up to.'

'Well, *we* know, don't we?' Mason picks up another letter. 'It's here. After he's seen Pole, Botolf writes to Philpot confirming the plan.' Mason paraphrases. 'Come the autumn, when the Lantern Gate is open to let in the herring fishermen…is that true?'

'It is. They've finished for the season and want to go to the taverns. It's left open for a day or so.'

'When that happens, Philpot and company - whoever they are - are going to overcome the gate's guards so their friends can walk in.'

'The French, presumably.'

'It'd have to be a large force, if the idea is to knock out the Calais garrison and then take the whole of the Pale. It's mad, I know. There's another letter to Philpot.' Mason sorts through the pile. 'This one. Where Sweetlips says he's going to see the Emperor to get his support.'

'Charles wouldn't have any truck with this.'

'I reckon they were on their way when we stopped them. Once you've left the Pale, the first good road north is at Tilques. It'd take you straight to Ghent.'

'Why weren't they going up along the coast?'

'Too risky, I suppose. The Pale's northern border is heavily patrolled.'

Wyatt gathers the letters together. 'If he *was* heading for Ghent, we might come across him.'

'We should make it our business to come across him.'

'In the meantime, these go off to Cromwell.'

'Send Frank.'

'It's not urgent. They can go in the next bag to Greenwich. I'll do a covering letter and take them to Pate in the morning. Who's this Clement Philpot?'

'He's also attached to the Lisles, according to Robert.'

'Whoever he is, he's a dead man. As is Sweetlips. And who's John Browne?'

'Just a manservant, I imagine. He's not mentioned in the letters.'

Mason looks about him. 'You got any more wine here, Thomas?'

Wyatt goes to one of the cabinets. 'I see you've got a new shirt, John.'

Misalliances

'Two new shirts! Do you like the lace round the collar?' Mason traces the decoration with his fingers. 'Smart, eh?'

'Very.'

'Is that girl with the flat iron still down the street?'

'The washerwoman's daughter? I think so.'

'She did your velvet.'

'And didn't ruin it.'

'I'll take my stuff along tomorrow. You said we won't be off just yet.'

'You can have a couple of days rest. I've got to see Pate and we need to hire horses.' Wyatt uncorks the wine. 'Did you find out how Cromwell's doing?'

'I was coming to that. I think he could be on his way out.'

'I guessed as much.'

'Stephen Gardiner's fronting a lot of it.'

'Well, that's a surprise.'

'Norfolk's in favour again…'

'That won't help.'

'Then apart from all that, the King doesn't much like the new wife Cromwell's brought him.'

'That might change. He's not known her long.'

'He doesn't *like* her.'

'How do you mean?'

'God, Thomas! You're not usually slow about such things.'

'You mean he's not sleeping with her?'

'He might be lying alongside her, but as for anything else...'

'That was your impression?'

'That's what they were saying. So Cromwell's in the dog-house over that. The word is he could be about to lose the Secretaryship and the Privy Seal. And he's not helping himself.'

'Go on.'

'He's been heard saying that if it comes to a fight with the King over the Church, then so be it.'

'Where did that come from?'

'Originally? I've no idea. I got it from Ralph Sadler, who swore me to secrecy.'

'I wonder who else he's sworn. He's close to Wriothesley. And if he gets hold of it…'

'And the King's hears of it…'

Wyatt gives the table an emphatic tap. 'It's treason.'

'It is indeed. And you know better than most how quickly it can get out of hand when things take that sort of turn. If Cromwell falls…'

'Then others would follow.'

'Including us.'

'Why would we be at risk? We've kept ourselves separate from all the Church stuff. And we've taken our orders from the King.'

'In which we're hardly covering ourselves with glory...'

'No. And in view of what I've been told to tell Charles, we still might not.' Wyatt picks up the pouch of letters. 'But this'll do us some good. And

Misalliances

if we come across Sweetlips in Ghent and manage to seize him...'
    'We need to send that straight to the King.'
    'He'd give it to Cromwell, anyway...'
    'I'm not sure he would the way things are...'

Chapter Twenty-four: Discoverings

Lizzie's in labour, which in one sense is no surprise because she's become huge and been in bed for the past two weeks. It's a Sunday, the first day of April. Damaris knows this because in a week's time it'll be Easter. Lizzie's always said she didn't think she'd be giving birth before the end of April, so it's come early, though Damaris knows these things can only be estimates. Babies who come very early are often in difficulty. She hopes everything will be alright.

She wants nothing to do with the birth, all the screaming, all the blood, but she's anxious for Lizzie and when the midwife's girl comes down she asks if she can be of help. She's relieved when the villager says 'No, mistress, we have it all in hand.' Jane, unusually, has opted to take herself off to the nursery to spend time with her son, and after a while Damaris leaves off sitting at the bottom of the stairs and retreats to the small sitting-room, where her thoughts return to what was preoccupying them all until Lizzie's labour began: where Tom has got to. He's been gone since yesterday.

She can't face the prospect of her and Jane being alone together at supper, so she goes across the passage to say she doesn't feel well, she'll have it brought to her room. But there's no one there. It's mid-afternoon; preparations should be underway regardless of what's happening upstairs. The fires have been lit, the big one at the far end and those under the stove, but there's no aroma of anything roasting or being baked. She picks up words being exchanged in the pantry behind her, whisperings which she can make no sense of until one voice – it's Cook's – rises above them.

'Well, it makes you wonder, don't it? Whose it is. After what Madeleine saw.'

Someone shushes at Cook and it all goes quiet. Janet and Ruth, Cook's two girls, must be in there with her, but not Madeleine and, therefore, probably not Miriam. Whoever it is, their silence says they know somebody's come in. Not for the first time at Allington, Damaris tip-toes away from where she'd rather not be, or not be discovered.

'Just gossip,' she says to herself once she's back in the sitting room. Nonetheless, she can't get out of her mind the image of Tom trying to undo Lizzie's gown, nor what he was saying to her and she to him.

Miriam is standing in front of her, a big smile on her face. 'It's a boy,' she says. 'A big, healthy boy. Mistress says, would you like to come and see?'

Jane's already there. What do you say about a new baby who's a big, healthy boy? That he's lovely? Damaris says it. That he looks a good weight. She doesn't say that. Jane, in between cooing and aahing, is gushing out some twaddle about its being the spitting image of its father.

Misalliances

Damaris asks how Lizzie is. She murmurs that she's alright, though she looks utterly exhausted. Stumped for something else to contribute, Damaris says: 'It's a shame Sir Thomas couldn't be here.' And then, at the sight of the tears filling Lizzie's eyes, she wishes the ground would open up and swallow her. 'Where's Tom?' Lizzie asks.

Jane steps in quickly. 'He went off to Malling first thing.'

'He's probably best out of the way,' Damaris adds.

Jane is staring at her. 'Thank you, Sister.'

The penny drops: Jane's not thanking her for supporting her story, she's dismissing her.

Later that afternoon there's the sound of feet on the gravel. She puts down her book – not the Bible, one of Thomas's - and pulls back the edge of the curtain to peer out. Edward and Tom come into view. Something's going on, an argument of some kind, though Edward's doing most of the talking. Whatever it is, it must be connected to the way he's dressed. Edward normally favours a leather jerkin, leggings and big, scuffed boots. Today he's rigged out in a long grey coat and his boots are knee-length and shiny.

She's always liked Edward and she trusts him absolutely. In the days after Thomas rescued her from St. Wilfred's, he made sure she was as comfortable as a young woman could be in a cart constantly bumping up and down, swinging from

Misalliances

side to side, on the rough roads from the south coast to London. He tended to her needs during the few days she spent in the house by the river. He was a young man then. The man she's got to know in the past five months has the confidence and authority that come to older men, as long as they've been fortunate enough to find themselves in situations which nourish those qualities. It's hardly a coincidence that in some ways he reminds her of Thomas himself. He's a good soul – she's sure of it - but at this moment his feathers have been well and truly ruffled.

They are coming level with the window so she draws back. Tom – hang-dog, dragging his feet – mumbles something. They stop. Edward's response is loud enough for her to hear.

'That's it. I'm not doing this. Your father can deal with it when he gets back.' Tom turns. His face is pale and drawn; his jacket is ripped at the armpit, and one of his pockets has been pulled out of his britches. He mumbles something else.

Edward takes his arm. 'Because while your father's away, it's my job. I'll ask you one more time. How much is it this time?'

Tom's back is towards the window again and that prevents her from hearing his reply but it causes Edward to recoil. 'What! How in God's name did you rack all that up? Do they know you? Where you're from?'

Tom nods.

Misalliances

'So they'll be coming here.' Edward grabs him again, pulls him close, face to face. 'I'll deal with it. But it's the last time. Do you hear?'

There's more, but she doesn't catch it because they're moving away. A few moments later she hears them coming in through the back door. If they're going upstairs, they need to be told the baby's come. But they're next door in Thomas's study. She can hear Edward.

- Look. Look at this. You're not rich. You once were, but these days we rely on what comes in. It's in this column here. D'you see? And the other one shows our outgoings.
- You itemise everything?'
- What comes in on the left-hand side, what goes out and what it's for on the right. It's the only way to keep Allington afloat. Not much has been coming in, as you can see. Wool prices have fallen and we've had two poor harvests. We've got the rents, but wool and grain are the main things we trade in and if they fall short...
- But...but that's not the whole story, is it?
- What do you mean?
- There's what's in our coffers.
- Hasn't your father shared that with you?
- Shared what?
- You'll have to ask him.
- He's never here. What are you saying?
- There's enough to settle your debts.
- And not much else?'

Misalliances

- Not a lot. In your grandfather's time, towards the end, things went downhill. Bills weren't paid. The bailiff was a thief. Sir Henry even had to sell land. For much of the time your father was in Calais, he wasn't being paid. In Spain, he used his own money. And he'll be paying his own way now.

There's the patter of soft shoes. 'So you're there, Sirs!' It's Madeleine. 'We have a baby boy!'

Damaris goes back to the sitting-room. Her patch of sunlight has gone. She considers calling one of the girls to light the fire but they'll be busy. Gathering her shawl round her, she tries to make sense of what she's heard. How does she square the Tom she's just witnessed with the one who's studied The Bible with her? She's never been sure how much piety is in him. His interest in God has always seemed more rooted in ideas and in arguments, more concerned with the question of how to worship than by the necessity of doing it. She is sure of this: gambling is no way to lead a Christian life. If there's one thing she's learned since she came out into the world, it's that you can never be certain of knowing someone. There's always another revelation waiting to disclose itself, and sometimes it contradicts what you think you know.

Misalliances

Part Three

Misalliances

Chapter Twenty-five: Brussels

As they enter the city, they see a line of ordinary folk filing into a church. Mason says: 'Is it Holy Week or something?'

'It must be,' Wyatt replies.

Anxiety flits across Rudston's's face. 'We'll not be going, will we? They're Catholics.'

'I shall insist upon it,' Wyatt says.

Mason bursts out laughing. 'He's jesting, Robert.'

Rudston calls out to Pitcher: 'What day of the week is it?'

'It's a Tuesday.'

'You don't go to church on a Tuesday,' grumbles Rudston.

'They do here,' Wyatt says. 'It's the Emperor's city.'

Mason is still chuckling to himself. 'Well, whatever day it is, what I want is a bath, a cut from a side of lamb, a flagon of Burgundy and a soft bed with a woman in it.' He steers his horse round a cart loaded with bales of wool. 'Where's this palace, Thomas?'

'That must be it,' Wyatt says, pointing to a long, high gabled building on the skyline.

'And that's where Charles'll be...'

'If he's in Brussels, he will. Let's go and see.'

'Well, it was worth a try,' Mason says, dropping his saddle-bags on the unswept floor of the room. It's smaller than the one in the Petit Nesle.

'We were never going to get lodging at the Koudenberg,' Wyatt says, sitting down on one of the mattresses, his back to wall.

'Who was that we saw? I don't remember seeing him in Spain.'

Wyatt stretches out his legs. 'I don't know. It wouldn't have hurt Granvela to come down himself.'

Mason goes out on to the landing only to immediately return. 'This place is as dismal as the city.'

'It's not Paris.'

With an 'Ah, that's better,' Mason pulls off his boots. 'Let's open the wine,' he says, massaging his toes.

'Just half a cup for me,' Wyatt says. 'Otherwise, I'll be dead to the world by the time Rudston and Pitcher get back.'

'Can't have that,' says Mason. 'I need to go and eat.'

It's a tavern with a side business in upstairs rooms, and Mason has led them to it, having shaken his head at several other houses with a dismissive 'No, no good.' While waiting for Rudston and Pitcher to stable the horses, he's occupied himself with the flagon of Burgundy rather than fetching water for a wash and changing his clothes as Wyatt has

Misalliances

done. The whores at the back of the room must have nosed this out because they've not responded with any eagerness to his enquiries. One of them appears to be interested in the least smelly member of the party, however.

She's typical of the young women Wyatt has seen on the street: blonde haired, blue eyed, pale skinned, and with that upturn of the nose he's always thought of as specifically northern European. He has a weakness for the type and can feel his commitment to abstinence wearing thin.

With the bravura that comes with her profession, she arrives at their table and addresses him in French. 'Do you like me, monsieur?'

The girl at Loches is suddenly in his head, with all her clumsy precocity. But this isn't her, nor Kate Howard. This woman is Lizzie's age.

'Monsieur?' she enquires again. There's a lilt to her voice which he likes, and for all its over-painting he also likes her face, the fullness of her lips. There's a light in her eyes, a sparkle almost, as if she's saying 'let's not make this more tedious than it has to be.'

Nonetheless, he says: 'I do like you. But forgive me. Not this evening.'

****

'See, I was right,' Mason says, when a messenger arrives from the palace. 'Now he's free of the French, he's willing to see you.'

Misalliances

Wyatt should be pleased to be climbing the hill, but he's thinking about the coolness of his reception at Loches, the number of times in Paris his requests for an audience were ignored, and he's been reading his instructions again.

When he's shown into a state-room that's of a piece with the Koudenberg's favouring of high-ceilinged, airy interiors and a mere scattering of furniture, he is not surprised to find Charles flanked by the two men closest to him, his first minister Nicolas de Ganvela and secretary Francisco Cobos.

Granvela, with his slight, hunched frame, now looks markedly older than his fifty-odd years, whereas Cobos, who's the same age but still muscular, could be taken for a man not far beyond Wyatt's own thirty-odd. This morning, as ever, Charles' secretary is wearing a tabard emblazoned with the vertical red sword of the Order of Santiago. It says he belongs to it and is, therefore, a Knight of Christ. What that means in practice Wyatt has never learned, though it does occur to him that since Charles is about to march an army up to the walls of his native city, it's not a bad idea to have the pugnacious Cobos by his side. The Emperor's two aides have brought their own, Alonso Idiáquez and Alejandro Calderón. Wyatt feels outnumbered, standing alone in the enormous room, and wonders if he should have brought Mason in with him.

Misalliances

Charles is in funereal black. He has one elbow resting on the arm of his golden throne and is leaning towards it. The attitude he seems to be at pains to strike is one of nonchalant forebearance. That's how Wyatt sees it, at least, for even though they once conversed at length in his private quarters, Charles has uttered no word of welcome, and in response to his visitor's bow has not so much as nodded his head in acknowledgement.

It's Granvela who speaks: 'You have requested audience, Sir Thomas.'

'Thank you, First Minister,' he says. 'I have been instructed by my king to raise a matter that is of grave concern to him.'

The Emperor stirs himself. 'Speak, Sir Thomas.'

Wyatt takes a breath. 'In your household, Majesty, is an English subject whom King Henry has declared a traitor. Robert Branceter. The King requests that in accordance with established practice you withdraw your protection and give him up.'

Charles sits up straight. 'I am aware of the established practice, as you call it. And in other circumstances, I would respect it, but your behaviour in Paris made a mockery of proper procedure.'

'We only wished to talk to him.'

'Tell me, what has he done to merit being hauled off to the scaffold? Because I'm certain that's where he will find himself if I were to return him to King Henry.'

'He's long been advocating a Holy War, encouraging yourself and the French to march against us.'

'You deceive yourself, Sir. Do you really think my decisions – I can't speak for King François – are so easily influenced?' Charles waves the foolishness away with his hand. 'You say he has been saying these things. He may well have. I am not a ruler of men's tongues. King Henry sets too much store by what is said in my realm.'

Wyatt takes a moment to moisten his mouth. 'Robert Branceter may be your servant, Majesty, but in the first place he is a subject of King Henry. If you persist in refusing to deliver him, the King must charge you with ingratitude.'

There is a jangling of ceremonial chains as the Emperor leans forward. 'Ingratitude? How dare he!' The words echo round the hollow chamber. 'I am the Holy Roman Emperor!' He stops; Granvela has stepped forward and caught his master's eye. Charles continues: 'Princes such as King Henry and myself...we mustn't talk in such terms, who should be grateful and who is not.'

The Emperor beckons Granvela. They whisper and the First Minister steps back again. 'Let us talk about alliances,' the Emperor says. 'I would like an assurance from King Henry that, in view of his recent marriage, he will not be entering into a further union with the state of Kleve.'

'We've talked about this.'

'I need more than *your* assurances, Sir Thomas.'

'Is this about Gelderland, Majesty?'

'Gelderland? It's about more than that.' The Emperor glances at Granvela, who gives a barely perceptible nod. 'You know of Gelderland?'

'I know of your interest in it and why you might view King Henry's recent marriage as a threat to it. As I told you at our – regrettably - very brief meeting at Loches, I have no reason to believe the marriage will lead to an alliance of arms and armies. In fact, and I would appreciate this being kept between ourselves, I have heard the alliance of the bedchamber is not going well.'

'Is that so?'

'I would go so far as to say that were you to ask King Henry directly what *his* interest is in Gelderland, you might receive an agreeable answer.'

Again the Emperor glances at Granvela. 'I may well do that.'

'Without, of course, mentioning what I have told you in confidence.'

'I don't betray confidences. Let us return to the question of Branceter. His place in my service is being reconsidered.'

'As to whether it will continue?'

'Or cease. Whichever.'

'May I relay that to King Henry?'

Misalliances

'You may. And tell him I wish to hear nothing more of ingratitude.' The Emperor shifts in his chair. 'Are we done, Sir?'

'One more thing. Does your Majesty know of an English gentleman by the name of Gregory Botolf?'

The Emperor turns to Granvela, who shakes his head, and then to Cobos. The Knight of Christ does the same. 'Should we know something?'

'The less you know the better.'

'Then it's good we know nothing.' The Emperor rises.

Granvela glances at Wyatt and raises his eyebrows, but doesn't say a word.

Chapter Twenty-six: Hampton Court

The chamber beyond the great hall is thronged with the King's favourites. It's the Easter dance. It's late afternoon, still light, and there's a concomitant lightness to everyone's step. All at once there's a commotion; the Queen is rising. Her ladies, the foremost ones, gather round. The King is on his feet, nonplussed. He calls out something to his wife's retreating back, but it's too late for her to hear above the noise of the viols and sackbutts.

    Catherine is similarly flummoxed. 'Something's wrong,' she tells Surrey, whose invitation she's accepted for no other reason than he's an uncontroversial partner. 'I'd better go.' As she turns to follow the Queen's party, which has already reached the door to her private chambers and is fast disappearing through it, she catches John Russell eyeing her. His expression – the tight set of his lips, the lift of his head - is unmistakeably one of scrutiny. 'Why is he looking at me like that?' she asks herself. But she knows why. It's because there's one other person who's been constantly eyeing her, and that's the King. For much of the evening she's been sitting to one side of the royal couple and Henry's been casting glances at her. Not just once or twice, either. And while she was dancing, she dared to look at him, and as on the previous occasion, their eyes had met.

In the long passage-way to the Queen's private rooms, she meets her fellow ladies-in-waiting coming back. Anne Basset takes her to one side and says: 'She's sent us away.'

'I'd better go and show my face. I don't want her to think badly of me.'

'I'd leave it, Kate.'

'What's upset her?'

'Something must have.'

It's only then it occurs to Catherine – alarmingly occurs to her – that the something mght be her. And not to present herself now, to absent herself, would compound the problem. It's not as if she's done anything wrong. Yes, in accordance with her uncle's instructions, she's endeavoured to be present whenever the King is, but as for more than that, she's not exchanged so much as a word with him, so she has nothing to feel guilty about. 'I'll just put my head round the door,' she says.

The Queen's closest companion is a woman of middle age, the Countess Van Ossenbruch, who came over with her and rarely leaves her side. Her bearing, her brusque manner, her refusal to humour even the most senior of the Queen's English ladies, such as Margaret Douglas, give out an unequivocal message, which is 'I am the authority here, don't assume we are friends.' She is there now, walking the length of the room with the Queen and speaking sharply to her. Catherine

Misalliances

can't understand a word, but she recognises the tone; it's one of admonition. They reach the end of the room, are briefly silhouetted against the rainbow shafts of late sunlight refracted through the thick glass of the window, and turn about. They freeze. The Queen flicks a hand at her and says to the Countess: 'Schick sie weg. Dummes Luder.'

Catherine feels she ought to say something, though the dismissive gesture was enough to tell her she wasn't wanted. She's framing a question when the Countess forestalls her. 'Go away,' she says. 'Her Majesty wants you gone.'

She's not sure if she should return to the dance but she goes anyway. Culpeper is lounging in an alcove outside, which is awkward because, to his consternation, she refused him a dance earlier and she doesn't want to go into the reasons why she did. It's the sad side of the game her uncle has told her to play; for if she had accepted, she wouldn't have trusted her lover not to betray by his behaviour towards her - his smiles and covert whispers - how affectionately connected they are and she didn't want the King observing that. All the same, she stops.

He reaches out a hand. 'Why do you dance with Surrey and not me?'

'Oh, please. I'm having a terrible evening as it is.'

'Come and sit,' he says, making room for her on the bench. 'What's wrong?'

Misalliances

'I think I've offended the Queen.'

'You don't say..'

'I haven't done anything.'

'Maybe not. But if the King is still gazing at you...'

'He's looking not gazing. Stop it.'

'But is he?'

'Yes.'

'There you are, then.'

'She should take it out on him, not me.'

'Is that why you're not dancing with me? Because it wouldn't do?'

'Well, it wouldn't, would it? Have you seen my uncle? I know he's here somewhere.'

Culpeper leans back and crosses his ankles. 'He's downstairs in the buttery with Brandon, plotting.'

'Plotting?'

'They've got their heads together, so it looks like it. I told you. They've got their knives out.'

'Who for?'

'Thomas Cromwell, of course.'

'Oh.'

'I ran across an old friend of yours a moment ago.'

'Who was that?'

'Francis Dereham.'

'He's no friend of mine.'

'That's not the impression he gave me.' Culpeper gives her a long look and smiles. 'He wanted to know if I was fucking you.'

Misalliances

'That was nice. Sounds like him.'

'I denied all knowledge of you. That kind, at least.'

'Thank you.'

He sits up. 'To hell with the King. Come and dance with me.'

'I can't.'

Thomas Howard listens and leads her away from where he's been sitting. 'Tell me again.'

'She'd left the dance in a huff of some kind and sent the others away. I thought I ought to go and present myself. And she was nasty to me.'

'What did she say?'

'*I* don't know, do I? But it wasn't nice.'

'Where is the King now?'

'Still at the dance, I imagine.'

'Well, you can't be if the Queen has left. It wouldn't look right. Make yourself scarce. Go to bed.'

'It's still early!'

'Do as I say. In the morning, just be yourself. Go to her as normal.'

****

When Catherine wakes after a fitful night's sleep, it doesn't take long for Anna von Kleve to fill her head. How dare she! Whatever the words were, it was rude. And who does the Countess think she is? Coming over here and throwing her weight

Misalliances

around. Ugly woman. Actually, they both are. No wonder the King has no interest in his new wife, all the greys and browns she wears. The palace dress-maker came to her with a selection of brighter fabrics and she rejected them! Wouldn't even consider trying the powder and rouge all the women of the court wear. On top of that, there's her apparently inborn inability to smile and laugh. Little wonder her husband can't take his eyes off real prettiness when it comes along.

She gets out of bed and goes to do her ablutions. When the idea comes to her she dismisses it. She's in trouble as it is. But it would show this dull excuse for a Queen what competition looks like. The gown goes with her hair and shows off her bosom.

'The green one,' she says to Margaret.

'The green one? Today?'

'The bright green one, and let's have some rouge and kohl.'

Still exulting in the spirit of devilment coursing through her, she's just about finished making up her face and eyes - 'Yes!' she mouths to the mirror – when there's a knock at the door. Margaret's announcement, 'It's the Queen's Chamberlain, my lady', shatters the self-admiring, devilish moment. She jumps to her feet. 'Get me out of this.'

Margaret stands stupefied. 'Which one now?'

'What I'd normally wear!'

'It's Easter Sunday. Had you forgotten?'

Misalliances

She had. 'Something dark, then. Grey, brown. Anything.' She begins to wipe off the rouge and kohl.

Minutes later – too many, really – she's in charge of herself again, demure in a dark grey, high-necked woollen gown with her hair concealed under a plain white cap.

She likes Thomas Manners and believes he knows that, so she's confident he won't be too cross at having been made to wait. Anyway, she'll flatter him with his full title.

'Good morning, Lord Rutland.'

Manners is in the process of returning her greeting when, on the verge of saying her name, he has to clear his throat of what must be a globule of early morning phlegm.

She fills the pause. 'What brings you here at this hour?'

Manners coughs and swallows. 'I am come to tell you the Queen no longer requires your service.'

Catherine takes a moment to straighten one of the daffodils in the arrangement on the nearby table. She takes it out of the vase, straightens it, and returns it. 'Oh,' she says, determined to maintain a show of composure. 'Am I to be gone immediately?'

'This morning.'

Her fingers are wet and she wipes them on the skirt of her gown. It occurs to her it might appear she's reacted too coolly, that her dismissal is something she's been expecting. She turns her back, dips into her pocket for her handkerchief, and dabs her eyes. 'This is an unexpected turn of events, my Lord.'

'I'm sure it is.'

'Do you have an explanation?'

'I do not.'

'No matter. Has the Duke of Norfolk been informed?'

'Not as far as I know.'

'Would you see it's done, please?'

'I shall.'

She waves him away. 'Thank you, Rutland.'

Just before noon, for she's stubbornly taken her time in packing up her things and saying goodbye to Anne Basset, she and Margaret are following Coxon and her baggage down to the outer yard when, at the foot of the stairs leading to the Queen's apartments, she comes face-to-face with the Countess. Catherine hesitates for only a moment. 'My Lady, a word if you don't mind.'

Van Ossenbruch takes several more steps before coming to a halt and making a half-turn.

Catherine advances. 'What exactly did the Queen say to me yesterday evening?'

The Countess looks her up and down. 'She said nothing to you.'

'About me, then? She called me a dumb luda. What does that mean?'

'Dummes Luder was the phrase. It means stupid bitch.'

'What?'

'We Germans do not mince words.'

Even while she's processing the insult, Catherine can't help finding the woman's self-referential pomposity amusing. 'Clearly not,' she says, stifling a giggle.

'There's nothing for you here any longer, Katrin Howard,' the Countess says.

'Isn't there?' Catherine calls after her. 'Well, just you wait and see.'

Chapter Twenty-seven: Ghent

Wyatt is drafting a letter to the King. He shows it to Mason and sits back in his chair, hands behind his head, fingers interlaced. 'It's mostly about my audience.'

'I can see that. I'm not sure about this, though.' Mason comes round the table and taps the paper. 'This paragraph here.'

Wyatt reads it through.

The Emperor may have refused your demands, but he is at least considering whether Branceter should continue in his service. I take that to mean he would rather we were friends. He remains concerned, however, about the prospect of your marital alliance becoming a martial one.

He unlaces his fingers. 'What's wrong with it?'

'I'd leave out the bit about the the marital alliance, that's all.'

'Henry likes that kind of wit. Marital, martial. And we don't know what's going on at Greenwich.'

Mason reaches for the last of their flagons of Burgundy and fills his cup. He does the same for Wyatt's, pushes it across the table and taps the paper again. 'If the marriage still isn't working, it'll be a sore point. And as you intimated to

Misalliances

Charles, it makes your martial alliance unlikely. In my view the marriage is doomed. Henry has his eye on Kate Howard.'

Wyatt is hunched over the text, mouthing the words as he reads them. He opens his writing-case and selects a sheet of paper. 'I'll start again.'

'You're not going to mention that Charles might be in touch about Gelderland?'

Wyatt begins to write. 'No, I'll stay out of that.'

'Did you hear what I said about Kate?'

'Yes.'

'Sorry. I should have told you before.'

'I can't see why.'

Mason picks up his best shirt which he's just had washed. He starts to fold it. 'She'll be loving it, won't she? She likes powerful men, and they don't come more powerful than Henry.'

'I've never been powerful.'

'You were to her six months ago.'

Raising his pen from the paper, Wyatt looks up. 'From here to Greenwich and back, how long?'

'Frank could do it in three weeks if the wind's on his side. But he'll have to wait for an answer, so...'

'He'll be meeting us at Ghent, remember. It's not far from the coast.'

'We're off, are we?'

'Robert saw soldiers on the street this morning.'

Misalliances

'Spanish?'
'Lowlander. Charles'll be gathering his army.'
'Let's go and see.'

About a half-mile away from the city wall, tents are being dismantled. There's a line of soldiers marching west.

'They must have come in during the night,' Wyatt says. 'From Charles's sister.'

Mason cups his hands to his eyes and peers into the spring sunshine. 'It's a big force. Mostly foot, but there's horse and cannon as well.'

'If they're moving out, Charles will be. It's time we were on the road.'

It's no more than a day's ride through terrain that is mostly flat on a road that's mostly straight and elevated where the area's streams have combined to form marshland. It's pretty country, not unlike Kent. There's no sign of life in village or field. When Rudston passes a comment, Wyatt says: 'They know there's an army nearby, that's why.' They have to cross fords, walk their horses through gaggles of chickens and geese, and shoo off the odd cow, otherwise the journey is disquietingly uneventful.

They're not far from their destination when they spy in the trees, a short distance back from the road, two men on horseback, evidently taking their ease because they're dressed only in hose and tunic. The sight of them prompts Mason to signal they should slow their horses to a walk. 'Soldiers,' he says.

'Are you sure?' queries Rudston.

'They're not farmers,' says Wyatt.

Before long they come upon an encampment, hundreds of tents, more than they saw outside Brussels. In the spaces between, Landsknechte are sitting with their armour beside them. Fires have been lit. The order of the day appears to have been 'stand down'.

Men carrying pikes spill on to the road. An officer on horseback arrives. He barks orders and with no great sense of urgency the pikemen arrange themselves into a loose formation and follow him.

'I wouldn't want to take that lot into battle,' Mason says.

'Doesn't seem to have been one,' says Wyatt. 'And nobody's much bothered about us, are they? Let's go on. The city can't be far.'

The road takes them through trees again. They round a bend and the sky opens. Even from this modest elevation they can see enough of the city to make them pause, to draw their horses to a halt and take it in. To their right, accessible by an off-shot track, is what looks like a clerical estate, given it's comprised of a large church and several other big buildings. It's ringed by a wide moat. The city, also circled by water, lies beyond.

'My, oh, my,' says Mason. 'How about that for a sight?'

'The place was built between rivers,' says Wyatt. 'The Lys and the Scheldt. It's moated by them. Look.' He points off to the left where, in the distance, the city wall curves to accommodate a wider water-way.

'That must be the Scheldt,' says Mason.

Rudston has come alongside. 'What do you think, Robert?' Wyatt asks him.

'It's big.'

'It is. And beautiful.'

A team of heavy horses dragging cannon, flanked by a crew of a half-dozen men, is clanking up the road behind them. The officer in charge canters ahead and calls out for them to halt.

****

Mason cuts another slice of the fried pork the monk has put in front of him. 'This is better than riding back to one of the villages for the night.'

'It'll do for now,' Wyatt says. He pulls another chunk off the coarse-grained loaf to mop up his gravy.

The refectory is a cool, square room which they have been let into through a side door. Its brick walls are bare except for a wooden crucifix and, on a shelf in the corner, a statue of the Madonna. The number of tables suggests it normally caters for a sizeable community. This evening, it's just them.

Misalliances

Mason puts the question. 'I wonder where the other monks are?'

The one who served them has quietly come up behind them. 'They've been taken into the city.'

Wyatt looks up into the long face. 'Why's that?'

'They're suspected of being rebels.' The monk sets down their wine. 'None of us was. People met here, that's all. There's talk of executions.'

'And what's the name of this place again?'

'It's the Abbey of St. Bavo. That's the cathedral over there.'

Rudston appears. 'We've each got a room,' he says, sounding surprised.

'Monks are known to look after their guests,' Wyatt says.

Mason is grinning. 'You know all about that, of course.'

'It's not the first time I've been in this kind of place, if that's what you mean.'

'Was that when you rescued the nun? The one now at Allington?'

'That's right.'

Mason pulls the flagon towards him. 'I have to say, Thomas, with all that water, it might not be the easiest of cities to get into.'

'We'll cross whichever bridge takes us there,' says Wyatt.

Mason smiles. 'Cross that bridge when we come to it, eh?'

Misalliances

They are at the table again, having breakfast, when Wyatt, who's facing the window, says: 'There's soldiers out there.'

Mason turns to look and sees two of them walking the monk out of the kitchen garden. An officer comes into view. The sight of him brings Wyatt to his feet. 'There's Courrières!'

Mason puts down the piece of bread that's on the way to his mouth and joins Wyatt at the window. 'So it is.'

Seconds later, the man himself is in the refectory, his eyes wide. 'What are you doing here?'

'We've come to see the Emperor,' Wyatt returns.

'I mean *here*.'

'It's where we were put when we came in last night.'

Courrières' men are at the door with their prisoner. 'I have to go,' he says. 'Give me an hour.'

Back at the table, Wyatt says: 'As soon as we've done, let's get the horses and wait out front.'

Now they're seeing everything in the light, they've got their bearings. The abbey - a squat brick building - stands on the perimeter of the enclave, several hundred paces beyond the cathedral, which they can now see is an ancient stone building of some size, with not one but three steeples. On the

Misalliances

road, closer to them, there's no traffic of any kind, military or otherwise. It's one of those April mornings when there's drizzle in the air, and the greyness adds to the inertness that appears to be lying over the city. From deep within – it must be a mile away - a column of smoke is rising. In ordinary times, a city's coming awake is accompanied by the sounds of the comings and goings through its gates - the clop of horses, the dull clang of iron wheels on cobbles, the shouts of wagon-drivers – but nobody appears to be visiting or leaving Ghent today.

When Courrières arrives with the same two guards, he addresses them from his horse. 'Good, you're ready. I would say welcome, but you've arrived at a difficult time. I'm taking you to the Prinsenhof, the royal palace. It's well into the city, so ride close. We only came in yesterday.'

'Walked in by the looks of it,' Wyatt says.

'Yes.' For the first time the Fleming graces the Englishmen with a smile. 'We'll talk later. For now, mount up and follow close.'

A causeway connects the abbey to the city. When it comes to the river the road bifurcates off to the right beside the bank, but Courrières' guards go straight on, across a bridge which leads directly to a gate. There are soldiers on either side of it but it's open.

At first sight, the narrow streets of Ghent seem to be similar to those of any other city, except for one striking difference: there's no one on them, apart from soldiers, standing in groups talking. There's an air of desultoriness about them, like they're unsure of their role or purpose.

After a few minutes Wyatt, Mason and Rudston find themselves being led into a large square, empty apart from a gallows in the centre. Further over, taking up the whole of that side, stands a building fronted by a long collonade. It's typical of a trading hall, though there's no one bidding there today.

Eventually the street they're on narrows to the point where they can only ride single file. Courrières stops and dismounts. 'We can walk from here,' he says. 'We're coming up to the palace barracks. You can stable your horses there.' He looks back at them with a smile that's apologetic. 'It'll take a while to get the city back to normal.'

Wyatt says: 'Is that what the gallows is for?'

Courrières walks on. 'I'll tell you how things are once we've got you settled.'

The street is opening out again. They're walking alongside a long, low building and a gate is coming up. Courrières says to his men: 'Take these horses to the stables with you. They'll need to be fed, watered and groomed. We'll be alright from here.'

While the handover is being done, a man in a hooded cloak comes out of a side-gate. He raises his hand in greeting to the two guards. By the time

Misalliances

he's level with Wyatt and Rudston, he's drawn the hood close his face.

Rudston whispers: 'That's Botolf!'

Wyatt looks down the street after the fast disappearing figure. 'What?'

'I'm sure of it. And those guards knew him.'

Mason is leaning in to catch the conversation. 'Sweetlips,' Wyatt tells him.

'Where?'

'Just gone by. Leave it for now.'

Ten paces ahead, Courrières is waiting for them to catch up.

The size of the Prinzenhof is difficult to gauge, because it stands behind high walls and like everything else in this city it's girded by water, a moat that even at its narrowest, where a bridge crosses, must be a hundred paces wide. For now, they're on a parade ground of sorts, an expanse of beaten earth from which a shuttered gate leads back into the barracks. Barring the way to the bridge there's a line of soldiers which parts with a shuffling of feet and a clanging of pikes at Courrières' approach.

They're in a courtyard bordered by big anonymous buildings, one of which has balconies on its upper stories. Directly facing them is an ornately decorated door way through which two figures in red and black livery have appeared.

'Wait there,' Courrières tells them once they're inside. 'I'll find somewhere to put you.'

Misalliances

The vestibule's tiled floor is its most attractive feature. It's barely half the size of the one at the Koudenberg and its low-ceiling and lack of windows explain its dimness, though the staircase climbing from its right-hand corner promises airiness and light.

'Well, it's better than a monastery, I suppose,' Mason sniffs.

After a while a servant presents himself and beckons them to follow him up the stairs. He takes them to a room bright with sunlight.

'Now, that *is* better,' Mason declares. There's a long sideboard laden with baskets of fresh fruit and a round table on which a flask of wine, glasses and bowls of sweetmeats have been laid out. In dumb show, the flunky shows them their bedchambers and a wash room. Finally, in halting English, he says: 'Food at noon,' and points off down the corridor they have just come along.

When Wyatt returns from washing, Courrières is at the table with Mason. Without helmet and breast-plate, he's more like the man they used to know. 'I've just been explaining,' he says. 'The Emperor had to keep you at a distance in Paris because of the French.' He selects a *bon-bon* from the dish beside him. 'And then there was the business with Branceter, which didn't help.'

'We weren't exactly welcome in Brussels, either,' Wyatt says.

'But you got your audience.'

Misalliances

'Eventually. And here we are in the Prinsenhof. I assume an alliance with the French is no longer on the cards.'

'It never was.' Courrières pushes the dish of sweetmeats across the table, as if another comfit is a temptation too far. He straightens his jacket and leans forward. 'This must stay between ourselves, understood?'

'As always,' Wyatt says.

'We always knew the *grandes fêtes,* the reception at Tours, the brotherly entry into Paris, all the gaudy show...' Courrières dismisses it with a wave of his hand, '...was nothing more than flimflam to soften us up about the Duchy of Milan, which we've been fighting over for years, as you know. We waited. And after a while it came. A proposal. No more fighting, they said. It's time we were allies, so we could take on the Mediterranean pirates, the Lutherans and yourselves.'

'That's from the Pope,' Wyatt says.

'No doubt.'

'And in return they wanted Milan. It doesn't sound like much of a deal. I take it the answer was no.'

'Charles will never give up Milan. And he has no interest in that kind of alliance. Where that leaves the peace, we shall have to see. We went our separate ways amicably enough. Then, after we arrived in Brussels an envoy arrived to inform us we were not welcome to travel back through France.'

Misalliances

There's a burst of laughter from Mason. 'So that's why we're here! You'll have to go back by sea and you don't want us to sink you.'

Courrières gives one of his engaging smiles. 'It is a consideration. Not that you would, of course.'

'*We* wouldn't...'

'But your king might. I know. I'll let the Emperor tell you why else you're here. You'll be seeing him before long. Now, tomorrow I have something unpleasnt to attend to.'

'You're hanging people,' Mason says.

'Some guildsmen. The ones who a year ago put the city's aldermen to death so they could take over the city. The aldermen were good men. They'd made Ghent peaceful and prosperous. Those responsible for their murders have to pay.'

Wyatt says: 'We heard it was about more than that. The guilds were not prepared to accept Charles' higher taxes.'

'That's true. And I'm sure we could have resolved that with negotiation. Instead, the guildsmen said they owed him nothing and wanted their independence. We couldn't have that. So we've taken the city and re-established our authority. The hangings tomorrow will be the first of several. The Emperor would appreciate it if you accompanied me.'

'Your doing some monks as well,' Mason says.

Misalliances

'Are we? There are no religious persons on tomorrow's roster.'

'We'll come,' says Wyatt.

It's barely an hour after dawn. Whether out of dissent or because it's early, the number of spectators is small. All the same, the square is lined with soldiers.

'Hundreds gather at these affairs back home,' Mason remarks, as they take their places.

The single gallows they saw the previous day has been extended in the Tyburn fashion: four uprights, three cross-beams. From each of the beams four nooses are hanging. The structure is designed to despatch twelve men simultaneously.

Wyatt has never had much of a stomach for this kind of show, but he's been to several at Tyburn and assumes it will work similarly, with the condemned men being despatched from the back of a cart, the 'cart's arse' as they call it. Restless, he looks around. Two priests are coming across the square. Rudston taps him on the arm.

'Sweetlips is standing to our right.'

'Has he seen you?'

'He's signalling. It looks like he wants to talk.'

'I bet he does. Make your way towards him when this is over. Find out what he's up to.'

Three carts have entered the square. There are four men in each, guarded by a pikeman. Though there's been little noise, silence falls; everything becomes still except for the theatre of the

Misalliances

manoeuvring vehicles. It takes several minutes to reverse them into position. One cart has to go back and forth before the alignment is right. When everything is set, the pikemen prod their charges to their feet.

Wyatt will look away at the moment of the drop but for now he's taking stock of what's before him. The condemned men look prosperous. Their clothes say that: the leather and velvet, the lace. These men – he takes them to be senior guildsmen – must have believed they were unassailable, yet here they were.

The bishop steps forward. He's saying something in Latin about penitence and redemption. The pikemen order the men to turn round so that they are facing the crowd. What's to be done must be seen to be done.

The hangman comes into view. Clad in black leather, hooded and masked, he climbs up on to each of the carts to hoop nooses over heads and tighten knots. That done, he climbs down, and blows his horn. There's a moment's hiatus, just the couple of seconds it takes for each cart-driver to look across to his colleagues. In unison the carts edge forward; the men totter and drop. A long 'oooh' goes up from the crowd. Wyatt looks up to view the grisly tableau. In all but two cases the hanged men's legs are still jerking about.

The soldiers nearest the gallows go to cordon it off. The crowd begins to disperse. Wyatt catches

Misalliances

sight of Rudston making his way crab-wise through a gaggle of spectators.

Mason says: 'Where's Robert off to?'

'Gone after Sweetlips.'

'So what are we waiting for?'

'What would we do with him? I'll talk to Courrières.'

But Wyatt is not sure he should. There's a chance his Flemish friend will know about Sweetlips, and that the Emperor will too.

'Here,' Mason says, pouring Rudston a glass of wine. 'Might as well enjoy this while we can.'

'What did you tell him?' asks Wyatt.

'I told him the King had them,' Rudston continues. 'You should have seen him. It was all a game, a bit of fun, they never meant to carry it through, blah, blah, blah. He says he's going to the Emperor.'

'He may have tried that already.'

'He knows Courrières' men, that we do know,' says Mason. 'You need to talk to him, Thomas.'

Alonso Idiáquez, Granvela's man, is at the door; the Emperor wants to see him.

He doesn't have a clean shirt. 'Can I have yours?' he asks Mason. 'The one in your bag?'

'Of course,' Mason says, 'but you can't go in that jacket, it's creased to high heaven.'

'I'll wear my coat over it.'

Misalliances

'I'll get it,' Rudston says. 'It'll need brushing. It's covered in mud and horse-dung.'

Idiáquez waits patiently, and eventually Wyatt is spruced up enough to follow him. After fifty or so paces down the hallway, the Spaniard turns left into a shorter corridor and brings them to a big, studded door. He knocks and ushers Wyatt through.

Things have changed. The space he's in has none of the regal vaultedness of the Koudenberg; it's not much bigger than one of the ground-floor sitting-rooms at Allington. The emphasis here is on comfort: the room is carpeted and contains two cushioned settles and a day-bed, on which Charles, dressed in a loose tunic, is sitting, eating an apple. Granvela is there, on the window-seat, perusing some papers, but there's no Cobos.

'Sir Thomas, it's good to see you,' the Emperor says, putting the apple down and wiping his fingers. 'Come sit by me.' The pleasantries continue. He's pleased they were able to attend the morning's events. 'I know King Henry and I are of the same mind when it comes to insurrection, ' he says. 'One has to quell it promptly.'

'Indeed, Majesty.'

There's a long pause before Charles speaks again. 'Gelderland.' The change in tone shifts the mood. 'I have written to Prince William and demanded he relinquish his claim on it.'

'Am I to convey that to King Henry?'

Misalliances

'He already knows. I wrote to him on the subject, as you recommended, and he's assured me it's no concern of his.' There's another pause. 'Thank you for your help in the matter.'

'It's what I'm here to do.'

Charles begins to scratch his beard, which isn't long in itself, but it does cover that chin. 'The Princess Mary has not found a husband yet, I believe.'

The question catches Wyatt off-guard. 'She has not, no.'

Charles is clicking his fingers to summon Granvela. They confer. The whispering goes on so long, with Granvela doing most of it, that Wyatt concludes the Emperor must be receiving advice.

'Another matter,' the Emperor says eventually. 'We have recently been approached about a scheme to capture the Calais Pale. Do you know of it?'

'It's the brainchild of Sir Gregory Botolf. Until recently he was residing in Calais. I mentioned him the last time we met.'

'And I told you we had never heard of him.'

'You did.'

'We have now. More recently he's been here in Ghent in the hope of obtainig an audience with me. The plan was to open the town gates and let in the French. Is that right?'

'It is. I came by letters which set it out in detail.'

'You should have mentioned them the last time we met.'

'I should have. But they indicated the scheme was hatched with the support of Cardinal Pole, you see, and, well....'

'Then the Holy Father must have known about it.'

'That was my assumption too.'

'Unquestionably. An enterprise of such consequence, he had to know.'

'Perhaps that's why Reginald Pole presumed to engage yourself in the scheme.'

'Did he?'

'That's what the letters said.'

'Via an undistinguished English knight...'

'Apparently.'

'Do you believe me to be a credulous man, Sir Thomas?'

'Not at all.'

'You believed I was prey to the blandishments of Roberto Branceter.'

'No. I had no knowledge of that one way or the other. What I was sure of was that he was in favour of the Pope's Holy War and was cultivating support for it.'

'I am not at Rome's bidding, whether it be in the person of Branceter, this Botolf, Reginald Pole or the Holy Father himself.'

'I am pleased to hear it. Any assault on Calais, whoever was behind it, would have led to war as surely as the sight of your galleons, or those of King François, crossing the Channel.'

'I have no plans to send galleons across the Channel. When you were in Spain with us, I assured you I had none and I have none now. As for François, what he decides is up to him. But I doubt he would ever contemplate such rashness without my support.'

'And he doesn't have that…'

'He does not. As for Gregory Botolf, I ordered his arrest this morning. Granvela informs me he fled before we could lay hands on him. But we'll track him down.'

'May I ask where things stand with Robert Branceter?'

'He has left my service, so I have no idea. He's probably on his way to Rome.' The Emperor picks up the apple. 'I assume *you* will be leaving us soon.'

'I assume that too.'

'Come and see me before you go. Thank you, Thomas.'

There's no sign of Mason or Rudston. Wyatt pours himself a glass.

When Mason does appear, clad in a singlet and rubbing his head with his shirt, the first thing he says is: 'Frank's back. And we've been called home.' He picks his jacket up, delves into a pocket and takes out a fold of paper. 'From Cromwell.'

Misalliances

Wyatt breaks the seal. 'It's time. Our work's done here. You've had a wash, John.'

'I thought it was time for that as well.'

'It was.'

'Well?'

'He says we'd *best* be home. I wonder what he means?'

Mason pauses in his pouring. 'Trouble?'

'He doesn't say. The King's just made him Earl of Essex, so presumably not.'

'Well, that's a step up...'

'Possibly. Wriothesley and Sadler are to be the King's Secretaries.'

'Both of them?'

'So he says.'

'Ralph Sadler's a good man.'

'Did Frank see Cromwell?'

'I imagine so. He can tell you himself when he comes back from filling his belly. Drink up. We're celebrating. How did it go with Charles?'

'Better then I expected.' They sit down.

'It's a triumph, isn't it?' Mason says when Wyatt's finished. 'Not only is there no alliance with the French, but Charles has told you – told you directly - he's not at the beck and call of the Pope. Also, he's thinking about Mary.'

'Not necessarily for himself. They *are* first cousins.'

'That doesn't matter.'

'It does in his family.'

Misalliances

'The chin, you mean? Possibly. Still, she's young and pretty enough.'

'Let's not get ahead of ourselves.'

'He wants closer ties with us, Thomas.'

'I wouldn't go that far. At last, he doesn't want war.'

'We've done well, Thomas!'

'We haven't laid hold of Branceter or Botolph.'

'Charles has banished one of them, and the other will soon be in a Flanders gaol. I think we've done alright!'

'If you say so.' They clink glasses.

There's something going on beyond the causeway and they're having to wait. The soldiers have no French or English. Wyatt shifts impatiently in his saddle. 'Any idea what they're saying?'

'It's obvious,' Mason says. 'Charles likes us so much he doesn't want us to leave. Tell me again what he said this morning.'

'That he wants to know more about Princess Mary and he'll be sending his best men to meet her. That was it.'

'He called you back in to say that. How was he with you personally?'

'All smiles.'

'I can see you coming back to broker the marriage.'

'I'm not coming back.'

'Oh?'

'I'm going to tell Henry this it for me. I've got another child on the way.'

'He won't be happy. And Cromwell certainly won't.'

'He might not have a say.'

'He will. He's in the aristocracy now.'

Pitcher interrupts. 'I think they're taking something down. They were bringing up cannon when I came in yesterday.'

They jump at the sound of ordnance being touched off. From somewhere in the distance comes the rattle and rumble of tumbling masonry.

The soldiers wave them on.

They cross the water and make it on to the road they came in on. To its right is a battery, its pieces smoking, and to their left a cloud of dust is rising. As they watch, it clears. The abbey is being demolished. It's already in ruins: one of its towers has gone, and there's a great hole in its frontage. Mason shouts at them: 'Let's keep moving! We need to find the way to the coast.'

They ride on. At the top of the hill they look back to see the other tower fall.

Pitcher says: 'Why are they levelling it?'

'It's where the rebels met,' Mason tells him.

'And where the next round of hangings will be from if I'm not mistaken,' adds Wyatt.

'Tell you what,' Mason says, 'if that's how Charles treats *his* monks, ours are getting off light.'

'You really think so?'

Misalliances

'We don't hang ours.'
'Oh, we do. I've seen it.'
'Where?'
'At Watering.'

Chapter Twenty-eight: Visitors

Damaris is feeling less of a stranger in the kitchen and has begun to work out how things are organised. It's smaller than the one at St. Peter's, with the stove on the right and the chopping tables on the left, but kitchens are kitchens. As customary, the paraphernalia for roasting, the spit and open fire – long-lit by the looks of it – is at the far end below the flue. As they're talking, Cook is wiping down the wall above the stove. 'Fat,' she's muttering more to herself than Damaris. 'You try to keep on top of it…' She turns. 'If it's veal you want, Mistress, they'll have to do some slaughtering.'

'Who do I see for that?' asks Damaris.

'Mister Edward.'

'But you can do venison for tonight?'

Cook exchanges glances with her girls. Janet goes to one of the larders and returns nodding. It's Rose who speaks. 'Enough?'

'Yes,' Janet says.

'We had it on Sunday in that pie we did,' Cook says. 'It's only Tuesday. It'll be alright.'

'Lamb for Thursday?'

'They're doing them today.'

'Pigeon for Friday, chicken roasted for Saturday and cold on Sunday.'

'Got all them. And they've been picking the early peas. We'll make it interesting with some

Misalliances

sauces like we always do.' Cook gives a half-smile like she also always does. Damaris is never sure if it's simply a concession to her authority, or whether in time the two them might get on, once the woman who has apparently run the kitchen at Allington for over twenty years has finished weighing her up. She thinks they might, for despite her brusque manner, intimidating bulk and tendency to grimace, particularly when addressing Rose and Janet, Cook has a kindly face somewhere under there. Damaris has glimpsed it when she's gone into the kitchen after supper to say 'that was excellent', and seen the three of them relaxing with their mugs of beer.

'I'll be back to do the sweets, then,' Damaris says.

Cook - displaying one of the tics that seem to be inseparable from the job, for the cook at St. Peter's, Marjorie, did it too – gathers up her apron and wipes her hands. 'If you like. You know where everything is.'

She goes back to the sitting-room and finds herself wishing again that Lizzie was there. She was more talkative this morning, but Miriam, who claims to know about such things, says it can take a woman badly, having a child, even if she seems alright. 'You know,' Miriam said, gesturing, 'even if she's alright down there.' So it must be how she is in her head that's kept Lizzie in her bed for two weeks. It's nothing to do with the baby. He's fine, and

Misalliances

being well looked after by the nurse. As for Jane, she's been keeping to her own quarters. Supposedly it permits her to keep an eye on Lizzie and little Francis, though there's been no sign of her when Damaris has gone up. It doesn't matter. She has no wish to spend time with Jane, though conversation at the supper table has been civil enough. And Tom's there.

It's barely noon and she won't be welcome in the kitchen again for a couple of hours. She likes what she's started doing there, drawing up the weekly menus, seeing that provisions are in hand, listening to this or that concern about what can be supplied and what can't. At first she bridled at Jane's request she oversee the kitchen. 'Recently there hasn't been the variety we would like, you see,' Jane said. It had made Damaris wonder if this was the way the others saw her, best suited to kitchen business rather than any other role in the house. But it is a role, and if it becomes clear that Jane's agenda is to treat her as a servant rather than as an equal in the house, she'll talk to Thomas when he returns.

She's looking forward to that. The house is ill-at-ease. That'll be because of the way things are with Lizzie, but she suspects it's also to do with whatever's happening with Tom. As she sees it, there's only one person capable of restoring some harmony and that's Thomas. The trouble is no one knows when he'll be back.

Misalliances

She's not yet taken her daily walk. At this hour the sun hasn't yet made much of an inroad on the path outside, but it doesn't seem like it's a cold day. There are weeds in the gravel. Robert or Peter should be seeing to them. Perhaps they've not been told to. Edward has been going into town a lot. And she saw him once with Tom and Jane, leaving in Lizzie's carriage, the one with the padded seats. It adds to her sense that things are going on she knows nothing about. But then, why should she? It's time to take the air. She picks up her shawl, drapes it over her shoulders and turns away from perusing the gravel, only to turn back when she hears the scrunching of feet on it. There's a knocking on the back door. Whoever it is, she'll let one of the girls see to them and then go out.

'Mistress!' It's Miriam. She's in the room. 'Mistress, it's someone for you. A man.' There's a look of consternation on the girl's face, though she always tends to look anxious, unlike the capable Madeleine.

Damaris is tying the ends of the shawl. 'Does he have a name?'

'An old friend. He said you'd know.'

'Then thank you, Miriam.'

The girl hesitates. 'Are things alright?'

'They are. I think I know who it is.'

He's standing back from the doorway. He was once plump-cheeked, but there's a gauntness in his face which makes her wonder if something has happened and it's that which has brought him here. 'James. How good of you to come and see me.' She takes a step towards him and offers her hand. He gives it a gentle squeeze and lets her have it back.

'I thought I'd see if you were still here, Sister.'

The appellation grates on her but she ignores it. 'I was just going for my morning walk...'

He steps aside to make way and removes his hat. He was growing his hair when she last saw him and now it's gone except for a circlet round his ears, like a monk's. Concealing her surprise, she says: 'Would you like to come with me?'

'Yes. I'd like that.'

She laughs, aware that she has picked up his nervousness and that she's sounding like her old self, a little shy. 'There's a park with deer. I tend to go there. Come.' She continues to do the talking. ' I walk out here most days. I like some time to myself.'

'You would, of course.' He falls into step beside her. 'All those years...'

It's not as warm as she thought and she gives an involuntary shiver. 'Have you come all the way from Dartford?'

'I have.'

'You must have business in Maidstone...'

'No. I wanted to see you.'

They stop. 'Has something happened? Is Marion alright?' His shoulders have slumped. 'What is it, James?'

'Marion died a month ago.'

'Oh, I'm sorry.'

'It was something inside. It had been wrong for a while.'

They continue walking, more slowly. 'You have the cottage?'

'Yes, she willed it to me. Not that I'd have been turned out or anything.'

'I don't know. These are strange times.'

They have skirted the row of the trees that separates the close from the park and are approaching the felled tree trunk. But intuition prevents Damaris from inviting James to sit there with her. There are deer ahead and she doesn't want to disturb them, so she stops and turns to him. 'You're shaving your head again.'

'Yes.'

'Gone back to being a monk…'

'In a way.'

'In honour of Marion?'

He struggles for words. 'Yes…though… that's not it. Not all of it.'

'You wanted to go back…'

'It's who I am.'

'You can't be, James. You don't have a house.'

'I think I can, Sister.'

'James, please don't call me Sister.' As she says it, she feels her heart lurch. 'I *was* a nun, but I am no longer.'

James looks as if he's about to weep. 'It wouldn't matter.'

'Did you come here thinking I might go back with you?'

'I thought you might.'

'I've moved on. There are things which keep me here. I'm sorry.'

'So am I. I'll go.'

It'll be their first and only embrace, and it's she who initiates it. James lays a hand on her arm. 'Safe home, now,' she says. And with that he replaces his hat, turns about and with purposeful strides - strides which signify there's no purpose in his being there any longer – goes.

****

It's the late afternoon of Catherine's second day at Norfolk House. Since early morning there's been noise from the gardeners out front and from the workmen in the vestibule, who are whitewashing the walls. In passing, Grandmother Agnes has ill-temperedly mumbled something about the front sitting-room being re-papered. And then: 'You know why?' Catherine does know. Her uncle has tipped her the wink. It's about accommodating the King. It's why Mary, Joan and Katherine Tilney

Misalliances

have been sent away to Chesworth House. 'Then play your part, girl,' the Duchess adds.

Now it's gone quiet and since it's warm she strips off her gown and lies down in just her shift. She's missing Culpeper. It's a weakness of hers, she knows it, to feel so utterly empty when she's separated from the man bedding her. It's always been the same. Even her first two lovers - despite her never being much enamoured of their personal qualities – had left a vacancy she had found intolerable after they had been ordered away.

When she wakes from her doze, her first thought is that it can't be much later because the light hasn't changed. There's a vase of primroses on the table. She calls out for Margaret.

The girl comes in from her room next-door. 'My Lady?'

'Have you been back long?' Catherine asks. She swings her legs off the bed and perches on the edge.

'No, not long. I didn't want to wake you.'

Catherine gives her head a shake to wake herself up. One of the shoulder straps of her shift is hanging down. She leaves it there. 'I was only dozing. I had to take my gown off. It's a winter thing and it's been warm today.'

'It's been lovely in the dells.'

Catherine gets up. It's done Margaret the world of good, going out to get some air. Ever since the girl came to her, she has quietly envied her prettiness – the blue eyes and dark brown hair

Misalliances

– and the two hours she's spent picking spring flowers with one of the housemaids has enhanced it. 'You've got some colour in your cheeks,' she says, picking up her hand mirror. 'Come and see.' Catherine holds up the glass for her.

'Oh, I have.'

'It suits you.' Catherine slots a stray curl back in place behind Margaret's ear. 'I think we'll have supper up here. I can't be bothered to put my gown back on.'

'I'll go and tell the kitchen.' Margaret looks up into Catherine's face. 'Just some cold meat and bread?'

'And some wine. A flagon. Enough for two.'

'Oh, you spoil me, my Lady.' Margaret hesitates. 'Since we're going to stay up here, we could unpack the new gowns. We've got a few more hours daylight.'

The latest presents from Catherine's uncle have arrived and are still in their bag. They are not gifts in the conventional sense, given out of affection, but investments, and so she has responded to their delivery with no great show of enthusiasm. 'If you like,' she says.

Catherine, her mouth half-full of cold beef, is watching Margaret as the girl unties the bag. She's struck by the look on her face. It's one of gleeful expectation. 'Tell you what,' she says, 'you try one on.'

'Me?'

'Why not? They'll fit you as well as they would me. I'd like to see you in something fine and you'll be doing me a service.'

Margaret is standing back from the box with her hands clasped, as if what's in there has outfaced her, deprived her of motion. 'Oh, they're lovely. Do come and see.'

Margaret's right. These seem to be a cut above the ones her uncle last sent. She lifts the top gown, a satin creation in pink with a frieze of embroidery round the neck. It's quite light. 'Mmm,' she murmurs approvingly. Beneath the pink is one in a pale green and below that one in yellow. Margaret is at her elbow, looking at her enquiringly. 'Don't you think?'

'Pick one.'

Margaret hesitates. Catherine can see her mind working. It would be getting above herself to be choosy. The girl runs her fingers over the one on top, the pink one. 'This one,' she says.

'Take it out, then.'

Margaret knows how to handle gowns. In a second she's got it hanging upright. She lets the fabric drop to take shape, kicks out a foot to remedy a kink in the hem and holds it up over her plain dress. Over the swag of satin, she beams at her mistress. 'What do you think?' She takes a turn round the room.

Catherine moves to the window. 'Come into the light.' At the sound of horses outside, she turns to look. There are guards, pikemen and, only now

Misalliances

coming into view, a litter emblazoned with the King's colours. She lets out a scream.

'My lady?' Margaret is still holding the gown up to herself.

Catherine snatches it from her 'Quick! Get me into this.'

'Get *you* into it?'

'Yes, yes. Hurry.'

She doesn't know what to make of the King, other than that he looks fat and old and out of place in her world which only a short while ago was full of silks and taffetas and the prospect of some giggly, girlish pastime. What on earth is he thinking, sitting here opposite her amidst the piles of stripped wallpaper and bare walls? He will have had to negotiate the stepladders and buckets of white-wash in the hall, too.

'I've come to apologise,' he's saying, 'for the way you were abruptly sent away from Hampton. It was none of my doing.'

At the sound of that voice - authoritative but thin, wheezing - she's stuttering. She never stutters! 'I...I understood, your Majesty.'

'I thank you for being so understanding, my dear.'

Henry's tight, little mouth parts in what he must take to be a smile. The mouth is sagging, tilting to one side and the sight of it unnerves Catherine further. The King gestures in her direction. His fingers hover there and the mouth opens a little wider. 'I believe you're wearing one of the gowns I sent.'

He sent the gowns. Catherine smooths down the skirt, flattens the stiffened petticoats which she and Margaret found just in time. 'I like this one in particular,' she says. 'I really must thank you. What a delightful surprise it was when they arrived.'

'Pink suits you, my dear.'

She looks down at herself. God knows how big he thought she was in the bust because Margaret has had to pin it at the back so that her bosom isn't too much on show.

Henry is talking about some other things that are on the way. He hopes it doesn't seem too forward, sending her these gifts.

Her head is reeling. Quilts? What does she need quilts for? 'No, Sir,' she says.

'And perhaps I can come again?'

'Yes, of course you may.'

He appears momentarily at a loss for words. He's looking down at his hands. 'The Queen,' he says, and stops.

'Sir?'

'The Queen is going to Richmond soon.'

'Oh?'

'She's going to Richmond and she will stay there.'

'Will she?'

He seems embarrassed. The King is embarrassed. 'I don't know whether you know, but things haven't been going well.'

'Really? I'd no idea.' She drags an errant strand of wallpaper under the stool with her heel.

'No, not at all well.' Henry sits up and peers at her, as if he's trying to work something out. Her, perhaps.

'Do you mean the marriage is at an end?'

'Yes.' The silence is uncomfortable and she wishes she were back upstairs with Margaret. The King says it again. 'Yes.' He is still looking at her with a steadiness she's finding disquieting. 'There are steps to go through, but that is my intention. So may I come again?'

She gives him her sweetest smile. 'But of course, your Majesty.'

He's slowly getting to his feet. The effort it's taking is obvious. Half way up, he stops, his head bent. He's contemplating what's on the floor. 'Renovation,' he says. It occurs to her that it's not a genuine interest that has made him pause; it's to mask his difficulty in rising. She hears him taking a breath, and another. Finally, he straightens up. 'Good.'

She realises she should be standing. She does so and feels something give. It must be the pin. Panic-stricken, because she can't have her titties falling out now, she presses one hand to her bosom and pulls the loose fabric back into place with the other

Misalliances

'I ought to get back,' he's saying.

She manages a curtsey. 'Thank you for coming, your Majesty.'

He's making his way out – or finding it, rather. 'Guards!'

Her grandmother's in the vestibule standing over one of the housemaids, who's apparently being tasked with moving the buckets of whitewash. 'It's a bit late now, Grandma!' Catherine says, sidling past. 'Why on earth didn't you show him into one of the rooms that *weren't* being decorated?'

The old woman lifts her head. She's only just seen her. 'Oh, child! I didn't show him anywhere. I was in the jakes. Taken short.' She clasps her hands to her shrivelled breast. 'Oh, the shame of it!'

'It's alright. I don't think he noticed.'

'What did he say?'

'He wants to come again.'

'Good, good. We'll have all this done by then.' The Duchess returns her attention to the hapless girl. 'Against the wall. Put them up against the wall!'

As Catherine climbs the stairs, up to the suite of rooms on the very top floor, which at least has the advantage of distancing her from her grandmother, she finds it difficult to keep it in, her relief that it's over, her first one-to-one meeting with the King, and despite the chaos and her fear of showing him much too much of her bosom, she brought it off. Her elation comes out in great gulping giggles. Wondering if her grandmother has heard, she looks down. The dowager duchess, still preoccupied with the buckets, is waving her stick around as the girl moves the last bucket to where her mistress wants it. The image tips Catherine into full-throated laughter. Once in the safety of her room, she falls back on the bed, swinging her slippered feet up into the air. Underneath her petticoats her legs are bare. In the rush they had not been able to find a pair of stockings. She met the King with bare legs and a barely covered bosom! How absurd! Margaret emerges from her room and stands stock still. 'My Lady? Are you alright?'

Catherine swallows hard. 'I'm fine.' She sits up and wipes her eyes. Another spasm of mirth bubbles up and she lets it out.

Gingerly, Margaret approaches the bed. 'Are you sure?'

Catherine straightens her legs, pulls down her skirt, and looks up at Margaret. 'Quite sure.'

'Was the gown alright?'

'It came undone.'

'It didn't!'

Catherine sits up and leans forward. 'Look! Just imagine if these two had come tumbling out.'

Margaret's hand is still at her mouth. 'I think, my lady, he'd have married you for sure then!'

It's a wonder the ensuing cachinnation of girlish laughter hasn't dragged the dowager up, got

Misalliances

her hobbling up to the first-floor landing, which is probably as far as she'd be able to get. Their noise must have drifted down. But there's no sound from below. Eventually Margaret stops her hooting, Catherine swallows the last remnants of the ridiculousness that has entered her life, and they look at one another. 'There must be some wine left,' Catherine says.

'Lots.'

'Pour me some.'

Chapter Twenty-nine: Out

Wyatt keeps turning it over.

'So there you are. After all these years, I'm out.'

'Because the marriage has failed?'

'And the alliance with the Germans. I heard *you* were against it.'

'I didn't think it was the right policy.'

'You let me down there, Thomas. But never mind. Henry was never going to go for it. Now they're talking about Princess Mary marrying the Emperor. Were you behind that as well?'

'I'm afraid so.'

'You might rue that.'

'I know.' Wyatt attempts to lighten the mood. 'You're now the Earl of Essex. That's worth something.'

'No more than a pinch of salt.'

'Why do you say that?'

'You know how it is. Once you're out, all it needs is one little thing…'

Cromwell hadn't finished the sentence. He'd left the words hanging in the air of his newly extended, ostentatiously grand house in the City, Austin Friars. Perhaps he already knew what that one little thing was, the comment or deed that would not only strip away these riches but do for him altogether.

Misalliances

Wyatt's glad he didn't press the matter. There are things it's best not to know. Back when he was making his way at court, and still with Elizabeth, his father was always saying to him: 'Keep your face in. Let the King see you. That'll remind him who you are and that you are there to do his bidding.' Now he thinks it's time to stop showing his face. At least for a while. Henry's pleased with him, told him he is, promised him rewards, and given his blessing for him to spend time at home. If that means he'll be forgotten for a while, so well and good. And if Cromwell is about to fall, he'd like the ties that bound the two of them to be forgotten too. The three weeks he spent in The Tower back in '36 taught him that loyalty and dependability count for nothing when the wheels begin to turn, as they now appeared to be doing for Cromwell. So until they've ceased turning, completed their cycle, he's going to take his face out of the picture and lie low.

He's out in the country, hawthorne and elder a-bloom in the hedgerows, and St. Thomas a Watering is coming up. It's always been the point where he's felt the city is behind him and he can begin to think of himself simply as Thomas Wyatt of Allington.

There are no bodies hanging at Watering. 'Well, that's something,' he says to himself.

Chapter Thirty: Elderflowers

When Damaris enters the kitchen, she's surprised to see Madeleine at the place she herself has come to occupy over the last few weeks. Apparently, the girl is preparing that day's sweet dish for she has a large jug of cream by her elbow and is cutting some little white flowers into slivers. Cook comes forward and says: 'I hope you don't mind, Mistress. It's her speciality, you see, and the elder blossom doesn't last long.'

A little put out, but deeming it not worth undermining the good relations she's been taking pains to foster in the kitchen, Damaris says: 'I don't mind. I'd quite like to watch.'

At the far end of the room Janet is turning the spit on which two joints of meat are fixed. The smell of roasting pork fills the air. Cook goes over and lifts her off the stool. 'Leave that. They're done. I've told you before. You don't have to sit there when the meat's cooked and the fire's gone down. The one under the stove needs seeing to.' Ruth is watching from where she's slicing cabbage. 'What's up with the girl?' Cook asks her, shaking her head.

'I think she's in love,' Ruth says.

Cook now has Janet by the arm, dragging her towards the door that leads outside. 'Wood, you shiftless thing. Go and fetch it!'

Misalliances

Amid the hubbub, Damaris takes a step towards her usurper. She considers this tall girl with the ready smile the most amenable of the servants. She fingers one of the flower stems. 'These are elderflowers, then...'

'They are.'

'I suppose it's the time of year for them.'

'It is. They're all over the hedgerows.' Madeleine stops cutting. 'I'm sorry, Mistress, they should have told you.'

'We didn't know till you came this morning with them,' Ruth says. 'So we couldn't.'

'It's alright,' Damaris says to Ruth. 'Honest it is.' She redirects her attention to Madeleine. 'What is it you're making?'

'Syllabub.'

'Oh.'

'Never had it?'

'I must have.'

'But not with elderflower, I bet.'

Neither the tone of gentle mockery in the girl's voice nor the sideways look she's giving her offends Damaris. 'Not that I know of,' she says.

'You do know what syllabub is?'

'Not really.'

Madeleine continues her lesson. 'It's cream with sugar and wine, and when you add elderflower it gives it a very special flavour...' She knits her brows. 'I don't know how to describe it.' She takes one of the sprigs and offers it. 'Here. Smell.'

Misalliances

The odour is sweet but with an edge of something else that's not exactly that, like the scent of new growth Damaris has picked up coming from the bushes in the park. A freshness. 'Does it taste like this?'

'Sort of. But you have to catch the flowers when they're new. These have come out in just the last few days along by the river. You must have seen them.'

'I don't go down there that often.'

'Why not? It's lovely.'

It's a justified rebuke. She really ought to widen her horizons now spring is here.

'Can I do anything?'

'Yes. In the room where you sit, there's a cabinet?'

'There is.'

'And in there are some special glasses.' Madeleine leans in, all confidential. 'I think they must be, 'cause they're not stored with the rest of the crockery. And Mistress Jane ticked me off the first time I used them.'

'You're still doing it, though.'

'I didn't take any notice.'

'Very wise. That's what I do.'

Madeleine's laughter is fresh, too. It reminds Damaris of the friends she had before she entered St. Agatha's, when she used to meet Eleanor and Alison in the fields above the cottage, relishing the temporary escape, the few hours' respite, from the attentions of her father. Madeleine can't be much

Misalliances

more than the age she was then. Her fine white teeth match the rest of her regular features and not for the first time Damaris wonders what brought this bright, personable girl to the castle. But that's a silly question: for a girl out in the country it's either work on the land or serve the local gentry, and Madeleine seems content with her lot. She's dusting off her hands. 'If you go and get the glasses,' she says, 'I'll fetch the wine. And then you can watch me put it together.'

The glasses are tall and narrow with short stems. They need washing. Once that's done, they glisten with a clarity superior to the vessels that usually grace the supper table. 'I think they're Italian,' Madeleine says. 'Sir Thomas spent some time there, you know.' She's spooning in the thick, creamy mixture from the jug. Dipping a finger in, she proceeds to taste it. 'Oh, that is good. Go on, try it.'

Damaris wipes her finger round the top of the jug and licks it. 'Mmm. I could get to like that.' She smacks her lips. 'Sir Thomas was in Italy, was he?'

'Years ago. When my sister was here.'
'Your sister?'
'Joanna. You're in her old room.'
'Come on, girls!' Cook is clapping her hands. 'We're about to dish up.'

'I have to be at table,' Madeleine says. 'Would you like to go down to the river one afternoon? There's an hour when I'm not much needed.'

'I'd like that. What about tomorrow?'

'Tomorrow. Yes. I know where to find you.'

****

They have come to the the little stone bridge across the stream that feeds the moat. 'This is where I come,' Madeleine says. 'But there's a nice spot further on.'

The river is immediately below them. The opposite bank is a mirror image of their own, overgrown with bushes and low-hanging trees. Midges are hovering there, between the lowest branches and the surface of the slow-moving water.

'The elder bushes are down that way.' Madeleine points to their right, where the path disappears into a mass of foliage thick with new greenery. 'We'll pick some before we go back. Shall we go along a bit? It's easy enough. It looks a bit overgrown but Robert has been clearing it.'

They come to a place where the bank has been embellished by half a dozen boards on stilts to form a makeshift jetty for the row-boat tied up next to it.

Madeleine steps out on to the platform, puts down her bag and holds out her hand. 'It's quite safe.' She kneels, folds her legs under her and,

Misalliances

motioning to Damaris she should do the same, removes her cap and unpins her hair. She shakes it out and runs her fingers through. 'Go on,' she says. 'You won't be seen from the house.'

'Are you sure?'

'Trust me.'

Damaris takes off her cap. She's never needed many pins in her hair and it takes only a moment to pull them out. She laughs, embarrassed, as she untangles her curls.

Madeleine is studying her. 'How old are you?'

'Thirty. You?'

'Nineteen next Michaelmas. My sister was quite a bit older. She'd be going on thirty-five now.'

Damaris is about to ask what happened when Madeleine forestalls her. 'Now, there's only one thing to do on a sunny day when you're by the river,' she says, pulling off her shoes. She reaches under her skirt to tug down her stockings.

'What are you doing?'

'I'm going to dip my feet in.'

'I can't.'

'Yes, you can,' Madeleine says. She makes a grab for Damaris's slippers.

'Alright, alright, I can do it myself!'

'If you're thirty,' Madeleine says, 'it's high time you got yourself a man.'

'What?'

'Well, you're definitely no longer a nun.'

'I've not been for a while.'

Misalliances

'That's what they call you, you know, in the kitchen. The nun.'

'Then I'll have to put them right. Have *you* got a man?'

'Not yet.' Madeleine gives a mischievous smile. 'Come on.'

With giggles and chuckles, they shuffle to the edge and drop their legs over the side. The water is ice-cold and Damaris, barely recognising herself, gives a girlish shriek. Madeleine swishes her feet from side to side.

'Whose is the boat?'

'It's ours. Robert uses it sometimes. He takes Janet out in it on a Sunday. It's cold fare, so Cook does Sunday by herself. It gives the girls some time to themselves.'

'Do you have any, apart from the occasional snatched hour like this?'

'Sometimes. It's not a busy house, is it? It used to be. In my sister's time. Lords and ladies coming, even the King once or twice. Then, what with one thing and another, people stopped coming, and everything sort of shrank.'

'Was that because of what happened to Sir Thomas?'

'It must have been. And the fact he's away most of the time. Or has been while I've been here.' Madeleine is undoing the top buttons of her dress. 'Oh, that's better. It's alright. As I say, it's not as if there's a lot of you.'

'There's one more now.'

Madeleine stops moving her feet. 'Oh, you mean the baby. Well, yes...'

Damaris detects a reservation. 'Aren't you happy for Lizzie?'

'I am...'

'But...?'

'Things aren't what they seem there, that's all.' Madeleine starts to swish her feet again.

'Go on.'

'Just between ourselves?'

'Of course.'

'I'm not convinced it's Sir Thomas's.' Madeleine gives Damaris a cautious glance. 'I'm not being fanciful.' She takes her feet out of the water and gives them a wipe with her stockings.

Damaris follows suit, though she'd have liked to enjoy the water a little longer. 'Because it came early?'

'Not just that.'

Damaris pulls her shoes on. 'Those sorts of things are easily misinterpreted, aren't they?'

Madeleine, on her feet, picks up the bag. 'Sometimes. Anyway, it's none of our business. Let's go and get the flowers.'

They cross the bridge and push their way through the undergrowth until they come to the cloud of whiteness that's the elder bush.

'It's pretty, isn't it?' Madeleine says. She gives Damaris the bag. 'I don't need so many this time,' she says, reaching up through the branches. 'They'll be done soon.'

Misalliances

When the bag's half full, they take a look. 'Will that do?' asks Damaris.

'It's more than enough.'

Before they reach the bridge Madeleine gives a half-turn and says: 'I know Tom and Lizzie have slept with one another.'

'How do you know?'

'I'll tell you when we get to the bridge.'

The span amounts to no more than a dozen paces but its parapet rises high enough for someone to comfortably lean on. Madeleine stops and waits for Damaris to join her. 'It was last summer,' she says. 'Sir Thomas wasn't back long from Spain and had gone up to London to see the King, like he always does when he's back from abroad.'

'Like now...'

Madeleine nods. 'Jane's father was ill so she'd gone to Bishopsbourne. A storm had been coming all afternoon and by the time I went to bed it was really windy. I got to sleep alright but then I was woken by something banging in the room beneath. Tom and Jane's room is below mine. I don't normally hear anything from down there. You wouldn't, would you? Not in this big place. So I figured it had to be a window left open. I thought Tom'd close it when he went to bed. But it went on. So after a while I went down. It must have been the middle of the night by this time. I knew there couldn't be anyone there, because no one'd be able to sleep through that racket.'

'And there wasn't.'

'Tom's bed was empty. But he was often out all night. Playing cards in Maidstone. I closed the window and went back to bed. In the morning, he came down for breakfast early – looking like he'd hardly slept - and I thought no more about it. Until I went into Lizzie's room. When you're a maidservant you know when a bed's had two people in it. And hers had. Bed linen tells no lies. I knew Tom was smitten with her. She'd only been here a few weeks when I noticed that. So I imagine what happened was, there came a time when they were alone in the house...and there you are.'

'And this was when?'

'Perhaps a week past the longest day?'

'July, then.'

'And that adds up, doesn't it? For a baby born at the beginning of April. And, you see, Lizzie wasn't sleeping with Sir Thomas then. They'd only just started to get to know one another again and they didn't sort out that side of things till well after he came back from seeing the King. And that *doesn't* add up to an early April baby. May, more likely. Well into May.'

Damaris has been weighing up whether it would be wise to share what she saw that afternoon in Lizzie's room and decided it wouldn't. She doesn't really know Madeleine yet, and she doesn't want to fall prey all over again to the very fancifulness which, for all her denial, the girl herself might have fallen into. 'Have you told anyone else?'

'Only Miriam.'

'Could she have told Cook and the scullery girls? I heard them talking the day the baby came.'

'Saying what?'

'What you're saying.'

'She better not have.' Madeleine takes the bag. 'We ought to go.'

Chapter Thirty-one: Lèse-majesté

'I've been given a couple of properties in the city,' Wyatt says towards the end of supper.
There's a groan from Tom. 'Not more abbeys. How many do you need?'

'I do need these.' Wyatt looks round the table. 'I don't like monks and nuns being put out on to the high-road, but the way things are we need these gifts.' His eyes dwell on Damaris.

Jane's spoon is half way to her mouth. 'The way things are? What do you mean?

'I mean we are not as well-off as I would like.' He lays his spoon down. 'That was good.'

'It's Madeleine's recipe,' Damaris says. 'Elderflower.'

Wyatt looks round. 'Madeleine? Are you there?'

She steps forward and exchanges a quick glance with Damaris. 'Sir?'

'That was excellent. I hope to have it again.'

Damaris speaks for her new friend. 'It's only possible once a year. They only bloom for a few weeks.'

Lizzie says: 'Thank you, Madeleine.'

'We need to fill up our coffers,' Wyatt continues, 'and one sure way of doing that is by renting these houses out, like I've done with Poynings at Boxley. The valuables in them have gone, which means the kind of work I asked you to

Misalliances

do at Malling, Tom, has already been done. There's one in Bermondsey, which I already have someone in mind for, another in Southwark, and an especially fine one near The Tower, which I'm thinking of keeping for ourselves.'

'The Tower?' It's Tom again. 'Haven't you had enough of that place?' He pushes away his empty glass, one of the fine ones from the sitting-room, and it topples over. Damaris rights it. 'Be careful,' she scolds, 'it's Italian crystal.'

Tom ignores her. 'I don't see how renting out a few abbeys is going to fill our coffers. If the King is so pleased with you, he needs to be giving you some coin.'

'That's coming.'

'How much?'

'Enough to see us right. I didn't get a penny for my time in Spain, nor my last jaunt across the water. Since I've emptied our coffers to serve the King, it's only right he fills them up again.'

'And he agrees, does he?'

'I didn't quite put it like that. But yes.'

'Do you trust his promises?' Lizzie asks.

'He's pleased with me. We'll see.'

When they leave the table to go into the parlour, Wyatt asks Damaris to wait. 'You do understand,' he says. 'It's how service is rewarded. And I can't afford to turn it down.'

'Literally can't,' she says, 'if your coffers are empty.'

'*Our* coffers,' he says. 'I was afraid I'd come back and find you gone.'

'No.'

'I'm glad.'

He's studying her and she laughs nervously. This evening she's put on one of the prettier gowns she got from Maidstone, the red one, which she's chosen because it's the most striking of the three. Is it that?

'You've left your old life behind, then,' he says.

'I have.'

'And you've been reading my books...'

'The Tyndale, yes.'

'And the English Bible...'

'Tom's been a help with that.'

'He said. Have you found some common ground?'

'A little.' She wants to tell him she also helped with the removal of valuables from Malling Abbey, but perhaps that's better coming from Tom.

'I hope you're joining us?'

'I am.'

'One of the things about being in France is that you can get your hands on some wines that are scarce over here. I thought I'd open one.'

'Lead the way,' she says.

'You first.'

****

Misallianges

Thomas is with someone in the next room. John Mason. She met him when they got back from abroad and she recognises his voice.

- They took him yesterday, at Westminster Hall.
- And he's gone to The Tower?
- Naturally.
- It can't just be about the marriage…
- That's at the back of it, for sure. And the folly of pressing for an alliance with the Lutherans. But the crux of it was what he'd been saying about fighting for the new Church.'
- Even if the King was no longer minded to.
- He said he'd fight *him* over it.'
- Not literally though.
- It doesn't matter. It's come to Henry's ears. A clear case of *lèse-majesté*. Enough to take Cromwell's head off. And there's a second thing, not a charge exactly, but it's got Henry fired up. As you might imagine, he's been exhorting him to make the marriage work and Henry told him there was nothing to work with, because he couldn't do it…you know, get it up. Now whether that's just a problem with the Queen or...
- Henry put it in those terms?
- In confidence, I'm sure. But then Cromwell told Wriothesley and next thing it's all over the court and the King's spitting blood.
- Who did you get this from?

Misalliances

- Ralph Sadler, so I'm sure it's true.
- Well, one thing's sure, if there's any suspicion Henry can no longer father a child it'll shorten the line forming to be the next queen. You thought his eye might have settled on Kate Howard...
- He's been visiting her at Norfolk House.
- Has he, now? With the connivance of her uncle, no doubt...
- And her grandmother presumably. All it needs is for Thomas Audley to start making enquiries about the young lady and we'll know it's serious.
- Enquiries?
- Whether she's had lovers and who they were. So you'd do well to keep quiet about your small part in it.
- Only you know about that. And it wasn't such a small part!

There's laughter

- Well, however big it was, it needs to shrink to nothing now. Our Lord Chancellor is cunning and he's thorough, so our Kate better have her wits about her.
- *She* will, it's grandma I'd be worried about.
- Why, what's she likely to know?
- There'd been others before me.
- And you think the old lady would have turned a blind eye? I doubt it.

Misalliances

- Wriothesley.
- What about him?
- Remember what I said?
- If anyone was going to betray Cromwell, it'd be him.
- He'd sell his soul for advancement. If he's the one who set the hare running about Henry's shortcomings in bed, my guess is he's behind the charge of *lèse-majesté* as well.
- You think he might have spread both stories...'
- It wouldn't surprise me if, like Gardiner, he'd been suborned by Norfolk and Suffolk to bring Cromwell down. Kill off the man driving the new Church and you up your chances of killing the whole thing off.
- Same goes for the German marriage. What's left of it.
- Leaving the way clear for Kate. Two birds with one stone.
- Thomas, I know what you said about us being the King's men. But we're also Cromwell's. Where do you think we stand?
- We've been out of the country these past three years, bar a few months. What would the charges be?
- They'll find them if it suits them, we know that. If I were you, I'd watch out for Suffolk in particular.
- Keep me informed.
- I will. As best I can.'
- You can't go yet. Stay for dinner.

Misalliances

- No, I ought to get off. How's the boy?
- Growing fast.
- Give Lizzie my best,
- I will.

Damaris hears them leave and expels a sigh of relief. Eaves-dropping may have become her new-found métier, but when it comes to affairs of state, she's out of her depth. It's bad enough carrying the other secrets. As for Thomas and his lust, she's not shocked but she is disappointed. Then again, if a good man like David could sin because of a woman, what chance did other men have? She knows nothing of Kate Howard, but with that name she's obviously high-born. And from what she's just heard, she'll be young and pretty. She tuts to herself. Has Thomas learnt nothing? It's the Anne Boleyn thing all over again. And if he were to – all over again - wind up in The Tower, what then?

Misalliances

Chapter Thirty-two: Audley

Gowns for this, gowns for that! All the measuring done by Mister Scott, the King's tailor. She says to Margaret: 'Well, at least I won't fall out of these!' And Margaret laughs, though there's something sad about her this morning.

'What is it?' Catherine asks. 'You've been down in the dumps a day or two.'

'You're going to have all those high-born ladies waiting on you.'

'So?'

'Will there still be room for me?'

'Why shouldn't there be? Anyway, what do you mean? High-born ladies my arse. It'll be the same old bunch you know already. Though I might get rid of a few.'

Margaret looks unconvinced.

'Come here,' Catherine says. She pats the place beside her on the bed. Margaret dutifully comes to occupy it. 'You have been with me since Chesworth, done things for me none of that lot would do.'

'It's what a personal maid does.'

'You're more than that. So with me you will stay. Anyway, we're still here in Lambeth.'

'Why is that?'

Catherine looks down at her painted nails, turns her hands this way and that. 'He says he's got to get the divorce done first.' She gives one of her high-pitched giggles. 'Do you think he'll actually propose? Do Kings do that?'

Catherine is not expecting a reply and Margaret is thinking about what she heard when the King stayed for supper. Catherine is thinking about it too, how after they had finished the meal they had made their way to the day bed, the introduction of which she'd had no say in, but which she would, of course, have agreed to, despite its being out of place in the dining-room and the obviousness of what it was intended to facilitate.

Margaret is at the window. 'My lady…is this him?'

Catherine's heart resumes its normal, healthy pace when she sees the litter crossing the courtyard. It's not the King. There's the usual number of pikemen, though, so it must be somebody important. And…no…it can't be. She doesn't want *him* here.

Margaret is craning her neck to see past her mistress's shoulder. 'Isn't that your cousin?'

'I believe it is.'

Culpeper draws back the curtain of the litter and reaches in to help a grey haired man bedecked with chains of office climb out. It's the Lord Chancellor, Thomas Audley.

Catherine waits, one finger raised to silence Margaret, who is hovering by her side, but there's no call, no tread on the stairs of a servant coming up to summon her. 'Come,' she says.

Misalliances

From the first-floor landing, her grandmother can be heard in the vestibule, unctuous in her greeting: 'Sir Thomas, this is an honour!' The Lord Chancellor's is brisk. 'Your Grace, somewhere private, if you please.'

'What if we get caught?' Margaret whispers, as they tip-toe down the stairs.

'Then we get caught. Now hush.'

The voices are coming from the great hall, a cavernous, echoing space at the best of times and not the most discreet choice for a private conversation. The vestibule is still smelling of whitewash and Catherine is careful not to brush her skirts up against the damp walls and thus give herself away later. She leads Margaret into the front sitting-room. Its furniture is back in its rightful place and she motions her to take the stool that's on the left hand side of the door into the hall while she lowers herself on to the one to the right. It's Audley who's speaking, his self-important tone at odds with his broad Essex vowels.

- You will know why I am here, your Grace.
- It's about Catherine.
- Indeed.
- The Duke told me you would be coming.
- The King has expressed an interest…
- Which, as her grandmother, I have been happy to assist in.
- You are her *step*-grandmother, in fact. You were the late Duke of Norfolk's second wife.

Misalliances

- I was. Catherine and I are not blood relatives. I hope you're not going to trawl through the whole of the Howard family line, my Lord.
- No, I was merely attempting to confirm the connection.
- The connection must be well-known, given the eminence of the Howard family and the years I served at court.

These days, around the house, the Duchess's voice rarely rises above a low grumble and now she's polishing its tone and raising its pitch. Catherine suppresses a titter.

- So, just to be clear, the Duke of Norfolk is your step-son, and it's his brother who was Catherine's father.
- He died last year. It was no great loss to her. Over the years she'd seen little of him. None of us had. There were difficulties. Catherine came to live with me when she was very young.
- Ah, yes. That was at Chesworth Park.
- Chesworth House. The damp country air wasn't good for my bones. Too near the sea.

    Catherine mimes a yawn.

- Was Francis Dereham with you at Chesworth?
- Dereham? No. He entered my service when we came here. The Duke recommended him.
- And what were his duties?

Misalliances

- He helped me manage my affairs.
- Your secretary...
- In a manner of speaking. He ran the household.
- And what was his relationship with Catherine?
- His relationship? A formal one. Like that of anyone in my employ.

Margaret sees Catherine stiffen.

- Dereham has been at court recently and has been heard saying the relationship was not at all, as you put it, formal.
- Then he's making mischief, that's all, pumping himself up into something he never was and never could be. Perhaps he tried to flirt with her and got a flea in his ear. She's a pretty girl. And pretty girls always attract unwanted attention. That's why I kept a close eye on Catherine the whole time she was with me.
- Perhaps you could ask her about Dereham.
- Certainly not. That would be insulting to her and demeaning for me. Does the King know of this claptrap?

There's silence. Margaret looks across at Catherine again but her mistress has her head bowed.

- Not at present.
- Then you must say nothing. I'll have my stepson deal with Dereham.

Misalliances

- The Duke?
- Who else? Dereham has been besmirching the Howard family name.
- Putting it in the hands of the Duke might create more of a fuss than is necessary, don't you think? Expose Catherine to more attention than either of us would want...
- Do I understand you, Sir? Are you saying we ought *not* to make a fuss?
- I'm happy to take your word, your Grace. If you're saying there was nothing between Catherine and Dereham then there wasn't.
- What you're saying, Lord Chancellor, is if the King were to hear from the Duke things which you haven't yet told him...
- I'll not make a fuss if you won't.
- You have my word.
- And you mine.

Catherine leaps up and motions Margaret to follow. She wants to be up the stairs. In the vestibule stands Culpeper. One eyebrow cocked, he is smiling at her. To Margaret she says 'Go!', to Culpeper she says 'In here, quick!'

For the second time in a few months, she's in the little space that only servants visit. The phrase 'hole-in-the-corner' comes to her and if it weren't for the likelihood of her being overheard by Audley or Grandmother she'd vent her vexation with a loud expletive. Instead, tugging Culpeper

Misalliances

away from the door, she whispers: 'Don't tell me you've been waiting for me.'

'I saw you go in. Eaves-dropping, were we?

'Keep your voice down!'

'Why?'

'Why? Because we can't be seen together.'

'That's going to be difficult when you come back to the palace.'

'You know what I mean...'

'Calm down. And stop biting your lip. For one thing, where else was I going to wait? Second, it's you who's dragged me in here and risked compromising us. Aren't you pleased to see me?'

'Of course I am.'

At the sound of voices outside, they both go quiet. He draws her to him. 'When *are* you coming back to the palace?'

She wriggles away, as far as the cramped space allows. 'I don't know, do I? Look, we can't stay here. You go first. Say you were looking for the jakes.'

'No need,' he says, reaching past her. 'Here's Audley's hat.' He gives her a grin and opens the door.

Margaret, watching Catherine pacing up and down and muttering to herself, is at a loss. 'Is it so bad?'

'It is, it is.' Catherine swings round and grabs at Margaret. 'You'd never say anything, would you?'

'About what?'

Misalliances

'About Dereham. All those nights he was in my bed. What if Mannox comes forward?'

'Who?'

'Mannox, my tutor at Chesworth...' She notices the slyness in Margaret smile. Dropping the girl's hands, she bats her away. 'Oh, you naughty thing! You had me there...'

Margaret collapses on to the bed and into her very own peculiar expression of hilarity, a series of hoots, the peculiarness of which always precipitates a fit of the giggles in Catherine.

Chapter Thirty-three: Tower Hill

The house is a short ride from the river, Wyatt points out, and where else in London is there a house like this at the rent he's asking? He's taken a liking to John Horsey, to the warmth in his voice, which he senses is as much due to his good nature as to his west country roots and easy-on-the-ear accent. What's more, as a justice of the peace in that part of the world and the newly chosen knight for the shire of Dorset, he would be a reliable tenant.

In spite of the warmth July has brought, Horsey is wearing a long, heavy coat. It's quite similar to the one Wyatt himself would wear when he's down at the farm.

His prospective tenant is taking stock of the second ground floor room he's been shown into, which like its counterpart across the passage, overlooks the well-tended garden. 'It's the old Abbot's house, you say?'

'It is. John Pope was given the abbey itself when they closed it. You can see it from here.' He goes to the window.

Horsey joins him and looks down the length of the garden to a row of roofs punctuated by a steepled tower. 'It looks a fine building.'

'It was. He's been knocking quite a lot of it down.'

Misalliances

'That's a shame. I'm more minded to think in terms of preservation. It's why I'm taking over the one at Sherborne.'

'Really?'

'I shall be paying for it, though.' Horsey claps Wyatt on the arm. 'We're not all as fortunate as you.'

'How much?'

'Somewhere in the upper hundreds. It's not settled yet.'

Wyatt whistles, more in sympathy than surprise. 'That's high.'

'It's worth it. It's a splendid building with a fine church.'

Wyatt considers the man before him. He might be wearing a country man's coat, but he's undoubtedly a man of means. 'Looking to expand your estate, are you?'

'Not at all. I've got what I need at Clifton Maybank. It's for the parish. If I don't take it over, someone like your friend over there will get it and demolish it. That would be a loss.'

'You'll give it to the village?'

'I'll take a payment, something minimal, just to make it legal.'

'That's very generous of you.'

'I like to look after my people.'

Wyatt returns to the matter at hand. 'So there's only the two rooms upstairs which, as I said, would suit servants. You and your lady could live quite comfortably on the ground floor, if you're only going to be here when parliament's in session.'

'Joan's quite happy to stay at Clifton.' Horsey offers his hand. 'This'll suit me very well, Wyatt. I'll move in next week if that's convenient for you.'

Wyatt hands him the keys. 'Whenever you wish, John.'

Horsey turns about to look at where they are. 'I do like these rooms at the back. But tell me, you're a favourite of the King, so this can't be all you've got.'

'It's not.' Horsey raises his eye-brows, and Wyatt doesn't mind telling him more. 'I've two in Kent, one in Somerset – don't know what to do with that - and three in the city. This, St, Mary Overy in Southwark, and the Crutched Friars near Tower Hill.'

'You were lucky to get the Friars. I hear it's splendid inside.'

'It's unusual. A lot of French influence. Not your average religious house.'

'Will you be renting it out?'

'At the moment I'm inclined to keep it for myself.'

'Well, let me know if you decide not to.'

'It's not much closer to Westminster than this.'

'That's not material. It sounds like it might be more to Joan's liking.'

'Ah, I see.'

Misalliances

'A man needs his woman with him.'

'Well, come and see it, anyway, once I've spruced it up a little.'

'I shall.'

****

Back at the Friars, after a sleepless night, Thomas Wyatt is pacing. On the trompe l'oeil floor of the entrance hall he is going back and forth, blind on this occasion to the ingenuity of the mosaic, which depicts a vertical cross rising into an azure heaven, or any of the other features which persuade him to keep the place. Last week, while walking round with Arthur to look over the alterations he'd had made, it struck him how much its elegance suited his taste, how well it met his vision of a town house appropriate to the stage he'd reached in life. It's much grander than the one he had at Westminster when he was still making his way. But today there's a more pressing matter. Having decided what he must do, he stops, pulls the silk scarf out of his jacket pocket, winds it round his neck, and pulls it up over the lower half of his face. Just at that moment, when he's screwed himself up to act, he hears Elsie, one of the servants he's recently taken on, come out of the kitchen. 'Will you back for supper, Sir?'

'Yes,' he says sharply, and opens the door. It's little more than a couple of hundred paces, he's measured it, a distance of no import on any other

Misalliances

day, but he fears he's going to be late, so he starts to run.

When he gets there, he despairs. The crowd is fifty deep. No. More than that. By standing on tiptoe, craning round this or that dirty neck, he can just see the scaffold. It hasn't happened yet, otherwise the crowd wouldn't still be here. He begins to push his way through but the mass of bodies is unyielding. Some mouth oaths, stick out an elbow or leg. In desperation, he summons up his most authoritative voice and shouts: 'Make way! King's man!' To his surprise, the sea of heads and shoulders parts. There's a swivelling of querying faces but no one's in his way. He does it again. 'Officer of the King! Let me through!' He's almost made it, mere feet away from where he wants to be, and the only obstacle before him now is the line of soldiers. It's then, as he sees a flash of recognition cross the face of the captain in front of him, that he decides to throw caution to the wind, lower his scarf and take one further step. The officer nods at him, utters one word, 'Sir', and steps aside to make room. Wyatt looks up.

He's been so intent on reaching the front that he's missed the moment when Thomas Cromwell has climbed up on to the scaffold. It must have been more than a moment ago, because the churchman has finished delivering his homilies and Cromwell is speaking now, about his Faith, about the sacredness of the Sacrament, about the ways of the Devil, words which Wyatt does not recognise as rooted in the man's beliefs or actions. It's then that Wyatt, not recognising himself either, begins to cry.

Cromwell falls to his knees and his hands come together in prayer. He closes his eyes. When he opens them, his gaze falls on the man in tears immediately below him, who is well aware that whatever his old friend might say now will be his final words. When they come, they shake him to the core.

'Oh, Wyatt, do not weep. If I were only as guilty as you were when you were taken, I should not be here.'

The leather-clad executioner lifts the head of his axe from the rough planks on which it's been resting. Cromwell gives a glance over his shoulder at the axe-man, and closes his eyes again. Wyatt, who throughout his life has always closed his own when witnessing something like this, does not do so this time. The axe falls, the blood spurts, and the head rolls away. As a satisfied murmur rises from the crowd, he takes a moment to see if any of the blood is on him. It isn't. Then he pulls his scarf back up over his face and shoves his way, all-a-tremble, back through the milling, shifting mass.

As he makes his way back to the Friars, he knows what he must do. The captain of the guard saw him, others might well have done, and - for all his reassuring words to Mason - a move against him is a possibility he can not discount. These days, when that happens, everything's at risk, everything you own, all your money, even those close to you. He has to talk to Tom and Edward.

Part Four

Misalliances

Chapter Thirty-four: The Tower

Wyatt and John Gage, have never been close so it surprises him to receive a word of sympathy from the Constable of The Tower. 'I'm sorry to see you here, Wyatt.'

'Do you know why, John?'

'I'm sorry. I don't.'

As he's taken across into the inner yard, he tells himself off for asking the question. He knows why he's here. It's because of his closeness to Cromwell, which he couldn't have more obviously demonstrated than by brazenly attending his execution. It's taken them seven months to move against him but as Mason predicted, it'll be Norfolk or Suffolk behind it, one or the other, perhaps both. He assumes Mason's also here. Or soon will be.

There are dungeons several floors down but like before, presumably because he's a knight of the realm and a sometime favourite of the King, he's been given a bare but quite sizeable room. It contains a table, a stool, a straw pallet and a bucket. The window looks out over Tower Hill and it consoles him to see the roof of his new house in the distance.

He seats hmself at the table. What he needs now, what he always needs to keep body and soul together, is pen, ink and paper - and a candle

Misalliances

because it's past noon and the light will soon begin to fade. The warder in charge of him has not changed much from the boy who tended to him last time, he's just taller and heavier. Robbie Skinner recognised him immediately.

'Sir Thomas! God's blood, have I got you again? What a coincidence.' And as he walked him up the three flights of steps: 'Let's hope it's not for long, eh?'

When Skinner appears with his supper, Wyatt studies him in the light held aloft by the boy with him. The once thick head of hair has been shaved to a stubble but the lopsided grin is still there, even if it's being given less readily than before. 'Now, Sir Thomas,' he says, as he sets down the tray. 'I've gone up in the world, so if I'm busy, the boy here'll attend to you.'

'As you once did,' Wyatt says.

'Like I did.' Skinner steps back and seems to relax. 'Lord, remember me taking you down to the grating?'

'I've never forgotten your kindness.'

'And then you were out of it for days.'

'I was.' Wyatt needs to be business-like. 'Robbie, I shall need thngs to write with.'

'I can do that, Sir. I've brought a candle. Let's set it up.'

Skinner fetches a holder from the window-sill, takes the candle out of his pocket and sets about lighting it. He smiles with satisfaction as the wick

Misalliances

catches and the flame flares.. 'Right. Pen and paper.'

'Plenty of it, please. And can you have a fire lit? Gets cold these winter nights.'

Skinner is at the door, jangling his keys. 'The boy'll be back in a twinkling.'

He draws the table close to the fire, checks the fullness of the ink-well – it'll do for tonight – and considers the pen. It looks like Skinner has brought him a newly sharpened quill. Good man. The chances are Arthur will have got away. He'll have ducked out the back, got on his horse and will by now be safe in Kent. When they saw the soldiers at the door, he'd said to him: 'Tell Masters Tom and Edward to do what I said if this should happen. Go now.'

The visit he'd made to Austin Friars, a month after Cromwell mounted the scaffold, had told him the likely course of events if they ever came for him. He'd not stayed long, just the time it took to peer through the window into the sitting-room where he'd been received only two months before. As expected, it had been stripped: the furniture, the silver plate, even Cromwell's framed copy of the Mappa Mundi, which had been on the wall in his old house. It was all gone.

He begins to write, jotting down as best he can remember the date and substance of all his letters to the King's late Secretary, because whatever they believe they have against him must lie in

Misalliances

Cromwell's papers. He racks his brains for instances when either of them, if only obliquely, were critical of the King, but he comes up with nothing. To be sure, there were conversations of that kind, but neither he nor Cromwell was careless enough to put into writing anything that could be construed as dissent, let alone treason. Of course, there might be memoes, aide-memoires, which refer to him, but nothing of his making. He's stumped. Of course, it wouldn't be beyond his accusers to come up with something so outlandish it defies commonsense and logic. That's what happened before.

When Skinner comes the next morning, Wyatt says to him: 'I have a request.'
'What?'
'I want you to show me the grating.'
'Why would you want to see that?'
'It's on the floor below, I think.'
'It is.' Wyatt takes out his purse and Skinner recoils. 'Put that away. I don't want your money. You might need it for other things, 'cause I reckon you're going to be here a while.'
'Come, Robbie. You might have gone up in the world, but you can't be earning much.' He takes Skinner's hand and presses some coins into it. 'Will you take me down?'
Skinner sighs. 'Sir, you're going to get me into trouble. Come on, then.'

Misalliances

It's a short flight of steps but it takes him back five years, to the dim, damp passage he stumbled along, half out of his wits, to watch Anne Boleyn being put to death.

They stop by an iron grating. 'It's here,' Skinner says.

Wyatt remembers it as square, and smaller than this. But it couldn't have been, not for him to get his head and shoulders in far enough see what was happening below. 'Can you open it?'

'I can.' Skinner bends his back and with a grunt lifts off the iron-work. 'That's all I'm doing. And don't be long.'

Wyatt kneels down. The aperture is crusted with dry leaves and the wispy, wasted bodies of several summers' flying insects. He brushes them away and leans in. It comes to him why he had such a clear view: whenever the grating was installed it was let into a recess much wider than the vent itself so that the thickness of the fortress's walls didn't get in the way at all. As before, he can see most of The Green, though it's desolate today; there's not so much as a raven on the overgrown grass. Wyatt withdraws his head. 'I didn't see it, you know.'

'What do you mean?'

'The moment she went. I couldn't bear it. I closed my eyes.'

'You'd have heard the noise, though. I know I did.'

'Yes.'

Misalliances

'It was just the one blow. Swift. Then the other noise went up. From them watching. It's always the same, that noise. Like a big wind getting up.'

'Yes, I remember.'

'It was then you folded. I was scared I wasn't going to get you out. I was just a puny lad and you were out cold.'

Skinner heaves the iron screen back into place. 'We'd best be getting back,' he says.

****

When the questioning comes it similarly takes him back to where he was five years ago, the seemingly endless days of interrogation about his relationship with Anne Boleyn. So strong is his sense of absurdity repeating itself that initially he feels nothing but disdain for his questioners, two men in ink-black gowns whom he doesn't know and whose names he initially has difficulty retaining. When he asks them on whose authority they've come, they tell him they are advisers to the King. Lawyers, he assumes, raised up from the Inns of Court to assist with the plethora of actions initiated by an increasingly litigious king. Simon, the younger one - small, pale-faced, not much more than in his twenties – is the clerk, here to do no more than scribe. The other, Shaw, is much older, a big man with a penetrating stare, which reminds Wyatt of Thomas Cromwell, though

Misalliances

Shaw's vowels belong to somewhere far north of Putney. 'There are two charges against you,' this man says. He's eyeing Wyatt's own stash of paper and the pen lying across it. 'Were you writing something for us?'

'Not yet.'

'Then let us begin.'

- You are charged with consorting with the rebel and traitor Reginald Pole.
- Oh, I know where this has come from...
- You are also charged with referring to His Majesty, vulgarly and traitorously, as being 'cast out of the cart's arse'. Sir Thomas, it's nothing to smile about. These are serious charges. They carry the severest penalty.
- I'm smiling because this has all come from Edmund Bonner.
- Doctor Bonner, the Bishop of London, and Simon Heynes, Dean of Exeter. They were in Spain with you.
- The offices they hold don't make them credible witnesses. Forgive my levity, but let me explain. In Spain, Bonner's poor judgement constantly threatened to undermine the work which, as the King's ambassador, I was taking pains to prosecute. I often had to put him in his place – I had to do it again in Paris last year - and he's never forgiven me. No, let me speak. He's a vindictive little man who's trumped up these charges to get his own back. As for

Misalliances

Heynes, he's a nobody, a parish priest who's achieved a prominence in the Church far above his deserving, probably by hanging on to Bonner's coat-tails. The question of whether I'm guilty of the charges you've just put to me comes down to this: whether my story or theirs carries the greater degree of veracity.
- Then we must have your story.
- I hope you are patient men.
- We shall have to be. Let us begin with your relations with Reginald Pole. That takes us back to the French town of Nice, I believe, three years ago. The Holy Roman Emperor and the King of France had arranged to meet there. What are your recollections of that event?
- They came in the *hope* of arranging a meeting. It was by no means cut and dried. Not long afterwards the Pope arrived too, because if the Emperor and King François were able to settle their differences, it would be to his advantage.
- And where was Reginald Pole at this time?
- On the Pope's galley, out in the bay.
- What contact did you have with him?
- I had none. He did make contact with me. He sent me a bottle of wine.
- Why was that, do you think?
- It was an attempt to sweeten me, I thought.
- To extend the hand of friendship…
- There has never been any kind of friendship between myself and Reginald Pole.
- It sounds like he wanted you to be friends.

- Since we were in the same neighbourhood, he was probably afraid I'd send assassins after him.
- That's how he thought of you? Someone out to assassinate him?
- So I was told.
- And that was understood, was it? That if you got the chance, you were to assassinate Pole.
- The King had given the order.
- But you made no attempt to act on that instruction.
- The opportunity never came my way.
- It came John Mason's way. He sailed with Pole and the Pope to Genoa, after the talks between the Emperor and the King of France had come to an end.
- He did. And he and Pole spoke. Mason set all this down in a letter to Cromwell at the time. Not long afterwards, Mason was called home, because Bonner – who was also back by then – had accused him of being in league with Pole. As soon as Mason arrived, the Duke of Suffolk had him arrested. Cromwell mounted an investigation and cleared Mason of any wrongdoing. This is old ground, and the only reason Bonner's raking it over is because Cromwell's no longer with us.
- Doctor Bonner claims Mason's links with Pole were never properly investigated. That's why he's asked for them to be revisited. So justice can be served.

Misalliances

- And this time he's dragged me into it. No doubt with the support of the Duke of Suffolk. Charles Brandon will be part of this. Cromwell's no longer here, so they think they can now make their lies stick.
- The Duke of Suffolk sits on the Privy Council.
- I know.
- So I would advise you not to slander him.
- It's no slander.
- You say Thomas Cromwell cleared Mason of any wrong-doing. Such a judgement won't carry much sway today, will it?
- It should. Whatever it was that took Cromwell to the scaffold, he was once the man the King relied on above all others. You practise the law, so I assume evidence is important to you.
- Of the utmost importance, it goes without saying.
- Then find Cromwell's report on Mason. It'll be a record of the facts. And talk to Mason. I assume he is here? Set our testimonies side by side.
- The facts, then. You were back in England while Mason was talking with Pole on the way to Genoa.
- I was.
- There's no need to go into that. We have the details. So did Mason board the Pope's vessel of his own volition? Or was it on your instructions?

Misalliances

- It was with my approval. After we got Pole's bottle of wine, we thought he might be willing to talk to one of us, if only to find out if we had orders to kill him. Since Mason had had some acquaintance with him in the past, it was agreed he should try to get himself into Pole's company.
- Not to kill him, I assume.
- No, no. That's not how such things are done. It was to gain intelligence. I remember us discussing it over supper before I left. Bonner and Heynes would have been there.
- They *knew* Mason would be seeking Pole's company?
- They certainly knew we needed to take steps to find out what the Pope was thinking, whether he would be prevailing on the Emperor and François to get his Holy War off the ground, since the talks had gone well. That's the intelligence Mason was after.
- And did Mason succeed?
- In the event, all Pole wanted to talk about was whether he was still a target for assassination, and that was the one thing Mason was not prepared to talk about. Nothing Mason did was against the interests of the King. As I said, he sent Cromwell a report. Look in Cromwell's papers.
- We will.
- And talk to Mason.

Misalliances

- In due course. That will do for now, Sir Thomas.
- You'll be putting what I've told you before the Council.
- We are obliged to consult with them.
- Beware of Charles Brandon, then. Test the veracity. It's all about veracity.

****

'Five minutes,' Skinner says.

Mason gets up from his pallet. 'Thomas!'

'How are you, John?'

Skinner turns away as the two men embrace. Mason seems alright, and his room, though smaller than his own, has a window and a fireplace, so he has light and warmth. 'I don't have long, John,' Wyatt says. 'You know what this is about. I thought they must have found something against us in Cromwell's papers, but it's Bonner.'

'I told you he'd make mischief.'

'Have you been questioned yet?'

'Not yet.'

'They're doing me first, then. They've been asking me about Genoa. But – and here's the irony – Cromwell's papers have gone astray, or been removed, so you need to tell them it was all investigated and you were cleared.'

'We could still do with it in writing.'

'I know.'

Misalliances

'Be quick, Sir,' Skinner calls. 'We're coming up to the hour they usually come.'

Wyatt takes Mason's arm and walks him to the far end of the room, beneath the window. 'John, I mentioned something you picked up from Branceter at Loches, that Pole was convinced we'd been sent to kill him.'

Mason is blinking in the pale February sunlight. 'But we weren't.'

'That's not the point. If they ask you about it, say I'd picked it up from Charles. They won't be able to check. As far as our story goes, the first time we set eyes on Branceter was when the French seized him outside that house by the Porte Saint-Denys. And we didn't exchange a single word with him, either then or at any other time.'

Skinner again: 'Sir!'

'Amost done, Robbie. So don't mention Loches, John.'

'I won't. I wouldn't have. What are our chances of getting out of here, Thomas?'

'They've got nothing. Stay strong.'

Skinner is grim-faced on the way back. 'Thank you for that,' Wyatt says, when they descend yet another flight of steps and, safe once more, have time to speak. 'It was important.'

'Don't ask again,' Skinner says. 'Now sit down at that table like you've been there all morning.'

****

Misalliances

- Sir Thomas, you know this as well as I, it's a saying used about criminals getting their cumuppance at the gallows, stepping out of 'the cart's arse' with a noose round their necks.
- That's not its only meaning. It was originally used to refer to items lost while travelling, when a trunk or valise fell out of the back of a cart or carriage, probably after some careless packing. So to say 'I'm out of the cart's arse' also means 'I'm lost' or 'I've fallen out of favour in this or that matter.' Rather like I have at present.
- And you're saying you used it like that in referring to the King...
- If I used it at all. Look, I may have. Two of the most powerful princes in Christendom had come together in friendship, and despite all the protestations they'd made to us of their continuing good will, we were out of the picture. In that situation I might have said to Mason or Blage, or one of the other good men I had with me, 'It looks like the King has been left out of the cart's arse.'
- That's not how Dr. Bonner remembers it. He says – and I quote - 'you feared the King would now be cast out of the cart's arse and, by God's blood, it would serve him right if he were.'
- That's nonsense. I would never say such a thing about his Majesty. Why would I have uttered such words – treasonous words, I agree – in the

Misalliances

presence of two men for whom I had little respect and whose judgement I didn't trust?

It's breakfast time. Skinner brings it. Despite saying the boy would be attending him, he's been coming himself more often than not.

'I've just heard they're on their way again,' he says, as he sets down the bread, pork and mug of ale.

'Do you know if they're questioning Mason yet, Robbie?'

'I don't. To be honest, I don't like to ask. We warders keep ourselves to ourselves. Bit fishy to ask what's going on on other wings. But I've heard something about somebody else. A Lord Lisle and his wife. They're here. Do you know them?'

'I did once.'

Wyatt's appetite for his breakfast has gone. Arthur and Elizabeth Lisle are there because of him, or rather the letters he sent to the King. That's sad. And what will have happened to Anne Basset, their daughter? For all her closeness to Catherine Howard, it's unlikely she'll have escaped the family's disgrace.

****

- So you admit you humiliated Doctor Bonner in Paris?
- Is this another charge?

Misalliances

- No, I'm simply trying to arrive at the full picture.
- He didn't need my help in doing that. He did it to himself constantly. Cromwell knew it. He might even have written a minute to that effect. Have you found the papers I said you should?
- We're still looking.
- I've just realised…you don't need them!
- What?
- It's only just occurred to me. It'll all be in the minutes of the Privy Council. Let's go back. Cromwell knew that Suffolk had played a part in the charges against Mason. In fact, he said Brandon was really aiming at me. There's long been bad blood between me and him. It's what put me here five years ago. Hear me out. Now Suffolk and Cromwell were sworn enemies as well. Their mutual loathing dates back to when Cromwell first became the King's Secretary, because he dislodged Suffolk – and Norfolk – as the King's key advisers. Now, Cromwell was meticulous about putting on record things which might be contentious. So, I would lay a pound to a penny that after he'd finished investigating Mason's alleged links with Pole, he made sure he informed the Council. It'll be in the minutes.
- I don't have the authority to delve into the Privy Council's records.
- Who's on the Council, apart from Suffolk and Norfolk?

Misalliances

- Thomas Seymour, Archbishop Cranmer, Thomas Cheyney…
- Thomas Cheyney's your man. As straight as they come and a good friend of mine.
- Favours shouldn't enter into it…
- All you're doing is asking for a copy of the minutes for…let me think…for October to December 1538. You asked for my story, Mr. Shaw. Are you inclined to give it any credence?
- I don't disbelieve it.
- Then I'm in your hands.
- And that of the Council. Very well, I'll talk to Cheyney. But even then, there's the other charge.
- Which is more serious.
- It is. What if you were to submit in writing an explanation of how that offence came about?
- I don't accept I committed an offence.
- Come, now. Let me speak to you as if I were *your* lawyer. In my experience, a little contrition goes a long way.
- I'd go so far as to admit I spoke rashly …
- That's it. And you intended no malice. If you could write something to that effect, I'm sure it would be helpful.
- I can do that.

Misalliances

Chapter Thirty-five: Queen Catherine

Three hours on the river and she's having to present herself at the dance! 'It's to celebrate your return from Richmond,' Jane Boleyn has told her. 'The King will expect you there.' But not to dance, she thinks, because he doesn't any longer. So here she is, next to him on the dais, itching to be on the floor, but fully aware she can't ask him to take her because he'd be sure to decline and that would embarrass them both. She gives it a while longer and then, having formulated a way of asking, she says: 'My lord, am I permitted to dance?'

She wonders if he's heard above the din the musicians are making, because he doesn't so much as turn his head. She follows the track of his gaze. It appears to be on a very attractive woman immediately below them, a red-head like herself, though the stranger's colouring is closer to orange. And she's older – well she would be, most of the women here are – though it's hard to be sure by how much. She dares to nudge his arm and also to rephrase the appeal. 'Sir, I would like to dance.'

Henry comes to and sits up. His bewhiskered jowls sway towards her. Their eyes meet. He blinks. 'Why, yes, my love. Why not?' He summons the nearest page. 'Bring me Lord Rutland.'

Thomas Manners is there in a matter of seconds: 'Majesty?' A conversation takes place, which consists of the King whispering in

Misalliances

Rutland's ear and the Lord Chamberlain nodding. The only part of it Catherine hears is Rutland saying 'Of course, Majesty' and 'As you wish, Majesty'. By the time the dance in progress comes to an end, Rutland has acquired an ebony staff with a silver ferrule and cap and has taken up position at the foot of the dais. It's a signal that all those on the floor seem to be acquainted with, for they retreat to the sides and a hush falls. Catherine realises with some trepidation that the King is slowly getting to his feet, that she must too, and that she is going to be at the centre of whatever is to happen next. Rutland goes into the middle of the floor, raps on it with his staff and announces: 'Ladies and Gentlemen, the King and Queen.'

'Come, my dear,' Henry says, placing one unsteady foot and then the other on the – thankfully wide – top step of the dais and offering her his hand. The descent is slow, almost cautious, so she's glad she's got hold of him. Eyes will be on them, but she's not going to look for fear of what the faces will reveal. Once they're on the floor, matters improve, for he leads her confidently to the spot Rutland occupied a few moments ago and gives nods of acknowledgement to the crowd. They elicit an immediate commotion of bowing and curtsying and a hubbub of murmurings. Someone shouts: 'Here's to the King!'

The Master of the Revels, Thomas Cawarden, steps forward to reclaim the role usurped by his superior, the Lord Chamberlain, and announces

Misalliances

that the next dance will be a pavane. It's the slowest in the book. Catching on, Catherine catches Cawarden's eye. The nod he gives her confirms her suspicion that the choice of dance is deliberate. But if the King is aware of the ploy, he shows no sign of it. A dozen couples rise to join them, one of which is the red-haired woman and her partner. Catherine recognises him from her days as lady-in-waiting to Anna von Kleve though the name eludes her. The viols, gambas, lutes and recorders strike up and, to her relief, the King capably leads her and the procession behind them round the floor. They circle it three times until the bass viols strike the final note.

'Once more,' Cawarden calls out. When they come to a stop for a second time, the King says: 'My love, why don't you continue with your cousin?' He's beckoning Surrey, who is standing on the sidelines without a partner. 'I need a word with Rutland.'

Catherine isn't fooled: the next dance will have to be something livelier – a galliard, perhaps – and Henry, who must have caught on that the unusual second run of the pavane has been for him, won't be up to its leaps and kicks. Surrey is there next to her, a gratified smile on his face. 'Cousin,' she says, offering him her hand. Cawarden calls out: 'And now, a galliard!'

Surrey's tendency to be physically forward with her must have been inhibited by her change in situation – when he's had to hold her in the dance he's done it unexpectedly loosely - but it doesn't seem to have exerted much of a check on the way he looks at her. When the dance comes to an end she doesn't want to give up her freedom yet so she says to him: 'Come, I need something to drink.'

'What's this, coz?' he says, as he steers her towards the refreshment table. 'Shouldn't you be going back?'

'He's talking to Rutland,' she says. Though he's not. The King is in conversation with the woman with orange hair, or rather – at this precise moment – backing away from her. Surrey has seen it too. 'Ah,' he says, 'the ever importunate Elizabeth Brooke.' He nods to the serving girl behind the table, picks up the glasses she's filled for him and gives one to Catherine. 'It's Gascon,' he says. 'Is that alright?'

She prefers claret but she's not going to quibble. 'Tell me about her,' she says.

'Elizabeth Brooke? What do you want to know?'

'Whatever you can tell me.'

'Are you sure?'

'Come now, cousin. I'm not a child.'

Surrey smiles to himself. 'Very well. There was talk about her and the King. Months ago. Before you.'

'Who is she?'

'She's the sister of the fellow she's with, George Brooke. And the wife of Thomas Wyatt.'

Misalliances

Catherine's heart misses a beat. 'The poet? Who's in The Tower?'

'Unfortunately.'

'It's because of his closeness to Cromwell, isn't it?'

'Apparently. It doesn't look good.'

'No?'

'It's his second spell there. If he does get out it'll be to walk no further than the scaffold.'

'You'd regret that by the sound of it.'

'I would.'

'You're friends.'

'We've exchanged manuscripts from time to time. .'

Catherine notices they are being observed by the serving girl, a pretty thing who can't be much more than thirteen or fourteen. She watches her out of the corner of her eye while Surrey is expatiating on the new verse he's writing. Despite her dislike of him, she has to admit he's cutting a handsome figure this evening in his dark grey doublet, with his hair curled over his ears. It's him the young girl is looking at, of course, and – what's more - he's returning her glances. Positioned as they are, he must be thinking he can ogle the girl unobtrusively, which means he'll be happy to stand here, answering questions about Elizabeth Brooke for as long as she wants him to. She brings him back to that subject.

Misalliances

'Tell me more about *her*,' she says. 'She's just been pestering the King. Do you think that'll be about Wyatt? Getting him released?'

'It'd be in her interests. If Wyatt goes to the block, all his land and money will go to the King. And that'd dash her hopes of a reconciliation.'

'She wants him to take her back?'

'So I heard. Though it won't be out of affection. They've been apart for years.'

'What, then?'

'Money, cousin. What else? It's common knowledge the Brookes are up to their ears in debt. And she has a case. She is still his wife. Personally, I wouldn't fancy her chances even if Wyatt weren't in The Tower. He stopped supporting her years ago, after it came out who she'd cuckolded him with.'

'Who was that?'

Surrey laughs. 'Oh, now you are getting into deep waters…'

'Tell me.'

'Charles Brandon. It made quite a stir when it all came out. At the time, he was married to Henry's sister and it got him banished from court.'

'Well, cousin, what a mine of information you are!'

'I keep my ear to the ground.'

Catherine is back in Thames Street, listening to Thomas Wyatt explain how he last wound up in The Tower, that it was Brandon who did for him. And as for Elizabeth Brooke, if she once finessed

Misalliances

her way into the Duke of Suffolk's bed, which others has she been in? Surrey's gaze has travelled yet again towards the refreshment table. Henry will be wondering where she's got to. She only has one more question. 'Has Elizabeth Brooke been in the King's bed?'

Surrey coolly empties his glass. 'What do *you* think?'

'Ah. And now I'm here, he wants rid of her.'

Surrey purses his lips. 'He won't want her being a nuisance, that's for sure.'

'She won't be. I'll see to that.'

The serving girl is wiping the table-top. Now there are fewer people around it, her gaze is fixed on Surrey in a manner that Catherine – well-versed in such matters – has no difficulty in interpreting. It's an open declaration of availability.

'You'd better go, cousin,' Surrey says.

'Get back to the kitchen!' snaps Catherine, as she passes the table.

The girl does a half-curtsey. 'Your Grace?' She's blushing.

'Back to the kitchen and stay there.'

****

Catherine keeps referring to Lady Rochford as Jane Boleyn, which is how she's always known her. 'Oh, you mustn't call her that, my Lady,' Margaret has told her. Catherine could see why, given the shame and scandal attached to the name

Boleyn, especially if Jane's husband George – late husband George – really did sleep with his sister, Anne, but it's hard to break the habit of a life-time. And, anyway, George was Lord Rochford, so it's not as if his widow is disowning all connection with him. Nonetheless, when Margaret announces Lady Rochford, Catherine doesn't demur, even though she's been on first names with the woman since she was small. Still, if they're insisting on ceremony, she won't get up from her mirror just yet.

'Lady Rochford,' she says, addressing her visitor's reflection. 'Welcome.'

'Your Grace.'

Catherine finishes adjusting her hood, waves Margaret away when she steps forward to assist, smooths down the front of her bodice and stands. 'Poetry, then. Who are we expecting?'

'It's not a large gathering. We don't seem to have those these days...'

'My cousin Harry's coming...'

'The Earl of Surrey, yes. And the Earl of Hertford...'

'Is that Edward Seymour, the late Queen's brother?'

'That's right.'

'Who else?'

'Myself and Margaret Douglas from your ladies. And Sir John Russell, Sir Thomas Cheney and the Duke of Norfolk. The King is in with them now.'

'My uncle. A bit of a family affair, then, with the four of us.'

Jane Boleyn is only family at several removes but she takes Catherine's meaning. 'Well, yes.'

In fact, however distantly they might be related, Catherine appreciates having this particular relative as one of her ladies, because once she became apprised of the whole story of the Anne Boleyn débâcle, she felt nothing but admiration for Jane's wiliness. The fact that this fourth or fifth cousin – whichever it is – weathered all that and retained her place at court, even after it was rumoured she was the source of the reports that led to her husband losing his head, was testament to her having a particular set of skills. The life of the court went on at several levels: that of King's privy chambers; the public life outside of that; and then the hidden, backstair life. Jane Boleyn, Catherine guessed, dwelt more in the latter, where making the right judgement as to what was said to whom and when was an essential skill. They might not be confidantes yet, but if she's got it right, her cousin could be the most useful of her ladies-in waiting.

'Are you reading something yourself, your Grace?'

Catherine takes the poem from the pocket of her gown. It's the only one she knows. She got Culpeper to make a legible copy of it. She quailed when she saw how long it actually was, but it's too late now. 'I am.'

Misalliances

The King is late, which leaves Catherine making small-talk with Edward Seymour about his nephew the prince. Now, here's the eye! He must be thinking 'What's a young girl like you doing with the King?' or 'You may be yet another of her successors but you'll never be the equal of my sister!' It's something Catherine has thought about, the women she's following. And Jane Seymour's brother would be correct in one respect, because as yet there's no sign of her succeeding his sister in the matter of supplying the King with another son. Or any sort of baby. And the way things are going with Henry in bed, that's the way it's likely to stay.

When he eventually arrives, accompanied by her uncle, Cheney and Russell, he's decked out in his usual heavy velvets, chains and furs. It irritates her, this tendency in him to overdress. It makes him look even fatter for one thing, but her main objection is this insistence on formality. For a gathering of this kind, he doesn't need to carry all the regal paraphernalia. As he sits down next to her, she's tempted to say something but in company she'd better not.

'Who's reading for us?' the King asks, as Norfolk takes the seat to his right.

She answers: 'Harry and myself.'

Henry pats her hand. 'Oh yes. Let's begin.'

'Shall I start?' Surrey asks.

Misalliances

'Please do,' the King says. 'We'll save the Queen till after we've had some music.'

Surrey reads two poems - neither of which Catherine finds engaging, though the one about some girl named Geraldine isn't bad - and then the King signals Van Wilder to come forward. Catherine isn't good with names but she's remembered his, not for his skill on his instrument, but because he's a handsome man. She's not fond of lute music; all that plinkety-plonking is a bit boring, especially when it goes on so long. Will there be refreshments, she's wondering, because she's beginning to feel nervous and her mouth has gone dry. At last, Van Wilder concludes his recital and – thank goodness! – sweetmeats and wine are brought in. She takes a glass of claret and finding that no one is apparently willing to engage her in conversation, she sips her wine and takes stock of the company she's in. They all know one another better than she knows any of them, she realises. So much for its being a family affair! Her uncle is talking with the King, Surrey with Seymour, and Jane Boleyn and Margaret Douglas are giving the lutenist all their attention. After her last encounter with Cheney and Russell, she rules out attempting to broach anything with them and, anyway, they appear to be content with their own company. Feeling increasingly apprehensive, she takes the poem out of her pocket and reads it through.

It surprises her to find Cheney standing in front of her. He bows. 'Good day, your Grace,' he

Misalliances

says. 'May I presume to wish you well in your reading?' He smiles reassuringly. 'I'm sure it will be a success.'

'Thank you, Sir.'

'May I ask what you have chosen?'

'It's something by Thomas Wyatt.'

'Ah.' Cheney's eyes open wide. 'That's a brave choice.'

'Because he's in The Tower? It doesn't make him a bad poet.'

'Indeed not.'

'Do you know how he's faring?'

'Quite well, I hear.' He lowers his voice and leans in closer. 'He'd be out if I had my way. But we'll see.'

The King is addressing her. 'Catherine, are you ready?'

'Excuse me, your Grace.' Cheney takes his leave and returns to his place.

The old man's twofold assurances have stilled her nerves. And, really, there's no one here she need be in awe of, so she takes a deep breath and begins:

> *That time that mirth did steer my ship*
> *Which now is fraught with heaviness*
> *And Fortune then bit not the lip*
> *But was defence of my distress...*

Misalliances

She hears Surrey murmur 'Good, good...' though whether that's about the quality of her reading or the poem itself she's not sure. But she can do this. Her voice is steady, and she likes what the verses are saying. They're quite moving. She tries to convey the emotion Wyatt put into them, this lament for a lost, much-loved woman, and feels it working. It's a skill she didn't know she had. She's almost at the end.

> *I suffered so that I might know*
> *That she were mine I might be sure,*
> *And should be while that life endure*

She lays the paper in her lap and looks up. At first, she doesn't know how to read the way they're all looking at her. Was it so bad she's stunned them into silence? Then the murmurs of approval come: 'Well done,' and 'Well read,' and 'My compliments, your Grace'. The King is the last to comment, but he is smiling, if only faintly.

'Whose poem is that, my dear?'

'Thomas Wyatt's, I think.'

'Ah, yes. Wyatt. I thought as much.'

'It's a shame he couldn't be here,' she adds.

'It is.'

The King joins her that night, his night shirt billowing around his portly frame like some fantastical wind has blown in and inflated it. His

Misalliances

greeting is always the same. 'Good evening, my dear.'

'Good evening, my Lord,' she replies, as she always does, moving over in the big bed to make room for him.

'I was wondering,' he says, as he climbs in and the mattress, depressed on his side, tips up on hers, 'would you read that poem for me?'

She's startled. 'Why, yes.'

'Do you have to fetch it?'

'No, it's here.' She rolls over and in the dim light feels for the paper she's only just put down on the side table.

'Ready, my Lord?'

Henry, propped up against the pillows, hands folded over his belly, closes his eyes. 'You may begin.'

When she's finished, she says: 'A man who writes like that can't be all bad.'

Henry still has his eyes closed. 'He's not. But he's foolish and outspoken. He disrespects people and makes enemies.'

'Is that why he's in The Tower?'

'He's in the Tower because he disrespected *me*.' The King sighs. 'Or that's what they say.'

'What they say? Who?'

'The Bishop of London. The Dean of Exeter.'

'And what do *you* think?'

'I'll take advice. I'm seeing Cheney and Russell again tomorrow.'

Misalliances

She's familiar with the moment when the King's breathing starts to become shallow. She's losing him. She'll have to mention Anne Basset and her return to court another time. 'Goodnight, my Lord,' she whispers.

She's climbing the stairs the following morning when she sees Cheney coming down. 'Good morning, Sir,' she says, making a point of stopping. She signals Margaret to wait.

Cheney removes his hat and bows. 'Good morning, your Grace.'

'What brings you here again so soon?' She flatters him with a smile; it always works with old men.

'Oh, you know,' he says, evasively. 'Just matters of state.'

Imitating his manner the previous afternoon, she leans in closer. 'And Thomas Wyatt?'

Cheney blinks rapidly. 'Yes. We did discuss his situation.'

'And how is he now?'

Cheney descends one step. 'He's well. Or he's soon going to be.'

Catherine resumes her climb. 'Good to see you. Thank you.'

It's warm for early March and she decides to go into the garden that afternoon. By that time, she's almost worked out what to say to the King and while her ladies are taking a turn around the lawn, she rehearses the lines, saying them to

Misalliances

herself. And then the King brings it up over supper.

'I'm going to free Thomas Wyatt,' he says, out of the blue, in between mouthfuls of roast goose.

'Are you?'

'He's accepted his fault, admitted he spoke out of turn.' Henry takes a chunk of bread and dips it into the gravy. 'He's always been a bit headstrong.'

'Has he apologised for it?'

'He has.'

'So when are you letting him out?'

The King chews for a while. 'Not quite yet. Your uncle thinks there has to be a punishment. And I agree.'

'From what I hear,' Catherine says slowly, 'Wyatt's a bit of a one for the ladies...' It's one of the lines she's rehearsed.

The King takes a drink and belches. 'No doubt about that.'

'As you can see, I've been finding out about him.' She laughs; it's one of her trills.

The King raises his eyes from his meal. 'You're becoming quite the admirer, Catherine.'

'Just his verses. I've never met the man. But if he does have a weakness for the ladies...'

'He does. I've just said.'

'Then that would explain why his marriage broke down.'

'That was years ago.'

'And I've heard he's not treated her at all well since.' The way the King is looking at her, a mixture of puzzlement and unease, makes her wonder if she's gone too far. Is he calculating what else she might have learned about Elizabeth Brooke? 'That's what I've heard at least.'

'I've heard that too,' Henry says. 'But it's none of *my* business.'

'On the contrary, my Lord, I think it is.' She narrows her eyes. 'If you're looking for a punishment for Thomas Wyatt, I have an idea.'

Chapter Thirty-six: Reprieve

'Good morning, Thomas. I'm to get you out of here.' Cheney waves a paper. 'I've shown this to Gage.'

Wyatt half-rises from his seat. 'At last,' he says, surprised at how croaky his voice sounds. His primary feeling is not relief at what his old friend has just told him but embarrassment at his seeing him here in this bare room with its noxious bucket, straw pallet and all-pervasive smell of damp. Rain has been seeping in from the underside of the window lintel ever since January's clear, frosty skies gave way to thick clouds and unremitting drizzle.

Cheney comes to the table and Wyatt, ashamed of the scatter of pages because they're stained with beer, shakes his hand and attempts a smile. 'The King's come to his senses, has he?'

Cheney takes one of the stools that are still there from the visits made by Shaw and his clerk, though they ceased weeks ago. 'We've been talking to him, Russell and I. And someone else has.'

Wyatt is gathering up his papers. 'I'm not at my most wholesome,' he says. 'Sorry.'

'It could be worse,' Cheney says, taking his fingers away from his nose.

Wyatt stands. 'My warder's been good. I knew him from before.' Despite the things whirling in his head, he's struck by the figure Cheney cuts.

Misalliances

It's not the quality of the man's silks and velvets, or the perfume wafting from the sexagenarian's neatly trimmed grey hair; garments of a similar fineness are waiting for him at Allington and he'll clean himself up soon enough. It's another kind of envy and one he's not finding it easy to rationalise. Through the work he's done for the King, Cheney has acquired influence and authority. Whereas he, Thomas Wyatt, has been rewarded with two confinements in The Tower. Though, that said, without the money the King sent the previous autumn, Allington would have been in serious difficulty. Then he corrects himself: he was owed the money, for God's sake! He shouldn't be commending Henry for settling the monetary debt whilst remaining unconscious of the other kind. 'I'll get my boots and cloak,' he says.

'Just take a moment,' Cheney says. 'I've got the order for release, but it's not quite the end of it.' Wyatt resumes his seat. Cheney leans forward and puts his hands together. 'There's to be a sanction,' he says. 'A punishment.'

'On top of being locked up for three months?'

'You know how this works, Thomas. You had to stay here until they'd completed their investigations.'

'Which they did weeks ago.'

'With you admitting your fault.'

'Such as it was.'

Misalliances

'A fault nonetheless. You spoke ill of the King. And as you know, there are those on the Council who've always been after your blood.'

'Suffolk.'

'And Norfolk. Your closeness to Cromwell did you no favours with him. Look, there's no need to make too much of this. The penalty is still to be settled on. And you won't be losing Allington.' Cheney immediately sees what's in Wyatt's face. 'Oh, you didn't know…'

'That they were minded to take it? I expected no less.'

'They haven't taken it. The order's been rescinded.'

'How far had it gone?'

'As far as I know, Richard Southwell went and sent everyone away and seized everything of value. The usual practice. He's a friend, isn't he?'

'He was.'

'I imagine he still is, which should make it easier to get your things back.'

Wyatt goes over to the pallet, pulls off the canvas slippers Skinner got for him and reaches for his boots. 'You said you thought someone else had been talking to Henry. Any idea who?'

Cheney gets up, takes Wyatt's cloak from where it's hanging behind the door, and walks over to where Wyatt is struggling to get his boots on. 'My guess would be Catherine.'

Wyatt puts the boots aside. 'How odd,' he says.

Misalliances

Cheney lays down the cloak. 'Your feet have swollen. Too little exercise.'

Wyatt picks up the slippers. 'Must have. It's not far to the Friars. I'll wear these.' He looks up at Cheney. 'I meant Catherine. If she had been speaking on my behalf, that'd be odd.'

'She's been taking an interest.'

'Has she?'

'Just these last few weeks she has.' Cheney laughs. 'I began to think there might have been something between you.'

'I barely know her.'

'It must be your verses, Thomas. She read one the other day at one of the King's gatherings.'

Wyatt takes his cloak gets to his feet and drapes it over his shoulders. 'I don't suppose you could send a message down for me?'

'To Allington? Of course.'

'I'm not up to the journey just yet. And I'm not even sure I've got a horse.'

'Get your strength back first. What do you want me to say?'

'Just that I'll be at The Crutched Friars. If there's no one at Allington, they'll be nearby at Boxley Abbey, Poynings' place. '

'I'll make sure someone comes up for you.'

'My man Edward.'

'I'll see to it. You've got servants at the Friars?'

Misalliances

'I should have.' Wyatt crosses to the table and gathers his papers. 'This punishment. Any idea what it might be?'

'It won't be much. He'll probably send you away again. That's what he usually does.'

****

He tells Elsie to boil some water so he can wash, and asks the cook what she has in for supper. He hardly knows these people, but they've stayed. Apparently, Arthur has been back several times to see them.

'He needn't have worried, Sir,' Elsie tells him. 'We wasn't goin' anywhere. We knew you'd be back.'

'We've been giving the place a good clean,' the cook says. Her name comes back to him: Mrs. Anders. Judith. 'The winders 'ere, never seen the like. We've been busy, 'aven't we, Els?'

'We 'ave. Made it as comfy as we could. Your room's ready. You go up when you like.'

'You'll need your rest after where you've been,' Judith adds. The women stand together, their hands clasped in front of them: Elsie small and wiry, Judith plump, forearms the size of hams. Both have kindly faces.

'Thank goodness you've been let out,' Elsie says. 'Some don't make it. We seen 'em, Jude, 'aven't we? Up on the 'ill.'

'We 'ave.'

347

Wyatt has begun to feel extraordinarily tired. 'I'm going to lie down,' he says.

It's a joy to be on a proper mattress again but he doesn't go straight to sleep. Allington's on his mind. Not its people; they'll have gone to Boxley as he said they should. And it'll be easy enough to get back the things they took. Unless they found the money. Money makes for venality, so it could be harder to get that back. His thoughts move on to what else Henry might have in store for him, and that question keeps him awake. It'll be as Cheney said, surely. Another sojourn abroad. When he last met the King he intimated as deftly as he could that he was keen to retire, that he wanted to spend more time at home now that he had a baby son; that barring some conflagration in France or the Low Countries which required his specific knowledge and expertise, he'd like to be done with travelling. It'd be just like Henry to deny him that now.

 He'll say nothing when he gets home. He and Lizzie had barely begun to renew their connection before he was sent off to France; they need to develop a family life together. Another separation would be a bitter pill to swallow, but they'd simply have to manage it.

 Underpinning all this, though, is the very something he doesn't know how to manage. It's been dogging him for years, ever since, on the old bowling-green at Greenwich, he revealed to Henry

Misalliances

he'd once been close to Anne Boleyn. Everything in his life since has been coloured by that confession. His three-year exile to Calais; his near-miss with the scaffold that took Anne; the second exile, to Spain; his half-year in France and the Lowlands; his latest incarceration, again against the backdrop of the scaffold, with a further sentence pending. If he's got anything about him at all, and he believes he has, he ought to put a stop to this continual cycle of being favoured one minute and disfavoured – persecuted - the next.

Lizzie's always said Henry's never got over Anne, that he's still tortured by the suspicion she never loved him; that Thomas Wyatt came first in her affections even after she became Queen. 'He's jealous of you, Thomas. That's the truth of it.'

His thoughts are getting away from him, drifting away into the mists of sleep. He's going under, but before he does the voice in his head says: 'It has to stop...'

Misalliances

Misalliances

Part Five

Misalliances

Misalliances

Chapter Thirty-seven: An Accounting

His head's thick from the wine - even Damaris was slurred of speech and unsteady on her feet by the end of the evening's celebrations – but he's risen early because he wants to take a look round before everybody else is up. According to Edward, it could have been worse. They hadn't found the money. He has the list, but he wants to see for himself what has gone. He begins in the parlour where most of the silver and gold plate was always kept. There's nothing there, apart from the pot in which Lizzie likes to put flowers. He surveys the bare walls; the tapestries must have been torn from their battens because all that's left are limp shreds of cloth. He had been expecting carelessness of this kind, but tapestries can be repaired. There's a good man in Maidstone.

    He moves on to the great hall. They've taken his father's banners. They're all very old and unlikely to still be in one piece after being carted up to Whitehall and then brought back again. Truth be told, he'd only make a fuss about the one marking the old man's attendance at the meeting between Henry and François, twenty years ago, at Balinghem, the gaudy affair that's come to be known as the Field of Cloth of Gold. He bought Jane a gown in that material as a wedding present; he'll have to ask her if it's still there. If they've taken tapestries and banners, they wouldn't have been above ransacking the women's garde-robes.

Misalliances

On the way upstairs he meets Madeleine coming down.

'Are you ready for breakfast, Sir?' she asks, straightening her cap.

'Leave it for now,' he says. 'I'll be down shortly.' Something occurs to him. Southwell had ordered all the servants to leave within seven days, but the only ones who had were Miriam and Peter. Madeleine said she thought that might have been for their own reasons rather than out of odedience to the King's man. She's reached the bottom of the stairs and he calls after her. 'Did you say you knew where Miriam and Peter were going?'

'Canterbury, Sir. She has a cousin there. I told Mister Edward.'

'They were a couple, were they? Her and Peter?'

'They were planning to be, I think.'

'Did you lose anything?'

She's fiddling with the waistband of her skirt. 'I did.'

'What?'

She comes back up. 'I can show you if you want.'

He's never been in Madeleine's room before. It's sparsely furnished – a bed, a garde-robe, a joint stool - but it has a big window and is not a bad place to retire to at the end of a working day. The principle of looking after his servants is something he's always believed in, and it pleases

Misalliances

him that at some point – probably in his father's time – that was put into practice.

She goes round to the other side of the bed and bends to pick something up. The clinking of loose glass tells him what it is. He knew she had it. 'Do you remember this?' she asks, as she lays the broken mirror on the bed. She stands back to see his reaction.

'Of course, I do,' Wyatt says. 'I bought it for your sister in Italy.'

'It looks like they tried to prise out the stones.'

'And shattered the glass.' One of the stones is almost out. He sits and presses it back in. 'These are emeralds. They were probably trying to pocket them.'

Madeleine goes to the garde-robe and takes out a green gown. Its fabric shimmers in the brittle early morning light. 'Which would explain this as well,' she says. She holds it up for him to see. It looks like a knife has been taken to it. It comes back to him: visiting the shop on The Strand with Joanna, her saying she couldn't wear something so fine.

'I bought her that as well,' he says. His tone has become sombre.

'I know. What use was this to them?'

He resists taking it from her. 'The stones round the neck, I imagine'

There are footsteps on the stairs. Lizzie's in the door-way. 'I heard voices,' she says. 'What are you doing?'

Misalliances

Wyatt only half-turns his head. 'Taking stock of what's gone,' he says.

'Oh.' Lizzie comes in and exchanges glances with Madeleine. 'That's a lovely gown. Whose is it?'

'It was my sister's.'

'Joanna's...'

'Yes.'

Wyatt gets up. 'We'll have it put right,' he says to Madeleine. 'And the mirror.' He turns to Lizzie. 'And we'll get your jewellery back.'

Thank God they hadn't taken any of the horses. Perhaps Allington's horse-flesh wasn't considered worthy enough. Arthur's there with the stable boy, grooming his mare. He stands there shy, hiding behind the dark thickness of his cowlick. 'Morning, Sir,' he says. 'Was she alright for you yesterday?'

'She was. I was glad to see her when I got back to the Friars.'

'I rode yours down that day they came for you. Thought he'd have the wind.'

'Edward said.' Wyatt goes over to the stallion's stall. It comes forward at the sight of him and gives a low neigh. 'Hello, old friend,' he says, stroking its nose. 'I'll take you out later.' He turns to Arthur. 'I'm surprised they didn't take this one. Did they come and look?'

'They did. More interested in gold, I think.'

'Which is all safe.'

Misalliances

'It is. All done like you said.'
'Have you seen Mister Edward?'
'He's gone off to Canterbury.'
'Ah, yes.' Wyatt remembers. They'd agreed last night they should try to bring Miriam and Peter back. He doesn't remember Edward saying he'd do it today, but never mind. 'Then it's just the two of us. It's time we went and got our gold. You and I can manage it, can't we?'

Arthur pats the mare's rump. 'I'm sure we can. I'll go and get a barrow.'

They cross the moat and take the path that leads to the farm and the fields. Workers are sowing seed in the nearest one. Wyatt turns to Arthur. 'Did anyone leave from here?'

Arthur follows his gaze. 'They weren't told to.'

'So it was only the house.'
'That's right. And Mister Edward told them not to till they were forced to.'

It's news to Wyatt. 'That was sensible of him.'
'And brave.'
'That, too.'
'Are we going back to the Friars? To finish the work?'
'We must. Though there's not much left to do, is there?'
'There is. All the painting we talked about.'
'It's been three months. We'll have lost those men you had.'

Misalliances

'The masons and joiners had finished. It's painters we need now. Decorators. D'you want me to go up and find some? Get things started again?'

'As long as you're not needed here.'

'Nothing that can't wait. Judith and Elsie are still there, are they?'

'They are. You gave them enough to keep them comfortable for a good twelve months. They weren't going anywhere.'

There's activity in the slaughter-house, blood on the brick floor behind it. 'They'll have been doing the spring lambs,' Arthur says.

They come to the woods which curl down from the park to run alongside the lake. A dozen paces in, where the shade begins to encroach, Arthur stops at a rise in the leaf-deep ground. At its base is a bush and a growth of bracken. Wyatt, reluctant to admit that he couldn't have been sure of finding the icehouse on his own, says: 'You did a good job hiding it.'

Arthur begins to hack at the bush's roots with the mattock he's brought. 'We just stuck this hornbeam in and put some ferns round it.' He carries on working away. 'You were right about them coming, Sir. How did you know?'

'I didn't. Not for sure.'

'But you thought they might...'

'There were signs. And I knew if they did, they'd be having a good look round.' The removal of the bush has revealed a rectangle of bricks framing an iron door.

Misalliances

'They did that alright,' Arthur says, giving the door a hefty tug. The door creaks open and out comes a waft of chilly air and the unmistakeable odour of meat. Only now does he give Wyatt a grin. 'But they missed this.' He hitches up his britches. 'I'll go down and then you hand me the lantern. It's not far.' He backs in, his boots clanging on the rungs of the ladder. 'Can I have the light?'

There were twenty bags of coin. Wyatt remembers counting them. A hundred sovereigns in each. And they're all in the barrow. It's his windfall from the king, who's as capricious about who he smiles upon as he is about locking them up. It wasn't as much as he'd asked for but it'll see them through. Arthur's still busying himself below. 'That's all of it, isn't it?' he calls down.

Arthur's voice rises and his head appears. 'Just the account books.' Wyatt's forgotten them. It was Edward's idea: 'If you think they might come,' he'd said, 'then we've got to hide everything 'cause what Allington's worth is all in there and they'll be wondering why there's not more in the coffers.'

Arthur hands up one leather-bound volume after another and then disappears for longer than usual. There's the sound of papers being shuffled. Eventually he appears with a book that's not fared its spell in the dark as well as the others. 'That's it,

Sir,' he says, as he hands it over. 'But be careful with this'un.'

The book's binding is broken and its pages have come unstuck. Wyatt waits till Arthur has finished closing the door. 'What happened here?'

'What, Sir?'

'This. It's in pieces.'

'Sorry. It was dropped when we was putting it down. I'll just climb up and uncover the vents. We don't want things going off now it's getting warmer.'

Wyatt closes the book as best he can and puts it under his arm.

Once the money's locked away in the strong room, he takes the book into his study to tidy it. He dislikes seeing any book damaged or in disarray. But it's not just that. It's last year's and he wants to look through it because it's a record of Allington's near-fall and revival, of how bad things had once been.

He wasn't sure it was going to happen. Last July, after the execution, he'd come back with images in his head that refused to recede: Cromwell's head bouncing across the scaffold floor; the excited ugliness of the crowd as he'd pushed his way through to get away; the moment he'd looked back to see if he'd been seen by anyone other than the Captain of the guard; the sight of the men with the buckets of water, sloshing away the blood. Then, despite his having

Misalliances

been there and been seen there, the money came. More than any smile or whispered word, it showed he was still in favour. Nonetheless, still nagged by an insecurity he could no more banish than the pictures in his head, he ordered everything – all the money except for a single bag of sovereigns - to be hidden in the ice-house. Rightly ordered it, given what happened in the first weeks of the New Year. As it was, according to Edward, Southwell's men had been surprisingly incurious about how little was in the coffers.

Only about a third of the book's pages are secure, where the glue has held. The rest are loose and been stuffed back in without much care; they're all out of order. Nobody had told him about the mishap. Perhaps they thought it didn't matter. He'll tell Edward to start a new book, backdate it with the records he's been keeping in his cottage.

It takes him a while to sort out the pages, to put them to rights, but it does him good, quietens the disorder in his head. He sets the book aside. Then, thinking he should tidy up his desk, he looks at what's on it. He can see the dog-eared corners of some letters from Cromwell. On top of those are the discarded drafts of the verses he was working on before he and Arthur went up to work on the Friars. And on the top of the pile – he'd just put it down there last night since he was dog-tired – is his statement to the Privy Council, which he'd copied out in the absence of anything else to fill his time once Shaw and Simon had stopped coming. He picks the document up and uncovers something he doesn't recognise. It's a quarto-size piece of paper, not the kind he uses, folded in two. He opens it. The hand is angular, child-like:

> *Sir Thomas*
> *The child is not yours. Ask Maddelin.*
> *M.*

'What in God's name...!' He realises he's said the words out loud.

Damaris is in the doorway. 'Excuse me,' she says, 'I heard you were in here and since we didn't have much of a chance to talk last night...'

Perplexity always tends to make him short-tempered, especially if he's being interrupted in the midst of it, and he's in a swell of it which will engulf him if he doesn't maintain his equilibrium. He's about to send her away but she's a good person and he needs some goodness on his side right now.

Damaris has seen him like this before when he's struggling with something, and his failure to greet her makes her think she shouldn't be bothering him. 'You're busy,' she says. 'I'll find you later.'

'No, it's alright,' he says, putting the note down. 'Come in.'

She seats herself on the settle next to his desk. 'I just wanted to say, I'm very pleased you're back, and...' She pauses like she's shy of finishing. 'And that you're safe.'

'For now,' he says.

'You said there might be something else...'

'Probably being sent away again. Nothing more than that.'

'Oh.' Damaris is conscious of his eyes on her. She's put on the red gown she was wearing the day he came back from the Low Countries. He liked her in it, she knows that, even if he hadn't said so. If someone were to ask her what she's doing, she wouldn't be able to articulate it – she's unversed in the he and she of things as that business with Tom demonstrated - but she likes it when his eyes are on her. She smooths down her skirts.

'It's better than going to the scaffold.'

'Did you think you might have been?'

Wyatt fingers the note, which is still looking up at him. He forces himself to be talkative. 'Oh, it was certainly on the cards but I managed to convince them I'd not done anything deserving that.'

'I was afraid you might have.'

'No, as I said at supper, I have enemies and...' He stops. 'What made you think that?'

'I was next door when Mister Mason came to tell you Thomas Cromwell had been arrested.'

He pushes the note away. 'That wasn't what got me into trouble. Or not directly.'

'I thought it might have been the other thing you talked about.'

'The other thing?'

'Catherine Howard.'

'You thought I was in The Tower because of her?'

'It crossed my mind, since she's now Queen. Didn't it yours?'

'No, it didn't. None of that matters. Otherwise, she wouldn't be the Queen.' He picks up the note again and looks at it. 'Did you hear everything?'

'Enough to know you must keep your distance.'

'I intend to.' He folds the note between his fingers and sits back. 'What do you think of me?'

'You know what I think of you.'

'Do I?'

'You err now and then, but all men do. I think you're a good man.'

'Whoever wrote this,' he says, handing her the note, 'must have thought so too, though I wish they'd shown it some other way.' She's taking longer to read the two lines of childish script than their brevity requires. 'It could have been left weeks ago,' he adds. 'I've only just found it.'

'It'll be from Miriam.'

'Will it?'

'I'm certain of it.'

'You know about this?'

'A little.' She sighs. 'Madeleine told me something a year ago that she'd also told Miriam. I

Misalliances

didn't think it added up to much. These girls lead unexciting lives. I think they let their imaginations run away with them.'

'Something that would explain this?' He taps the note.

'It could. It's best you hear it from Madeleine.'

That evening he sits up late. He's thought of talking to Edward to find out what he knows, but decided it's best restricted to the small circle already involved. It's very late. The conversation he has to have with Lizzie will have to wait till morning.

Wyatt does believe in Fate and he's not surprised it has other ideas. At this hour, the tread outside his door can only be one person's. She's in the doorway in her nightgown.

In the light of the candle Lizzie's face is pale and creased with sleep. 'Thomas, why are you still up?'

'Come and sit,' he says.

She takes the place Damaris occupied earlier, puts her candle down on his desk and draws her shawl around her. 'What is it?'

'I got this today.' He pushes the note across the desk and watches her face as she takes it and reads. 'I've spoken to Madeleine about it.'

Lizzie retreats from the light of her candle. 'Did she send it?'

Misalliances

He pulls his candle closer so she can see his face. 'She says Miriam must have, before she ran away with Peter.'

She puts the note back on the desk. 'What nonsense! I'm surprised you've given it a moment's thought.' Her voice rises. 'Francis is yours, Thomas. How could you begin to think I...' Her voice dwindles away.

'Madeleine says that Tom spent the night in your bed once. After I'd come back from Spain. I was up at Greenwich. Jane was at Bishopsbourne. You were the only two in the house.'

'Madeleine's a silly girl. They all are.'

'Not so silly to share with Miriam something she'd made up.'

Lizzie rises. 'I'm going back to bed.'

'Please sit down.'

'I'm not staying here to have my character blackened by the word of a couple of serving girls.'

'Sit. Please.' He picks up the note. 'I'm sure this is nonsense. But I don't think it all is.'

Lizzie sits back down and slumps. 'Thomas, it was ages ago.'

'But it did happen...'

'It was nothing.'

'Then tell me about it.'

'Tom came in that night, soaked to the skin. It was wild outside. He knocked on my door.'

'And you let him in.'

'He looked unwell. He'd been drinking.'

Misalliances

'He was drunk...'
'Not being loud or anything.'
'What did you say?'
'I must have said something about the state he was in. Asked where he'd been. I was concerned.'
'What did he say?'
'None of it made much sense...' She lifts her eyes. 'He asked if he could stay.'
'As in spend the night with you?'
'He didn't say that. He needed looking after. I lit a candle, sat him down on the bed and helped him out of his wet clothes. I went to put them in the dressing-room and when I got back he was fast asleep. I pulled the covers over him and went back to bed.'
'Next to him...'
'Yes, next to him.' Lizzie comes into the light. There's sorrow in her face. 'It was nothing.'
'You should have told me.'
'How could I? And you weren't here as usual.'
'Oh, thanks for that...'
'And by the time you came back, it no longer mattered. Things went on as normal. I've never brought it up with Tom, nor he with me.' She takes to the shadows again. 'I suppose you'll be talking to him.'
'No. I don't think so.'
'May I go back to bed?'
'Of course you may.'

Misalliances

The next morning he looks for Damaris and finds her in the chapel. It's chilly and she's wrapped up in her winter coat. While he's waiting for her to finish praying, he notices one of the windows is broken.

'I'm sorry,' he says. 'May we talk?'

'Here?'

'It might as well be.' He sits down next to her. 'I've spoken to Lizzie.'

'Has it all been sorted out, then?'

'Not really.'

'What did she say?'

He tells her. When he's finished, she says: 'And you don't believe it *was* nothing...'

'I don't know. What do *you* think?'

'What do *I* think?'

'What with one thing and another I've been away a lot. You've been here.'

'I wasn't then.'

'The thing is, the baby came early.'

'Not by much. It's hard to be exact with these things, isn't it?'

'It came very early. And was as healthy as could be.' He's staring at her as if what he'd like to say might be better left unsaid.

She speaks for him: 'You'd have been happier if it had come later.'

'I would.'

'She always said April.'

'The end, not the beginning. I thought she might have got it wrong. Being with child the first time. And the middle of May would have made more sense.' He's looking round the chapel like he's seeing it for the first time. 'I must get that window fixed.' He turns to look at her. 'Have you ever seen anything between her and Tom?'

'Like what?'

'Anything that was out of place.'

'Thomas...'

'Haven't we always been honest with one another? Me with you and you with me?'

'Thomas, don't...'

'You *have* seen something...'

'It was just the once. I didn't know what to make of it.'

Misalliances

Chapter Thirty-eight: Letters

Catherine has letters. For a month or so after the wedding she was receiving a good dozen each day, mostly from the heads of minor families offering their congratulations and presuming to offer their services should she be in need of maid-servants, horse-grooms and the like. Since then, her daily delivery has shrunk to two or three and more often than not they are responses to something she has ordered or requested. The first is from John Scott and contains swatches of material for the gowns they discussed when she last received him; the second is from Anthony Browne about the horses she'll want to take to the North when they begin the royal progress; and the third – the handwriting is feminine, so she skims down to the signature – is from Mary Lassells. The last she heard of her she was at Chesworth House with Joan and Katherine. She reads the opening lines which contain nothing more than the flattering felicitations she's become used to and puts the letter down. She'll read it later. A visit to the Master of the King's Horse is a more exciting prospect than anything Lassells is likely to be offering. Or importuning.

****

Wyatt has decided to leave things as they are. If he brings up what Damaris saw that afternoon, or has

Misalliances

it all out with Tom, the furore doesn't bare contemplating. Things will get better. Lizzie will begin talking to him again, she'll come back to sharing his bed, and they'll go on as before. Time heals. It always does.

He's in the stables preparing to take a horse out, not for any purpose but to ride round the park, when Madeleine comes to tell him a messenger has come from the King. They've not spoken since he and Damaris sat down with her. But in the normal run of things they wouldn't. Now, as he follows her back to the house, she lingers.

'I'm sorry, Sir,' she says, as he comes alongside.

Striding on, he addresses her over his shoulder. 'What for?'

She catches up with him. 'If Miriam hadn't made mischief like she did, there wouldn't have been any reason for me to say anything. And I wouldn't have.'

'Things will out,' he says. 'They always do. It's not always a bad thing,'

Her face crumples and she pulls out a handkerchief. 'I think it is. It might be best if I went.'

'Went where?'

'There's a place going in town. Edward's told me about it.'

Wyatt stops. 'It'd be a shame,' he says.

'But you think I should?'

Misalliances

'Go and see. Get Edward to take you. And if you're to their liking, say you can start the first day of May.'

'I am sorry. I don't make mischief, Sir.'

'People do,' he says. 'And more often than not they make something out of nothing. Which is what this was. Where's this messenger?'

'In your study.'

The letter is from the King, though the hand is likely to be Wriothesley's or Sadler's.

> *Sir Thomas.*
> *I send you greetings. It would please me to see you at Dover Castle*
> *on 20th. inst. There is a matter between us that requires resolution and*
> *there are some others concerning the Calais Pale which I want you to be*
> *apprised of. In the first instance, report to William Fitzwilliam, the Lord*
> *Privy Seal*
>
> *Henry R.*

He weighs up the tone. It's cordial enough. Calais. There was a time he knew it intimately. In his time as High Marshal, he reckons he laid eyes on every flood-gate, every channel, every furlong of crumbling embankment within the Pale's twenty or so square miles; and later, when Henry recalled him to conduct a survey of the town's vulnerabilities, not just to the sea but also to the French, he became familiar with Calais' gates, walls and watch-towers, all of which were showing signs of salt-induced decay. Somewhere he has a copy of the report he submitted, much of it informed by the expert eye of George Lambert, a local surveyor, though that was no more than a dry reduction of their spray-soaked experience out at the Rijsbank Tower or on the wind-buffeted ramparts of the castle. Apart from Lambert, no one knew the Pale's endemic weaknesses as well as he did back then. Fitzwilliam, a former captain of Guînes and Lieutenant of the Castle, has a smattering of that knowledge, though his mainly resides in that of a military kind, how best to deploy the Pale's troops along its porous borders. Cromwell's successor has never quite left his days at Calais behind him and his presence at Dover suggests something other than flooding is rising across the water.

****

Mary Lassells as one of her ladies-in-waiting? No, no. She doesn't even like her. She screws up the letter, takes it over to the fire and watches it burn. She's still there, warming herself, when Jane Boleyn enters. 'Oh, you're back,' she says to her. 'Come and sit.'

Misalliances

Jane seats herself on the end of the daybed and casts a wary eye round the room. 'Are we alone? No Margaret?'

'She's gone to lie down.' Catherine giggles. 'I think I must have worn her out. We spent most of the morning choosing horses and the afternoon riding them.'

'She doesn't have much stamina, does she?'

'Unlike you, you mean...'

'I don't do so bad.'

For an older lady, she doesn't, Catherine has to give her that. Though, when the moment's right, she might suggest she tone down the rouge. It really doesn't go with the wisps of grey hair that have begun to show. 'So, tell me,' she says. 'What have you found out?'

'Well...' Jane Boleyn moves closer. 'The gentleman in question has been unwell...'

'Has he?'

'So I had to risk going to his rooms. It's alright, he was alone. I told him that Coxon would soon be introducing himself, and that he'd be bringing messages in future.' Jane pauses to fiddle with the straps of her bodice. 'As for meeting, he doesn't think there'll be an opportunity till we're in the North.'

'But there'll be more people around us than ever then. Thousands of them.'

'He thinks there'll be opportunities.'

'Very well.'

'Are you absolutely sure of Coxon?'

Misalliances

'I am. A little favouring goes a long way with a man.'

'Then he can take your next letter.'

'I'm about to write it.'

'Good.' Jane Boleyn smiles, and if there had been an observer to this tête-à-tête they would have said smiling wasn't her forte. 'Will you need me again? There's some favouring of my own I'd quite like to attend to.'

'No. Margaret will put me to bed.'

Telling herself off, she lights a candle. She really ought to write her letters when it's still light. But at least there'll be no summons from Henry. He's spent the day with *his* horses and sent word he's tired and would she mind keeping to her own bed tonight? Silly man; she doesn't mind at all. She dips the quill in the ink, ponders for a few seconds, and begins to write.

Master Culpeper
I pray send me word how you do. I've heard you are sick, which will trouble me until such time as I see you and speak with you, which I trust will be soon...

Chapter Thirty-nine: The Sentence

Wyatt's sleepless night at the castle means he's not at his best. But something has come from it because now he's sure what he must do when he gets home.

He's about to take his horse through the first of the gates when he sees John Russell coming out to his carriage. 'I'll see you this evening, John,' he calls. 'I'll send a man down to wait for you. In case you've forgotten the way up from the road.'

Russell puts his hat on. 'Thank you, Thomas. I may well have.'

Wyatt rides on, pleased that Russell is still intending to take up his invitation to break the journey back to London with a night at Allington. Like Thomas Cheney, John Russell has been at court a long time and if anyone has an insight into what he's being ordered to do, where that could have come from, it's likely to be him.

He'd spent the previous afternoon participating in an inspection of the Dover seafront and the castle's fortifications. 'That's why you're here,' Fitzwilliam had told him that morning, presumably unaware of the other reason. 'I requested it. No one else who's coming knows the first thing about rebuilding a castle's defences. You and I do. Dover's safe enough. The real

Misalliances

problem is the fortifications at Guînes. I want you over there to see what needs to be done.'

After that, he felt certain his sentence was going to be a couple of weeks in the Pale, a month at most. But what the King had in mind was something quite different, as he'd learned after supper.

He had only once before been invited to so late a private audience. That was at Richmond Palace, the occasion when Henry insisted he tell him what he knew of Anne Boleyn's time at the French court. Still in his twenties then and making his way, he'd been terrified of revealing what he'd learned from someone who was there.

As he winds his way out of Dover's streets towards the road north, he takes consolation in the fact that this time, oddly, he hadn't been apprehensive at all about being alone with Henry. Whether this was due to the toughening of spirit that comes with age and facing life's challenge - he's no longer the untested young man who William Brereton ushered into a much grander, though just as dimly lit, chamber a decade ago – or to his having lost all respect for the man, he's at a loss; the mind governs in mysterious ways what causes fear and what doesn't. He even wonders whether it's because he's resolved to free himself – some way or other – from his ungrateful King.

At Richmond, he'd come to the conclusion that Henry's advanced state of drunkenness was the only possible explanation for his reacting so measuredly to what he was being told, which was, in a nutshell, that Anne had been known by many men in France. But last night, though the King was again well in his cups, what he had to say was, ultimately, anything but measured.

'What most concerns me about you, Thomas,' he began, 'is your lack of governance. You seem to find it difficult to do what reasonable people – and I include myself in that number – would consider right.'

At that point Wyatt had dared to interrupt: 'If you are referring to what I said about your good self, Majesty, I admit I was headstrong. Again, I apologise.'

'It's not that, simply. It's in the way you live your life.'

'Majesty?'

'You know why you are here?'

'It's to be punished, chastened, for speaking ill of you.'

'Chastened, yes. That's the word. I find it wanton, the way you live your life. It's time you had a greater regard for consequence. It's come to my notice that you have never done right by your wife.'

'My wife? What has she got to do with any of this?'

'Hush. So what you will do is take her back.'

'Your Majesty, you demand too much...'

'Enough! You will take her back.' Then came a pause for breath and a menacing embellishment.

Misalliances

'If I find you are still with the Darrell woman or, mark this, in the company of any other woman, you'll pay with all you have. *All* you have. Do you understand?'

He said he did, whereupon Henry reached for his glass of wine, took a gulp, and said: 'Good. It would pain me, Thomas, to see you on the scaffold so see it's done. You're pardoned. We want you at Calais within the fortnight.'

He's on the London road; it's longer in terms of miles, but it carries traffic from the coast so it's well looked after and an easier, faster route than cutting across country through barely traversible lanes. By the time he stops at Canterbury to rest and water his horse, he's worked out what he needs to say to Lizzie, but what's still eluding him is why, or how, Henry has come up with this particular punishment. It's tantamount to gelding him.

It's nothing to do with morality, he's sure of that. Henry presents himself as an advocate of right Christian behaviour, but it's never been in the forefront of his driving forces. Malice has, though. Can it really be that the King is still jealous of his relationship with Anne Boleyn ? So much so that he'd come up with this? There's a piece missing somewhere.

A sexton or verger has sidled up, a slight man with crooked legs, which explains his shuffling gait.

Misalliances

'Sir, you can't have your mare here. It's not allowed.'

'Is that so?' Wyatt gets up. 'Then good day to you, vicar.'

The man takes a step back and cracks a smile. 'It's Sir Thomas, isn't it? I've only just recognised you.'

'It is.'

'I do apologise. It's an honour to have you here. The King came through only a few days ago.'

The man is still smiling but Wyatt's not feeling much disposed to reciprocate. 'I'm on my way back from seeing him.'

'Well, then. Please. Sit as long as you like. Can I get you anything? Some wine, perhaps?'

'Tell you what,' Wyatt says, moving towards his horse, 'stuff your wine up your arse. And your precious grass.'

Supper turns out to be a quiet affair. For his part, he simply tells them the King wanted him to take part in a review of Dover's fortifications. Only Damaris seems minded to query the succinctness of his story and then only tacitly: a long stare and a raise of the eyebrows.

By the time John Russell's carriage draws up, candles have been lit and Lizzie, for one, has gone to bed. While his guest eats, he tells him what's happened and how perplexed he is by it. For that

Misalliances

matter, what makes Henry think Elisabeth Brooke will want to come back to him?

'I think she might,' Russell says, eyeing Madeleine as she brings another flask of wine.

Wyatt starts to pour. 'What is it you know?'

Russell finishes wiping his plate. The thin, crinkly skin under his eyes is dark with fatigue. 'That was good, Thomas, and I needed it. All this journeying, it takes it out of me these days.'

'There was a time we rode up and down Italy,' Wyatt says.

'Long behind me. And you, I imagine.'

'I'll go as far as Calais if I have to.'

'As will I.' Russell looks round the darkened room.

'We are alone,' Wyatt tells him.

'Well, then. What I know is the Brookes have money troubles. Serious ones. And the lady herself is no longer welcome at court.'

'Not welcome as in sent away?'

'I believe so.'

'That only happens when someone has displeased the King.'

'Or Queen.'

Wyatt sets down his glass. Something Mason said to him in Paris, that he wasn't usually slow about matters of the bedchamber, has popped into his head. It stung him, but – by God! – he has been slow. 'Are you saying there's been something between Henry and Elizabeth?'

Misalliances

Russell purses his lips. 'She was a favourite for a while. I know that much.'

'So it's Catherine who's had her sent her away?'

'It might be. It's not unusual, is it? New queens tend to get rid of their husband's former bedfellows.'

'And she's had her sent her back to *me*...' It's a second epiphany. 'Ah, I see it now...'

'See what?'

'She's getting even.'

'Getting even? For what?'

'She's behind the whole thing.'

'Good God, Thomas! Don't tell me you've been up to something there.'

'It was a while ago. It's alright.'

'I don't think it is. Who else knows?'

'John Mason.'

'No one else?'

'Well, there's you now...'

'Make sure it stays just me and Mason.' Russell heaves another sigh; this one migrates into a cough. 'Fill that up for me again.' It provides a welcome interregnum. Russell looks across the top of his glass. 'What are you going to do about the situation here?'

'As I've been told. What choice do I have? Things aren't good, anyway.'

He sees Russell to his room and on the way back goes into the nursery, The nurse is asleep in her chair. She wakes as he goes over to where the children are. He puts a finger to his lips to say 'it's alright' and is relieved to see her close her eyes again. Henry is going on three; he's been sleeping in a cot this past year. Francis is still in his crib. They are very alike. As well as sharing the Wyatt nose, their hair is exactly the same shade, light brown going on fair, the same as Tom's was when he was their age. Francis is in the sleep suit he got for him before coming home from the Friars. But even the sight of these boys of his – and they are both his, one way or another - can't move his thoughts on from the conversation he's had with Russell.

When he climbs in beside Lizzie, she stirs and he holds still for a moment. He doesn't want an exchange of words now. But they'll need to talk in the morning.

****

'Well, that suits you, doesn't it?'

Lizzie has changed colour. She's gone so white, he wonders if she's going to vomit.

'Suits me? Taking Elizabeth back? How could it?' It's still early. He's seen Russell off and found her outside, sitting on the felled tree-trunk in the park. It's a fresh morning, prevented from being uncomfortably chill by the sunshine percolating through the alders.

Lizzie looks pained rather than angry. 'Why would he do that?'

'Resentment. Malice.'

'No, what he's doing is turning you back to where he wishes you'd stayed.'

'To before Anne, you mean?'

'He's never got over it. That she loved you more than him.' Lizzie reaches for a handkerchief and for a second he thinks she's about to cry, but she puts it to her nose. 'And you've never got over her, have you? I was in her shadow when I first met you and I've been living under it these past two years.'

'That's not true.'

Lizzie raises the handkerchief to her eyes. She gives them a cursory dab before putting her hands back in her lap. 'You're certain he means it?'

'He had me in The Tower for three months. I'm sure he does.'

Lizzie scrunches up the square of white silk. 'You and your damned King, Thomas. I asked you years ago why you work for him.'

'I know.'

She straightens her back. 'Where are Francis and I to go?'

'Boxley,' he says. 'Poynings is away but Kat's there. And you get on with her. It's not far. I'll come over.'

'And break your word to your precious Henry?'

'He's not precious. I despise him.'
'Yet you always do as he says.'
'Would you rather have me dead?'
She stands. 'I really don't know at the moment.'
He looks up at her. 'You'll be taking Francis, then?'
'What?' Her look of incredulity dwarfs anything he's had from her so far. 'Of course I will. You don't think he's yours, anyway.'
'Is he?'
The look she gives him is no answer and if it's meant to make him ashamed for asking it doesn't achieve that either. She starts to walk back to the house, and when he catches up with her and tries to walk beside her she moves away. 'There's no hurry,' he says. 'You don't need to go right away.'
Reaching the door ahead of him, she turns: 'Oh yes, I do, Thomas. The sooner the better.'
'I'll take you.'
'No, you won't. Edward can.'
'I'll need to explain...'
'Write something. Say we're in difficulties. There's no need to say anything else, is there?'

He can hear raised voices on the stairs. A baby's crying. Francis.
Tom appears. Judging by the state of his clothes he's slept in them. As he comes closer, the stale beeriness on him becomes pungent. Wyatt

wafts it away. 'God, have you been in a tavern all night?'

'Never mind about that. What's this about Lizzie?'

'She's going to Boxley.'

'I know that. Why?'

'It's the King's doing.'

'The King? What's he got to do with it?'

'It's my punishment.'

'You spent all that time in The Tower. Wasn't that your punishment?'

'I told you there'd be something else. For reasons best known to himself, the King has decided that since Lizzie and I aren't married she has to leave.'

'Oh, our virtuous King has decided that, has he?'

'And I have to take your mother back.'

'That's ridiculous.'

'I know.'

'Lizzie belongs here more than her.'

Wyatt feels his temper rising and, correspondingly, things slipping away. 'If you're that much attached to her, you can take her to Boxley.' And now they're tipping beyond recovery.

'Attached to her? What do you mean?'

'You slept with her, the summer before last. When I wasn't here.'

'Oh, that. Yes.'

Misalliances

'You were probably too drunk to know what you were doing.'

'She wasn't.'

It's a revelation that hits Wyatt like a hammer blow. His fists bunched, he takes a step forward.

Tom doesn't move. 'Go on, then...'

'No,' Wyatt says, unclenching his fists, 'that's not going to help.' Father and son stare at each other. Wyatt steps back. 'It must have occurred to you,' he says slowly, 'that Francis might be your son.'

'It had. I'm sorry. I didn't...'

Jane has come in. 'What's all the noise about?'

Tom walks away from his father. 'Lizzie's leaving.'

'I know. Are either of you going to tell me why?'

'Apparently,' Tom says with a wave of his arm towards nothing in particular, 'she and my father are living in sin and the King's not having it.'

'Oh.'

'And my mother's coming back.' Tom's making for the door. Jane gives Wyatt one last glance and follows. 'Tom! Wait!'

Damaris comes in from next door. She looks shaken. 'I'm sorry...' she says.

Wyatt gives her the best smile he can muster and raises a forefinger to signal her to be quiet. They listen.

Misalliances

Jane's doing all the talking. 'What are you so upset about? She never belonged here anyway.' They're moving away, but Jane's voice carries at the best of times. 'Don't walk away! I want to know where you were last night.'

Damaris says: 'Are you alright?'

'Are you?'

She gives a shrug. 'It's out now...'

'It is. For good or ill...'

She comes to stand by him. 'You had to do that. Have it out.'

'I know. We'll get past it.'

'Yes. And it's not as if that's the reason why Lizzie's leaving...'

'No. That's all the King. Quite a turn-up if you think about it.'

'Why would he have put that on you?'

'To get at me. He's never needed an excuse.'

'But why that specifically?'

'Catherine's idea. I'm sure of it.'

'To also get at you?'

'Presumably. I'd better go and find Edward. Lizzie's set on going today and she won't let me take her.'

'That's probably for the best. You're sure it'll be alright with Kat?'

'I'll send an explanation with Edward. That there's been a falling-out. Something like that. They don't rent the hospitium, the second house. She can go there. I wanted time to get it ready,

Misalliances

but...' He puts his hand to his forehead. 'What a mess.'

She takes hold of his wrist, brings his hand down and folds it into hers. 'We'll get past it.'

Chapter Forty: Elizabeth

It's a steeper track up to Cooling Castle than he remembers. The pace of his horse has been reduced to a steady clop. But that's alright. He's in no hurry to be there. He has meetings with Kings and Emperors, but he's been more apprehensive about this one than any of those. He's in an unkind world, but that's not news.

There was a time, as a young man courting Elizabeth Brooke, he liked visiting Cooling. He admired it, not simply as a fine building twice the size of Allington, a couple of hundred paces from the bank of the Thames, but as a house that exemplified aristocratic wealth: its expansive, well-tended grounds; its liveried servants; its stables stocked with well-bred horses. In those days, it represented an affluence which Allington could only aspire to, and Elizabeth in her fine clothes epitomised it. The last time he'd been here it was to collect his son, who'd been staying with his mother while he was in Italy. Tom had just had his sixth birthday, so it had to be fourteen years ago. The remnants of a sickness picked up abroad had collapsed him, there in Elizabeth's sitting-room, and she'd been more than keen to get rid of them both. Not long after, Charles Brandon had admitted to having been his wife's lover and knocked him down; did it in his own home when

Misalliances

the King was visiting. That had put an end to his son's visits to Cooling. And his own.

Since then, rumour had matured into accepted truth, throughout Kent at least, that George Brooke was anything but a steady custodian of the Cobham fortune, and that his weakness for cards, gambling large sums on the turn of one, had significantly depleted the family coffers. Wyatt never doubted it; he could always tell when George was on a losing streak by the letters that came asking him for a prompt payment of Elizabeth's allowance. He had stopped paying it after the fracas with Brandon. Nonetheless, despite George's prodigality, the Brookes had somehow managed to fund their regular appearances at court. Wyatt has long suspected that's likely to have been at Cooling's cost and as he rides up to the first of the castle's gates, looking forward to sheltering from the chill wind that's a left-over from March, his suspicions are confirmed. There's no porter; he rides into the castle's outer ward without hindrance.

It's where he used to go with Elizabeth to escape from the watchful eyes of her parents. They would climb down from the causeway and walk through the closely scythed grass to the curtain wall and back, stopping now and then to kiss. Now the area is so thickly populated by dock, thistle and couch grass that the weeds have begun to encroach on the raised road. He's approaching the moat. Its width used to be a feature renowned in the county – no other castle boasted anything like it - but it's been narrowed by the unchecked spread of bull-rushes. The planks of the bridge across it look sound enough, but he sets his horse upon them cautiously.

At least there's someone at the inner gate. Two burly men appear in front of him, neither of them in livery, though the swords they're carrying proclaim a status of some kind. 'Don't you keep anyone at the outer gate?' he says to them. At the appearance of a boy with dirt-caked fingers, the men withdraw, still without a word, to wherever they are meant to be stationed. 'You let us know you were coming, Sir, that's why,' the boy says, taking hold of the horse's bridle. 'I'll look after him.' His accent and tacit authority do not square with his being a stable-lad.

Wyatt dismounts. Through the grubbiness of the boy's face he discerns a resemblance to Elizabeth, and deep in the mess of hair lurks the characteristic Brooke tint. 'And you are?'

'William, Sir. Someone'll be with you soon.'

Wyatt looks at where he is. Structurally nothing much has changed, but there is an air of desuetude about his surroundings: the stone-work is flaking, one of the top windows is broken and a recent attempt has been made, no doubt by William himself, to extract the weeds proliferating between the yard's paving-slabs and snaking up the walls. A pretty girl appears in the doorway at the base of the yard's tallest tower. Her hair is tightly tucked under her coif but he can see enough of it to tell she's a member of the family. She beckons him. 'Sir Thomas? Do come this way.'

Tentatively, he takes the child-like outstretched hand. 'I'm Elizabeth,' she says. 'Though everyone calls me Beth.'

The moment of déjà vu lasts only a few seconds but it disposes him to be less cool than he had planned to be with whoever was to receive him. He knows who the girl is: she's George's daughter and, if his arithmetic is right, fourteen years of age. With patent obviousness, he says: 'To avoid confusion with your aunt...'

'Indeed.' She's beaming at him. 'I'm pleased to meet you at last.'

Her niceness, her smile, her pale prettiness disarm him. Even in the dimness of the tower's stair-well he can see how much she's like her namesake: the straight nose with its upturned tip, the generous mouth. He casts about for words. 'There's no reason why you should have, the way things have been.'

'You *are* my uncle.'

'I suppose I am.'

'You've met William,' she says, leading the way out of the tower's stair-well into an open lobby to the left. Now they're in the light he sees her green gown matches her eyes, and that the piping round its neck is frayed. He knows where they're going. He used to enter the family's quarters from the other side through a similar airy

Misalliances

lobby. 'My brother,' she adds. 'He likes to get his hands dirty.' She opens the door they've come to, walks him on a dozen paces and stops at the foot of a staircase. 'My aunt's rooms are up there. She's waiting for you.'

'Will I be seeing you again?'

'I don't know.' She's already moving away. 'It depends on what you say to one another.'

Elizabeth Wyatt, née Brooke, rises from her chair. 'Thomas. Welcome.'

The peeling back the years he's been experiencing has not been unpleasant so far, but now, in front of this woman who is no longer really his wife, he doesn't know what he feels. He can't help but associate the room with her heartlessness the last time he was here, and his subsequent conviction – on the strength of his son's testimony - that the Duke of Suffolk was in the castle that morning, waiting for him and Tom to be out of it. Coming across Elizabeth at Greenwich was one thing, but meeting her here, in the intimacy of her own domain, is a different matter. As he had noted on the last occasion, eighteen or so months ago, she's weathered the years better than he. They are the same age but her hair has lost none of its rich colour nor her eyes their brightness; apart from a hint of crow's feet, she could be taken for a woman in her early thirties, whereas with his paunch and thinning hair no one would think him anything other than what he is, a man approaching his fortieth year. It looks like she's dressed up for him. When they were first married, and the Cobhams were rich, she used to send to Paris for her head-dresses, French hoods of the newest design, embellished with emeralds, sapphires and rubies. She's wearing one now - perhaps she should sell the stones to help the family finances – and her blue velvet gown shows none of the wear he saw on her niece's.

'Sit,' she says, and gives him a smile that is incongruously warm. 'So we're to be reconciled.'

'That's what I've been told.'

'Then we have to do it, don't we?'

'What we have to do is make a show of it until such time it's safe to go back to where we were.'

'You think there'll be such a time?'

'I don't know.'

'And what's happening to your lady in the meantime?'

'She's gone.'

'Has she, now?'

'She had to. That was the second thing Henry demanded.'

'My God, Thomas, he's really got his knife in you.' The green eyes narrow. 'Let me tell you how I see it. You're the one at risk, not me. So I'll help you in this show, as you call it, on two conditions. You will assign me rooms at Allington – three or four will do – and recompense me for the indignity of pretending to be your wife again.' She pauses.

Misalliances

'Except I am, aren't I? And you haven't supported me for years.'

'After Charles Brandon admitted to being your lover.'

'Having been my lover. It didn't last that long.'

'A fair while.'

She sighs in exasperation. 'Thomas, I haven't had anything to do with Brandon since Catherine of Aragon's time. Let it go.'

'I would if he would. He was behind my latest spell in The Tower. It's not his doing, is it? Your being sent away from court?'

The remark brings her up short. 'That's to do with George.'

He's not minded to contradict her yet. 'Which explains the state this place is in.'

'We're going through some temporary difficulties.'

'Temporary? Cooling's been in decline for years by the looks of it. George's son is weeding the courtyard!'

'It keeps him happy.'

'And where are your servants?'

'What do you want from me, Thomas?' Her voice has risen to a pitch and a sharpness that he finds altogether more acceptable than the coolly enunciated pretences of a moment ago. She takes a breath. 'Alright. All our money, the Cobham money, has gone on keeping George at court, or on its numerous card tables. Anne – George's wife -

Misalliances

has some, but she needs that. So, if I'm to do this for you, conspire to prevent you from getting on the wrong side of Henry again – or that silly chit Catherine – I shall want rewarding.'

'There's no danger of me getting on the wrong side of Catherine. That's you, isn't it?'

'I don't know what you mean.'

'How many times was it you slipped into Henry's bed?'

'Oh, Thomas, that's unworthy of you, considering you got Catherine into yours more than once.'

'Where did you hear that?'

'Don't dissemble with me. I know you, remember.'

'It was nothing.'

Elizabeth laughs. 'I'm sure it was something. And if Henry were to hear about it...well, I think it would do for you once and for all.'

'You'd wish that on me?'

'No, I wouldn't. Your secret's safe.'

'It has to be, doesn't it? If you're looking to me to get you out of the mess you're in. How much *do* you have left?'

'I don't know exactly.'

'Yes, you do. How much?'

'Practically nothing. There!'

'Well, well, the grand Elizabeth Brooke is throwing herself on my mercy.'

'I don't want your mercy. I want your money.'

She's glaring at him, whereas he's smiling, because the tables are turning and for the first time in days he's feeling a kind of satisfaction. 'How did you hear about Catherine? No, I can guess. Anne Basset.'

'That's right. She didn't spell it out. But you just have.'

'You're friends.'

'Friendly. She's half my age. I got to know her last year, while the King was struggling to make something out of marrying the German.'

'And while you were still angling for advancement.'

'I had to.' She's picking at the skirt of her dress.

'Which is why we're here. Though I still don't understand *how* that's come about.'

'You know how. It's because the King has commanded it.'

'He has. Out of spite and to please his equally spiteful wife. But he didn't come up with it on his own and since she's even more witless than he is, neither did she.'

'I don't see what you're getting at.'

'Well, did you kick against it? Say you'd rather starve than go back to Allington?'

'No. I've always liked it. You know that. And Tom's there.'

'How long has George been putting it about that it'd be the best solution to your money troubles? I'm not stupid, Elizabeth. What was it?

A word over a card game? A whisper in Wriothesley's ear? Or were you doing the whispering? In the King's ear.'

'You weren't supporting me, Thomas.'

'No, I wasn't.'

'And now you'll have to.'

Wyatt takes his time. He adjusts the collar of his shirt and straightens his jacket. 'Let me tell you how *I* see it. I need your help no less than you need mine...'

'I need yours a lot less.'

'No, you don't. So you come to Allington. Once there you'll live in the style you've been accustomed to and be well looked after. You'll have your own rooms.'

'Thank you.'

'But I'm not in the business of covering George's debts.'

'I need something, Thomas, if only to help things here.'

'Should I tell the King you've changed your mind?'

'No, don't do that.'

'Then let's make this work.'

There's a knock on the door. A small voice asks: 'Is it safe to come in?' Without waiting for reply, Beth enters. Her eyes skitter over Wyatt. 'Lemon juice and cakes,' she announces, stepping aside for William carrying a tray. He sets it down and bobs a bow. 'We're not staying,' the girl says, before hooking an arm round her brother's neck and steering him out. The door closes.

Wyatt takes a cake. It's a plain thing with currants but the pastry is moist and he's hungry.

The interruption has given Elizabeth time to regain her composure. She fills a glass for him. 'How *are* things at Allington? I heard all your servants were sent away.'

'Only two went. Richard Southwell was in charge and he didn't make a fuss.'

'Is that the Southwell whose life you once saved?'

'The same. You heard about that?'

'A sword-fight outside Westminster Abbey? That sort of news even makes its way down here. See, Thomas. Good deeds do pay.'

'Perhaps.'

'Henry was quick to seize it.'

'That's how things are these days. I doubt he'd got as far as deciding what to do with it.'

'A pretty castle on the Medway with some good land. I'm sure he had.'

'I've still got it so it doesn't matter. Southwell has promised to return everything they took by the end of the month.'

She puts down the jug and takes a cake herself. 'Including your money?'

'They only got their hands on a little of that.'

'That was clever of you.' She takes a cake. 'Going back to Anne Basset, in case that's worrying you...'

'No more than anything else...'

'She's no longer at court. Her father's in The Tower...'

'I know. I put him there.

'Did you?'

'I uncovered a plot he was part of. Long story...'

'That must have put you in Henry's good books.'

'Not for long, it seems.'

'Well, it's that, and there's been some other things. She's gone. So you're safe.'

'As long as you don't tell on me.'

'I'd never do that.'

'Then let's hope she never does.'

Elizabeth brushes the crumbs from her lap. 'You must come and spend an hour with the family before you go. Beth has taken a shine, I see. I might bring her down with me. Would that be alright?'

'She'd be welcome.'

'Unlike me, I take it.'

'I can't speak for the others. You'll have to make of it what you can. I'm not going to be there for a while.'

'Why's that?'

'I've been ordered to Calais. I'm leaving on Friday.'

Chapter Forty-one: The Pale

They've come to the point where the river goes under a wooden bridge before, further on, turning east in the direction of Ardres. Fifty or so paces away, alongside the bend in the river, a herd of cows is grazing. The day is warming up and some of the cattle are lying down, chewing the cud.

'Here we are, Sir,' says Sergeant Crabtree. 'The coswade. Or the *coursoide*, as the French call it. As I said, it's just an ordinary cow pasture. A few acres of grass.'

Wyatt is making sense of what's before him. 'Perfectly ordinary,' he says. 'Except for its being right on our border. That's the offending bridge, I take it? The one you keep chopping down.'

'That's right.'

'Because the French farmer, whoever he is, keeps bringing his cattle across it and on to our land.'

'Yes.'

Wyatt looks back down the river. 'So the border runs alongside the water to here...'

'And then goes across to the top of the woods there.' Crabtree gestures to their right.

'Whereas the river turns off into France. What's it called again?'

'*Le Moulin*.'

'*Du Moulin*, I would imagine. There must be a water-mill somewhere. So at this moment we're directly on the border...'

Misalliances

'We are.'

'And we're looking at this pasture that's in France...'

'That's it.'

Wyatt shakes his head in exasperation. 'To be honest, Sergeant, I don't see the problem. This Frenchman quite rightly wants to graze his cattle on *his* pasture, and if the only way to get them on to it is to take them over that bridge, who can blame him for doing it?'

'But that brings him, and them, into the Pale.'

'I see that.'

'The cows wander up, you see.' Crabtree gestures again, this time to the meadow behind them. 'Then we have French cows in the Pale.'

'Well, we can't have that, can we?'

'Sir John says it's setting a precedent.'

'Wallop's been ordering you to take down the bridge?'

'It's only been a problem since he came.'

Wyatt trots his horse over and Crabtree follows. It's a rickety structure that's evidently been repaired more than once. 'We take it down and they put it back up,' Crabtree says.

'They?'

'Soldiers from Ardres. They must see it as a *cause célèbre.* It's got no military value. If they wanted to attack us they wouldn't need to cross the river at all.'

Cause célèbre. It's not the first time the sergeant has used words Wyatt would not have

Misalliances

expected from someone of his rank. The young man has had some education. 'What's your story, Crabtree?'

'Story, Sir?'

'Sergeants work their way up through the ranks. But you sound like you're from a good family. Why aren't you an officer?

'The family fell on hard times.' Crabtree directs his gaze towards the cows. 'I couldn't carry on at grammar school, so I joined the army.'

'I see.' Once again Wyatt surveys the ground: the bridge, the invisible border, the pasture and beyond it, over the horizon, the garrison town of Ardres. 'Why don't they build a bridge further down?'

'I imagine it's because the water's a lot wider there. Or because there's always been one here.'

Wyatt puffs out his cheeks. 'All this fuss about a few cows straying into the Pale.' He scans Crabtree's fair-complexioned face; a man of his background must have an opinion. 'What do you think of it all?'

'The Coswade?'

'The situation as a whole. The French doubling the size of the garrison, us drafting men into Guînes. It can't be all because of this.'

'It's not. They've been reinforcing Ardres for months.'

'Do you think they want war?'

'Just waiting for an excuse, as I see it.'

Misalliances

'Well, I can't believe this is it, but in case it is, let's deprive them of it. All it needs is a fence, with a gate in it. We let the farmer bring his cows across, on the understanding he takes them straight on to the *coursoide* and closes the gate.'

On the other side of the bridge, two riders have appeared. The Frenchmen are wearing breastplates but, like their ostensible adversaries, nothing else in the way of armour. One of them – the older of the two - takes off his cap and flourishes it in greeting. Wyatt does the same. 'They're not looking for trouble,' he says. 'So let's hope it doesn't come to it.' He turns his horse. 'Let's go back.'

Wyatt would make more of this chamber on the second floor of the keep if he were in charge: a new coat of whitewash on the walls would be a start. This is his third time here and he doesn't relish the prospect of a fourth. He expected them to be on better terms, he and John Wallop, not only because they have in common the indignity of having been sent here, but because they worked well together ten years ago when he was High Marshal and Wallop Lieutenant of Calais Castle. He assumes it's nothing personal, but a reflection of the other man's resentment at the downturn in his career. Until recently he was the resident ambassador at the French court, Bonner's replacement, and now he's the Captain of Guînes, a posting of little prestige, even though it's the

Misalliances

fortress closest to where the greatest number of French soldiers are massed. Wallop's loss of favour is, like his own, without much justification: he'd been in the habit of corresponding with Richard Pate, who – it's recently been discovered – has been using his position as ambassador to the Emperor to lay the groundwork for his defection to Rome. According to John Mason, who knows all about the affair, Pate's letters contained nothing about his plan to go over to the other side, but the fact of the correspondence was sufficient to have Wallop demoted.

A whiff of something, like cabbage that's been stored too long and begun to turn, is coming across Wallop's desk and Wyatt's wondering how long it is since the old man bathed. He's finished outlining his plan to resolve the problem of the coswade and in the silence that's fallen he says: 'It's simple enough. Could be done in a morning.'

'No,' Wallop declares, 'we can't do that. We let one Frenchman bring his cattle on to the Pale and we'll have hundreds doing it.'

Wyatt tries again. 'It's a situation that needs the heat taken out of it. As I see it, the way things stand, we shouldn't be giving François any reason to send in his soldiers.'

'Over a cow pasture?' Wallop's sounding tetchy. 'He'll not do that.'

'He might. His armies have been standing idle since the truce. He's never been in a better position to kick us out.'

Misalliances

Wallop shifts in his chair. 'Very well. I'll put it to the rest of the Deputies tomorrow.'

'What's it got to do with them? You're the Deputy here.'

'Because it'd be setting a precedent...'

'And they might have to follow it. I'm familiar with the argument.'

'You come, too. The Duke of Norfolk's going to be there, before he goes on to Paris with Fitzwilliam.'

'They're talking with Montmorency, I hear. About the reinforcement of Ardres, presumably.'

'We're demanding they scale it down.'

'Then,' Wyatt says, rising, 'it might be politic for us to make a concession.'

Wallop is shuffling papers. 'Just a minute, Wyatt. This report of yours, from your surveyor. You're remortaring the battlements.'

'They've been doing it today.'

'Will that be enough?'

'Aginst French ordnance? I doubt it. This old castle wasn't built to withstand cannon fire. I'm seeing Lambert tonight to find out what else he can suggest. What time are we meeting tomorrow?'

'Noon.'

'At the castle?'

'The Staplers' Hall.'

Wyatt has no intention of riding in Wallop's carriage, though it's conceivable he might bathe before setting off for Calais. 'I'll see you there,' he says.

****

The Deputies who have furthest to go, those from Oye and Gravelines, are on their way out. The three officers from the Calais garrison – men who are unlikely to have had much interest in the coswade or reports from the various districts about shortages of grain and meat – are going too. The banners ranged around the walls of the hall are stirring in the air coming in from the open door. Wyatt has just noticed they all celebrate - in diverse images and types of script - the great meeting at Balinghem, like the one his father brought back. He's ready to leave but Fitzwilliam is coming towards him. Till now, chairing the Deputies' meeting, he has had his austere public face on. Now it relaxes. 'Well done, Thomas,' he says. 'That should solve the coswade.'

'So the French ambassador has been making representations to the King about it. I didn't know that.'

'Neither did I until Norfolk told me this morning. The commander at Ardres must have referred it up the line. Silly, I know. All this fuss about a bit of pasture. But that's where we're at with them at present.'

'You're off to try and calm things down.'

Misalliances

'There's five hundred men at Ardres. We need to know why that is.'

'Don't let Norfolk get on his high horse. The French won't wear any of that.'

'Now, now. If he hadn't supported your plan this afternoon the Deputies would *still* be discussing it.'

Wyatt looks across the room to where the Duke is in conversation with Wallop. He'd have quite liked some personal acknowledgement from Thomas Howard, but never mind.

Fitzwilliam glances towards Norfolk. 'I'd best get back,' he says. 'How's the work at Guînes going?'

'We've made a start.'

'Good.' Fitzwilliam goes to move off. 'By the way,' he says, stopping, 'when I get back, I've got an envoy from the Emperor coming.'

'Here?'

'It's easier for him and for us.'

'Do you have a name?'

'Another Montmorency. No relation, I'm told.'

'Jean de Montmorency, Seigneur de Courrières?'

'That's him.'

'I know Courrières.'

'Then you must come and have supper. I'll be in touch.'

Misalliances

He's about to mount his horse when he hears a familiar voice. 'Wyatt? What are you doing here?'

He turns to see Henry Howard in a blue velvet doublet topped off with a yellow hat. Surrey's get-ups always prompt Wyatt to examine his own; he doesn't always come off worse but he knows he does today. Guînes isn't the place to play the peacock, and he's been settling for grey and black fustian. On top of that, his hair and beard need trimming.

'I could ask you the same, my Lord.'

The Earl of Surrey swaggers over. 'My Lord? I'm Harry to you, Thomas.' He offers his hand. 'Why do you *think* I'm here?' He smiles to offset the sarcasm. 'Is he in there?'

'He is.'

Surrey takes his arm. 'Right. Let's walk the other way. He'll ask me what I've been doing and since I've been down at the Lantern Gate all afternoon I'll be stuck for an answer.'

The late afternoon sunlight is lending the streets adjacent to the Staplers' Hall a dappled charm, though beyond the residential quarter there's little that's pretty. These turnings where the town's administrators live quickly peter out to an area neither fed nor crossed by recognisable by-ways. Calais' function as an entrepôt requires storehouses and workshops and that's where they are, randomly spaced in clutches of two or three according to trade – fishmongers, vintners, sail-makers, ships' carpenters - beneath the eastern perimeter of the wall. Once as Marshal, Wyatt took the night watch down that way, came across a band of robbers and found himself with a box of mackerel tipped down his front and facing a seven foot blond giant who, thankfully and astonishingly, thought better of taking him on and fled. Calais town is no longer the drab, neglected place it was when he first spent time here. Money has been put in to level the surface of the once barely negotiable main street, and the buildings lining it have been re-roofed, their frontages cleaned and painted. Even the castle, looming above the town, seems less forbidding today now that it's acquired a background of blue sky.

Wyatt, mindful of the journey he'd rather complete before it gets dark, extricates his arm. 'Look, Harry. I must be off. Perhaps we can meet when you're back from Paris.'

Surrey's mouth, which has always had a tendency to adopt a scornful curl, pouts petulantly. '*I'm* not going. He insisted I come and now he says I've got to stay here till he gets back.' He brightens. 'But *you're* here as well! I've got some verses you might be interested in.'

'I'm at Guînes at the moment.'

'Where's that?'

Wyatt points. 'Ten miles inland. Near the border.'

'What are you doing there?'

'Working on the castle's defences.'

'What do you know about that?'

'More than I thought.'

'You do that all the time?'

'The surveyor I have does most of it. Testing mortar, identifying stones that need replacing, checking the stoutness of doors and gates. I write it up, get approval and he gets the work done.'

Surrey yawns. 'How tiresome. A waste of your skills it seems to me. Do you really have to be off?'

'I do, yes. It's not the best terrain when it's pitch black.'

'What if I came out to see you? How about that? I could do with taking a look at the lie of the land. It'll impress the Duke.'

'You're welcome to.'

Surrey, cheered, claps him on the arm. 'Excellent. What about tomorrow afternoon?'

'That'd suit. But come early.'

'Is it safe?'

'For now it is.'

'How do I find you?'

'There is a road. You'll find it.'

Surrey holds out his hand again. 'Good to see you, Wyatt.'

Wyatt, sensing in Surrey's farewell something of his usual superior manner, feels the need to fire a parting shot. 'You too. But beware of those Lantern Gate girls. Pound to a penny some of them'll have the pox.'

****

Misalliances

Wallop is spooning up his soup. He wipes his mouth. 'The Earl of Surrey? Is he a friend of yours?'

'Yes.'

'Why's he coming here?'

'To talk about poetry.'

Wallop pauses in his slurping. 'Oh, yes, the other thing you do. Use the council chamber. You can't entertain him in that room of yours.'

Wyatt likes his room in the north west tower. The bakehouse immediately below means it mostly warm and it's pleasing to wake to the aroma of fresh bread. Nonetheless, he sees Wallop's point. Like most of the tower rooms it's small. 'Thank you.'

'Tell the kitchen you're to have our best wine.'

He's thought of putting on his newest doublet. He bought it on the Strand the same afternoon he spied Francis' sleep-suit in a shop he was drawn to precisely because it appeared to specialise in clothes for infants. Both purchases were tokens, celebrations even, of his new freedom. Its dark blue twill is no match for Surrey's velvet, even with its gold piping, but it's smart enough. In the end, he decides not to. It's too smart for Guînes and it would undoubtedly elicit a ribbing from Lambert who is up on the ramparts supervising the remortaring and would be bound to catch sight of him greeting his visitor. He goes to check that the council chamber is as he would like it.

It's not much used these days, he understands, because the practice of the Pale's deputies taking turns to host the monthly meetings has been suspended while the French are being difficult; and no one wants to come out to Guînes with hundreds of heavily armed French soldiers only a few miles away. With its high ceiling, polished panelling and window overlooking the flowering kitchen garden, it's the only room in the castle with pretensions to civility. He's asked for some of the flowers to be cut and placed in a suitable vase; 'silver' was what he wanted but the request was met with a blank stare. The wine is there, and two reasonably clean cups.

Surrey seems happy enough. He's unpacking his manuscripts, sipping his wine and talking idly about what a good ride he and his men have had. He hasn't asked what Wyatt has written lately, which is as well because it amounts to very little. 'Look,' he says, taking a further sheet out of his bag. 'This is what I've been working on. A translation of Virgil's *Aeneid*.'

Wyatt picks up the first page. 'What's made you go to that?'

'Why not? It's a great work. Apart from sharpening up my Latin, which I thought I was in danger of losing, it's not been done in English. Or not properly,' Surrey runs a hand through his hair.

Misalliances

'To be honest, it keeps me sane.' His voice has taken on what is for him a surprisingly introspective quality. 'It gets me away from the hurly burly.'

'How do you mean?'

Surrey's eyes flash. 'At court, Thomas! What else? Having to do this, having to do that. Show my face at the dance, show up in the lists, please my father...dance attendance on my cousin.'

'I thought you and she got on.'

'We do sometimes.'

Wyatt, sensing that they might be getting on to the subject of Catherine and preferring not to, says: 'So it's good to lose yourself in something like this now and then, you mean?'

'Don't you feel that?'

'When it happens, I do.' Wyatt's about to say that three months in The Tower was not good for his verse, but since Surrey's father was no doubt one of those keen to keep him there, he says nothing. Instead he begins to read. His recollection of Virgil's poem is scant , but he likes what's before him.

 O Sacred mother was it then for this
 That you me led through flame and weapons
  sharp
That I might in my secret chamber see
Mine enemies, and Ascanius my son,
With Creusa my sweet wife
Murdered alas! The one in the other's blood?

Misalliances

Thy servants! Then bring me my arms again.

Surrey is smiling to himself. 'You know it, of course,' he says, when Wyatt breaks off and lifts his eyes. 'The Greeks have taken Troy, set fire to it, and Aeneas, who's fled, is reflecting on his escape.'

Wyatt's eyes return to the page. 'There are no rhymes. Was it too hard?'

'Of course it wasn't.' Surrey sounds offended. 'God, Thomas, I expected better from you. I *chose* not to rhyme it. Could have done if I'd wanted to. Virgil's didn't rhyme.'

Wyatt is still contemplating the text. ' Well, it's certainly different...'

'It's still verse, Thomas. It may not rhyme, but it has a regular rhythm.'

'In Chaucer's old meter...'

'But without his awful rhymes.'

Wyatt raises his eyes. 'So we've got a ten syllable line...'

'I prefer ten. Eight syllables aren't enough for even half a thought.'

'It's new, I'll give you that.'

'It is.'

'What are you going to call it?'

'Do I have to call it anything?'

'The new verse. What about that?'

'That's not very exciting.'

'Then something about its having no rhymes. Its blankness. That's what it is, blank versifying. I like it.'

'Then *you* must try it. Time to break away from old habits, Thomas!' They drink some more. 'I mean it. Don't stop writing.'

The remark encourages Wyatt to open up. 'I won't,' he says. 'Fortune's not been on the side of it lately, that's all.'

Surrey nods sympathetically. 'It won't have been. Is your wife back?'

'She will be by now.'

'Well, that'll please someone I know.'

'Dare I ask who?'

'Better you don't.' Surrey is sorting through his pages. 'Now, look at this,' he says. 'I think it might be the best of it.'

****

Lambert's age is beginning to tell. He's visibly no longer as agile as when they first worked together and his formerly greying hair is now silver. He's been bringing his boys with him, his sons by his French wife, one on the cusp of adulthood, the other a few years younger. They're big strong lads who have recently completed their apprenticeships as masons. It appears to be a successful combination of skills: Lambert's to identify in apparently superficial symptoms the likelihood of a building's more deeply seated ills, the boys' to

Misalliances

apply their tools to put right what their father has diagnosed. This morning he's demonstrating why the castle's battlements – or at least these, the ones facing Ardres – need to be buttressed and capped. 'We've remortared as far down as we can, but it won't take much to knock these old stones out. If the French ordnance is as good as they say, you'll be open to the sky, ready targets for their arrows and shot.'

'You think their cannon have that kind of reach?'

'It might.'

The elder boy, Charles - Wyatt has heard Lambert pronounce it in the French manner when he forgets himself – climbs on to the nearest battlement, takes out his knife and sinks its point into the stone. It doesn't need his comment - 'This is very old' – to make the point.

The other brother, Denis, adds: 'They all are.'

'Couple of good lads, George,' Wyatt says to Lambert.

'They are. Wish I'd had them when we were doing all that work on the castle in town.'

'I'd gone by then, remember,' Wyatt says.

'Back to your palaces. I do remember.' It's Lambert's perennial jibe but Wyatt, who's not sure he'll see much of such places again or will want to, doesn't smile back. 'They've got some Italian working on it this time,' Lambert says. 'Did you know?'

'I did. No skin off our nose.'

Misalliances

'None at all. Too big a job for me anyhow.'

Wyatt moves the conversation on. 'You have the stones for this?'

'Bricks. We need bricks.'

'How long will it take?'

'Just this stretch? Three or four days to see it done right. But if you wanted all four sides doing, I'd have to bring in more men.'

'Let me consult. Would your lads be any good at putting up a fence? We need something on the border between here and Ardres.'

'Are we putting up fences now?'

'It's just a short one. A couple of hundred feet.'

'That's still a good length. You need a carpenter for that.'

'Do you know someone?'

'Several. Leave it with me.'

****

It's a long time since Wyatt was last in the state room of Calais castle. It's benefited from having its window embrasures glazed, but it's a cold space, even on a warm May evening.

Pleased he's chosen to wear his blue twill – it'll keep him warm - he walks the length of the room, to where Courrières is standing by the hearth talking to Fitzwilliam. His Flemish friend has grown his hair and cast off the soldier's uniform he adopted at Ghent. Decked out in a pink

Misalliances

doublet and white ruffled shirt, he's the old Courrières, the one Wyatt has always been comfortable with. He has time to do little more than take his hand and say 'Good to see you, old friend,' before Fitzwilliam, dressed informally this evening, says: 'Come and sit, gentlemen. Next to me, Thomas.' On the other side of the table, a servant – one of the Lord Privy Seal's liveried people from London – is pulling out a chair for Courrières.

No other guests have appeared. It's just the three of them.

Fitzwilliam begins. 'Monsieur de Courrières is here to convey the Emperor's warm wishes for a speedy resolution to our difficulties with the French.'

'That's good of him,' says Wyatt, giving Courrières a quick smile before dipping his spoon into the bowl of soup that's been placed in front of him. 'I was hoping you'd already resolved them, William.'

'We've made some progress,' Fitzwilliam says.

Courrières says to Wyatt: 'I was telling Lord Fitzwilliam, the Emperor is in Regensburg,'

'Talking to the Lutherans?'

'*And* the Catholics. Tempers need to be cooled and Charles decided it was time he went himself.'

Fitzwilliam says: 'I imagine the problem you have there is that the Lutherans no longer think of him as their Emperor.'

Misalliances

'They have no choice but to,' Courrières says. 'That's not up for negotiation. As you know, there are three seats of power in the Emperor's domain, Spain, Rome and Germany.'

'And the New World,' Wyatt says. 'That'll become a seat of power.'

'It is already, in the viceroyalty,' says Courrières. 'New Spain.'

As if he's remembering, Wyatt says: 'That's Cortes, is it?'

'No, he's on his way back to Spain.'

'Some would say you're losing Germany,' Fitzwilliam says.

'I wouldn't say that.'

'The Lutherans have rejected Rome.'

Courrières smiles indulgently. 'But the Empire is more than Rome.'

'And France is closer to the Pope than you are.'

'Our relationship with the Holy Father is complicated.'

'Not as much as your relationship with the French.' Fitzwilliam signals to the servants behind them and waits for dishes to be removed. 'Tell us where that stands,' he says.

Dishes of venison have arrived and Fitzwilliam waits until they've been set down and the servants have withdrawn.

There's a pause for eating. Eventually Courrières says: 'Where we stand with France...'

Fitzwilliam looks up. 'If you don't mind.'

Misalliances

'I don't mind at all. It's what I'm here to discuss. There is a misunderstanding abroad that we have become interested in an alliance with the French. As Thomas knows, because he was there at the time, they have broached such a thing with us but we were not interested. There is no such thing. Currently, we have called a truce in our endless arguments over who owns the Duchy of Milan and this or that part of Burgundy, and that is all. It does not mean we are friends. In fact, I can assure you we've had no part in the agitations on your borders in the Pale.'

Fitzwilliam skewers a piece of meat. 'I spoke with your namesake about that last week. He claims the agitation, as you term it, is all in our heads.'

'He would say that, of course,' puts in Wyatt.

Courrières eyes the side dish of fritters and selects one. 'I think there's little doubt that Montmorency and François are weighing the wisdom of launching a campaign against you. In the Pale, I mean. That would mean a wider war, of course. Personally, I doubt they have the stomach for that. For now, they may be content to simply stir up a little mischief.'

'Like that ridiculous plot that came to light last year,' Fitzwilliam says.

'The one that Thomas uncovered. Yes.'

Fitzwilliam turns to Wyatt. 'Was that you?'

Courrières answers for him. 'It was Thomas who intercepted Gregory Botolf's letters.'

Misalliances

'I didn't intercept them,' Wyatt says. 'John Mason did. I simply passed them on to the King.'

'Anyway,' Courrières continues, 'it never got off the ground, so it's easy to dismiss it as ridiculous, but I believe it was being taken seriously in Paris. It's no coincidence that at that exact same time the Ardres garrison received a supply of troops that doubled its size.'

Fitzwilliam chews for a few seconds. 'You really think they could have got the better of us here in Calais?'

'If your gates had been opened, they might. As it is, though the plot was nipped in the bud, it did you harm. It led to Arthur Lisle being taken to The Tower of London. And he was one of your main men here, I understand.'

Fitzwilliam nods. 'For many years.' He picks up a fritter. 'François swore to the King he knew nothing of the scheme.'

'He swore the same to the Emperor.' Courrières looks across at Wyatt. 'Thomas didn't believe it. Did you, Thomas?'

'No more than you did,' Wyatt says.

'So you see,' Courrières says, turning in his chair and holding up his glass to be refilled, 'we do not trust the French.'

Fitzwilliam says: 'Do you trust *us*?'

'Why else would I be here?'

The fire has been lit and while Courrières is in the jakes Wyatt and Fitzwilliam stand in front of it, warming themselves. Wyatt says: 'I've finished at Guînes.'

'Do I need to come and look?'

'No. It's good work. It'll keep them out if they do come. How's it gone here?'

'This place is solid enough. And we've strengthened the gates.' Fitzwilliam gives a wry smile. 'We just need to make sure they're kept shut.'

'Is there anything else you want me for?'

'I don't think so. Let me have your report and get yourself a boat. I won't be far behind you.' Fitzwilliam goes over to the table and picks up the remaining fritter. 'What do you make of our friend?'

'He's a good man. You can count on what he says.'

'I didn't know it was you who uncovered the Botolf business.'

'Mason did, on the way to Paris. We nearly caught him in Ghent, too.'

'Well, we've got him now.'

'So I heard.'

'You stand high with them, don't you?'

'With Charles and his people? I did do.'

'You still do. It's obvious. We ought to use you better than this.'

'This?'

'What we've had you doing in the Pale.'

'It was useful work.'

'True, true.'

Misalliances

'What would you have in mind?'

'Let's wait till the King has forgotten whatever it was he fell out with you over. Then we'll see.'

As Wyatt leaves, he finds Courrières waiting in the vestibule. 'Time to say goodnight, Jean,' he says.

His friend comes over. 'Henry's had you in The Tower again, I hear.'

'He has.'

'Why do you put up with him?'

'He's my King. I have no choice.'

Courrières draws his cloak round him. 'There are always choices. You just need to recognise them and take them. If you ever need a bolt-hole, my friend, across the water, I have a place outside Brussels. It's yours if you ever feel the need to flee. Just a thought. In case things go wrong again.'

'Thank you. And the *quid pro quo*?'

'There wouldn't be one. Though we could certainly use you.'

Wyatt holds out his hand. 'Good to see you, my friend. Travel safely to wherever you're going next.'

On the road to Guînes in what's left of the light, the words go through his head. 'He is my King. I have no choice.' It's what he's said so often. To Courrières, to Tom, to Lizzie, to Damaris. It's the only justification he has for service which profits him nought. And it's not enough.

It's when he's packing his bags, getting ready to take the noon ship, that he thinks about what awaits him at home. He's kept it at bay by keeping busy, by wilfully refusing to dwell on the fact that Lizzie and her son have gone and that Elizabeth will have come. For the first time ever, he's not happy about going home. But at least Damaris is there, his safe harbour of honesty and good sense. And fondness. It's been different between them since the business with Lizzie. All the talking they did. And he's glad of it. There have been times, up on the battlements with Lambert, or while he's been riding to or from Calais, when her image has leapt into his mind and cheered him. The thought of her does the same now as he walks down from the castle towards the main gate and the dock.

Misalliances

Part Six

Misalliances

Chapter Forty-two: In the North

While Jane Boleyn is tightening her laces, Catherine is occupying herself with looking out the window at the sweep of lawn. She lifts her eyes to the squat church tower which is peeking above the perimeter wall. 'What a little place this is,' she grumbles.

'The house is alright. Better than a draughty castle.'

'The house is fine. But this Hatfield is no more than a village.'

'Be content,' Jane says. 'The hunting's good.' She turns Catherine round, tugs at the waist of the bodice to straighten it and give a firmer shape to the bosom. 'It could do with coming down a bit, you know.'

'That'll make me look like a tavern wench..'

'Isn't that what we all are, when all's said and done?'

Catherine giggles and though she has never been much given to nervousness it comes out jittery.

'Stand still,' Jane says. She makes the adjustment and nods approvingly. 'That's better. And you're still decent.' With both hands she fluffs out Catherine's skirts. 'Now, I've told everyone that the travelling has tired you out, you're having a lie-down and must not be disturbed. Margaret will be in the ante-room just in case.'

Misalliances

'She'll hear everything.'
'She'll be by the outer door.'
'And he'll be coming up the back stairs?'
'Through there,' Jane says, pointing to the door in the corner. She goes over and unlocks it. 'I'd leave it ajar. Best not to have him knocking. But lock it once he's here.' She folds her hands together in front of her to signify she's finished. 'I'll leave you now.'

****

Culpeper gets out of bed and reaches for his boots. Catherine, her back to him, is pulling on her skirts. 'You could stay, you know,' she says. 'He's not going to be back till morning.'

'We can't risk it,' he says. 'It only needs for the hunt to have gone badly or the lodge not to be to his liking and he'll be back.'

'You're right.' She sounds more forlorn than she means to.

He walks round to her side of the bed and sits next to her. She hasn't yet attempted to put her bodice on but he resists the temptation to reach up and touch her breasts. 'You know I'd stay if it was safe.'

'Of course I do,' she says brightly, though she's finding it hard to banish the thought that now he's had her, he wants nothing more than to be off.

Culpeper bends to sort out out some wrinkles in his hose. 'Are things any better in bed with him?'

Catherine is busy looping her hair into a loose knot. 'I'm not telling you anything more about that,' she says, though she wishes she could tell someone. Something else she can't banish is the thoroughly unpleasant sensation of the wetness on her thighs after last night's awkward coupling.

'So he's still not managing to get it up, then.'

Catherine turns on him. Well acquainted with the sharpness of her nails, he's on his feet. 'No, you don't,' he says, laughing. The slipper bounces off the back of his head. He picks it up, chuckling.

'If you're going, go,' she says over her shoulder.

'I thought I'd just sit here for a minute.' She still has her back to him, is making a point of still having her back to him, but it's alright; he likes these moments, when he's watching her tidy herself, when she's female to him in no other way than as an exemplar of loveliness, to be admired and nothing more. A thick lock of hair has escaped from the knot and the sight of it, its auburn strands curling on her freckles, makes his heart lift.

She's fiddling with the clasp of her pearl necklace. 'Let me do it,' he says, climbing on to the bed. She sits still while he secures it. 'It suits you,' he adds.

'What does?'

'All this finery.'

Misalliances

'I've always had finery.'

'I know. But not as much as now.'

She half-turns. 'It's becoming tiresome. I get something new every day.' She holds up her wrist to show him the diamond bracelet. 'It was this yesterday.' Holding her bodice up in front of her, she says: 'I'll have to get Margaret in to help me with this.'

'Hook your arms in,' he says. 'I can do it.'

She does as she's bid and he gathers the laces between his fingers. One has come out of its eyelet and he has to rethread it.

She mocks his slowness. 'You're all fingers and thumbs.'

'Sit still,' he tells her. 'It's not something I do a lot of.'

'Isn't it? And there was I thinking you'd done it dozens of times.'

He has the laces where they should be and pulls on them as hard as he can.

She lets out a cry. 'Not so tight! I can't breathe.'

'Serves you right.' He lets in some looseness, ties off the laces and gives her back a gentle shove. 'There. All done.'

Now she turns. 'Where next?'

He gets down and straightens his jacket. 'York possibly,' he says.

She gets up and comes to him. They kiss. 'York, then,' she says.

He's making for the door. 'I'll send a message.'

Catherine goes next door to get Margaret who, as Jane had promised, is seated sentry-like by the door leading out on to the landing. 'Thank you, my sweet. All well, I take it?'

Margaret is not comfortable with lying, but what good could come of telling about Margaret Douglas, who – ever bustling, always hurrying – had got half-way to the bedroom before stopping in her tracks and turning on her heel, though not at anything Margaret had said – she'd got no further than saying 'Wait, my lady!' - but at the clearly audible sounds of sexual congress coming from inside. So she says: 'Yes. All well.'

Catherine is fingering a damp, straggly strand of her hair. 'Good,' she says. 'Would you come in and fix this for me?'

Misalliances

Chapter Forty-three: How are we all?

The new girl Marjorie, one of Elizabeth's, has been in to announce supper is ready and Damaris is waiting to hear him move. When it looks like he's not going to, she goes in. 'It's supper time,' she says.

'I just need to finish this line,' Wyatt says. He looks up. She's still wearing the summer gown she put on earlier to go out in the park with Beth. In pale yellow, it has a lower neck-line than the ones he's used to seeing her in. It's not the provocative plunging kind Kate Howard had on when she came to him but it dips enough to show off her shoulders where she's caught the sun. Two nights ago when he got back from the Pale, her initial greeting, when she was with the others, had been formal, cool, a simple 'Welcome back, Sir Thomas.' But when they happened to pass on the stairs later, she said 'I'm glad you're back' to which he replied, not altogether truthfully, 'I'm glad to be back.' She's been in his head ever since, though how much he's in hers, exactly what place he has in hers, he doesn't know.

She comes to stand in front of him. 'You can't avoid him at supper, you know.'

He finishes writing and lays down the pen. 'What makes you think it's him I'm avoiding? I'm avoiding everyone.'

Misalliances

She picks up the quill and puts it in the inkwell. 'Not me, I hope?'

Wyatt pushes back his chair. 'No, not you.'

She's fussing with the inkwell. 'I thought I'd go to Boxley tomorrow. Is that alright?'

'Yes. Have you been going?'

'I've been a couple of times.'

'What do they know?'

'Thomas Poynings is still away...'

'With the army in Scotland. And Kat?'

'She knows it's to do with the King. Lizzie must have told her.'

'And nothing about the other business?'

'I don't think so. She wouldn't have mentioned that, would she? And needless to say, I haven't.'

'I feel bad about not seeing Kat myself. But what with one thing and another...'

'Then come with me. I think you should. If only to express your gratitude. Kat has taken Lizzie and the baby in without so much as a quibble. You don't have to see Lizzie.'

'I don't want to.' He picks up what he's been writing. 'By gratitude, you mean some money?'

'It might be appreciated.'

'I've got something at last,' he says, showing her the paper.

'Any good?'

'I don't know yet. It's like a letter to an old friend. I'll let you read it when it's finished.' He puts the paper down. 'Alright, I'll come.' He holds out his hand.

They arrive at the parlour door the same time as Tom does. Without exchanging a word, father and son back off from one another and then simultaneously advance and collide in the doorway. Wyatt gives Tom a push. It's harder than it needs to be. 'Stop it!' Damaris whispers.

Elizabeth, Beth and Jane, who are already seated, turn their heads. As the late arrivals take their seats, Elizabeth says: 'Well, how are we all?'

****

They are coming into Sandling. Damaris, anxious, says: 'You're sure?'

'I am. You were right. I ought to.'

The village has grown little since Wyatt was a boy. It's still three short intersecting streets of farm cottages and is sleepily quiet on this June morning. The rumble of barrels being rolled down into the cellar of The Black Horse inn is the only sound. A single villager is out, a young woman with a basket of turnips and carrots over her arm. She's crossing ahead of them and Edward slows the cart for her. Though she's wearing a shapeless smock with her blonde hair all but hidden by a coarse head-scarf, her prettiness catches Wyatt's attention. She sees him looking and he gives her a quick smile which she shyly returns. He's very aware of that side of himself this morning, his susceptibility to pretty women, not least the one beside him.

'I hear you've been out riding,' he says to her.

'It was Beth's doing. She used to have her own at Cooling. You don't mind?'

'Why would I? I didn't know you could ride.'

'I learned when I was small.'

'And did it all come back?'

'It's not something you forget, is it?' She strokes her hands down from her hips to her thighs. 'Though these parts of me clearly had. It's getting better.'

It stirs him, seeing her do that, though not as much as Edward's description of her mounting the mare he chose for her. 'She hoisted her skirts and swung herself up into the saddle like a boy,' he said.

'It's going to be nice,' he says. 'We should go out this afternoon.'

Her face darkens. 'I normally stay for the day when I come.'

'Oh. Perhaps tomorrow, then.'

Sandling is behind them and the Abbey's two buildings, the gabled main house and the low-roofed hospitium –the house where the monks would have lodged visitors - are visible on the skyline. Wyatt hasn't been here since he and Poynings came to look it over, but it seems to be being well-looked after, judging by the closely mown grass on either side of the approach. 'Do

Misalliances

you know who's she got managing the place while Poynings is away?' he asks Edward.

'I don't. But whoever it is, I don't envy them. I only come to collect the rent and that's enough.'

'Been getting the sharp end of her tongue, have you?'

'Just for dragging in some mud one time.'

'Sounds like her.'

'I don't find her difficult,' protests Damaris. 'When you went into The Tower, Thomas, she was the only one of our neighbours to come and see how things were.'

'We'll see how she is today,' Wyatt says. 'I'm showing my face, that's all.'

'And your gratitude,' Damaris says.

Wyatt wouldn't claim to know Kat Poynings well but the few times they have met he found her fussy and brusque, not easy to take to.

Their reception does nothing to change his mind. 'Welcome, Damaris,' the lady says when she meets them in the vestibule. 'Come in, come in.' And then, sharply: 'No, not you, Sir Thomas.'

Damaris, her mouth open like she's scrabbling for words to ease the awkwardness of what's just happened, resists the arm shepherding her away. 'He's come to thank you, Kat,' she says, freeing herself.

'About time,' Kat snaps. 'You go on into the parlour. I want a word with Sir Thomas.'

Damaris is hovering. 'I'll see you this evening, then,' she says to Wyatt.

Misalliances

'Someone'll have to come and fetch you,' Kat says.

Edward says: 'I can do that.'

So far Kat Poynings has not so much as acknowledged Allington's bailiff. Now she gives him a cursory glance and says to Wyatt: 'Your man should wait outside.'

'Stay, Edward,' Wyatt says.

Kat draws her shawl round her; she's a stout woman, and she makes a dramatic show of the manoeuvre. 'If you've come to see Lizzie,' she says, 'you're going to be disappointed. She doesn't want to see you.'

Wyatt's tempted to brush her and her impertinence aside and go and say to Damaris, 'You're not staying here, we're leaving.' But there's nothing to be gained from making an ugly situation more so. Instead he says: 'I've not come to see Lizzie. You've helped us out at a difficult time, Kat, and I wanted to thank you, that's all.' He takes the bag of sovereigns out of his jacket pocket. 'And give you something to help with expenses.'

Kat expels a breath. 'Don't insult me further, Thomas. You send Lizzie here with only the briefest note to explain things and don't have the courtesy to show up yourself. At least your son had the good grace to come and apologise.'

'When was this?'

'That same day.'

'Has he been since?'

Misalliances

'Two or three times. Unlike you, he's been concerned how things are.'

'I've been in Calais.'

'Listen,' Kat says. 'I have no wish to get involved in your disagreements with the King, or how he came to interfere in the arrangement you've had with Lizzie. It's none of my business. All I'll say is you could have handled it better.'

'I could, yes. It's the story of my life at present. I'm sorry.'

'She'll be staying for the foreseeable future, I take it?'

'Yes. She'll have to.'

'I'll say good day, Sir Thomas.'

He's not going to press his case. There's no way he can. He thought he should come, and he's done it. What he's really disappointed about is that he's leaving Damaris there and they won't be riding in the park together that afternoon.

****

Back at Allington, Wyatt goes to the stables. If Damaris and Beth are going out riding he wants to be sure everything's being done right. Since Arthur left for the Friars, it's all been left to the boy, who divides his time between the horses which belong to the family and the larger number of heavier beasts down at the farm. That must be where he is, though the stallion and mares have

Misalliances

been fed, there's fresh straw in their stalls, and saddles and tackle look newly soaped.

It's almost midday. He has some bread and fruit, swallows half a mug of small beer and sits down down to work on his poem for John Poyntz, which he still hasn't got quite right.

Abigail comes in. She's been promoted from house-maid to lady's maid since the departure of Miriam and Madeleine and she's all tentative curtsies and diffident hesitation.

He looks up. 'Yes?'

'Sir, Lady Elizabeth would like to see you.'

'Where is she?'

'Outside with her niece.'

They're sitting in the shade of the back porch. Beth immediately gets up from her stool. 'Good afternoon, uncle!' She flashes him a smile, all white-teeth and bright eyes. As part of her toilette today she has lightly rouged her lips and braided her hair in a fashion he's seen some young girls in the Low Countries do, not at the back but at the front and side, with the plaits hanging in front of her ears and framing her face. The style suits her, though it makes her look younger than her years, which he doubts was the intention. She's wearing what he takes to be one of her new gowns. Elizabeth said they'd been into Maidstone to get the girl something decent to wear. It's a similar shade of green to the threadbare one he first saw

Misalliances

her in. It'll be one of her favourite colours, of course, because it sets off the red of her hair.

Elizabeth shades her eyes to look up at him. 'Thomas.' During the day, his wife has taken to dressing plainly in loose linens, embellished by a simple girdle. Equally, he's noticed that until supper-time she does little to her person. Only in the evening does she powder her face, rouge her lips, and put on one of her French hoods. Like she once did at Greenwich or Beaulieu, he supposes. He prefers, he's realised, the unadorned Elizabeth, plainly herself, wearing a plain white cap instead of one of her French creations. It's a more authentic version of her, more honestly reflective of her age.

'You wanted me,' he says. She's squinting up at him as if just being out in the light is hard for her. 'You should take a walk in the park, the two of you,' he adds, 'rather than sitting here in the shade. It'll be pleasant at this hour.'

'That's what I've been telling her,' says Beth, squirming on the hard seat, her legs moving this way and that.

'I have no fondness for grass,' Elizabeth says to her niece. 'I've told you. It stains, and getting it out of the hem of an expensive gown is the devil's own work.'

'You're not wearing an expensive gown.'

Elizabeth screws her eyes up to Wyatt again. 'I need to talk to you about my bed,' she says.

'Your bed?'

Misalliances

'That'll do,' Elizabeth says to Beth, who is making no attempt to suppress the bout of giggling that's bubbled up in her. 'God knows how old it is, Thomas. But it's most uncomfortable.'

'It'll be the mattress. You're probably used to feathers,' he says. 'It'll be stuffed with wool. Might even be straw.'

'No, what's needed is a new bed. Every time I turn over the whole thing shakes.'

A loud chortle bursts from Beth's lips. Then, like the child she still is rather than whatever maturer version of herself she aspires to, she instantly straightens her face and murmurs: 'Sorry'.

'Once more and you'll go in,' her aunt tells her.

'I said I was sorry.'

'And I heard you.'

In a show of petulance, her face creased by an unbecoming grimace, the girl slips off her stool. 'I think I will, anyway,' she says.

'Good.'

'Can I play with your necklaces?'

'As long as you put them back.' Elizabeth gives the girl a slap on the bottom as she saunters past and disregards the 'Ow! What was that for?' She invites Wyatt to take the vacant seat. 'Now,' she says, 'I assume there's a joiner in Maidstone who can make a bed to specification.'

'There's nothing wrong with the bed,' he says. 'I'll have one of the men come up and tighten the joints. That's all it'll be.'

'Indulge me with a new mattress, then. As you say, a feather one. Is there someone there who does that?'

'There must be.'

'Then would you measure it up and get it done, please?'

He's tried to avoid visiting the rooms he's given them. But since Beth is up there somewhere, he ought to be there while Robert's taking measurements. Wondering where she has got to, he wanders along the corridor. She's in the room which used to be his father's. It has little of the old man about it now; what was there was too much marked, too much stained, by the emanations of illness and old age, so they'd emptied it except for a settle and the old account books on the shelves in the closet. It's an odd place for her to be. Or perhaps not, because here she is, seemingly content with its musty bareness. She's seated on the floor with her legs tucked under her, not with her aunt's jewellery in her lap, but a sheaf of yellowed papers.

She sees his face and scrambles to her feet, pulling her gown down over her striped stockings with one hand and doing her best to hold on to the papers with the other. What they were fastened with falls to the floor. 'Oh, I'm sorry. I shouldn't have. They must be yours.'

He bends to pick up the piece of twine. 'Some of my old poems,' he says. 'I'd forgotten they were there.' It's come back to him. They're his earliest efforts; he put them there for safety before he went to Spain. She's still looking at him anxiously, but he's not angry. Every intelligent, curious child likes to explore. He'd have done the same at her age. 'It's alright,' he says. 'I don't mind.'

She puts the papers down on the table and picks up the topmost one. She tugs on one of her plaits as she reads it to herself. 'I like this. Or I think I do. Some of it I can't make out.' She comes to show him. 'What's this word for instance? And this line, it's just squiggles!' She laughs to excuse the slight.

He takes the poem from her. 'You're right. I'm not sure what it says either. I'm a writer who's never been much excelled at penmanship.'

'I think it's about a woman you loved. Love.'

'Loved. Past tense. These things are years old.'

She goes back, kneels down and studies another text. 'This one's a bit easier.'

'Choose half a dozen,' he says, 'and I'll read them to you.'

'Really? When?'

'Not now. Let me see them first.'

Misalliances

She's picking up paper after paper, dismissing some, setting aside others.

'Nothing too long,' he says. 'Otherwise we'll lose our audience.'

'Then let's make it just the two of us,' she murmurs. Then quickly: 'I've got three so far. All very short.' She looks to him for approval. Can we take them down to the river tomorrow? Damaris says it'll be nice down there now.'

'It's only a stone's throw. How is it you haven't been yet?'

'I have, with Aunt Elizabeth. But you know what she's like. It was all overgrown and she didn't like it. We didn't stay long.'

'We'll go tomorrow, then. With Damaris. I'll tell Robert to go and clear the path.'

'You, me and Damaris?'

'Yes.' She seems disappointed. 'Would that be alright?'

'Of course. I like her. And you'll read to us...'

'I promise.'

She beams at him and flourishes the poem she has in her hand. 'Just half-a- dozen?'

'I think that'll be enough.'

****

Damaris doesn't return until immediately before supper and there's no opportunity then for them to speak. Afterwards, he finds her in the kitchen lighting a candle, though it's still light.

Misalliances

He stands by the door to put the question. 'Did you have a good day?'

'Yes,' she says. 'It was nice to see Lizzie and the baby. But I'll not go again.'

'No?'

'Not if Tom's visiting.'

He comes in and leans one elbow on the chopping table. 'You didn't know?'

'I'd no idea.'

'I think we both know why it wouldn't have been mentioned.'

'Well, I'm not going to get caught up in all that. Or be party to more of Kat's rudeness.'

'She had a point.'

'It wasn't fair. It's my fault. I shouldn't have made you come.'

'No. It was right you did. But like you, I'll not go again. I've got enough on here.'

The kitchen goes dark; a cloud must have passed over what's left of the sun. She lays her hand on his. 'Please don't fight with him...'

'It won't come to that. I won't let it. I was thinking more of Elizabeth.'

'You seem to be getting on alright so far.'

'It's only been a few days...'

'And Beth's lovely.'

'She is. She'd like us to go down to the river tomorrow. The three of us. She's found some of my poems and wants me to read them to you both. It's a nice idea. Poetry by the river.'

'It is. We'll do that, then.' She's holding up the candle like she's ready to leave and he moves aside. 'Are you off to bed?'

'I am. I'm tired.'

He lets her pass and follows her out. 'I'm thinking of going up to the Friars,' he says, calling her back. 'As soon as I hear from Arthur.'

She turns. 'Oh?'

'It'll make things easier.' In the dark of the stair-well she's a pale, hesitant wraith and he very much wants to go and embrace her. 'Goodnight, then,' he says.

'Goodnight.'

Misalliances

Chapter Forty-four: Strong passions

There's no sun but it's another warm day. He leads the way, listening to the girls chatter as they make their way down by the stream which feeds the moat. Girls. Damaris is hardly a girl, yet in Beth's company she's talking like one, almost breathlessly. It's all quick exchanges - 'I like your hair' 'Do you?' and 'I could never do mine like that, it's too curly'– interspersed by Beth's little giggles. He feels like an outsider, but he'd rather be with the two of them than with Elizabeth, Tom or Jane.

    He looks up and down the river. At that moment the sun comes out and, sifting down through the trees, it plays on the water in luminous patches. Apart from the midges gathered in discrete swarms underneath the trees on the opposite bank, all is still. Beth and Damaris come and stand on either side of him. He's noticed that when Beth looks up at him something playful enters her eyes, like she finds something in him that's amusing or entertaining. Damaris, on the other hand, now she's stopped being a girl again, is regarding him like she always does, with a steady gaze that for a while now he's been interpreting as a sign of their closeness, the trust and understanding that's grown between them. 'I imagine the elderflower has gone,' he says to her.

    'So has Madeleine,' she says. 'No more syllabub.'

Misalliances

'Or not with elderflower. There used to be a place to sit a bit further along.'

'It's still there.'

Beth is tugging on his arm. 'Let's go, then.'

Damaris takes over leading the way till they arrive at the jetty where she came with Madeleine.

'Yes, this is it,' Wyatt says.

'Sit, then,' says Damaris. He does so where he is, just off the path, draws up his knees and folds his arms on top of them. 'Don't sit back there,' she chides. 'The boards are safe.'

Beth is already out on the platform, at the edge of the water. He calls to her. 'I've brought the poems.'

'Let's just sit for a minute,' Damaris tells him. She joins Beth. 'Don't tumble in. It is quite deep.'

'Are there fish?'

'Somewhere,' Wyatt says, from behind.

'Tell you what,' Damaris says to Beth, removing her shoes and reaching up under her skirts. 'I don't think Thomas'll mind.'

'What are you doing?' he says.

Damaris's stockings are quickly round her ankles and Beth's aren't far behind. To shrieks of laughter they swing their bare legs over the side.

Beth casts a challenging grin back at Wyatt. 'Come on, uncle. You, too.'

'Unfortunately,' he says, 'my hose are not so easily removed.'

'Get him to go and do it,' Beth whispers to Damaris.

Misalliances

But Wyatt, shoeless, is already there beside them. 'Oh, why not.' There's a big splash as, still in his hose, he drops his feet into the water.

'You can't do it like that,' protests Beth.

'I'm not doing it any other way.' He's laughing. Then they all are. He wants to tell Damaris it's good to hear her laughing, but he doesn't.

'Let's have some poems,' she says. A bird pipes up on the other bank. 'Though it sounds like you've got some competition.'

> 'Alas, madam, for stealing of a kiss
> Have I your mind so much offended?
> And done so grievously amiss
> That by no means it may be amended?
> Then take revenge, and next is this,
> With one more kiss my life is ended.
> The first my heart into my mouth did suck
> The next shall out of my breast it pluck.'

Beth is looking up at him. 'Are all your poems about women and love?'

'Not all. Most of them, though. It's common.'

Damaris is giving him that look again, the one that says 'we understand each other, don't we?' What she actually says is: 'Do you remember when you first read your verses to me?'

'I do. It was when I brought you up to Westminster from St. Wilfred's.'

'Do you know what I thought?'

Misalliances

'You were a novice nun, so I dread to think. All that love and lust.'

Beth gives a nervous hiccup of a laugh.

'I thought they were wonderful,' Damaris says. 'They put me back in a world where a man – one man – wished nothing but good for the woman he was in love with. Very different from the world I'd entered, and from the one I'd been in before. And that's when I knew you were a good man.'

Beth is wriggling uncomfortably. 'Oh, stop!' She lifts her feet out of the water.

'None of it was real,' Wyatt says.

'It was,' Damaris says. 'Some of it was.'

Beth has backed off from them to dry herself. 'Are we going to walk along a bit?'

'There's two poems yet,' Wyatt says.

'Let's hear them later.'

Damaris is slipping her feet into her slippers without drying them. 'I hate trying to put stockings on when your feet are wet,' she says.

'That's a good idea,' Beth says, doing the same.

'Let's go that way,' Wyatt says, 'where Robert's cut it back.'

Beth is at his side. 'You don't mind?'

'Mind what?' He scoops her up, swings her out over the water and dangles her there. 'Shall I?' he says to Damaris.

Beth's alarm, such as it is, is coupled with a kind of glee: 'Don't you dare! Put me down!'

Misalliances

'There was I thinking you liked my verses.' He lowers her to within an inch of the surface.

Beth, her knees raised, red in the face, has realised it's more dangerous to struggle than be still. 'No, don't. Please.'

Laughing, he brings her back and deposits her on the bank. She slaps him on the arm, picks up her stockings and walks on, kicking her feet.

He turns to Damaris. She looks displeased. 'Just a bit of fun,' he says.

'Don't flirt with her, Thomas.'

'What?'

'She likes you. Didn't you know?'

'Of course she does. I'm her uncle.'

'Not just like that.'

'Don't be silly.'

'Young girls have strong passions.'

'I know that.' He slips his arm round her waist but Beth is not far ahead so he doesn't leave it there. 'Shall we see if there's some elderflower?'

'Even if there is,' she says, 'it'll be useless now.'

****

Oh, silly of her to show her jealousy, she tells herself. After concealing her feelings for so long. He'll know now.

Once again, because she revisits it often, she's back in the monk's cell at St. Wilfred's with a Thomas Wyatt who still has a full head of hair and has come in with a promise to help her. She couldn't admit then how much she was attracted to him. Didn't admit it. Even on the long journey up from the coast when they sat side by side and talked and talked, about Cardinal Wolsey and the state of the Church and ancient theologians. She knew she liked him, this somewhat troubled man who was involved with some lady at court and had strong views about religion but didn't, he confessed, pray that often. But as for feelings stronger than that, she couldn't let them into her head or any other part of her.

When she saw him again, just the one time, when she was filing out of the church at Westminster with the other sisters and he was on the street, her heart had started beating fast and when his eyes fixed on her and they exchanged smiles it leaped up in her breast. She knew then, didn't she? Why else, years later, would she have set out for Allington?

She's no longer a nun, no longer *feels* like a nun; is no longer what she was or who she was. She has an idea of what kind of woman she wants to be but what she doesn't know yet is whether the recent changes between them will be right for that woman. What she *does* know is how he makes her feel. Every time she's with him there's such a rush of emotion in her breast, such a stirring in the woman part of her, that she feels she's about to burst. All the looks, the smiles, the seekings out, the hushed exchanges...

Misalliances

She has got this right, hasn't she? He *is* drawn to her. And that is the behaviour of a man in love, isn't it?

But this is Thomas Wyatt. He writes heartfelt poems about loving women but he also lusts after them. She doubts even the prohibitions the King has laid on him will stop that. She wants him to *love* her, but she's afraid.

Chapter Forty-five: Departure

The new mattress has arrived. It's outside on the flags. It looks fine enough. Wyatt, testing it with his fingers, is relieved that it feels good too. 'Feathers,' he says to Edward. 'The coming thing. Too soft for me, though.'

'It's because you've become accustomed to straw.'

'In The Tower, you mean? It was only a thin layer at that. We slept on the ground that time in Italy.'

'Young men then. Do you want me and Robert to take it up?'

'Yes. If this doesn't suit her, nothing will. If there's a problem, you know where to find me.'

Edward's downstairs again before Wyatt's turned the first page of the account book he's inspecting. 'She wants you to go up.'

'She's not happy with it?'

'I think so. She just wants you to see it in place, I think.'

'I see wool prices have risen.'

Edward comes to look over his shoulder. 'And meat. The lamb and pork all did well at the market. The harvest's promising as well.'

'What about outgoings?'

'Since you got back from Calais we've mostly lived off the land, what we kill and what we sell.'

'We've not touched the King's money...'

'Not at all. The money for the ladies' gowns and what Arthur needed for the work on the Grange I took out of what came in.' Edward leans over to turn a page. 'It's all there.'

'And Tom?'

'Only what you said I should give him. Shillings, that's all.'

'No more racking up debts in town?'

'He's not been going in as far as I know.'

Wyatt closes the book and hands it to Edward. 'We might make a profit this year. I'd better go up.'

'Elizabeth?'

'I'll be out in a minute, Thomas.'

The mattress fits perfectly. It's a plain thing but the ticking is linen rather than canvas. He slips his hands under the bedstead and gives it a shake. It's sturdy enough now. Whatever Robert did, it worked. He'll have Marjorie come and make up the bed.

His wife comes in from the dressing-room. She's still in her nightgown, though she's tidied her hair, combed it down to her shoulders, and rouged her lips.

His immediate reaction is: 'Are you not well?'

'I'm very well.' She comes over and strokes the ticking.

'You approve, then?'

Misalliances

'I do. It's very much what I wanted. Thank you.'

'I don't need thanking,' he says. 'I want you to be comfortable.'

'Try it yourself. Come and stretch out.'

He takes a step back because he's begun to feel uncomfortable. 'That's alright,' he says. 'I'm busy. I should get on.'

But he doesn't, because the sight of Elizabeth Brooke lifting her nightgown to expose her nakedness is something he can't for the moment walk away from. In shape and firmness it's not so different from the last time he saw it. That was when he burst in on her in Thames Street and – the opposite of what's happening now – she was trying to cover it up, after having spent the afternoon with Charles Brandon in the bed there.

'Don't you still like this?' she's saying. 'Come and lie down with me. I am your wife.'

He takes a further step back. 'We talked about this. No, Elizabeth.'

She lets the hem drop. 'Oh. And I thought we were getting on so well.'

'We can't go back.'

One of her daytime gowns is laid out on the wicker chest beneath the window and she reaches for it. 'Then I'd better get dressed.'

'I'm sorry,' he says.

Half-way to the dressing-room she stops. 'Is it the nun?'

'What?'

Misalliances

'It is, isn't it? I've seen you looking at her.' She's clutching the gown to her like she's attempting to retrieve the situation and at least some of her dignity before this man who's just seen her naked but doesn't want her. 'Or is it Beth who's taken your fancy?'

'Beth? Are you mad?'

'She's only a bit younger than Catherine Howard must have been.'

'That's enough!'

'Is it?'

He's made it to the door. 'Enough! Get dressed.'

****

Sweaty, smelling strongly of horse, Arthur picks up the mug of beer that's been put in front of him. 'So that's it,' he says. 'All done. The main house *and* the smaller one.'

'The Grange.'

'The Grange. So it just needs Mistress Lizzie and yourself to come up and get it the way you want. It does need some furniture.'

Wyatt doesn't shy away from it. 'It'll just be me. Mistress Lizzie is living at Boxley.'

'Oh?' Arthur looks at Edward, who says nothing.

'I'll come up in a week or two,' Wyatt says. 'Perhaps stay a while. We can take some furniture

Misalliances

from here. Where did the stuff from my father's rooms go?'

'The outhouse next to the stables,' Edward says. 'There's not much. We burned a lot of it.'

'I'll take a look.'

'Oh, yes,' Arthur says. 'I meant to say. We've done nothing with the chapel. I didn't know what you had in mind.'

'You did right,' Wyatt says. 'I want it to stay as it is.' He turns to Edward. 'Have you seen Damaris today?'

'She's out riding.'

'I've got to go in before I wee myself,' Beth says, levering herself out of the saddle. 'Can you take the horses?'

Damaris dismounts and takes the smaller mare's bridle. 'Off you go, then.'

The girl dashes off. She's in such a hurry that she doesn't give a second glance to the young man making his way out of the close. But then, she wouldn't know who he is.

Arthur waves and comes over. 'Sir Thomas is looking for you, Mistress. He's in the outhouse.'

Damaris's skirts, the French-style ones she and Beth have had made to make riding easier, are caught on the top of her boots; she pulls them free. 'Which outhouse?'

He points to the shed next to the stables. 'That one. He's looking for furniture.'

Misalliances

'Is he?' She's hot and Arthur smells. All she wants is to get to her room, bathe her face and put on something loose.

'For the Friars.'

'So you've finished there...'

'Except for some dribs and drabs. Are you well, Mistress?'

'I am,' she says, gathering up the horses' reins. 'Good to see you, Arthur.'

'I didn't know you could ride, Mistress.'

'Didn't you?' Arthur's eyes are on her legs, travelling up them and she feels herself blushing. It's the divide in her skirts that has got his attention.

'They're nice, these two, aren't they?' he says, stroking the younger mare's nose. 'Shall I take them in for you?'

The outhouse is stacked with cast-offs: cabinets and side-boards, chairs and bed-steads, broken joint-stools and settles.

Though its coolness is welcome, the place is filthy and Damaris stays in the doorway. Wyatt hasn't heard her come in. 'I didn't know all this was here,' she says to announce herself.

'Oh, hello,' Wyatt says, giving another tug at the table he's trying to pull out. It doesn't look much bigger than the one they play cards on in the parlour but time has piled on to it an accumulation of items turfed out of the stables: dray-horse collars, bridles, rusted chains, a child's saddle.

Misalliances

'Arthur said you wanted me.'

He dusts off his hands, wipes them down his grubby shirt and joins her in the doorway. 'I hadn't seen you at breakfast, that's all. It was nothing.'

'I came down late and went straight out.'

'Well, since you're here, take a look at this.' He returns to the table, throws off the heavier things on it, and pulls it clear. He brushes the loose dirt off. 'It's pretty, isn't it?'

She ventures in. 'It is.'

'It was my father's. He used to sit at it when he was doing the accounts. It must be older than me. It occurred to me the other day I hadn't seen it. It should never have been put here.'

'Or had all that junk dumped on top of it.'

'It's with me being away so often. Things happen I know nothing about.'

'They do indeed.'

'Yes.'

She strokes her finger-tips over it. 'It's got scratched. What a shame. But it should polish out.' Beneath the patina of grime something is peeking out. 'What's this?' She takes out her handkerchief and begins to wipe. In the centre of the table there's an inlay: a rose. 'Marquetry,' she says. 'Very well done, too.'

'It's the Tudor emblem,' Wyatt says. 'An early version, I'd say. Might have been done in honour of the old King, Henry's father.'

She runs a finger along the finely carved edge. 'Must have been. Look at these crowns along the apron.'

'Is that what they call it?'

'A deep edge like this? Yes.'

'You know about carpentry?'

'A little. We had an excellent man who did things for us when I was a child. Is it going to the Friars?'

'And a few other things.'

'How long will you be going for?'

'I don't know yet. Three or four weeks. Maybe longer.'

'Oh.'

'I wish you could come with me.'

She steps back. 'I can't. With Elizabeth here it wouldn't be right.'

He closes the gap between them. 'What if she weren't?'

'But she is.'

'She won't be forever.'

'Won't she?'

'It's a show. That's what we agreed.'

'You said.'

'I took her back because I was ordered to. But it doesn't mean she has to stay, or that she will. All it needs is for George Brooke to roll up one day with a bag of gold sovereigns and I reckon she'll be gone. Would you come with me then?'

'I don't know. You're forgetting the other thing.'

Misalliances

His hands are on her, drawing her close. It'd be their first ever embrace. 'No, Thomas,' she says, freeing herself. 'I'll see you at supper.'

****

George Brooke, Lord Cobham, comes clattering across the drawbridge in a carriage and four with two liveried servants riding postillion.

The apparition startles everyone but Wyatt. Having told Robert to get the horses seen to and and Abigail to bring beer, he meets his visitor at the door and extends his hand. 'George. It's been a long time.'

'Hello, Wyatt.' Brooke takes out a handkerchief and mops his brow. 'I thought I'd come see my daughter.' He pauses. There's a whistling in his chest. 'Damned hot today.'

'Come into the hall, it's cooler there,' Wyatt says. 'I'll send for her.'

George Brooke's fortunes may have taken a turn for the better but he hasn't. His complexion has always tended towards the roseate, but since the last time Wyatt saw him it's acquired the ingrained ruddiness of the heavy drinker. And he's clapped on some weight. 'The horses'll need water,' he wheezes, as he lowers himself on to the nearest bench.

'They're being seen to,' Wyatt says. 'Your men as well. Beer for us, I thought.' To his relief, because it will help the flow of conversation,

Misalliances

Abigail is bringing it now. Behind her is Beth, in her green dress.

'Father?'

Wyatt doesn't greet Beth like he usually would. This is a moment for father and daughter. Brooke doesn't rise to the occasion at all – perhaps he literally can't – and says only: 'There you are. Come and sit.' Beth remains standing at the end of the table, from where she says: 'What are you doing here?'

It's not Wyatt's idea of a reunion. If this delightful girl were his daughter, he'd be rushing across to hug her and ask how she was after not seeing her for three months. But she's not his, and it's not for him to say anything.

Elizabeth's here now. She's found the time to throw on her evening wear, a satin gown, a French hood, a pearl necklace. 'George?'

'Elizabeth! May I speak privately with my sister and daughter, Wyatt?'

'I'll leave you.'

What he leaves them to is brother and sister embracing, gripping each other's hands, and Beth standing apart, looking forlorn. She flicks a glance in his direction, looks away again, and sits down.

The smallest sound carries in the great hall, which means he hears every word. Brooke and Elizabeth are doing all the talking.

- I'm back on my feet.

Misalliances

- Are you?
- I got into a card school with Henry. And since he never repays his debts with coin, I got that prime piece of land I had my eye on in Lambeth.
- The Sack Friars?
- And sold it within the week.
- How much for?
- More than enough to put Cooling to rights. And I got him to agree to having you back.
- He must be tiring of Catherine.
- He's not had her crowned yet. *And* – quite apart from all that - I've got the young'un here a place. Did you hear, Beth?
- Yes, you've got me a place. What kind?
- At court. Probably at Greenwich. I'll take you up to show you off. Someone'll be sure to snap you up.
- But I like it *here*, father.
- I've had to pull strings for this, child. So no shilly-shallying. You'll come today. We'll go up to London, get you some proper clothes and take you up to court.

At the sound of Tom's voice – 'Mother? What's going on?' - Wyatt retreats, goes into the kitchen, picks up a flagon of wine and goes into the parlour.

    Cup in hand, he walks back and forth, listening. By the time Abigail shows Brooke in,

Misalliances

he's on his second cup. 'So you're taking them with you,' he says to him.

'You heard...'

'Why else would you have come?' Brooke is eyeing the flagon but Wyatt wants him gone. 'The King might not like it,' he says. 'Elizabeth's only been here a few months.'

'Leave that to me. You did your bit. I'll have a word in his ear.' Brooke picks up the flagon and gives it a sniff. 'Is this Gascon?'

'It is. If you'd like to wait in the hall, I'll get someone to help them pack.' He leads Brooke out.

Tom has come to see them off but Jane hasn't and neither has Damaris. Wyatt doesn't know where she is. He waits till mother and son have said their goodbyes before approaching Elizabeth. 'That wasn't so bad, was it?'

She gives him her hand. 'D'you know, Thomas, it wasn't bad at all.' She kisses him on the cheek. 'We did what we had to. It'll be alright. I'll see to it.' She laughs. 'Who knows? I could be back.'

He gives Beth the hug her father should have done. She's sobbing. 'Now, now,' he says, 'we'll see each other again.'

'Will we?'

Her lashes are brimful of tears. One of them escapes and trickles down her cheek. He catches it with his finger. 'We will.'

Misalliances

Brooke is holding the carriage door open for his sister. He gives Wyatt a half-hearted wave.

'Goodbye, George,' Wyatt says.

Beth hasn't moved. 'I don't want to go,' she says.

'You've got to. I'll see you soon.'

'Promise?'

'I promise.'

He finds Damaris in her usual place in the park. He sits down beside her.

She gives him a glum smile. 'I'm going to miss her.'

'She was never going to stay forever.'

'She's only fourteen. She'll be lost at court. You know what it's like there.'

'She'll be alright.'

'When are you leaving for the Friars?'

'In a day or two.'

He's never seen her crying. At first, he's not sure she is, because there are no tears, just a convulsive shaking, a rise and fall of her shoulders, a heave of her breast and a dipping of her head. She takes charge of herself enough to say: 'Don't leave me here, Thomas.'

'Then come with me.'

'How would we do it? After what the King said to you?'

He puts his arm round her and this time she lets him draw her close. 'Don't you think I've thought of that?'

Part Seven

Misalliances

Chapter Forty-six: At the Friars

'The Mistress's new gowns have come,' Elsie says. 'I've put them upstairs.'

Wyatt is about to go and tell Damaris but decides to go and see them for himself first. It pleased him, taking her to the draper's on The Strand to choose fabric and patterns, seeing her eyes widen with pleasure at the colours and quality. He kept a look out for soldiers and anyone who might know him, but if someone should spy them out and about and report it to the King, which was unlikely, then she's his cousin.

'*Do* you have a cousin my age?' she asked.

'Several,' he replied. 'I even see some of them now and then. Henry's not going to know they're all men.'

Every day he gives thanks – just to the air - for how things are going. It wasn't easy at first, but he hadn't expected it to be. They're past the awkward early stages of sleeping together, and she's happier than he's ever seen her. Rescuing Madeleine from an unhappy placement in Maidstone and bringing her with them has played its part. 'Not to be my maid,' Damaris insisted. 'She'll be my companion.'

He assumes Elsie will have put the gowns in Damaris's room, one of the three first-floor bedchambers created by partitioning the old dormitory, but they're not there, they're laid out

Misalliances

on the bed in his. He wonders if he should say something, tell Elsie and Judith to be discreet in what they say outside. But *his* sense of discretion tells him to say nothing. What were the chances of gossip from his housemaid and cook ever reaching the King? And they'd be foolish to jeopardise their comfortable position by gabbing about their master to the baker, butcher or costermonger down the road. It does occur to him at times he's tempting Fate, living as he is, a stone's throw from Tower Hill, less than a mile from The Tower, but it's about time he took Fate on.

 Anne once told him he had an eye for which colours suited her - he's never forgotten her telling him that, because what happened later between them was memorable for other reasons – but he had no part in choosing the fabrics from which the half-dozen confections he's now inspecting have emerged. Damaris's choices were wholly her own. It was something that registered with him: by not consulting him – no 'What do you think of this?' - and relying wholly on her own predilections and taste, it was like she was in the act of becoming the woman *she* wanted to be.

 He spends a few moments examining the garments, carefully lifting them and assessing the quality of the work. The seamstress in Maidstone was skilled, but these – in the precision of the cutting, shaping and stitching – are of a different order. She will be pleased. And seeing her in them, so will he.

'No,' she says to him. 'Go. I'll come down and show you when I'm ready.'

'It's not as if I haven't seen you undressed,' he says.

Surprisingly, she's colouring. 'This is different. Madeleine's going to do it.'

'Did I hear my name?' Madeleine says, coming through the door.

'Tell him to go, Maddy.'

Madeleine takes hold of Wyatt's sleeve and steers him towards the landing. 'My apologies, Sir. There are some things best left to women.'

He hears their laughter as, ever aware of the absence of a banister, he descends the stairs. It's not the first time he's told himself he should have had a new staircase installed; this steep open stone affair might have been alright for the monks but it's not what he's used to and it doesn't suit the women of the household. Even Elsie and Judith, who must be more used to it, go up and down with a hand on the wall to steady themselves. It's one of several features he wants to revisit now he's living in the house. He'll recall the builders, have the two sitting-rooms they made out of the chapter hall knocked into one again, reinstate the space. There's a big enough fire-place. He imagines it thronged with merry guests on Christmas Eve, servants handing out cups of mulled wine and offering assorted sweetmeats; Yuletide like they used to have it at Allington in his father's time.

But he'd want them to devise it in their own fashion: insist that everyone comes to dance; bring in the best musicians he can find; a lord of misrule, perhaps, as long as she's of the same mind, that it's acceptable to have a little foolery on the eve of Christ's birth. It's a vision he can't see being realised the way things are, but in time it might be possible. Circumstances change. It's their nature.

'Goodness me!' It's not an exclamation as such, rather an exhalation of wonderment.

'Those stairs! Maddy's had to help me down.'

'I'll see to them.'

He knows what she's doing. Nervous of his reaction, seeing her like this, in the orange gown with its layered skirt, daringly scooped neck and tight waist, she's talking about anything but that. That's what they're both doing, though the only thing on each of their minds is how she looks. She's rouged her lips and on her head is not her usual plain coif but a French hood.

'Well?' she says.

'It's you,' he says. 'This is how you should be dressed.'

She laughs dismissively. 'Not every day, I think.'

'Some days,' he says, reaching out for her hand. 'My lady, shall we dance?'

'We don't have any music!'

'I'll hum, then.' He leads her down the room, adding a galliard-like skip or two. By the time they

Misalliances

do the turn she's laughing too much to continue, so he takes her in his arms and kisses her. 'Where did the hood come from?' he whispers.

'I got it the same day,' she whispers back. '*You* paid for it.'

'We'll have some made for you,' he says. He holds her at arm's length, drinking her in. Later, he will undress her, unpin her hair and bury his face in its curls.

She withdraws her hand; the smile vanishes. 'No. Don't do that.'

It flicks through his mind, the preposterous notion she's somehow read his mind and no longer wants him. But it's not that she means. 'What's wrong?'

'When would I wear them?' She waves a hand down the dress. 'When am I going to wear this?'

'You'll wear it for me.'

'Yes, I know...' She gives an exasperated shake of her head. 'But at what other time? You're out for supper tonight...'

'At Horsey's,' he says. 'A tenant. It'll be business.'

'But he's also a friend. Will he ever be invited here?'

'I'll talk to him.'

'No, don't.'

'He'll understand. His wife's not the sort to gossip.'

'Gossip about my being your mistress, you mean?'

Misalliances

'Not that,' he says. 'You know what about. You are *not* my mistress.' He draws her to him.

She puts her hands up between them. 'I can't be your wife.'

'Stop.'

She detaches herself. 'I'll go and change.'

****

One gloomy November afternoon, with fog clawing at the window, when they're side by side in the kitchen having an early glass of wine, she says: 'Can I ask you about Lizzie? Have you done anything for her?'

'I sent something before we left.'

'You didn't have to.'

'I thought I should. It's enough to keep the wolf from the door. For her and the child. That's all I'm doing. What Tom does is up to him.' Wyatt looks into his wine glass and swirls the liquid around. 'It's not as if I've led a blameless life myself...'

'You mean the women you've had...'

'The funny thing is, while I was in France, after that foolishness with Catherine, I took an oath to do better.'

'And did you?'

'I did. There were temptations enough, but I ignored them. Waved them away. Then the woman I was doing it for...well...'

'Some might say it served you right. Divine justice.'

'Justice of a sort, certainly.'

It comes to her. '*That* explains why you were so interested in the penitential psalms...'

'You figured that out, did you?'

'It was how I excused you. I thought if David could be led astray by his lust, then you certainly could.'

'David and I. Not so different. In that respect, at least. Otherwise I wouldn't put myself in his company. He was a better man than I could ever be.'

'I don't think that's true.'

'Thank you.'

'So where am I in all this penitence?'

'Where are you? Don't you know? You're this repentant sinner's heavenly joy.'

She takes his hand. 'Oh, Thomas, that's lovely...' Tears have sprung.

'I mean it. Even though I don't deserve your love, I hope I have it.'

'You do deserve it and you have it.'

'And you have mine.'

She lifts his hand to her lips and kisses it. 'Then we'll be alright.'

Judith comes bustling in. She stops on the threshold. 'Oh, sorry.'

Wyatt gets up. 'It's alright. We'll go. You'll be wanting to get supper ready.'

Misalliances

Elsie's there too now. 'Mistress, I meant to ask you. It's half-way through November and I was wondering what you'd both be doing for Christmas.'

'We'll be here,' Wyatt says.

Dislodged, they make their way into the parlour. 'Christmas in our new home,' Wyatt says. 'It'll be like christening it.'

Damaris removes her hand from his and goes to the window. She stands there, looking out.

Knowing her, he waits. 'What is it?'

She turns. 'This is going to be our home, is it?'

'Of course it is. I thought that was understood.'

'No more Allington, then?'

'No. I'll go down now and then and see how things are, but otherwise...'

'Christmas,' she says,' but we can't have guests. I'm your heavenly joy but no one must know because of the King.'

He goes over to her. 'It doesn't matter, does it?' He puts his arms round her.

'Yes, it does.'

****

Damaris finds out from Elsie and Judith who best to go to for cushions and curtains, people who'll come and size up the house, give their opinion on what it needs and whether the work can be done by Christmas. She's also been talking about

Misalliances

replacing the settles in the sitting-room with daybeds, the kind Wyatt's told her about which grace the King's and the Emperor's palaces. 'To be a home,' she says to Wyatt, 'it needs to be homely. When we do have guests we can't have them squashed up on these old things or sitting on the floor.'

They've talked further and Wyatt has come up with a list of who they might safely invite to the Friars, who among his friends would be discreet about the ménage there, who would never be tempted to reveal its character in order to gain personal advantage. It comes down to a handful: Mason, Cheney, Russell, and possibly George Blage, who after Mason was the most dependable and likeable of those he had with him in Spain. Blage's being related to the Brookes is not necessarily a bad thing: he might know what's happening with Beth at Greenwich.

Damaris, coming in from a walk with Madeleine, says: 'Come and see.'

Wyatt puts down his pen. 'What?'

She holds out her hand. 'In the garden. I want to show you something. The sun's out. You don't need a coat.'

Reluctantly, Wyatt follows her. The space between the main house and the grange is almost the size of the close back home. Beyond the stables it slopes down to vegetable beds, and behind them is the row of trees and shrubs lining the lower boundary wall. It's in that direction

Damaris, smiling to herself, is leading him. 'With this amount of land to look after, we need a gardener,' he says.

'It'll wait till spring.' She's picking her way through the weed-strewn beds. 'Look. Look at them all.' They're standing in front of a tall holly bush crowded with berries. 'They're early, aren't they?'

'I don't think so. It *is* the end of November. And we had a warm summer then a cold snap. It's suited them.'

'I'm going to cut some,' she says.

She's wearing her new surcoat, a pretty thing with patches of brocade on the sleeves. The prickly bush would tear it to pieces. '*You're* going to?'

Her smile is teasing, mischievous. 'No, you are.'

'It's work for a gardener. Then you can have your holly.'

'Thomas...'

'What?'

'Surely you can do it?'

'With what?'

'One of those swords you've got...'

Pricked and prickled, he carries in an armful of cuttings, dumps them inside the door and holds his old broad sword up to the light. Toledo steel, it shows not so much as a nick. 'There you are!' he calls out; he has no idea where she might be. He takes out a cloth to wipe the blade.

'Oh, thank you!' She's there, coming to embrace him.

'Mind,' he says, turning away to stand the sword up in the corner by the door. He gathers her in.

'You smell of garden,' she says.

'We should be lighting up. It's getting dark.' He gestures towards the holly blocking the doorway. 'That can wait till tomorrow. What's for supper?'

'I don't know,' she says, as they move towards the sitting-room where the fire has been kept banked up all day. 'I've left Judith and Madeleine in charge,'

'I've been thinking,' he says. 'Arthur's people did a good job in the grange. It could take a tenant.'

She draws him down on to the settle that has become their love seat. 'Could it?'

'You're the one who wants to see more of my friends.'

'Who, then?'

'John Mason. He lodges at the palace when he has to come up from the country. I'm sure he'd like somewhere of his own.'

'Does he have a wife?'

'He does. She mostly stays in Abingdon. Why do you ask?'

'Just curious.'

'You want more woman friends?'

'I don't have any woman friends!' She's laughing.

'There's Madeleine. And Elsie and Judith come to that.'

She picks a holly leaf from his jacket sleeve. 'I do have Madeleine, but I used to have the company of lots of women.'

'Did you feel like this at Allington?'

'Sometimes I did. Having Lizzie helped.'

'That's why you went to visit her.'

'I told you why that was. We'd become friends. And the baby was there.'

Madeleine comes in. 'Supper's nearly ready,' she says.

Wyatt gets up. 'Are *you* happy here?'

'Me?' Madeleine looks from Wyatt to Damaris and back again. 'Why wouldn't I be?' She sees the holly branches. 'Oh, you got some!'

'Do what you want with it,' Wyatt says.

'You've misunderstood,' Damaris says, as they go in. 'I'm not unhappy.'

He stops. 'But you could be happier.'

'I want it to be perfect.'

Someone – it has to be Elsie – has taken a sprig of holly, stuck it in a vase and placed it between the steaming pots on the table. It is her, because she's smiling. 'Well, it's *almost* Christmas,' she says.

Misalliances

Chapter Forty-seven: Trouble

John Mason stomps his feet to shake the mud off his boots, steps inside and looks down into the tromp l'oeil which he's standing squarely in the middle of. 'That's clever, Thomas,' he says. 'Good to see you, old friend.' He takes off hat and cloak, looks around for someone to give them to and seeing there isn't anyone puts his hat inside his jacket and folds his cloak over his arm. 'How long have you been here?'

'A couple of months.'

'I've been down to Allington.'

'I'm sorry. I should have let you know.'

'So, what's the story? Are you living here now?'

'Come into the sitting-room.'

Madeleine is on a stool trying to hang a bunch of holly from a beam. 'Sir Thomas has hammered in this nail too far,' she calls down to Damaris. 'It's not going to work.'

'Come down now,' Damaris says. 'We have a visitor.' She helps Madeleine off the stool. 'Mister Mason. Good morning.'

'Good day, Mistress,' says Mason. He shoots a glance at Wyatt. 'Is there somewhere we can talk? There's trouble with Catherine.'

'Let's fetch some wine,' Damaris says to Madeleine.

Misalliances

Wyatt catches her arm as she passes. 'No, I'd like you to stay.' He motions Mason to sit. 'You remember Damaris?' he says to him.

'I do.'

'She knows everything about me.'

Mason lays his cloak over the arm of the settle. 'Does she?'

'She does. What kind of trouble?'

'So,' Mason says, only now reaching for his wine glass. 'She's at Syon Abbey pending her trial. Dereham, Culpeper and Jane Boleyn are in The Tower. The grandmother is likely to follow.'

'And this all came out from someone who was at Norfolk House with Catherine...'

'Mary Lassels.'

'That's not the same Lassells as John, who worked for Cromwell?'

'Brother and sister. For reasons best known to herself...spite of some kind ...Mary told John what she knew about Catherine and Dereham and he went to Cranmer. Chose him, I imagine, because the Archbishop has never been close to the Howards.'

'Why would he have done that? Gone all the way up to an Archbishop?'

Mason picks up the jug. 'May I?' He carries it over to Wyatt and fills up his glass. 'Mistress?'

'No, thank you.'

Mason retakes his seat. 'Because what he had wasn't mere tittle-tattle. It had substance. My theory is it's because of what happened to

Misalliances

Cromwell. There was a bunch of them, wasn't there? Cromwell's acolytes, all full of hatred for Rome, all agitating for the new Church. You were one of them once. What better way to get back at the man who did for Cromwell, the man who has been doing everything in his power to get us back in bed with the Pope, than bringing down his niece, the Queen. He was aiming at Norfolk as much as Catherine. And he had what it'd take.'

'You and I would never have taken on Norfolk.'

'We didn't have the wherewithal. Lassels did. And I imagine as soon as he realised he did, he set the hare running. Cranmer chased it and found out about Culpeper, as well as the part Jane Boleyn had been playing in setting up his and Catherine trysts, where they met and so forth. By fair means or foul old Cranmer got confessions. From all of them. Dereham and Culpeper have admitted to knowing Catherine carnally so they're going to the block. It's scheduled for the second week in December.'

'That's hard on Dereham. It must have been three or four years ago.'

'But the King feels he's been hood-winked. He's in a rage and Dereham, poor fellow, has been caught up in it.'

Wyatt, still standing, looks at Damaris who, seated opposite Mason with her hands folded in her lap, has so far not said a word. Now she does.

'What of Thomas? Has his name been mentioned? There was a time he knew her carnally too.'

'I'm sorry, Mistress,' Mason says. 'This must be distressing.'

'It would only be distressing if Catherine were to offer up his name.'

'Why would she? It would only make matters worse for herself.' Mason glances at Wyatt. 'And she'll know what it would mean for you, Thomas.'

'I doubt that's been in her mind.'

'It might have. She got you out of The Tower.'

'Is that what went around? That I was a favourite of some kind?'

'Weren't you?'

'Not at all. That's not how it was. I've not been a favourite of anyone for a good while.'

'Well, certainly not the King's, after what he laid on you.'

'Is that common knowledge?'

'Of course it is. Which brings me to ask, Thomas, who else knows about you and Catherine apart from me and the Mistress here?'

'John Russell does. He figured it out and I told him.'

'He'd never give you up.' Mason puts down his glass. 'Is anyone else likely to know?'

'Anne Basset. She and Catherine were friends at the time. But she's not been at court for ages, because of her father.'

Misalliances

'That could be a problem. Lisle's imprisonment isn't the only reason she was sent away.'

'Why, what else was there?'

'As I understand it, she was banished with Henry's other mistresses after he married Catherine.'

'I'd no idea.'

'You wouldn't, would you? You need to be at court to know these things. Her relationship with the King goes back some years apparently. It started after the death of Jane Seymour, well before Catherine came to court. And it didn't stop when he married the German. Though that's hardly surprising given the kind of marriage it was. What I'm getting at is this, Thomas. You have to count on Basset's staying away. Henry was once very fond of her - obviously – and his bed is empty again. There's nothing like pillow talk for the yielding up of secrets.'

'Lisle's still in The Tower. Been there well over a year.'

'Then, for your sake, let's hope he stays there.' Mason gets to his feet and drapes his cloak over his shoulders. 'I ought to be off.'

'Stay a while. We'll be eating soon.'

'No offence, but I've stayed long enough. Look, let me say this. How you live your life, Thomas, and you yours, Mistress, is none of my business. And in my view it's none of the King's.

But are you out of your minds? Living here in the city, you couldn't be more visible.'

'We're taking pains not to be.'

'Thomas! If Henry meant what he said, about you being with no other woman but your wife, you have to be *invisible*. Especially with all that's going on. Get yourselves back to Allington, that's my advice.'

'Thank you, John.'

'I'm sorry to have brought all this to your door, but you needed to know. I'll see myself out.'

He finds Damaris on her knees in the chapel. He's made sure it's exactly how the monks left it: the chalices and patens, together with the missal, are still on the altar; the shrine to the Madonna hasn't been touched. Elsie has instructions to dust everything and wash the altar cloth once a week. It pleases him that Damaris goes there regularly, though she rarely visits this late. She has lit the candles. In their light, she looks ashen, like some devotee doing penance or about to undertake a vigil of some kind. 'Come to bed,' he says gently. In rising, she nearly tips over and he gets there just in time to steady her. 'You're tired,' he says. 'Come.'

'Do you know what I was thinking?' she says, as they climb the stairs, he behind her just in case she falters. 'Silly, really. John Mason won't be taking the Grange.'

Misalliances

'We didn't get a chance to put that to him, did we?'

'He wouldn't have considered it for a moment. You must have seen how keen he was to be off.'

'He came, that's the thing.'

'Then saw I was there.'

'He's a friend, no matter what.'

'Is he?'

Since it takes him no time at all to get out of shirt, britches and hose, he helps her, and by the time he's folded and neatly laid aside her bodice, gown, kirtle and stockings she's under the covers. She's lying clenched, like she was the first time they made love. Not that he's thinking of their doing that now. He touches her shoulder. 'We'll be alright.'

'I think Mason's right. We would be safer at Allington.'

'If they come for me, because of Catherine or because of you, it doesn't matter where I am. Other than abroad somewhere.' He blows out the candle.

Her voice – subdued, still anxious – persists. 'And you don't think this Anne Basset poses any danger.'

'Not as long as her family's in disgrace. We stay here regardless.'

'Hiding in plain sight...'

'Not hiding,' he says. 'Being invisible.'

****

Misalliances

Elsie picks it up on the street. There's going to be an execution at Tyburn, on Thursday.

'It'll be Culpeper and Dereham,' he says. 'Shame it's not on the hill, but I could do with a ride.'

'Don't,' Damaris says to him. 'We said we'd be invisible.'

'This'll help,' he says, pulling the brim of his hat down. 'And who's going to be interested in me out alone?'

'They'll see you're here.'

'So what? It's a free country.'

'It's not, that's the trouble.'

'I won't stay long. I hate these things. I'll get the feel of the crowd and be back.'

He's not been to Tyburn since the hanging of Elizabeth Barton, however many years ago that was. Seven, eight? He'd been forced to go, been inveigled into it as a proof of loyalty. It literally turned his guts; along a deserted stretch of Tyburn stream he'd had to stop and empty his liquefied bowels. He knew why it had affected him so badly. It wasn't just because Barton was a nun, and a young one at that. However mad she was for speaking out against the King's abandonment of the Catholic church – or principled, depending on how you looked at it - he felt it was wrong for the machinery of state to be taking *her* life, when Henry was without principle, had little sense of

Misalliances

moral rightness. As it turned out, the King would, privately, continue to follow Roman ideas of faith and worship – the things he'd had Barton hanged for - while paying only lip-service to the reforms which Cromwell said he must embrace if he was going to show those potential allies who had also turned away from the Pope's Church that he was serious. Cromwell was gone, and it looked like Norfolk could soon be, if not to the scaffold like his niece, then to his Sussex estates, out of favour and out of power. With its strongest opposing advocates gone, where would that leave the English Church?

As for his own position, he's no longer sure what it is. Once upon a time he considered the Roman Church irredeemably corrupt and its zealotry without rational foundation. The Inquisition had declared him a heretic. But he's living with a former nun, and the purity of her devotion has touched him. Ever rational, he has always inclined to the view that, no matter where one's religious sympathies lay, it was the same God.

As he expected, the turn-out is huge. The composition of the crowd is the same as always: just ordinary folk, rude in feature and gesture some of them, smelly most of them, and all of them as varied in character as those of his own class. He's sure none of them has much idea who the condemned men are.

Misalliances

Even if he wanted to, he wouldn't be able to get near the platform. There's no pushing through today with 'Make way! King's man!'. He lingers at the back of the crowd with the other latecomers and tries to calm his horse, which even at one remove from the excited hubbub has become restless.

He hadn't tried to explain why he felt compelled to come. To be sure, watching Cromwell die had been such a terrible experience it should have deterred him from ever again attending one of these public spectacles. The truth is he feels some kinship with Culpeper and Dereham, even though he doesn't know the former well and the latter not at all. What he has a more tangible relationship with is the scaffold. It's got close to him twice. That's what's brought him here.

One of the men on the fringes – a thick set fellow in a leather apron - looks like he's about to have a go at him, this high-and-mighty lord in his fine clothes on his fine horse. The smith, or carpenter, whatever he is, is looking up, assessing, and his expression is close to a sneer, but the sally turns out to be chummy: 'Should have come earlier, mate! You'll not get through now.'

'I know. Here'll do me.'

'Gonna be a good 'un. One of them's gonna get the works.'

'The works' means a man is half-hanged, taken down to have his belly opened so his entrails can be pulled out, and then, finally, subjected to the axe and chopped into four pieces. He wonders which one of them it will be. Whichever it is, it's a thing he has no wish to be party to, even at a distance. Sheepishly, he turns his horse round and trots away.

Arthur's at the Friars when he gets back. 'I've put him in your study,' Damaris says.

With his head bowed over his mug of ale, Arthur's looking somewhat abandoned, but his greeting is cheery. 'Hello, Sir! I've been sent up to see if you're coming for Christmas.'

Wyatt concocts reasons why they're not, though each contains a grain of truth: there are still things to do at the Friars, Mistress Damaris fancies staying in the city, it could be hard travelling. How are things at Allington? Is Edward managing everything? The accounts and so on?

'I've brought them, so you can see.' Arthur reaches for his bag. 'It's only the one book.' He takes it out.

'Good. I'll look them over before you go. You'll be staying the night...'

'No, that's alright. It promises to be a clear one with a good moon and it's not a bad road. I'm happiest on a horse.'

Wyatt takes the book and opens it. 'Are Master Tom and Mistress Jane well?

'I think so. Lord Cobham's been down once or twice.'

Misalliances

Wyatt looks up. 'Has he? What for?'

'To take Tom up to the palace.' Arthur peers out from under his cowlick.

'Which palace?'

'Greenwich, I think. He was only gone a week or two.'

So George Brooke has been taking Tom up to court. Wyatt lets it sink in. It's something he would have done himself by now if things had been different. He returns his attention to the ledger. 'So it's the same as every year. We're storing half our crop and selling the rest. That's a lot of wheat gone.'

'It was a good harvest. We kept the same amount as usual. Some went to be milled. The rest is in the big barn.'

Wyatt closes the book and hands it back. 'Good. Tell Mister Edward I'll be down in the New Year. I need to see how much we've got in the coffers.'

'I think we're thriving, Sir.'

'We are, if the Autumn figures are anything to go by. You must have some food before you go.'

'Had some, Sir. While I was waiting.'

'Good. Did you see to your horse?'

'I did.' Arthur, on his feet, grins shyly. 'If you don't mind me saying, you could do with a stable boy. And some servants. I was at the door ages before someone came.'

Wyatt takes him out into the hall. 'Arthur, you do know how things are here?'

Misalliances

'Between you and Mistress Damaris, you mean?

'Yes.'

'I do, Sir. I'm not daft.'

'Then will you tell Mister Edward that if anyone official, anyone from the palace, comes looking for me, it's alright to say where I am, but it's best they don't mention I'm with someone. A lady, I mean. Tell him to make that clear to Master Tom as well.'

'I think that's understood, Sir.'

'None of you is daft, eh?'

Arthur grins. 'I wish you luck, Sir. And a happy Christmas.' For the very first time in the many years he's served the Wyatts, he presumes to offer his hand.

Wyatt takes it and gives it a pump. 'Happy Christmas, Arthur. Ride safe.'

****

As December draws to a close, the house gets a daily dusting of snow, but that's all. After Mason's warning, they decide not to invite guests but the days of Christmas are pleasurable nonetheless: heapings of good food, gallons of good wine, much late sleeping and every afternoon, amid an extravagance of candles, an hour or two of convivial card-playing. Wyatt insists Elsie and Judith join in.

Misalliances

On one of the days between Christmas and New Year Judith asks Damaris if she might bring her niece. The girl is going through some hard times and could do with the experience of working in a big house. 'I thought she could 'elp me in the kitchen a bit. It's a busy time for me, what with all the poultry and puddings, cakes and comfits. It's always busy, really.'

'What you're saying is, you'd like us to take her on...'

'If you like her. She'd be no trouble.'

Lily - Judith calls her Lil - is a pretty girl: big blue eyes, a nose as perfectly shaped as the rest of her, and a full-lipped mouth that Wyatt guesses has had its fair share of kissing, given that even when she's sitting still she tends to adopt a particular posture, as if somewhere in her history she's learned that this is the way to get attention from men. It's one he's found a certain type of woman adopts: back straight, bosom thrust forward, lips set in a pout, eyes staring ahead to scan the room. Sometimes – usually when the eyes alight on an eligible man – this type of woman tosses her head back and fiddles with her hait. Plenty of women at court adopt this style of behaviour to invite themselves to this or that bedchamber. In the wider world it's not so common, but it's the stock-in-trade of women who work in establishments where a bed has a monetary value. He sets his prejudices aside until he's seen more of her, though when they sit down

Misalliances

for a hand of fifteen, which Wyatt says must include the girl, he notes how confident she is at handling the deck when it comes to her turn to deal, and how she lifts her chin whenever their eyes meet, which is often.

Everyone's late to bed. Just as Wyatt is dozing off, Damaris says: 'Poor Lily. We should have asked her to stay the night.'

He rouses himself. 'She said she doesn't live far.'

'What did you think of her?'

'I think she's been making her way as a whore.'

'Do you?'

'It's everything about her.'

'I did see her looking across at you a lot.'

'Any man's a meal ticket to a whore.'

Damaris raises herself on one elbow and looks into his face. 'I'd like to do something for her.'

'What? Try to save her?'

'It's been known. A lord of the manor rescuing a poor girl from the streets.'

'Usually so he can bed her.'

'What do we do? Talk to Judith?'

'No. I'll see to it.'

'Thomas...'

'Leave it with me.'

On her first day Lily came dressed simply in a plain skirt and blouse, cap and shawl. On the next she turns up in a thin taffeta bodice with her lips rouged and her eyes kohl-lined. Wyatt hears Judith remonstrating with her and when the girl next appears, with an apron covering her top, the rouge is gone, though the kohl, which he imagines must be harder to remove, remains. As soon as Judith and Madeleine go out to buy fresh meat, Elsie's upstairs cleaning and Damaris is settled in the sitting-room, he puts his plan into action.

Lily is putting a pan of water on the stove. 'Sir?'

He puts his arm round her waist, draws her away from the heat, looks straight into her startled eyes and says: 'Where can I find you, away from here?'

'I don't know what you mean,' she says. But she hasn't tried to get away.

'Yes, you do. I'm happy to make it worth your while.'

'I'll have to think.'

'Good. I'll be in my study. Do you know where it is?' She shakes her head. 'Go past the staircase and through the arch,' he tells her. 'You'll come to some wooden steps. I'm up there.'

He hears her mounting the creaking boards a few minutes later. 'Sir,' she says, and lays a piece of paper down in front of him. His first thought is that she's literate, though what's in front of him is barely legible. The note says:

Misalliances

Magpie Alley, Whitefriars. Brown door.

'Then I'll see you there this evening,' he says.

'Alright, Sir.' She gestures behind her. 'I'd best get back.'

'You must. And this has to be kept between ourselves, you understand?'

She gives a nervous smile. 'I know that.'

Whitefriars is less than a mile away, a warren of darkly dwindling alley-ways. His knowledge of similar places and the services they offer prompts him, just for a moment, to visualise her there behind the brown door, ready for him. Then he gives his head a shake and goes to find Damaris.

Lily is before them, her posture part apprehensive, part defiant.

'What's wrong?' Her eyes are on Wyatt. 'Have I done something?'

'You're a whore, Lily,' Wyatt says.

'You tricked me,' she says.

'I did. Your aunt brought you here in the hope we'd take you on. I had to find out who you were.'

'Where is she?'

Damaris says: 'I've told her to stay in the kitchen. She says you're going through a hard time. What is your situation?'

'I ain't got one, Mistress. I was working in a tavern. Upstairs mostly. You know. I got kicked out. Nothing I'd done. Or not done. Honest.'

Wyatt holds up the scrap of paper. 'And this?'

'It's a friend's place. I would have been there.'

'That's a point in your favour, is it?'

'I'm not a bad person. I don't let people down.'

'Not if they've got a full purse, eh?'

Damaris lays a hand on his arm to shush him. 'If we're to take you on, all that has to stop.'

Lily is clutching her left hand with her right, twisting her fingers. 'It will.'

'You ought to be doing better,' Wyatt says, 'a girl who can read and write. Where did you learn?'

'At the monastery in Whitefriars. I was a good girl once.'

'Are you from there?'

'Born there. I'm sorry, Sir, for that business with you. It's how I've been getting by. I will change.'

'You have to,' Wyatt says. 'If there's any sign of you going back to your old ways, we'll not keep you.'

'I understand. Thank you.'

'And the Mistress and I will help you with your reading and writing.'

Lily's face brightens. 'I'd like that.'

Later Damaris says: 'Was that you atoning for your sins?'

'If you like.'

'It was, wasn't it?'

'I did something similar in France.'

'What was that?'

Misalliances

He tells her about the girls in Loches. 'Mason said they'd go back to it as soon as the money was gone.'

'I don't think Lily will.'

'You don't?'

'She wants to improve herself. And she'd be a fool to throw away a place here. Elsie and Judith stayed on when you were in The Tower because they were being well looked after.'

'Very well looked after.'

'Then let's do the same for her. Put a little extra money her way, so she can buy things for herself, dress better.'

'I hear the nun speaking.'

'No. Like you, I'm simply trying to do the right thing.'

****

The month of February has sharper teeth than usual. Each day finds everyone at the Friars staying as close as they can to a fire or stove. If they must go out in the cold – Wyatt to collect his rents, Elsie and Madeleine to go to the butcher's or baker's – they come back with their scarves and hats stiff with frost, their noses red and streaming. It's only now, with the river below The Tower ice-bound, that the King has signed the warrant for Catherine Howard and Jane Boleyn to be taken out on to the rime-silvered square that's known as The Green and have their heads cut off.

Misalliances

Elsie picks the news up on the street again. It'll be in three days' time. At this distance, they won't hear anything of it. If it was happening on the hill, a public affair, they would. What they do hear on the day, first thing in the morning, is the sporadic tramp of feet. The crowd won't be let in, but it'll gather outside, waiting for the proclamation. Wyatt doesn't mention what day it is and neither does Damaris. When Judith makes a comment – 'It'll be about now, won't it? They always do them before noon' – she moves away.

****

Towards the end of Lent, the subject of simnel cake comes up. Judith says: 'The baker down the road does one. I'll go tomorrow, early, before they're sold out.'
    Lily is grinning. 'This baker of yours that you're always going on about. Did you say he's a widower?'
    'Hush, it's nothing like that.'
    Damaris, in the kitchen to check on the week's fare, says: 'It better not be. We don't want to lose you.'
    Judith throws up her hands. 'Goodness gracious. You're worse than the fish wives down at the market. He's just a very good baker. And you know I'm not much good at baking bread.'
    'You have tried,' Damaris says.

Misalliances

'You ought to go and see for yourself, Mistress. He does some lovely cakes. If you went now you might still get a simnel.'

She finds Wyatt in the stables grooming the mares. 'Come to the baker's with me.'
'The baker's? Why?'
'To get some simnel cake. It's Easter soon. We have to break our fast.'
'Fasting in this house? It's a wonder we're not all popping out of our clothes.'
'Come on,' she says, 'it's a lovely day and it's only down the alley.'

The baker is a balding man of middle years. He is evidently accustomed to receiving a certain kind of customer, because as soon as he lays eyes on these unlikely ones – Wyatt in his smart doublet and velvet cloak, Damaris in her brocaded coat - and hears their request, it sends him into a panic. Apparently unsure whether he should bow, he catches himself half-way and goes hurrying off into the bakery with a 'Yes, Sir'and a 'Yes, my lady' and returns balancing a cake on each palm. 'These are my best,' he says quietly. 'Reserved for my best customers.'
'Then we'll take them both,' Damaris says, taking out her purse.
It *is* a lovely day, one of those late March ones that announce Spring, and it makes Damaris smile, exchanging the yeasty and very pleasing aroma of

Misalliances

the shop for the breathy freshness of the air outside. 'Judith likes him,' she says. 'Elsie and Agnes tease her.'

'Poor fellow,' Wyatt says. 'Do you think he knows who we are?'

'Would it matter?' She hooks her arm in his. 'Catherine's gone. You're safe, Thomas.'

They turn into their street and immediately Wyatt pulls her back into the alley. 'Stay there!'

She does as she's bid, eyes wide with alarm. It takes her a moment to find her voice. 'Thomas? What is it?'

Pressed against the wall, poking his head round the corner of it, he signals her to be quiet.

The soldiers, pikemen, about fifty of them in breastplate and helmet, go clanking past. When they've gone, he waves her up to join him. 'Let's wait a moment,' he says.

She's hanging on his arm. 'You don't think...'

'I don't know.'

In the sunlight, the tall gables and porticoed frontage of the Friars stand out in the otherwise ordinary street. The soldiers are coming level with it. There's no shout of an order, no dispersal of the line. It crosses over and turns into the road which leads to The Tower.

'Must have been a drill,' Wyatt says. 'It's alright.'

They walk out. He takes the basket from her. 'Let me carry that.' He sees her face. 'I'm sorry. When they came for me that time, it was exactly like that. A whole troop for one man. On a January morning they took me out without jacket or coat. Paraded me manacled through the streets.'

She brings them to a halt. 'Would any of them be the same men?'

'Could be.'

'Then it only needed one of them to recognise you and see you in the company of a woman.'

'You're my cousin.'

'Were we behaving like cousins, hanging back frightened in an alley-way?'

'But it wouldn't go up to the King, not from a common soldier.'

'It wouldn't have to directly, would it? You've said yourself what it's like at court, everyone angling for advantage. It only needs to be picked up by someone whose turn is served by passing it on to Sadler or Wrothesley.'

'Wriothesley...'

'According to Mason, everyone knows what Henry told you.'

'People forget. *He* probably has. I want to live with you in our London home.'

'Under his nose.'

'It's time I defied him.'

'I've just seen how that's working. Are you going to hide every time we come across soldiers? There's a lot of them round here.'

'Not that many. And I wasn't hiding. I just wanted to see if they were going to the Friars.'

507

'You made *me* hide. We've been worrying about you and Catherine and forgotten the other thing.'

'I'm safer than I was...'

'But you're *not* safe. It's no way to live, Thomas.'

Misalliances

Chapter Forty-eight: Known

There's a peremptory rapping at the front door and Lily, keen to show she's worth the faith that's been placed in her, rushes to answer it. The visitor pushes past her and announces himself.

'William Fitzwilliam for Sir Thomas. Is he here?'

The Lord Privy Seal's presumptuousness catches Damaris off-guard. That morning she decided to put one of her fancy gowns – she likes to do it for herself as well as Thomas – and its long skirt slows her escape. By the time Fitzwilliam has stepped over the tromp l'oeil and raised his head to get his bearings, she's reached only the bottom step of the staircase.

What tears Fitzwilliam away from the sight of her is Wyatt. 'William?'

'Thomas! I hope you don't mind me dropping in like this. I was on my way to The Tower and thought...' Fitzwilliam's eyes stray back to the staircase. 'I hope I'm not intruding.'

'You're not.'

'I have a proposition for you.'

Fitzwilliam sits back and crosses his legs. He must be on his way to a formal meeting because he's in his full regalia; sables and chains of office decorate the shoulders of his coat. 'It's April and the elections for knights of the shire are coming

Misalliances

up. As you know, they're one of the mainstays of the Commons. Canterbury will be nominating somebody or other and we'd like the other to be you.'

'I'm flattered, William.'

'You're a known landowner and a knight. I said I'd get something for you...'

'I thought you meant abroad.'

'That's still a possibility.'

'You said we. Who's the *we*?'

'Russell, Cheney, Sadler.'

'The King?'

'This sort of thing doesn't go up to him and, anyway, at the moment he only wants to be bothered if it's something's really pressing.'

'It's bad, eh?'

'It almost did for him when he found out about Catherine. But now it's done, he's starting to bounce back.' Fitzwilliam looks round the room. It still gives off the odour of fresh paint. 'You've been working on this place.'

'A little.'

'And spending some time here.'

'Just a month or two, to get it how I want.'

'So, Knight for the Shire of Kent. What do you say?'

'Put me up for it. It's a good idea.'

'Excellent.' Fitzwilliam looks round again. 'Is this the only house you've kept for yourself?'

'It is. I like the size and it has some nice features.'

Misalliances

'Except that staircase, Thomas. That looks unsafe to me. If I were you, I'd think about that.'

'I'll be careful.'

'Elizabeth's at Allington, is she?'

'At Cooling for the time being.'

'You know she's been up to court?'

'No...'

'Straight after the execution. Henry was in no mood to receive *anyone*. Stupid of her. He sent her away.'

'I didn't know.'

'And this might be of interest to you. Arthur Lisle died last week.'

'In The Tower?'

'The day after Henry pardoned him. He'd only been out a few hours.'

'So the disgrace on the family has been lifted...'

'Just as they've lost him.'

'That's sad.'

'You weren't responsible for it, Thomas. It was foolish of him to get mixed up in that Botolf business.'

'He was good to me when I first went to Calais.'

'He was a good man. We all make mistakes, eh?' Fitzwilliam gets up. 'I'll send your details to the sheriff – it's Henry Isley now - and he'll no doubt be in touch.'

Misalliances

'That's good news,' Damaris says. 'The Parliament sits at Westminster, doesn't it?'

'The Commoners meet at Saint Stephen's Chapel. Except when the King comes. Then the whole parliament, the Lords and the Commons together, meets in Westminster Hall.'

'Will you have to be there a lot?'

'Three or four times a year, I think. Only for a week or two.'

'He saw me.' Damaris lifts the hem of her skirt, runs the silk through her fingers and lets it drop. 'In this.'

'And he made a comment about the staircase.'

'What kind of comment?'

'He told me to be careful. I took it he meant you. He's a friend.'

'And the Lord Privy Seal.'

'It'll be alright. Otherwise he wouldn't be going ahead and nominating me. And he's the least of our worries. Lord Lisle has died. Henry had just pardoned him. Poor man must have been worn to the bone, because he walked out of The Tower and dropped dead apparently.'

'Where does that leave Anne Basset?'

'It means the attainder on the family will be lifted, like it was with me. She could be returning to court.'

'And out to settle a score with you, because you put her father in The Tower...'

'She's not going to know that.'

Misalliances

****

Arthur's back again, still in the same mud-caked leggings and sweat-stained riding jacket.

'You got here early,' Wyatt says.

'So I can get back early. You've not been down, so I've brought up this quarter's accounts and what you said you wanted, the tally of what we hold. It's in Mister Edward's letter.'

Wyatt takes the book, extracts the letter, puts it to one side and runs his finger down the figures for January to March.

'It's a quiet time,' Arthur says, 'though we've sold the rest of the wool and the rents are all in. You're collecting the ones in the city.'

'I am.'

Arthur starts on the bread and dripping and takes a drink. 'There's something else. Mistress Elizabeth is back.'

Wyatt doesn't look up. 'Is she?' He turns over a page, sees it's blank and flips it back again. 'By herself?'

'Just with those two maids she brought last time.'

'And she's settled back in alright?'

'She seems happy enough. And Master Tom's pleased to have her there.'

'Is he?'

'Mother and son, Sir.'

'Has she asked where I am?'

'I think there's something in the letter.'

Misalliances

'Good.'

'Are you coming down, Sir?'

Wyatt hands back the book. 'Not for the time being. Come up each quarter, like you're doing now.'

He opens the letter and skims through Edward's message. What he's really interested in is the figure at the bottom of the page. Two thousand and twenty. Sovereigns, not ducats. A tidy sum. Twenty bags of coin. It's not that he has a plan what to do with it. But it is there if he ever has to come up with one. He reaches for the other document on his desk. Like the money, it's about making provision. At the top, in his best hand, he's written: **Thomas Wyatt: Last Will and Testament**. He considers the empty page for a moment, turns it over and makes a note of the sum, turns it back and pushes it across his desk. There might come a time for it, but it's not now.

Damaris pulls back the covers. She stays sitting up a few moments while she untangles her hair and then settles down. 'She won't have been taken in by what Edward told her, you know.'

'That I'm here doing the place up? Why not? It's not a complete lie.'

'She'll know you're here with me.'

'It'd not be in her interests to make trouble.'

'Will things be better for you, being a member of parliament?'

Misalliances

'It depends who I run into. I'm going to be showing my face. That's not always a good thing. I'm known. It'll remind everyone I'm still around. But John Horsey's there. So I'll have one friend.'

****

It's one of those evenings pitched between the end of summer and the beginning of autumn when Damaris notices a reddish glow in the sky to the west. She calls Wyatt over to the window. 'Is that just the sun setting?'

The view from the parlour is limited but with the sky blanketed all day by low cloud the light has to be from something man made. 'I think it's from Smithfield,' he says. 'Let's go up to the landing.'

The tall window at the top of the first flight of stairs tells them enough: the sparks flying haphazardly into the air above the old city wall can only mean one thing. 'Yes,' Wyatt says. He grips Damaris's wrist. 'They've put someone on the stake.'

She doesn't expect an answer to her question but she puts it all the same. 'Who?'

'It could be anyone these days,' he says. He's back at Ardres, ten years ago, taking his party, which included his young son, into the main square and finding himself and his men, and Tom, on the edges of a scene that no young boy should be thrust into, a young woman being burned alive.

Misalliances

The smell, and the sight of the febrile crowd's excited faces, stayed with him for days.

'That's your new Church for you,' Damaris says. 'It's just like the old one.'

'No Church is mine when they do that,' he says. 'Some of the new clergy are fanatical. They're doing as they please and Cranmer daren't stop them for fear of upsetting the King.'

'Is that what you've heard?'

'I'm sure it's true.'

'So it'll be Catholics they're burning...'

Her eyes are searching his face for answers he does not have. 'More than likely. Though I've also heard he still says his prayers from the Roman missal, like you do.'

'Then the world's gone mad. Let's go down.'

The following day he's on his way to Westminster when he meets Elsie and Lily coming back from the market. They wave him down.

'The burning, Sir,' Elsie says. 'It was a couple of nuns caught doing a Catholic Mass. Should I tell the Mistress?'

'No, leave it to me.' He turns his horse round.

He doesn't know what to say, thinks it's best to let her vent it, her outrage and distress.

'Two of my sisters, Thomas! For doing what I do in our chapel every day. For what I imagine thousands of English men and women are still doing every day!' He releases her, lets her walk

Misalliances

the floor again. She comes back and clutches at him. 'Can't we go somewhere *safe*, where I'm not going to be hauled off to the stake for worshipping my God as I want to? Where you're not in constant fear of what the King might find out about you?'

'There's nowhere here,' he says.

'What?'

'I don't mean *here*. We can do what we like in our home.'

Her body is taut with anger, and he's expecting her to rail forth once more against whichever powers have brought them to this pass, or to demand from him a solution to the manifold predicaments they find themselves in, but when the words come they take the form of another kind of challenge. 'Come and pray with me, then,' she says.

'Gladly,' he says, surprised at how easily the word has come.

Kneeling beside her in the chapel with, like her, his eyes closed and his hands clasped in front of him, also comes easily. He knows the Latin and when she begins reciting the prayer he joins his voice to hers.

> Sancta Maria, Mater Dei,
> ora pro nobis peccatoribus,
> nunc, et in hora mortis nostrae.

Misalliances

Afterwards, she says, 'It's their sins I'm asking the Holy Mother to pray for, not ours.'

'I know.'

'You're going to be late,' she says. 'Go. I'll be alright.'

****

He bids farewell to Horsey, who is going back to Clifton Maybank until the Commons sits again in November, and walks over to Westminster Hall. He likes being one of those privileged to enjoy it, this enormous, hallowed space in which the King holds forth once or twice a year on what he wants his parliament to do, though everyone knows, or those in the know do, that the really important decisions are taken in the Privy Council. The Hall is empty today; he's climbed up into the gallery for the simple pleasure of being close to the oak buttresses of the hammer beam roof and admiring what the previous century's carpenters were able to do. There's a similar one at Hampton Court but it's not as magnificent as this. The span of it has to be more than fifty feet. And once it was erected, they still hadn't finished. Other carpenters, those skilled in fine-chiselled ornamentation, went up and did the decorative work.

On his way out the big-bearded swaggering bulk that's Charles Brandon, the Duke of Suffolk, shoulders its way past him, and sends the papers he's collected from the clerk's office tumbling to

Misallianges

the floor. Brandon's man, whose swagger rivals that of his master, steps on one of them and at Wyatt's 'Mind out, you fool!' he turns, his hand going to his sword. Brandon, who has retraced his steps, slaps the hand away. 'Don't do that. He'll be better than you. Or he used to be.' Brandon puts his hands on his hips. 'Wyatt? Are you still here?'

Wyatt, straightening papers, gets to his feet. 'No thanks to you.'

'You didn't enjoy your little sojourn in The Tower then?'

Wyatt puts the papers under his arm, gives a sideways glance at the other man who is the short and wiry type, more terrier than mastiff, and takes a step forward. 'I thought we might have done with all this, Brandon.'

'Done with it? You and the whore queen had me sent away from court twice. That's not playing by the rules.'

'You seduced my wife and knocked me down in my own house. Neither was that.'

Brandon waves his man away and steps forward himself. There's spittle on his lips. 'The trouble with you, Wyatt, is that you've never understood. It's men like me who *make* the rules. And I've not done with you. You're bound to have been up to something you shouldn't have.'

Smarting, Wyatt watches them go and, to his surprise, realises his sword is a third of a way out of its scabbard. He pushes it in, leaves the Hall and heads across the square to where his horse is.

Misalliances

****

The message from Fitzwilliam says to come and see him at Greenwich that afternoon, or failing that no later than first thing tomorrow morning.

Now it's stopped raining, Madeleine and Lily are walking to Aldgate High Street to fetch beer and at the last minute Damaris has decided to join them. He catches her as she's putting on her coat. With the coming of September the air has turned cold.

'Will you be back?'

'Of course I'll be back,' he says.

'You're not going to be sent abroad again, are you?'

The girls are waiting; the front door is open. He draws her away and to one side. 'I don't know. Anyway, I'll refuse. I'm not doing that again.'

It's as if she hasn't heard him. 'Because I'm not staying here alone.'

He says it again. 'I'll refuse.'

She moves away. 'Then I'll see you this evening.'

Greenwich. It's on the other side of the river, but if he gets a move on and is lucky with a ferry, he should be able to get there by midday. That'd give him time to seek out Beth. There's a queue at the horse-ferry so he decides to cross by the bridge.

Misalliances

It's always busy, its traffic slow, but it'll be quicker than waiting.

It doesn't take too long to get past the usual bottle-neck at the gate. The careless and the laggardly quickly scuttle out of the way of the big horse. Then everything comes to a halt. There's been an incident of some sort opposite Saint Thomas's Chapel; there's someone on the floor and lots of blood. It's brought a crowd. He begins to think he'd have done better to strike out along his side of the river through Wapping and Limehouse, and taken his chances on getting a ferry from opposite Placentia. Things begin to move. He doesn't linger where the heads are. Even if he weren't in a hurry, he has no interest in seeing if Dereham's and Culpeper's are still there. By now, they'd not be recognisable, anyway. Bit by bit, steering his horse this way and that, he gets through.

The narrow by-ways of Southwark restrict them to no more than a trot; it's not till he's on Kent Street that he's able to urge the horse into a canter. The watery sun is high in the sky by the time they reach Deptford and its creek. His way is no longer straight; he has to go out of his way to where the tributary narrows to a ford. The rain has swelled it but his horse breasts it without floundering. Now it's back to the Thames; two miles at most. And at last the tops of Greenwich Palace's cupolas come into view.

Misalliances

In the stables, he takes off his hat and straightens his clothes. The water trough looks reasonably clear, so he dips in his handkerchief and wipes his face. After taking several deep breaths, he makes for the palace's rear entrance. It takes him past the enclosure where the kitchens dump their waste, and where, on a sunny morning almost exactly three years ago, he first met Catherine Howard. He doesn't give it so much as a passing glance.

As expected, he encounters guards on the way to the stairs up to the Queen's floor. They are posted at ten yard intervals, a stricter prescription than in his day, but these are less settled times. The trick, he tells himself, is not to make eye-contact, to stride past them as if the corridors and passage-ways of Placentia are as familiar to him as those of his own home, as indeed they once were. After a while, his confidence returns. He's here on legitimate business, even if it's elsewhere than the rooms to which he's presently bound.

There might not be a queen at present but, as he'd been hoping, the ladies of the court are still assembling in her presence chamber. The door is open, and he can hear their voices and laughter well before he reaches it. There's a guard on either side. One of them promptly draws aside the shaft of his pike to let him through, while the other, an older man, nods and greets him with 'Morning, Sir Thomas'. He *is* still known.

He picks out Beth immediately. She'll be one of the junior members of this sorority, one of those

Misalliances

who wait on ladies-in-waiting, in the outer rather than inner circle, which explains why she's seated near the door. The change in her shocks him: the rouged lips, the line of kohl round her eyes, the décolletage of her gown. She's busy talking. It's only when he walks towards her that she sees him and then, without a moment's hesitation, she's jumping to her feet and, with an abandon he would have cautioned her against had he not been so pleased, she's throwing her arms round him. 'Thomas! You came!'

Yes, she couldn't be happier. Terrible, a year ago, after she'd just arrived. And it was horrible for months. But things are better now. She's with Lady Clinton, who was *never* part of all the bad stuff. And, oh yes, she saw cousin Tom a few weeks ago. Is he going to be coming regularly?

Wyatt is conscious of time passing. He tells her that, for his sins, he's here on business, and that he must go soon, but that he will see her again. He's about to get up when her demeanour changes, the joy goes out of her face and, putting a hand on his arm, she says: 'Wait a moment.' She's seen something over his shoulder. 'It's Anne Basset,' she whispers. 'You don't want to meet her.'

'I really don't,' he says. 'Has she seen me?'

'I don't think so.' They sit frozen for several seconds, before Beth says: 'It's alright. She's gone again. She was looking for someone. Do you know her?'

Misalliances

'We have some acquaintance. She can't have been back at court long.'

He doesn't have to say anything more, it spills out of her. 'Just a few weeks. She's been trying to make a friend out of me. But then I realised she was more interested in talking about you. She doesn't like you, does she?'

'Probably not.'

'She blames you for what happened to her father. Says it's your fault he was put in The Tower. Was it?'

'In a manner of speaking.'

She grips his hand. 'Thomas, she says she knows something about you that will put *you* in The Tower.'

'She may do.'

'Oh, you can't be going there again! I'm sorry. I should have let you know.'

'It's better that you didn't. Who is she friendly with?'

'Well, lots of people.'

'Among the high-ups...'

'I saw her talking to the Duke of Norfolk once, but he doesn't seem to be here much now.'

'What about the Duke of Suffolk?'

'Well, she'll know him. We all do. That's not why you're here, is it? Because of her?'

She's squeezing his hand so hard it's beginning to hurt. He removes it and gives it a pat. 'I don't think so. I have to go.'

'I will be seeing you again, won't I?'

Misalliances

He kisses her on the cheek. 'Of course you will,' he says.

Fitzwilliam's rooms will be downstairs, along the passage on the left. He's about to turn into it when he sees Anne Basset and Charles Brandon talking at the far end of the corridor. She must have met him at the main entrance. They've stopped to talk. If they're going to Brandon's private rooms, they will be coming past. He slips into the passage-way and, just as he did when he and Damaris were coming back from the baker's, he presses himself against the wall and waits, not this time to see what he can see, but what he can hear. It's one of those serendipitous moments, because the snatch of conversation he picks up leaves him in no doubt of its subject. Him. He heard Brandon say his name.

Fitzwilliam has taken over Cromwell's old rooms. Half-rising from behind a desk almost as cluttered as the late Mister Secretary's used to be, he exclaims: 'Thomas! Sorry to have given you such short notice but that's all we've had ourselves. Our friend Courrières is coming to talk about a treaty and who better to meet him than you?'

Chapter Forty-nine: Resolution

Damaris takes the key out of her pocket and opens the door. 'Did I tell you? Thomas was talking about renting it out to John Mason, but I don't think that's going to happen now.'

'Oh, you've brought the cushions in,' Madeleine says, putting down the jug of small beer and going to the seat beneath the big window.

Damaris fills each of their cups and takes them over. 'I did it yesterday when you were out fetching this.' To express her gratitude, she toasts her friend. She doesn't much like Aldgate High Street and is glad Madeleine has taken on the task of fetching the beer.

'Are you going to find someone else?'

'I don't know,' Damaris says.

'It's a shame to leave it empty. It's such a pretty house.'

Damaris turns to look at the way the sunlight is dancing on the yellow walls of the Grange's sitting room. 'It certainly gets the light,' she says. 'It must be the way it's facing. The Friars *is* dark. Thomas was talking about returning the sitting-room to its original size. It used to be the chapter hall. That might make it lighter.' She pauses. 'But, I don't know...things are a bit uncertain at present.'

Anxiety fills Madeleine's face. 'You're not thinking of going back to Allington, are you?'

'Goodness me, no. What makes you say that?'

'Well, I know things are not easy for you in the city.'

'They'd be far worse down there. Thomas's wife is back. And then there's all the other stuff. With Tom.'

Madeleine puts down her cup and, drawing up her knees, swings her feet on to the window seat. 'I couldn't go back there.'

'We have talked about getting away. You know, somewhere safe.'.

'Where?'

'I don't know.' Madeleine has gone quiet. Damaris copies her, lifts her feet on to the seat and sits back against the sill. She pulls her skirt down over her shoes. 'It'll probably never happen,' she adds.

'If it did, what would happen to the Friars?'

'I suppose we'd sell it.'

'Oh.'

It's only now Damaris sees what's happening: the girl is on the verge of tears. 'Maddy, what's wrong?'

'You'll leave and I'll be all alone.'

'No, you won't, you silly. We'd take you with us.' Damaris closes the space between them and takes Madeleine in her arms. She tips up Madeleine's chin. 'I promise.' There's the sound of horses' hooves. 'That's Thomas. Come. Let's go and see what they wanted from him at Greenwich.' She pulls the girl to her feet. 'Who knows? It might be the answer.'

Misalliances

****

The house is asleep so they're talking in whispers. Damaris has found the riding skirts she had made in Maidstone. She puts one in her bag and lays the other on the bed.

'Don't pack too much,' he says. 'We need to leave room for at least one bag of money.'

'What are you taking?'

'A couple of shirts and a change of hose. Just a jacket over my britches.'

She's holding up her riding coat. 'Shouldn't I wear this?'

'We'll be riding hard each day. Getting a sweat on. But, yes. You'll need something for once we're at sea.'

'And you don't think Madeleine could come?'

'No, she'd slow us down. Courrières will be pulling into Falmouth in three weeks give or take a few days. It's a long way.'

'You said.'

'And neither we nor our horses can ride all day and night. We'll have to stop.' Her bag tips over and he moves the candle just in time. She stuffs another kirtle in the bag, closes it and eases it off the bed on to the floor. He does the same with his. 'If there's anything we've forgotten, we can get it at Allington or at Clifton Maybank when we see Horsey.'

'He'll be happy to take this place on, will he?'

Misalliances

'He's always wanted it.' Wide-eyed, she's stopped what she's doing and is staring at him. 'What is it?'

'I can't see how it's going to work.'

'How else are we going to escape?'

'What if Courrières won't help?'

'I told you, he offered to when I saw him in Calais.'

'He's coming to see the King.'

'That's right.'

'Keep your voice down, you'll wake everyone. Come and sit.' He brings his candle over and puts it next to hers. 'Listen,' she says. 'I'm sure Courrières is a good friend and if circumstances were different we could flee to Flanders and live in his house. But he's coming to see the King, Thomas! He's never going to go along with what you're suggesting, telling Fitzwilliam and the King you've been taken ill when all the time he's got us hidden on his ship. It's not going to stand up, and from what you've told me about him, he'll see that it won't.'

Wyatt gets up, picks up his bag and puts it on the bed. 'What do we do, then? How else do we get away?'

'Let's say we did, the King is bound to find out where we are. Then he'd send one of his assassins. Like he did you with that Branceter fellow. He'd be after you till the day you died. I think it might be better to...well...brave it out.'

'Say I never knew Catherine Howard, you mean?'

'It's not as if they're going to get anything from her.'

'They'll be getting it from Anne Basset.'

'So?'

'She's been the King's mistress!' He picks up his bag, swings it by its strap like he's preparing to throw it across the room, and then lowers it again. 'Damn!'

'I'm sorry.' Damaris holds out her hand. 'Come to bed. Things might look better in the morning.'

Wyatt's face lights up. 'That's it!'

'What?'

'What you said. He'd be after me till the day I died.' He goes to her. 'That's the answer. I have to die!'

Misalliances

Part Eight

Misalliances

Misalliances

Chapter Fifty: Over the waves

They're beginning to feel the swell of the sea. In the forecastle it's experienced as a slight dipping and rolling, a louder creaking of timbers. After they come in from watching the shores of Cornwall ebbing away from them on either side of the widening estuary, Damaris asks if there's anywhere she can lie down.

Wyatt comes to her side. 'Are you feeling sick?'

She leans against him. 'No, I'm just dog-tired.'

She's bound to be; they haven't slept in a bed for two nights. So is he, but he's not going to embarrass himself by asking for a hammock to be strung up when they're only an hour or so into the day.

'You can have the Captain's bunk, Mistress,' Matthias says, indicating the adjoining alcove. 'Pull the curtain over. It'll be private.'

'Thank you,' she says. 'I only need an hour or two.'

Matthias is the man in charge of getting them safely across the water. The Captain is Diego, the mate from Courrières' galleon, who with half of that big ship's crew is taking them in this leaky caravel north-east to the Zwin and up to Brugge.

Wyatt and Matthias have met before, or have laid eyes on each other at least. It was at the Abbey of St. Bavo in Ghent. It turns out the man who he

Misalliances

thought was merely one of the Seigneur's guards is his lieutenant in the Low Countries. Less solemn and steely-eyed than he was that morning, he has been a cordial and solicitous presence since he took charge of them.

'Let's try some of this wine,' he's saying. 'We insisted they leave two barrels for us. Do you think your lady would like some?'

Wyatt takes the cup. 'She'll be settling down,' he says. 'Best to leave her be.' He tastes the wine. 'It's good. Here's to pirates.'

They're sitting at the big oak table. Matthias picks up one of the charts which someone has rolled up and placed at the end of it. 'I've been looking at these,' he says. 'They've been down to Africa.'

'Pirates do, I'm sure,' Wyatt says.

'There was a pile of gold plate in the hold. Our pirates were doing well for themselves. Your coast guard picked them up foundering off the Lizard so I imagine they were bound for Ireland.'

'What's happened to them?'

'The Master at Falmouth has them in gaol. And we have their ship, all in one piece and bound for Brugge.'

'And then on to Bijgaarden.'

'South west of Brussels. Two days at the most after we land.'

'And you'll be with us all the way...'

'I'll introduce you to everybody, then go on to the Koudenberg, which you know, of course.

Misalliances

Diego and the crew will return the ship to Falmouth and wait for the Seigneur.'

Normality, such as it is, is suddenly altered. The cabin tips backwards. Like Wyatt, Matthias has taken hold of the edge of the table. 'Ah,' he says, 'we're out in open sea. You know this kind of craft?'

'The caravel? I've been in a few.'

'Then you will. There'll be a lot of this because they sit low in the water. It'll be very wet and not exactly comfortable, but I'd take this kind of vessel over a big galleon any day if I wanted to get somewhere quick.'

Wyatt smiles. 'Which we do.' He goes over and draws back the curtain to looks in on Damaris. She's asleep. He buttons up his jacket. 'I'm going to go out again,' he says.

'Stay aft,' Matthias advises. 'They'll be hoisting the main sail.'

He stands, wedged against the frame of the cabin door, looking out over the rolling grey expanses of water. They are well away from the coast. He nods to the man at the wheel. Though the sea isn't particularly rough, the deck is awash. He's been on many voyages, on seas more turbulent than this, but he's glad he's never had to what the men below are doing, moving about with a kind of preternatural balance as they pull on hoists and davits to raise the canvas. For the first time he's hit

Misalliances

by spray; the wind has changed, or perhaps their course.

It's more than three weeks since he was at Allington. Going on for a fortnight since he met Horsey at Clifton Maybank. Tom must have been up to Greenwich by now with the news. He hopes to God he has, or else it's all going to unravel. 'If you want to keep Allington, this is what you must do,' he'd said. He couldn't have made it any clearer: if he was arrested again, even if he didn't go to the block, the King would take everything. The only way out for all of them was to pretend he'd died, stricken by a fever on the road. He's going abroad. 'Wait ten days after we leave. Then go to the palace. Present yourself to Household. Tell them you've received a message from John Horsey. John Horsey at Clifton Maybank in Dorset.' Ever querulous, Tom had asked why *he* couldn't simply send a message to Greenwich. 'Because you're my son,' he'd explained. 'It's less likely to be questioned, coming from you in person.'

There was sadness underlying it all, of course. And the parting was painful, for all their differences. When Tom said 'Will I be seeing you again, father?' it had struck him to the core, as had his necessary reply: 'I don't think so. Allington is yours now.'

Damaris doesn't stir till the lamps have been lit, well into the afternoon. He's had his head down on

Misalliances

the table, dozing off when they're running smoothly and waking whenever a big wave causes the ship to jolt and shake, as happens frequently. 'Have you managed to sleep?' she asks, when he raises his head. Struggling for balance, she steadies herself against the table.

'Off and on.'

'Is there anything to drink?'

'There was some wine. Matthias must have taken it with him.' He looks round the cabin. 'Or to the galley. I'll go and look.'

When he comes back she's already found two cups for them. 'It's good,' he says.

As she drinks, she gives him a limp smile. 'How far out are we?'

'I don't know for sure. In the Channel possibly.'

She squeezes his hand. 'What do you think is happening back there?'

'I was working it out,' he says. 'If all's gone well, Tom should be home, the job done. We just have to hope he kept his nerve.'

'He will have. He wouldn't have wanted to risk losing Allington. It's Horsey we need to worry about. You didn't die on the road and you're not buried at Clifton Maybank. They only need to go down there and start digging around...'

He laughs. 'With spades, you mean?'

'It's not a joke. What if he loses *his* nerve? I know it was a *fait accompli*. By the time we got there Tom would have already declared you dead and all that, but...'

'He's not going to give the game away. It'd be more than his life's worth. And he's got the Friars out of it.'

She pulls her coat around her. 'I wonder what time we're eating? I'm starving.'

'They're cooking up something in the galley. Listen, we're on the way. It's a fine house we're going to, according to Matthias. You'll improve your French, me my Flemish. We'll be alright.'

She arches her back and raises her arms, stretching. 'Do you think Madeleine will come?'

'If it's gone to plan she will.'

Matthias comes in. 'Food's coming,' he says. 'Mutton and dumplings.'

'We'll talk later,' Wyatt says to Damaris.

Though whether because they've exhausted the topic or it comes too near to too many unknowns to continue to be gnawed away at, they don't talk about their situation again until they are in the house at Bijgaarden, a two-storied, double-fronted, white-washed villa surrounded by tall trees, with a big green and a duck-pond in front.

Having filled themselves with a sausage and vegetable stew served by mother and daughters Inge, Lotte and Famke, and utterly exhausted after five days at sea and two days on the road, they go to bed as soon as it begins to get dark.

Misalliances

Though her eyes are ringed with fatigue and she's speaking through intermittent yawns, Damaris voices the obvious question. 'What do you think?'

'I like it. A big house, off the beaten track.'

'Supper was good.'

'I think we're going to be well looked after.'

She yawns again. 'Oh, it's good to lie down at last!' She's shuffling about, getting comfortable. 'The bed's a better one than ours.'

'This is ours now,' he says. He kisses her and blows out the candle. 'Sleep well.'

Her voice drifts up out of the dark. 'When will we know we're safe?'

'When we hear it from Courrières, I expect,' he says, sliding under the covers. 'Or when the King's assassins turn up.'

'Don't...'

Misalliances

Chapter Fifty-one: Messages

It's two weeks before Christmas. Damaris, heavy with memories of the previous year, has been trying to explain to Bert, Inge's man, that she's looking for holly. Finally he understands and, with an exclamation she doesn't, he beckons Famke, his youngest daughter, and gives her an instruction. Damaris likes Famke and it's good the girl has some French. Communication with the others is still halting, words grasped here and there on both sides.

The girl leads her down the garden, which is white with frost, and on to a path that runs along the back. There it is: a huge holly bush, just as full of berries as the one at the Friars would be now. Bert is coming up behind them with a saw.

Wyatt, meeting them at the back door, says: 'Are we doing this again?'

Bert, encumbered though he is, waits. 'Waar?' he queries.

'Oh, bring it in,' Wyatt tells him. He makes some hand gestures. 'Lay it on the floor.'

Bert, happy to deposit his prickly load, says: 'Goed.'

It's early afternoon, but already dusk. Wyatt has sat down with a cup of mulled wine; Damaris is spreading sprigs of holly along the window sills. When they hear horses they exchange glances, but not of especial concern because they've had a message from Matthias to expect the Seigneur any time in the coming week, and now Damaris, leaning forward to peer out the window, is waving and Inge is on her way to the door.

Courrières, lowering his hood and unbuttoning his riding coat, strides in, a big grin across his wind-scored face. He gives Inge a hug. 'How are you, my love? Thomas, you clever dog! Where are you?'

Behind him, hanging back on the threshold, is the young woman he's brought with him.

Madeleine, still in scarf, coat and hat, is fussing with bits of holly. 'Oh, it's just like old times!'

Damaris takes her hand, embraces her yet again, and leads her to the table. 'Supper's ready. Come and sit. Aren't you tired?'

'I slept most of the way from the coast. And on that big ship.'

'At least take off your coat,' Wyatt says. 'I assume you are staying?'

'Of course I am.' Madeleine hands her coat to Famke and undoes her scarf. 'I have no choice, do I?'

'There are always choices,' Wyatt replies, raising his glass to Courrières. 'I learned that a while ago. But yours now, Maddy, are nowhere but here.'

'I know that,' she says. 'Oh, it's so good to see you both! And this place – what a lovely house!'

'It's nice and light,' Damaris says.

Misalliances

'It's good to see *you*,' Wyatt says. 'How are things at the Friars?'

'Sir John's there. He's looking after everyone.' She looks from Wyatt to Damaris. 'Honestly, when that soldier turned up with your letter...'

'Jannes,' Courrières says. 'I was off to see the King and it was best not to be seen there myself. I'm sorry you had to wait so long, Madeleine, but at least you were ready when we came back for you.'

Wyatt leans forward. 'And you told no one...'

'Not a soul. The others thought I was going back to Maidstone.'

Inge comes in with Lotte and dishes of carrots, parsnips and cabbage. She checks the platter of pork to see if there's enough. Muttering to herself, she goes back to the kitchen.

Wyatt picks up one of the bags that Courrières' man has placed at the end of the table. He shakes it to make it jingle. 'Listen to that,' he says to Damaris. 'Another two hundred.'

'You can spend English sovereigns in Brussels,' says Courrières.

Wyatt puts the bag back. 'Can we? Is it safe?'

Courrières is smiling to himself. 'I believe it is, because I have another gift for you.' He reaches inside his jacket and takes out a fold of paper. 'I got this at Greenwich from Eustace Chapuys.'

'Chapuys? Is he still there.'

Misalliances

'This is his fourteenth year as the Emperor's ambassador. He likes England.' Courrières opens the paper. 'He sent this to Charles three weeks ago. I'll not read all of it. It's the opening lines that will interest you. And I'm translating it into English, remember.' He clears his throat. 'On the third of this month arrived the Seigneur de Courrières at Falmouth, upon notice of which the King ordered Mister Wyatt to meet him as far as possible, who about eighty miles hence took ill and died within two days so that de Courrières missed his company and had no other than that of the Captain of Falmouth and his son-in-law who were bringing hither a French corsair...' He breaks off. 'That's your caravel.'

Wyatt is on his feet. 'We're safe!'

'You have been officially pronounced dead, my friend.' Courrières is looking round for a servant. 'Lotte! More wine!'

Once Damaris has taken Madeleine up to her room, Courrières fills up his and Wyatt's glasses. 'Now, Thomas,' he says, 'let's talk about the rest of it. What you can do for us.'

'Ah, I thought as much, the *quid pro quo*.'

'No. What I have in mind won't be a condition of your staying here. Nor would I be expecting you to betray your country.'

'So what would it be?'

'Simply asking if we might from time to time draw on your knowledge and good judgment.'

Misalliances

'My good judgement...'

'Yes. For example, you were told to assassinate Robert Branceter and yet you took steps – perilous ones, I would say - to keep him safe.'

'He told you.'

'He was grateful.'

'Did Charles know?'

'No, no. That would have compromised you and the mission you were on. There are always things it is best not to share with the Emperor.'

'We did that, Mason and I, to prevent you falling-out with Henry and sending your ships up the Channel. You were talking to the French at the time and we didn't know what was going on.'

'I understood. The trouble with princes is that they often let who they are get in the way of what they should be. They lose perspective. It takes a singular kind of diplomacy to counteract that kind of blinkeredness. And you are skilled in practising it.'

'I've always ploughed my own furrow when it comes to averting war.'

'And that's precisely why you can be of use to us. Let's get down to details. As you know, Henry writes to Charles. Chapuys is in charge of despatching these letters and he copies everything to Mary.'

'Charles' sister.'

'She's at Binches, as you know, a day's ride from here. Now, what if I were to arrange for you to receive copies as well, with a view to making whatever comments on them you thought useful? They'd come by special messenger, and he would return in a week, or say ten days, to collect whatever you'd thought fit to write. It's exactly what an ambassador to the Emperor might do when he meets him. The very role you've played on more than one occasion.'

'And which I can play no longer...'

'But you can!'

'You would want me to interpret the King's letters...'

'As a poet as well as a diplomat you know better than most how the choice of words and the way they're phrased conveys meaning.'

'I'd be looking for what's hidden.'

'Hidden, implied, hinted at. All in the cause of better understanding and the avoidance of war.'

'I can do that. But I'll not be party to anything else. If you want secrets, you must look elsewhere.'

'I think we have that side of things sewn-up. Is it a deal?'

Wyatt offers his hand. 'It is.'

Misalliances

Chapter Fifty-two: Postscript

They haven't been into Brussels since that first Christmas when, in the first flush of their new freedom, they decided one morning to ride in and see what the city on their doorstep had to offer. They took Madeleine that time. Today, she's stayed at home with a cough and runny nose and they've taken the children, Jean five and Anne four, without her.

This time, because they've seen the Koudenberg and been round the Grote Markt, he takes them down the back streets where Mason, Rudston, Pitcher and he used to go and eat. His wife doesn't care for the district. 'Thomas, I don't think this is a place for children.' And when he recognises the tavern where, for the last time in his life, he was in the company of whores, he has to agree.

They find a more proper establishment in the Place de Dinan and then, since the days are still short, they set off back home.

Their house is at the end of a long lane. There are no other houses along it. So when they hear someone galloping up behind them, they both turn to look, though it's now too dark to see more than fifty paces either way.

Damaris's voice is tremulous. 'Are we expecting anyone? The messenger from Binches?'

'Not at this hour.'

'Courrières?'

Misalliances

'He's in Spain. And Matthias came last week.'

'You don't think...'

'Take my sword out,' he tells her. 'Are the children still asleep?'

She turns to see. 'Yes.'

'Leave them be. If they catch up with us, I'll jump down and meet them in the road. You take the reins and get home.'

They hear Jean's small, sleepy voice. 'What is it?'

'Nothing,' Wyatt tells him. 'Close your eyes. We're nearly home.'

They reach the house before the phantom rider and hurry inside. When Madeleine comes out to ask if they've enjoyed themselves, Damaris says: 'We have visitors. Ones we don't know.'

'Oh, Lord!' Madeleine exclaims. 'Not after all this time surely?'

'Let's take the children upstairs. Are the servants abed?'

The door locked and barred, Wyatt waits in the entrance hall with his sword at the ready. It's some minutes before he hears the sound of hooves slowly skirting the pond and several more before there's a rapping at the door. 'Who is it?' he demands.

'Matthias. I have news.'

There's much talking. Prince Edward will take the Crown but he's only nine. His elder sister Mary, a

Misalliances

fierce Catholic, will want it for sure. England could find itself enduring years of struggle for the Crown and the Church. It's only when Matthias leaves them to go to bed that Damaris begins to sob.

Wyatt puts his arm round her. 'Hey, what's this? You're not crying for Henry surely?'

'No,' she says. 'For us. I was always afraid he'd find out you were still alive and they'd come.'

'The assassins, you mean?'

'You thought it might have been them tonight.'

'I did wonder. No more assassins, then. Or not Henry's.' He begins to laugh and a second or two later – it takes her that long to see the jest – she starts to laugh, too.

'It's finished,' he says.

Misalliances

Afterword

This novel is underpinned by what we know of the later part of Thomas Wyatt's life. The book is, however, an imagining of that life.

There is no evidence that he had intimate relations with Catherine Howard, though when Queen she intervened to have him released from The Tower.

More than ten years ago when researching *Mistrustful Minds*, my first novel about Thomas Wyatt, I concluded the official account of his death was unconvincing. In *Misalliances* I offer an alternative scenario.

The other piece of complete fiction in the novel is the character of Damaris.

My thanks to Susan Brigden and her excellent biography of Thomas Wyatt *The Heart's Forest* and to British History Online. Without those resources I would not have been able to support this novel with the skeleton of factual detail it has.

Printed in Great Britain
by Amazon